4 Steps to Freedom

KALLE GAYN

ART QUILL & CO PTY LTD

LAKE MACQUARIE, AUSTRALIA

Art Quill & Co Pty Ltd

First Published in Australia 2019

This paperback edition published in 2019

Wikipedia has been instrumental for many of the facts interwoven in this story, although the author takes full responsibility for how they have been interpreted and included. Every reasonable effort has been made to trace copyright holders of material reproduced in this book, but if any have been inadvertently overlooked the publisher would be glad to acknowledge them.

Art Quill & Co Pty Ltd
PO Box 892
Warners Bay
NSW 2282
Australia

www.blogspot.artquill.com.au

Design and layout by Marie-Therese Wisniowski, Art Quill Studio
Set in 11/16 Minion Pro
Printed and Bound in Australia by McPherson's Printing Group

A catalogue record for this book is available from the National Library of Australia, State Library of New South Wales, New South Wales Parliamentary Library and the University Library of Sydney.

ISBN 978 0 9873013 2 1

Front Cover Photograph
Model: Elfriede Jäkel
Photographer: Franz Jäkel
Back Cover Photograph
Photograph of Author: Kalle Gayn
Photograph Courtesy: Marie-Therese Wisniowski
Front and back cover photographs are the property of Art Quill & Co Pty Ltd

CONTENTS

ACKNOWLEDGEMENTS

I would first like to thank Marie-Therese Wisniowski, who enabled me to stitch isolated stories into a narrative. Marie-Therese has acted in a number of different capacities to make this book happen: critic, proofreader, as well as being the design and layout artist for this book.

My sisters and Marie-Therese have unwittingly played a role in the creation of this novel. None of the female characters in this novel are based on anyone of them and yet many of the female traits in this novel have been inspired by all of them.

My mother has been the source of inspiration for the main female character, Magrete. However, this book does not reflect her or her life. It is because of her willful but compassionate nature that as a seven-year-old boy, I was convinced that men were the second sex - not women! My view has not altered to this day.

My father, brothers and friends have inspired a number of male characters in this novel. However, all the male characters in this novel are not centred on anyone of them.

I wish to thank Tricia Dearborn for copy editing the manuscript and for trying to forge it into a readable book. All the final exclusions and inclusions have been of my own choosing.

Finally, I wish to dedicate this book to the person who has inspired me the most: Marie-Therese Wisniowski.

Kalle Gayn

PART ONE

The Rise

1

George Nagy sat in front of a Romani gypsy and smiled. She was reading his tea leaves. He was born in Hercegfalva, Hungary, in 1908, where his parents owned a mixed farm in the district. He went to a Catholic boarding school in Budapest and completed his baccalaureate in 1925. He was in the top percentile, and so had been accepted by the Technische Hochschule of Berlin (Technical University of Berlin) to do an electrical engineering undergraduate degree, and because he was travelling to Berlin alone, his fiancée, Julia, wanted to know what the future held in store for them and so she paid a Romani gypsy a gold coin to foretell George's future.

'You have a colourful past,' the gypsy said looking sternly at George, 'but your future will be far more telling.' George smiled at her, not believing a word of it. 'You'll deny your real circumstance to a woman imbued with spiritual energy,' the gypsy continued, looking more deeply into his cup, 'and in doing so your future will unlock a road with a series of forks, and the path you choose at each fork, will take you into another woman's reality.'

George yawned silently but Julia was transfixed. 'Once you leave Hungary,' the gypsy added, 'there will be no turning back. Each step on that road will take you further away – from past lovers, from past skills, from past cultures. You'll become unknown, but not alone, in a land where the first dreams were shaped by a tribe of wandering whisperers.'

The gypsy indicated the session was over. Julia was confused and devastated about her predicted loss, whereas George smiled and remained aloof. How silly, he thought.

2

In 1934 George Nagy graduated with a PhD in material science under the supervision of Dr Wilhelm Heinrich Westphal, who held a professorship at the Technische Hochschule of Berlin. George's PhD was based on his work in developing nickel-based superalloys that are extremely resistant to high temperatures, pressures, as well as to centrifugal force, fatigue, and oxidation. After he graduated he took up a position at the Kaiser Wilhelm Institute for Chemistry in Berlin as a senior researcher.

In 1928 Professor Otto Hahn became the director there, and established an investigation on the proof and separation of many elements that arose through nuclear fission. Hahn was interested in purifying radioactive uranium-235 from its other isotopes. Uranium is mined as a uranium oxide (yellow cake) and depending on the source of natural uranium, it contains approximately 0.71% of the radioactive isotope ^{235}U and some 99.28% of nonradioactive ^{238}U and 0.1% of ^{234}U. George proposed to find a volatile uranium compound, from which he could enrich radioactive uranium. Professor Werner Heisenberg believed that such an approach would fail, and that they would always be working with impure uranium. Hahn decided to take a risk and he hired George.

As a senior researcher with a budget to contend with, George was required to visit the business and accounting section, which he did in January 1935 – the most boring morning he could envisage. As he stood outside the accounting office window with his mentor, Dr Gunther Feldman, his eyes settled on Magrete, and he was immediately smitten. Her brownish blonde shoulder-length hair, her blue eyes, her natural red lips, her figure, was that of an actress rather than an accountant.

Gunther brought George back to reality with a jab in his back. 'She's been engaged for a year. She's marrying a shopkeeper, Herbert von Appen,' he whispered. 'All us single men have already made our enquiries.'

'Hang on,' George whispered in return, 'I know Herbert von Appen! I went to the university with his brother Simon, who died in a car crash. Herbert is the sole surviving child of the second-largest department store owner in the German Reich.'

'She'll end up rich, but marry into a brain-dead life. Living with me would have been so much more exciting for her – poor, but exciting,' Gunther observed.

George heard, but did not pay him any further attention as they entered the office and instead he immediately went to Magrete and addressed her. 'Madam, my name is Dr George Nagy. I'm a senior researcher in the material science section at the Institute. I knew your fiancée's older brother Simon von Appen quite well. He was studying engineering management when I studied electrical engineering. We fenced competitively against one another. I had lunch with him on the day before he died. Simon gave me a ceremonial épée when I won the intervarsity fencing championship. I always wanted to return it to his family as a reminder of him.' He bowed and handed her his name card.

Magrete looked at his card then back at him. Her first impression was that he was seriously good-looking. He had dark cropped hair, piercing brown eyes, a broad chin and a subtle smile. She stammered at first, and then regained her composure. 'Dr George Nagy,' she read slowly from his name card. 'I am certain my fiancée will get in contact with you.' She smiled at him suddenly and then blushed. 'Simon was loved very dearly, and his loss was severely felt,' she added. George nodded, turned, and retreated with Gunther to continue the rest of the induction tour of the Institute.

3

Two days later, George Nagy received a card from Herbert von Appen inviting him to attend dinner at the von Appen's villa, located on the shores of Lake Wannsee in Berlin. The villa was a landmark in German architecture. It had been built by Simon's father, Peter von Appen, and designed by Alfred Messel, a famous German architect. The villa contained a vast living area as well as a large garden, which measured some 7,500 square metres. Messel's student, Paul Baumgarten, had built two other villas nearby, one for the painter Max Liebermann and another much larger villa for Ernst Mailer, an industrialist of considerable wealth. It was one of the most exclusive suburbs in Berlin.

George arrived at the von Appen's villa ten minutes early, steadied himself in front of the famous villa owned by a very rich family, and rang the doorbell. Two large doors swung open and a butler greeted him. George presented his name card, and was shown into a large drawing room. The butler removed George's coat, accepted his scarf and gloves, and silently retreated. George could hear two voices getting louder as they neared him. Another door opened and in strode Herbert and another man slightly older in age.

'You must be Dr Nagy,' the chubby man said. 'I'm Herbert.'

'Please call me George.'

Herbert walked towards him, and the two men shook hands. 'Let me introduce you to another guest, Helmut Gruen, our company solicitor.' The guests shook hands. 'My father will join us for dinner, as will mother and Magrete. Simon spoke often about you. He considered you the most brilliant student he had met. He also thought you were a talented fencer. Simon used to say it was the Magyar blood!' All three of them smiled.

'I've an épée on the back seat of the car that I wish to return to your family,' George said.

Herbert walked across to the wall and tugged gently on a cord.

Silently the door opened and the butler emerged. 'Tomas, could you please retrieve Dr Nagy's épée from the back seat of his car?' Herbert turned to the guests and asked, 'Would you both care for a drink?'

'Not for me, thank you,' George answered.

Herbert asked forcibly, 'Helmut, how about you?'

'A gin and tonic would be nice,' Helmut replied.

Herbert opened a cupboard. The shelves displayed an array of alcoholic beverages, glasses and a bucket of ice. He poured Helmut and himself a gin and tonic, and that is when George noticed two large autographed photographs glaring at him from above the cupboard – Hitler and Himmler!

While not political, George was nevertheless shocked. He recalled the 5th Party Congress, held in Nuremberg in 1933. It was called the 'Rally of Victory'. The word 'Victory' related to the Nazi seizure of power and the victory over the Weimar Republic. Hitler announced that from now on, all rallies of the German Reich would be held in Nuremberg.

Herbert, handing a drink to Helmut, followed George's eyes to the two photographs. 'Ah, I see you are intrigued. I've known Himmler for some time, but Hitler only recently. They make a commanding duo! Himmler is one of the best managers in Hitler's inner circle, but it's Hitler who captures the imagination, railing at our lack of patriotic zeal. So, are you a fan?'

George was stunned by suddenly having to offer an opinion to his host. 'I've only two passions – material engineering and fencing! I've never had time for anything else, and being Hungarian in the German Reich makes me even more remote from politics.'

'That's exactly what Simon would have said,' Herbert observed, 'except it was engineering management and fencing, and that he had a deaf ear and so could not hear all this political shouting. To Simon!'

'To Simon!' Both George and Helmut reiterated the toast, even though George was without a drink.

The butler re-entered the room and gave a package to George and then slid out of the room unnoticed. George was about to hand the package to Herbert when Herbert touched his wrist. 'Please give it to my father,' he said softly. 'It'll make him so happy. I think we should now retreat to the dining room. I'm sure Magrete, my mother and father will be waiting for us.'

4

The dining room was immense. There were at least two Titians, a van Eyck, and a Raphael that George could identify – the identification of the other paintings needed someone with a far greater expertise. The housekeeper greeted them, and ushered them into a corner of the room where a special table had been set. Magrete looked magnificent, and glowed before her guests. Her future mother-in-law had a welcoming smile. Peter von Appen rose and greeted the two guests as they approached the table. It was clear he had difficulty walking.

'Hello, Helmut! You must be Dr George Nagy,' Peter von Appen said, shaking George's hand.

'Please call me George.'

'This is Elfi von Appen,' introduced Peter, 'and you know Magrete.' Both women gave George a faint nod, acknowledging the introduction.

George got straight to the point of his visit. 'Herr von Appen, I'd be pleased if you would accept this épée that Simon gave me.'

Peter accepted the sword and immediately unsheathed it. It was pure gold, with the family crest of the House of von Appen evident on the hilt. He displayed the sword to his wife. Tears welled in both their eyes. 'This is a family heirloom that I gave Simon on his twenty-first birthday, the year he died. It was a sword given to my family by Frederick II from the House of Hohenzollern in 1763 for our contribution in the Seven Years War, a war in which we stood side-by-side with Britain to defeat the French. My son said to me he would gift it to the greatest warrior of his time, and that's why he gave it to you.' A tear wound its way down Peter's cheek. His wife moved beside Peter, supporting him.

'It has now returned to its home as a reminder of your son,' George said, glad that a piece of German history had rightfully returned to the House of von Appen.

Peter placed his free hand on George's shoulder and said softly, 'Thank you!' Lady von Appen simultaneously nodded thanks.

They were seated at the table with Peter von Appen at the northern end, the head of the table, with his wife at the southern end. Magrete was seated to Peter's right and opposite Helmut, with Herbert beside his fiancée and opposite George.

'Gertrude,' Peter softly addressed the housekeeper, 'you may serve the meal.'

During the meal several conversations arose, with subjects ranging from the art on the dining room walls to music to theatre. All were impressed with the well-rounded education exhibited by George on most of these topics. More surprisingly was his candid admission of his lack of knowledge on several sub-topics. He oozed confidence. The conversation finally centred on business, a subject George knew interested all of them except him.

'Well, Dad,' Herbert said, 'it appears the Aryanisation of business has begun.'

Peter looked at his son to indicate this might be best discussed in the drawing room, but when his eyes fell on Magrete he remembered that she had graduated in 1934 from the Vienna Commercial Academy for Girls in business and accounting. He nodded for Herbert to continue.

'Our opposition, the Wertheim family, appears to be in strife. I hear that Göring has demanded that Georg Wertheim transfer 51 per cent of the family stock to his wife, Ursula. She is non-Jewish and almost 30 years his junior – the old swine!'

Lady von Appen raised her eyebrows to indicate that her son should tone it down in front of their guests; her demeanour suggested that talking business at the dinner table was uncouth. Then she saw that Magrete was fascinated by the revelation. Typical, she thought, of these young women who drive cars and have a professional career. Like her husband, she allowed the conversation to continue, though she was dismayed by the topic.

'At any rate,' Herbert continued, 'I hear that Göring and Hitler are not that pleased and want to annex the company in the not-too-distant future.'

'What are your Nazi friends doing with their workers?' Peter asked.

'As I understand it,' interceded Helmut, 'all Jewish employees have lost their positions by government mandate.'

'Let's have no more conversations about business,' Elfi said determined to change the course of the conversation. 'We have a guest who can entertain us on more interesting matters. Now George, please explain to us what nylon is, and why they believe it will replace silk in women stockings.'

George was shocked. Nylon had just been invented and patented by DuPont. Very few material scientists had heard of it, let alone the public. How could he explain the chemical intricacies to someone who knew nothing about it? He could see both women smiling.

'Don't worry George, I'm only teasing you,' assured Elfi. She looked around the table and saw that all diners, including George, were relieved. 'Now that we've finished here for the evening, perhaps you gentlemen can go to the drawing room, while Magrete and I attend to a few domestic matters.'

The men went back to the drawing room, where the conversation reverted to politics and business, only interrupted by the offering of port and cigars. It was clear that Herbert had joined the Nazi party, whereas Peter was a supporter of President Hindenburg and the

Weimar Republic. George and Helmut kept their counsel during the conversation between father and son, because at times it became heated. Thank goodness I'm Hungarian, thought George.

The night ended on a friendlier note, with Helmut playing a musical selection of Mozart on a grand Steinway in front of the residents and guest in the music hall.

5

In the weeks that followed the dinner, Herbert, Magrete and George saw each other on a regular basis. Herbert would often call at the Institute during lunch, and drive Magrete and George to some restaurant nearby. Herbert was really fond of George, who reminded him of Simon. They were of a similar age, had a passion for fencing, and both had broad knowledge across a wide range of subjects. Neither enjoyed politics, which suited Herbert because politics was the only subject in which he held strong views, and so conversations between them were always easy and enjoyable. Magrete was also fond of George. She never had a brother, only a sister, Mimi, and so she enjoyed being immersed in a brotherly love of sorts.

On one of these outings Herbert said, 'George, my family history is well known and publicly documented. What about you? What's known about your family?' Magrete leaned forward, eager to hear his reply.

'Well,' George said, feeling suddenly awkward, 'I'm from a humble background. I'm the only child. My parents were farmers on the Hungarian plains. We had a vineyard and stocked cattle. It was red wine to veal, if you get my drift. My father died of influenza during the pandemic in 1918, and our whole world turned upside down. Our extended family gathered around us and supported our farm. After I finished my baccalaureate in 1925, I went to Berlin. My mother died that year from cancer. As you can imagine, I was devastated. I sold the farm to my uncle, and started a new life and career here in Berlin.'

Magrete looked at him in disbelief. He seemed so composed, and yet he still must be hurting from the loss of both parents within such a short time frame. She felt for him.

'So now I've revealed all. I know very little of your bride-to-be Herbert. What about you, Magrete?'

Magrete blushed under George's gaze, glanced at Herbert and saw him nod.

'My story is not so tragic. It is very boring, really. My family on my mother's side fled Norway one hundred years ago-'

'Now I understand why your first name is spelt the way it is,' interrupted George.

'It has been the bane of my life! I was named after my mother's grandmother. Every day there is some reason why I have to spell it to somebody. Anyway, my family on my mother's side were Catholic and so wanted a safe haven. They decided on Austria, because Germany had become Lutheran. My grandfather on my mother's side was the mayor of Vienna from 1922 to 1923. He is Sture Nordholm. My mother, Eva, married my father, Hans Holweg, who is the Deputy Commissioner of the Vienna Police. Scotland Yard trained him. He suggested that I do an accounting and business administration diploma, because in 1931 Germany had issued a presidential decree, backed by company law, which mandated annual audits for large public firms and institutions. I graduated from the Vienna Commercial Academy for Girls in 1934 and took up the position at the Institute in August of that year. My sister Mimi – she was christened Wilhelmina – teaches piano in Vienna and still lives with my parents. One of her former students is now playing for the Vienna Philharmonic Orchestra.'

Magrete stopped, wondering if George thought she was boastful. Herbert, nevertheless, looked pleased with both of their accounts.

6

The three of them, Magrete, Herbert and George, appeared at most gala events, from performances at the Berlin Opera House to orchestral events to theatre and the cinema. Magrete was the glue that held them together. Typically, they would saunter around Berlin with Herbert on the right, Magrete in the middle and George on the left, each of her arms interlocked into one of theirs. They would sing together, laugh together and when they went dancing, Herbert would encourage Magrete to dance with George. Herbert was never jealous of the affection that Magrete showed George, because it was purely based on friendship. Their wider circle of friends nicknamed them the drei (three) amigos. The only adventure that two of the three would never entertain was being a passenger in Herbert's American Waco O series biplane. Although there were better performing biplanes and monoplanes on the market, the O series gave Herbert a sense of danger, adventure and freedom. When he flew it, he felt he was riding on the back of an eagle.

Magrete and Herbert spent countless hours trying to matchmake George with some of Magrete's inner circle of girlfriends, but to no avail. When George invited a female companion, she was always welcomed and embraced by the other two amigos. None of his relationships lasted long enough to be considered serious. Herbert and Magrete nicknamed him the social butterfly. George would laugh it off in good humour.

In December 1935 Magrete resigned her position at the Institute and announced she was getting married in April 1936. Both sets of parents were pleased that she was leaving her career behind and planning to have a family with her fiancée. Mimi would be her maid of honour and George would be Herbert's best man. At last Peter and Elfi would meet Hans and Eva Holweg.

At the end of 1935 elaborate preparations were well underway for the August Summer Olympic Games in Berlin. A huge sports complex was under construction, including a new sports stadium and state of the art Olympic village to house the athletes. Magrete wanted to be married before the Olympics and nationalistic fever tainted every other event in Berlin. A spring wedding, she thought, would be ideal. However, there were religious difficulties associated with the marriage. Magrete's family was Catholic, whereas Herbert's was Lutheran. Although Magrete and Herbert were not religious, both wanted to honour their parent's religious beliefs.

When Herbert joined the Nazi party, he linked himself to the German Evangelical Church. It viewed itself as one of the pillars of German culture and society, with a theologically grounded tradition of loyalty to the State. During the 1920s, a movement emerged within the church called the German Christians. The German Christians embraced many of the nationalistic and racial aspects of Nazi ideology. Once the Nazis came to power, this group sought the creation of a national Reich Church and supported a Nazified version of Christianity. This horrified Herbert's parents and moreover, would have horrified Magrete's.

The Catholic Church was not as sharply divided as the Evangelical Church. Catholic leaders were initially more suspicious of National Socialism than their Protestant counterparts. Nationalism was not as deeply embedded in the German Catholic Church, and rabid anti-Catholics such as Alfred Rosenberg, a leading Nazi ideologue during the Nazi rise to power, raised early concerns among Catholic leaders in Austria, Germany and at the Vatican. In addition, the Catholic Centre Party had been a key coalition government partner in the Weimar Republic during the 1920s and was aligned with both the Social Democrats and the leftist German Democratic Party, pitting it politically against right wing parties like the Nazis.

Herbert's parents were strong supporters and completely sympathetic to the Weimar Republic, but as Lutherans, Catholics were generally abhorrent to them.

The entrenched views of both sets of parents resulted in a longer engagement than what Magrete and Herbert had anticipated.

George came to the rescue. He reminded both Magrete and Herbert that civil marriages had been instituted by Napoleon in certain German principalities, through his Code Napoleonic. They could marry in a civil service and then, at a later date, marry as either Catholics or Lutherans whichever made their life easier.

'Good idea, social butterfly,' Magrete said, 'but that does not solve our problem if one set or both sets of parents dig in their heels.'

'Okay,' George replied, 'try it and see which set of parents does care and which set doesn't, and go with the set that will remain intransigent. If both stand on their high horse, tell them you'll live together in sin and have children out of wedlock. That will shake them up a bit, to have grandchildren that are bastards!' He laughed at his own solution. They were not amused.

The amigos then sketched a simple plan of attack: Magrete would coax her parents into agreeing to a civil wedding and Herbert would coax his.

7

Magrete knew her father would not be against a civil wedding. She was the eldest child, and he had doted on her from the day she was born. He also only paid lip service to his religion in order to placate her mother.

When Magrete moved to Berlin and took up the position at the Institute, she was living in the von Appen's villa at Lake Wannsee. Herbert and Magrete slept in separate bedrooms and behaved civilly toward one another, only giving each other a peck on the cheek when greeting each other. Occasionally they would hold hands, when they meandered through the gardens, but once out of sight of prying eyes, they would become more intimate.

The great advantage Magrete had living in the villa was unlimited telephone access. That was her second most popular form of communication with her father, after writing letters. Her father, as Deputy Commissioner of the Vienna Police, also had telephone access. He had informed his switchboard that if she rang they must immediately put her through. He knew she would use the telephone sparingly and in most cases for emergencies. Magrete thought that her marriage was an important enough issue to warrant a telephone call. She picked up the telephone and after going through several switchboards she finally reached her father.

'Hi Papa. Busy?'

'Always mein Schatz (my sweetheart)!' Hans was worried about the reason for the call and so asked, 'How's Herbert and family?'

'They are doing fine. Herbert and I are planning to get married, as you know, but this is the difficult part: we plan to get married in a civil wedding.'

'Oh,' her father said, somewhat surprised by the news.

'Papa,' Magrete continued, undaunted by his surprise, 'I know Mutti (Mom) might not approve of a civil wedding, especially if we decide not to get married in the Catholic Church after the civil wedding, but-'

'That could be a problem,' her father interrupted, 'especially if you have children because they'll need to be baptised and -'

'Papa,' Magrete interrupted in turn, 'let us not get ahead of ourselves. Let us take it one step at a time. How can we persuade Mutti to agree to a civil marriage?'

'Well,' Hans paused and with that pause Magrete knew she had him onside, 'perhaps, we could suggest to Eva that the civil wedding is a compromise, because you're not getting married immediately in any church.'

'Papa, please talk to Mutti and ring me back as soon as you know what she thinks. Love!'

'Bye, Schatz.' He placed the receiver on the telephone cradle and looked at it in deep contemplation.

As Magrete rang off she thought, better Papa than me!

8

Hans knew he had to broach this subject very carefully. Magrete had been very tomboyish as a child, whereas his youngest daughter, Mimi, was feminine to the core. It was Magrete's tomboyishness that had always endeared her to him, but not to Eva. She wanted Magrete to be feminine, well mannered and cultured, and so took it on herself to try to curb Magrete's tomboyish ways. When Magrete was quite young, Eva took her to singing, dancing and music lessons. The first two quickly became established failures, whereas her piano teacher thought Magrete was gifted. Mimi, two years younger than Magrete, demanded to learn the piano as well. Mimi was always in competition with her older sister. Mimi felt that whatever her older sister did came too easily to her, whereas she could only compete through sheer hard work.

Hans sat opposite Eva and gently began his opening submission. 'There was a time when we never wanted our two girls to grow up, but now look at them, young and vibrant women.'

Eva smiled and nodded with a bemused look on her face, as if to say, 'Go on.'

'Well,' Hans continued, choosing his words carefully, 'Magrete is engaged and Mimi is getting there with her new companion Albert. Magrete and Herbert are thinking of getting married soon. Magrete has already vetoed getting married in Herbert's church, the German Christian Church, who really are a bunch of Nazi diehards.'

Eva nodded in approval. Both of them favoured the Christian Social Party and intensely disliked the Austrian Nazis, who started terror campaigns within Austria to bring the government down. They had shot Chancellor Dullfoss, and the retaliation by the government had been hard and swift, with the army and Hans Holweg putting down the revolt, and inflicting heavy casualties on the Austrian Nazis.

'Magrete has also ruled out getting married in a Lutheran Church, in which Peter and Elfi are congressional members,' Hans comtinued. 'Peter is an elder in the church. Magrete did that out of respect for your family, Eva. She respects that the Nordholms fled Norway due to 300 years of Lutheran persecution. She appreciates your family's history to the extent of going against her in-laws' wishes.' Hans paused, eyeing Eva carefully, and was encouraged by her faint smile of satisfaction and pride.

'You know that Magrete has distilled in her soul a sense of fairness,' Hans continued. 'It's the only gene of mine she has inherited.' Not likely, thought Eva. She is her father's child through and through. 'She has decided with my blessing' – and here Hans held his breath – 'that the only alternative for her is to marry Herbert in a civil wedding.' He paused to allow for an interruption, but none was forthcoming. 'Later on, when they have a family, they'll get married in the Catholic Church so their children can be baptised.'

As he said the word 'baptised' he could see Eva descending into a deep reverie. Hans knew Eva was thinking of a tragedy that sat between them. He rose and came over to sit on the arm of her chair, placing his arm around her shoulders. Eva did not respond. Hans whispered tenderly in her ear, 'I'll make us a cup of tea', and silently left the room.

Eva travelled in her mind to a time when she was in her middle forties and found herself pregnant – a change of life child. Both Mimi and Magrete had just started another year at St Ursula's, where they were boarding full-time. Eva and Hans agreed to keep her pregnancy secret from their children at that point as both children were in their early years in high school, and to have another child so late in Eva's life might be disquieting for them.

It was a difficult pregnancy. Eva was plump and motherly in statute, which concealed her early months of pregnancy. In her twentieth week it was becoming noticeable, and so she stayed indoors as much as possible. Hans had been recently promoted to the position of deputy commissioner, which gave them more financial leeway, and so he decided to hire a non-resident housekeeper, Rachel Sulzer, who he knew well. She had a young baby daughter, Anna. Hans hired her to work during school terms, in order to suit his budget. She kept the house and kept an eye on Eva's needs.

Eva felt she could always guess the sex of her baby-to-be and on two occasions she was right. She felt this was a boy, just by the way he kicked: that is, harder than the initial butterflies in the stomach feeling that her other two girls imparted to her. A pregnancy to her, in concept, was like a drop forming from a much larger mother drop. As the gravity of the life grew stronger a teardrop emerged from the mother drop; the bigger the teardrop grew, the greater the pull to separate. At that critical point when the teardrop fell away from the mother drop, the child became complete in body and soul, but up until that point in time, both drops were interconnected – their souls and bodies were intricately linked.

It happened in her twenty-fifth week of her pregnancy, on a Friday afternoon. Hans was at work, but Rachel was by her side. Eva had the worst abdominal pains she had ever experienced. She nearly fainted several times. Rachel quickly got the doctor and summoned Hans. When the doctor examined Eva, he turned to Hans and said, 'You'd better get a priest. Your wife and child might not survive the night.' A priest arrived with a nun and within two hours the child arrived stillborn, but the mother had survived. The nun placed the child in a basket, covered its body with a small towel and took it from the house in order to dispose of the body in a mass grave at the nunnery. The doctor gave Eva a sleeping draught. Before the stillborn was whisked away, Hans and Rachel both saw that the child was a boy.

When Eva awoke some twenty hours later, Hans told her what had transpired. Rachel never left her side. The doctor paid her regular visits, and she slowly recovered her strength. The Catholic Church expected Eva and Hans to immediately let go of any emotional attachment to the stillborn, for he had not been blessed. Eva would cry alone and in private. No one could comfort her. They decided to tell Magrete, but not Mimi for she was too young. Rachel became a permanent fixture in the household as a non-residential housekeeper. Often she would bring her young daughter Anna with her, and having a child near, comforted Eva for the loss of her own.

Slowly Eva recovered physically, but mentally she felt that the soul of her teardrop was still attached within her and would forever be a part of her, to be released upon her death. Now and then she would think about how their lives would have been transformed with a healthy birth: Magrete would not have been so tomboyish, Mimi would not have been so jealous, Hans would have been more involve with the family, and Eva – well, she and her child would have been complete. Eva had picked a name for her stillborn baby, Francis, to remind herself that there was more to him than being unblessed.

Eva re-entered the now and saw Hans placing two cups of tea and biscuits on the table in front of her. 'Are you alright?' he asked, looking concerned.

'As good as can be expected,' Eva replied gripping his hand. She said gently, with a tinge of sadness in her eyes, 'I'll support a civil wedding, and I'll only make one request of both Magrete and Herbert – that they'll baptise their eldest son Francis, after my favourite saint, Francis of Assisi.'

Tears dropped from Hans' eyes as he turned his head away from her and said, 'I know she'll agree.' Hans knew why she had wanted that name in her family, and how God had denied it to them.

9

Herbert's plan was to raise the fact that he definitely did not want to marry in a Catholic or Lutheran Church, but rather in a German Evangelical Church, which he would name the Reich Church. He was hoping that it would frame a more productive and creative solution to his parent's dilemma if he started the conversation in context of his political views.

Herbert found both parents in his father's study and immediately tackled the subject. 'Magrete and I plan to get married in spring of 1936. I would prefer us to be married in the Reich Church that I've been recently attending. Our minister has agreed to officiate. His son is an important member of the Nazi party.'

'What does Magrete's parents think about your plans?' Peter asked. 'Aren't they Catholics?'

'I haven't discussed it with them,' Herbert said. 'I wanted to seek your advice before talking to Magrete's family.'

'Our preference would be a Lutheran service, as you know,' Elfi suggested, 'since your father is an elder at St Mary's.'

St Mary's Church was originally a Roman Catholic Church, but had been a Lutheran Church since the Reformation. The church personified the religious differences between the families: both believed in the tenets of Christianity, but their religious practices were worlds apart.

'Well,' Herbert decided to change tack, 'clearly we can't get married in my church, because both families would be distraught, and if we get married in a Catholic Church, us Montagues would refuse to go. And if we get married at St Mary's, the Capulets would abstain.' He could see his parents understood the Romeo and Juliet analogy and both looked distinctively worried. 'Magrete and I don't want to live in sin, nor do we wish to have children out of wedlock. So why don't we have a civil wedding, right here in our villa? We have the grounds, and the means to make you respectable grandparents!'

Herbert scrutinised their reaction and noted a flicker in his mother's face, which informed him that it would be she, and not Frau Holweg, who would be orchestrating the wedding. He quickly pushed that idea. 'Having the wedding here is critical to both of us and so, Mum, you'll need to be the cornerstone in organising it, of course, in consultation with Frau Holweg.'

His father spoke first. 'Elfi, they can't live here forever as an engaged couple.'

'No,' Elfi responded. 'It's the era of the youngsters! Civil weddings are all the rage now that the Nazis are in power. But once you have children they'll have to be baptised in the Lutheran Church.' Herbert nodded, knowing that bridge would have to be crossed at a much later date. He sighed. Magrete would be pleased, but she would have to convince her parents that the wedding needed to be held in Berlin and not in Vienna. Thank goodness, Herbert thought, that the Nazis have made Austria such a dangerous place for them to marry there!

10

It quickly became apparent to the Holwegs that to have the wedding in Austria would be problematic. As the Deputy Commissioner of the Vienna Police, Hans was responsible for operations against the criminal elements of the Austrian Nazis. If they could shoot the Austrian Chancellor, Hans reasoned, murdering a deputy commissioner's wedding party would be of little consequence, especially if it meant that the command behind police operations against them would have taken a significant blow. The irony of this was not lost on Hans – that the German Reich was a safer place for his daughter's wedding than in a neoliberal state such as Austria.

The price Hans was glad to pay was to install a telephone in his family home. He knew that Eva wanted a direct input into this civil wedding, especially because Hans insisted that the Holwegs would pay for the event. The latter was a condition for the wedding to go ahead. The von Appen's understood their position and agreed, even though they were far wealthier. This did not stop Elfi from providing under the table financial support. After all, Herbert was now her only child and so no expense would be spared.

A spring wedding gave both families three months to prepare. Mimi, Eva and Hans would stay in the villa for at least a fortnight before the wedding. This would enable Eva to have a direct hand in the final preparations and enable them to attend several rehearsals. The two mothers had already agreed to hold the wedding in the villa's expansive gardens. A pavilion-like marquee would provide protection from the weather. The large reception hall in the villa would be used to host guests for the reception. There would be speeches from the bridal table and a musical ensemble would play so the guests could dance on the sprung parquetry floor. The villa's cooks and in-house staff would be supplemented by outside staff paid for by the von Appens, a cost that would be unknown to the Holwegs. Some of Magrete's Viennese friends from her high school days at St Ursula's would also attend the wedding. They would arrive a week before the wedding and share rooms in the villa.

The time flew between December and April. The bridal party gowns, dresses, jewellery and, more importantly, the bridal dress, veil and ring had to be sourced, fitted and bought. The guest list needed to be assembled, and the honeymoon needed to be planned. Organising the wedding became a full-time occupation for the bride-to-be, her mother and her future mother-in-law. Magrete had little time for Herbert, let alone for her friends, including her recently adopted de facto brother George. Without Magrete, their inner circle of friends now knew them as the zwei verloren (two lost) amigos.

George and Herbert had been determined to keep the biweekly lunches and dinners intact, but because George's work commitments and Herbert's wedding arrangements were eating into their free time, going out to social events had been somewhat curtailed. Only occasionally, if Magrete was available, did the three amigos catch the odd Hollywood movie or have a night out at the opera.

A month before the wedding, Herbert and George met at Café Buchwald in Berlin. The café had opened its doors in 1900, and its decor was reminiscent of a bygone era: kitschy wallpaper, floral curtains and simple furniture. It always gave them an authentic feeling of dining in an old-fashioned parlour.

The waiter appeared, pen and pad in hand. Without consulting the menu George ordered a dobos torte and an espresso and Herbert a Berliner and an espresso. The waiter withdrew and within minutes their order was completed.

'How did Magrete and you get together?' George asked.

Herbert, who was playing with his Berliner with his fork, looked up at George and began to unlock a little piece of history. 'We met when the family business established a department store in Vienna. We'd established ourselves in Germany and central Europe before the Great War, with stores in Berlin, Frankfurt, Munich, Leipzig, Dresden, Magdeberg, Prague and Budapest. But the competition in Vienna was too severe. Then the Great Depression wiped out some of the competition and because we'd minimised our debt levels in the 1920s, we were in a position to expand. I flew my Waco into Vienna in January 1931 and by February I'd established a two-storey department store in Kaerntnerstraße. We invited as many dignitaries as possible to a preview of the store, including the Commissioner of the Vienna Police. He couldn't attend because he was in London visiting Scotland Yard, and so he dispatched his deputy, Hans Holweg.'

'Magrete's father?'

'That's right. Magrete accompanied him to the opening. Apparently her mother, Eva, was unwell at the time. I couldn't take my eyes off her. I gave them a special tour of the store before the opening. The German currency crisis then hit and I stayed on to manage the store through this rocky period. While I was there, I kept seeing and going to social events with Hans, Eva and Magrete. They guessed my intentions, so we became very close. By late January 1933 the store was doing well, and we appointed a manager to run it. I was needed back in Berlin. Unemployment was up to astronomical levels by then, nearly 30 per cent. More importantly, the Nazis had gained power and I needed to be close to the seat of power, so that if our company needed a capital injection it would have access to sympathetic ears within the German Reich. I flew back to Berlin in late February 1933. In the same month I asked Magrete's parents if I could marry her, and they agreed I could put the question to her. I did, and thank goodness she accepted, or I don't know what I would've done. I'd been seeing her for just over two years. Once she graduated from the Vienna Commercial Academy for Girls, she came to Berlin as my fiancée, much to the consternation of Eva and Hans. But we convinced them that we planned to get married within a year, and so they relented.'

'What happened? Why weren't you married within a year?'

'Because of the religious issue, remember? One set of parents being Lutheran, and the other Catholic. But then you suggested a civil marriage, and voila - now I don't see my fiancée at all. Thanks, George!'

'Anything to help a friend,' George said with a smile.

11

On 7 March 1936 the German Reich's military forces marched into the Rhineland. The Nazis gambled that England and France would not respond militarily to an action that violated the terms of the Treaty of Versailles and the Locarno Treaties. The German Reich's political assessment was that appeasement was the most likely outcome from both countries. They also reasoned that President Roosevelt was isolating the United States from the international arena and so Europe was of little concern to US administration.

The remilitarisation of the Rhineland changed the balance of power in Europe, transferring power from France to the German Reich, making it possible for the German Reich to pursue a more aggressive attitude toward the countries on its southern and eastern borders, as its western front was now secured. It validated to the German people that the terms of the Treaty of Versailles, in particular the loss of territory and reparations, were disproportionately unfair and needed to be rectified.

On the following Saturday Mimi Holweg and Albert Kuebler announced their engagement and set their wedding date for March of the following year. Eva, Hans, and Magrete were delighted. It did not diminish Magrete's own future wedding, but rather reinforced the notion that their generation was forging its own destiny and not just reflecting a past generation.

The weather could not have been any better for Magrete's wedding. It was a beautiful spring day, with a maximum predicted temperature of 18 degrees Celsius. Magrete adjusted her beautiful wedding dress, inspired by a Hollywood collection. Made of luscious silk satin, with a flattering gathered bust set into a bias cut body, it flared out from the knees and draped to the floor, with a short gliding train behind. She looked stunning.

Her father gently tapped on her bedroom door. Magrete positioned her tiara on her head to further secure her veil. The tiara was handcrafted, gold-plated and glittered because of the encrusted multi-coloured rhinestones. Magrete opened the door and her father faltered. 'Schatz,' he said, 'I've never seen you more radiant in all of my life.' Hans was wearing a ceremonial deputy commissioner's uniform. He placed her arm within his and proudly strode towards the marquee. He knew people would stare at her beauty.

To Magrete the ceremony felt as if it was conducted in an echo chamber: she heard words as if from a distance. She saw Mimi and her other bridesmaid Maria, and smiled at them. Magrete saw her father give her arm to Herbert, and then she saw George handing the ring to Herbert. She said 'I do' and moments later heard Herbert repeat the same phrase. He turned to her and they kissed. At that moment the echo chamber disappeared, and Magrete found herself a little surprised by the noise that suddenly flooded her senses. The recessional music being played was Handel's Water Music.

The reception hall was filling quickly as the guests were ushered to their designated tables. The bridal table sat on a platform facing them all. A small string sextet consisting of four violins, a viola and a cello were seated discreetly to the left of the bridal table. They were playing Haydn's Baryton Trio in A major.

Once all the guests were seated and the musical interlude was over, the master of ceremonies, Helmut Gruen, introduced himself, and welcomed everyone to the reception. He introduced the bridal party as each was seated. Then Helmut announced, with great enthusiasm and applause, the bride and groom's arrival into the wedding reception area. After they were seated, everyone else followed suit, and an entrée was served.

Hans Holweg made a toast to the bride and groom. All guests stood up with a glass in their hand, which they raised in a salute to the bride and the groom. The main course followed the bridal toast. The ensemble played Haydn's String Quartet No. 5 in F Minor.

After the musical piece had concluded, dessert and coffee were served. Helmut introduced the groom, and Herbert gave a short, sharp speech describing his love for Magrete. He raised his glass and thanked the two bridesmaids, Mimi and Maria.

Helmut then introduced the best man, George, who talked lyrically of each member of the bridal party. He raised his glass, and toasted Eva and Hans Holweg.

Helmut reintroduced the father of the bride, who gave a humorous speech about his in-laws, concluding his speech with a toast to Elfi and Peter.

Helmut then introduced the father of the groom, who thanked his in-laws. Peter then welcomed the special guests of honour –

Margarete and Heinrich Himmler! The guests gasped as the spotlight descended on them, for few were aware that this power couple was present. Himmler and his wife stood up, with Himmler nonchalantly giving a Nazi salute. Without encouragement from the master of ceremonies, the male guests stood up and returned the salute. No one except Magrete noticed that the two male guests, who had not stood up or returned Himmler's salute, were her father and George.

Johann Strauss' The Blue Danube filled the hall. The bride and bridegroom took to the floor and danced a waltz. Every guest stood and applauded the newlyweds. George noted that Margarete and Heinrich Himmler did not look pleased, and concluded they would have preferred a German composer to an Austrian whose Jewish grandfather had been airbrushed out of existence by the Nazis.

The last act of the ceremony had Magrete and Herbert holding candles trimmed with flowers and ribbons, which they used to light their unity candle that stood in the centre of the bridal table. They concluded the ceremony by placing each of their now unlit candles on either side of their lit unity candle.

12

Himmler requested a meeting with Hans Holweg after the wedding reception had ended. He directed his request to his friend Herbert von Appen. To defuse any tension, Herbert asked Himmler if he could invite his father and his best man George as well. Himmler consented. Perhaps they could smoke cigars and have a cognac or two, Herbert proffered. Himmler was pleased.

After the wedding reception, the five men greeted each other in the drawing room. Herbert poured out the drinks and in doing so released the conversation. Himmler was the smallest of the five men at only five foot eight inches tall, the same height as Hitler. Reichsführer Schutzstaffel (SS) Himmler (chief of the SS units) was advocating to be appointed as the chief of the German Reich police, and he hoped that when the Anschluss (connection) was in place he would be Hans Holweg's superior. He therefore directed his significant presence to the Deputy Commissioner of the Vienna Police. Holding his cognac in his left hand and swilling it before he took a sip he said to Hans, 'When the Anschluss occurs, we'll finally be one. Your past actions against our German-speaking people will not be forgotten nor forgiven! You do realise in the latest incident in Vienna 140 of us died and 600 were injured, 13 were executed, and over 4,000 imprisoned without trial. Many thousands of us were arrested, and some 4,000 fled across the border to the German Reich and Yugoslavia. Herr Deputy Commissioner, as a true friend of Herbert I must advise you to resign from your commission as soon as possible, and in your resignation letter state that you can't support a regime that's acting as a bulwark against German Reich hegemony.'

'Herr Himmler,' Hans said, stretching to the full height of his six foot two inch frame, 'I appreciate your advice, and understand that you and I want my son-in-law and my daughter to live a fruitful and happy life. However, I'm a simple servant of the people, and when the people enact rights and laws to make the Austrian way of life safe and civil, who am I to disagree? If I felt that the current laws were against my moral and ethical beliefs, I would resign and seek another vocation. But to murder innocent citizens for an ideology is beyond my comprehension. Our democracy, unlike a dictatorship, will endure. I hope that you appreciate my position.'

Himmler looked first at him and then at Herbert. Brother, his eyes said to Herbert, how can I keep your family safe with a father-in-law that is so defective?

Herbert suddenly directed his attention to Hans, although he was really speaking to Himmler. 'Hans, life is more malleable than what is written in black and white and enacted in law. As Himmler has suggested, there's a higher order to life. When the German-speaking peoples were in the ascendancy there was no distinction between the

Anglo-Saxons, the Dutch, the Germans, and Austrians. We created calculus – think of Leibnitz! We created music and opera – Wagner. What's more, we created philosophy – Nietzsche. It's our destiny to lead and to reunite the German peoples as one. You're becoming older and perhaps you should spend more time with Eva and your family. I hope you don't think I'm impertinent when I say retiring might be an option well worth considering.'

Himmler looked pleased but George looked dismayed. How can you see all human accomplishments through a Germanic lens, he thought, and still remain credible my friend?

Peter was silent, bemused. The Nazis always know what was patriotic and what was treachery. They had destroyed the Weimar Republic because it was deemed by them to be unpatriotic. The German Jews, Romani (gypsies), and communists were unpatriotic: their allegiances did not solely lie within German culture. The Nazi's notion of Aryanism was built on a racial ideology, in order to claim a racial superiority. As Lutherans, Peter reasoned, we pray to God and his manifestation on Earth, Jesus. No wonder they hate the Jews and religion in general. In the act of being Christian and praying to a Jew, we are subtly confessing that Aryans are not the master race.

Hans stood up and handed his glass to Herbert, giving his comments the recognition that they deserved – none! 'Make your family the centre of your happiness and the source of all your inspirations,' he advised Herbert.

He then turned to Himmler and said, 'Hopefully Austria will always display the independent spirit forged and framed by the Hapsburgs. I'm a nationalist, I'm just not a German Reich nationalist!'

Himmler looked at him in disbelief. He did not trust or like people who were unafraid of him, and Hans Holweg was just that: a man who had dealt with powerful people before. He knew when to hold his ground.

'The unification of German peoples,' Himmler declared, 'is the sole wish of our Austrian Emperor Hitler. Sieg Heil!' Himmler gave a Nazi salute that Herbert and, reluctantly, Peter mimicked. Himmler's remark that Hitler, leader and Chancellor of the German Reich, was an Austrian Emperor was not lost on Hans or George. Hans smiled and walked out of the room, ignoring the salute. It was the second time that night George had remained seated and did not respond to a Nazi salute, but this time no one noticed, because all were staring at the back of Hans Holweg as he departed.

13

On returning to Vienna Hans Holweg was deeply troubled. He had never suspected that Herbert was a Nazi sympathiser or, God forbid, a member of the Nazi party. It was now clear that he was one or the other, and his eldest daughter had sealed her fate with him.

Hans was worried about his Jewish connections. Rachel Sulzer, his late non-residential housekeeper, had been murdered in 1932 in the Café Sperlhof by two thugs wearing swastikas. While he could not lead the investigation, due to his seniority, he nevertheless made it known to his investigative team that he had a personal interest in the case. Hans was briefed daily on the progress and when they amassed evidence and arrested two Austrian Nazis and charged them with her murder, Hans made certain that the best Viennese prosecutor took on the case. Both men were found guilty and were jailed for the rest of their natural lives.

The murder of Joseph Sulzer in December 1935 placed his family in further jeopardy. Hans reassembled Rachel's investigative team to oversee the case. What was troubling for him, then and now, was that no evidence could be found to link the murder to anyone or any group. The only evidence that they had was the bullet, which had been left in the corpse. It was issued from a Luger P.08 sidearm. This make of gun was a favourite for the German Reich army and the SS.

The investigative team reported to Holweg that all the indications pointed to a professional hit ordered by a high Nazi official such as Heinrich Himmler. In the light of his daughter's wedding, alarm bells were now sounding in his mind.

Hans knew Rachel's daughter Anna was in Berlin; the investigative team had tracked her there. He needed to permanently sever this Jewish connection in order to protect his wife and two daughters. He needed to secure new identity papers for Anna Sulzer. He also needed to doctor or destroy the team's report about the death of Joseph Sulzer. Hans chose the former strategy, to doctor the report, since the case needed to remain officially open in the Vienna police files.

Gaining access to the team's report was easy: Hans called, and it was delivered. He got rid of any reference to a professional hit attributed to Himmler by removing one page from the report. He now turned his attention to Anna's whereabouts. This information was contained in the last paragraph of the last page. Using a pair of scissors he carefully removed the last paragraph. This page was now shorter than the rest, but as it was the last page and none of the pages had footers it did not appear out of the ordinary. However, the page numbering in the header was no longer in sequence, because of page he had removed. He tinkered with the idea of renumbering each page, and then he realised it would create more problems than it solved. He would leave the numbering as it was. The numbering might be seen as a typing mistake, he reasoned, or it might be concluded that a page had gone missing, but either way it would be considered trivial, because none of the team would dare to mention that they suspected Himmler of ordering a murder in Austria.

The following day Hans visited Births, Deaths, and Marriages, a major department in the Austrian government. He addressed the receptionist in the foyer: 'My name is Hans Holweg and I'm the Deputy Commissioner of the Vienna Police. I wonder if it's possible for me to talk to Deputy Director Karl Doppler, please? It's a police matter.'

The receptionist picked up the telephone and rang an internal number. She spoke softly into the receiver, and then placed it back on its cradle. 'He's waiting for you in room 102,' she said politely. 'Just go up these stairs and turn to your right.'

He knocked on the door and Karl immediately opened it and greeted him. 'Hans, so good to see you! The last time we spoke was at the opera in the interval of Don Giovanni. How can I help?'

'I've come because of one of my open cases: the murder of Joseph Sulzer. The investigative team on the case did an excellent job, but one of the pages of their report has gone missing. It's an open case, and so we need to retype the information it contained and reincorporate it into the document.'

Karl queried, 'Missing?'

'Yes, we don't know what happened to it. We've speculated that the page may have been waylaid during the typing of the report, fallen on the floor or found its way to a rubbish bin. Either way, the page did contain the identification of a possible suspect, an Austrian Nazi called Schmidt. I wonder if it's possible for me to look at your records to see if I can locate his birth certificate?'

'You don't have to do that, Hans. I'll call in one of my clerks, and he'll recover the file for you.'

'There's an additional problem. I only have his last name and without further information it would be impossible for your clerk to find him in your records. However, I do have a general description of him from memory, and several other pieces of information that would make the search much faster if I did it myself.'

'Okay, but don't say I didn't try to make it easier for you.' Karl opened the door and shouted, 'Franz!' A small man in an ill-fitted suit appeared. 'Could you please take the Deputy Commissioner of the Vienna Police, Hans Holweg, to the record storage area and give him every assistance in his search for a Herr Schmidt.'

In the storage area the clerk marched past large volumes of cabinets and stopped in front of one marked 'S'. Hans pointed to a chair nearby, indicating that the clerk could be seated while Hans checked the records. In reality, he was searching for a birth certificate of a female born roughly in the same year as Anna, fitting her description in terms of eye colouring and living in Vienna, and who was still alive. He could see that the more he searched the more disinterested the clerk was in watching him. Occasionally the clerk would nod off, then snap back into consciousness.

Hans pushed past many files, discarding them because his criteria were not met on one ground or another. He was starting to panic when he reached the 'Sch' section of the cabinet. Suddenly he sighted a file marked Anna Schuster. The first names matched, which was handy but not really important. She was two years older than Anna Sulzer. Hmm, he thought, we can live with that, and he read on. She had the same eye colouring, and she had been born in a poor district in Vienna. She was Catholic. He turned to see what Franz was doing. He was snoozing. Hans returned to the file. There was no death certificate. There was no marriage certificate. He slid out her birth certificate, looked in the direction of the clerk, saw he was still snoozing, slipped the birth certificate into his pocket and went on with the search, but now he was searching for Ilse Schwab. He found her. Hans turned to Franz, who had changed his position in the chair, but with eyes still closed. He located Ilse's birth certificate and replaced it with another. Hans located a Schmidt who was alive and in his thirties.

'Franz!' Hans said the clerk's name loud enough to wake him. 'I think I've found my man. Could you please retype this file and send it to my office.'

Hans went back upstairs and said goodbye to Deputy Director Karl Doppler. For the next stage of his plan he would have to wait until Magrete returned from her honeymoon. He would ring her and ask her to do him a favour. He had no idea at that time how Anna would use her new identity. All that interested him was to isolate his family from this Jewish connection.

14

Elfi and Peter von Appen paid for Magrete and Herbert's one-month honeymoon in Venice. Their presidential suite overlooked the picturesque Canal Grande. As raw sewage was pumped into the canals, a slight foetid odour lingered in the air. In the mornings, Magrete and Herbert would walk to the marble steps outside the hotel where a private gondola was moored, waiting to take them anywhere they wished to visit. They visited St Mark's Square, the Doge's Palace, the Bridge of Sighs and the Rialto Bridge. Although neither Magrete nor Herbert were devout Christians, they prayed in St Mark's Basilica, Madonna dell'Orto and Santa Maria della Salute. They bought ice cream from the Gelateria Nico and strolled arm in arm down alleyways that meandered through the inner city. They visited three of the lagoon islands, namely Murano, Burrano and San Lazzaro degli Armeni, the latter lies between Venice and the Lido, and houses the only local monastery that was not suppressed by Napoleon. Monks from the Armenian order now occupied this remote place. Magrete and Herbert understood why Lord Byron, the English poet, loved its serene and tranquil ambiance. They read Byron's poetry as they picnicked on its shores, in love with the poetry, in love with the island, and madly in love with each other.

There was an undercurrent bubbling in Venice that Magrete was aware of, but that Herbert seemed oblivious to. She had noticed that whenever they were guided through a church, a chapel, or a historic building, the link between Imperial Rome and Venice was always highlighted. Venice, her guides claimed, was founded just as Rome fell and continued to expand Roman heritage and influence in the Mediterranean. In Vienna, Magrete had been well educated in history by nuns who were in particular knowledgeable about the Roman Empire, and she felt if such a link existed, the nuns would have taught it.

She suspected that, as Venice was a tourist gateway, Mussolini was aware of its potential to advertise his particular form of Fascism as a legitimate consequence of the Roman Empire. Venice was described by the Italian Fascist propaganda as being the principal heir to the Roman Empire. Magrete could see that important allies in the establishment and re-enactment of such a myth were the Catholic Church in Venice and the city nobles. This rewriting of history, she reasoned, was Mussolini making a claim that his people were the master race, as exemplified by the Roman Empire.

She wanted to test her hypothesis on Herbert, but on each occasion she raised the subject he was dismissive or disinterested. In fact, on one occasion he said quite angrily to her that Italians could not possibly belong to the master race, because they were not Aryan. It saddened her that he believed in the Aryanisation of the German Reich and that Aryans were the master race. Like so many newlyweds before her, Magrete suddenly came to the realisation that she knew very little of what really mattered to her husband.

15

When they arrived back at the villa in Wannsee, they noticed that massive changes had been made to both the interior and exterior. The villa had been totally renovated in the month of their absence, which suggested that planning for this work had occurred over several months, if not years, without their knowledge or input. The villa was now reconstructed into two living quarters. Downstairs were the parents' living quarters, namely a bedroom, two bathrooms, a guest room, lounge room and a study, as well as the kitchen and a large dining room. The large reception hall and drawing room no longer existed. The upstairs quarters now consisted of three bedrooms, two bathrooms, a playroom, and study.

Peter von Appen was particularly proud of the outside rear entry to the upstairs rooms, which gave the newlyweds a private entry into their living quarters. The cellar had an entry via the kitchen and so remained the province of the kitchen staff. The attic was another space allocated to Magrete and Herbert to do with as they pleased.

The service quarters had been relocated to a newly renovated gatekeeper's house situated near the entrance gate to the villa. The gardener, Max, had vacated the premises when he got married and had children. The garage that used to be a barn had been extended, in order for it to house six cars. The chauffeur was particularly pleased with this renovation.

Peter proudly gave keys to Magrete near their outside private entrance and said to her, 'Please live here for the rest of your life. As you can see, there are plenty of bedrooms that need to be filled with the sounds of children laughing and crying.' He smiled and winked at her.

'This must have cost you a fortune,' Magrete said gratefully. 'Thank you so much for wanting us to live with you – it will be an honour for both of us! In your autumn years, it will be so important for your grandchildren to learn so much from the two of you.' They hugged and kissed one another.

'Now, there's one other thing we women need to discuss,' Elfi said to Magrete. 'Go, boys, to the house!' Both men did as they were ordered and retreated. Elfi then turned to Magrete. 'We've currently four servants in the house: Tomas, Gertrude, and the two cooks, Lotte and her daughter Emma. The gardener and chauffeur are non-residential. We've plenty of room in the servant quarters for another woman servant. I want you to talk to Gertrude and interview a young woman to be your personal maid, one that would primarily keep the upstairs quarters clean, and look after our grandchildren. Of course, she'll be under your instructions, and when you're not home under Gertrude's.'

'Perhaps, Mum,' Magrete carefully proffered, 'it might be best if I make the initial enquiries and bring Gertrude into the picture near the end of the appointment process.'

Magrete has something in mind, thought Elfi, but whatever it is, she's showing me that she's more than capable of managing the staff on her terms; she'll do the initial culling, and Gertrude's opinions will be listened to, but at the end of the process. This side of Magrete was new to her.

16

Scheunenviertel (Barn Quarter) was a neighbourhood of Mitte (Middle) in the centre of Berlin. It was situated to the north of the medieval Altberlin (Old Berlin), east of the Rosenthalerstraße (Rosenthaler Street) and Hackescher Market. It was regarded as a slum district and had a substantial Eastern European Jewish population.

Magrete took the train to Hackescher Market and made her way along Rosenthalerstraße. It was a cold and windy but cloudless day. She was wearing sunglasses, and a heavy overcoat. She stopped at a small door in an alleyway off Rosenthalerstraße. Magrete looked to her right, then to her left and knocked. An old woman wearing a beautiful silk scarf answered the door and immediately embraced Magrete, kissing her on the right and left cheeks. 'Magrete, please come in.' Ester was in shock. She recognised Magrete from a photograph in the newspaper.

The corridor was short and narrow and led to a steep stairway. The women were talking as they entered a large room, which served as a kitchen, bedroom and dining room. Sitting on the bed was a small fourteen-year-old girl, with big oval hazel eyes and long dark brown hair, wearing a grey sack dress and sandals. 'So this must be Anna,' Magrete beamed. 'Come and give me a hug.' Her grandmother gestured for Anna to get up and hug the visitor, and Anna complied.

'You look the spitting image of your mother,' Magrete observed, cupping her hands behind Anna's ears to bring Anna's face closer to hers. 'You're beautiful,' she added.

'Thank you ma'am,' Anna said, blushing with embarrassment.

'I was honeymooning in Venice when the household received your letter,' Magrete informed Ester. 'When I read it I did not know what to do, but after I spoke to Papa, I now think I have a solution. Here is a complete dossier that Anna needs to memorise. One mistake and all will be lost! Here are Anna's new identity papers. Her surname is Schuster. Do not ask me where I got them. If asked, she needs to be fluent and confident about her new past. She is now two years older than her actual age.'

'Leave it to me! I'll make sure that Anna studies this well,' Ester replied determinedly. A tear dropped down her cheek – she was so relieved that Anna might find a way out of this Jewish ghetto. Ester knew her fate was sealed, but she hoped that Anna would be spared.

'I am so sorry about Rachel,' Magrete said, looking distressed. Then, looking at Anna, she said, with emphasis, 'You only have a month to get it perfect.' Then she looked in turn to each of them. 'Rachel was special to me; she was so important in my mother's recovery! Do not see me out. I will see you, Anna, at Wannsee.'

Rachel was at the wrong place at the wrong time, thought Ester. She had been in a prayer room in the café Sperlhof in 1932 when she had been severely beaten by the thugs wearing swastikas. She died two days later. Ester's granddaughter, Anna, was only ten at the time. Anna's father Joseph Sulzer helped organise the Jewish Self-Defense Brigade that conducted street patrols and took action against Hakenkreuzler (the thugs bearing swastikas). He was murdered in December 1935. Friends of the family could not locate Joseph's sister, Ayelet, who was secreted somewhere in Berlin. However, they did locate Ester, who was also in Berlin. They paid for Anna to go to Berlin to be reunited with her grandmother.

In late March, when Ester bought the Berliner Tagblatt, an important liberal newspaper, she read an article in the society pages describing one of the most important weddings of the year: 'Magrete Holweg, daughter of the Deputy Commissioner of the Vienna Police, Hans Holweg, will marry Herbert von Appen, heir to the von Appen fortune on the 4th of April …' The photograph of them was romantic and respectful. The article ended on a slightly humorous, but pointed note: 'Herr Herbert Holweg is well respected amongst the Nazi hierarchy. Is this the beginning of the Anschluss?'

It was then Ester had remembered Magrete's connection to her family. She wrote Magrete a letter telling her of Rachel and Joseph Sulzer's deaths, and of her own precarious existence in Berlin. She begged Magrete to take in her granddaughter Anna. Ester waited for a reply, but none was forthcoming. She concluded that Magrete had wanted to forget a shared past, because acknowledging Anna, or her, might jeopardise Magrete's family. Now she realised Magrete had been honeymooning when she had sent the letter and, more importantly, that she had not forgotten her love for Rachel.

Ester knew what a risk Magrete was taking, not only for herself, but also for her family and her in-laws. Why? It must be because her daughter had been critical to Magrete's mother Eva not committing suicide after the birth of her stillborn child.

Ester vowed that Anna would pass any test.

17

It came as a surprise to Elfi that Magrete had proposed that both of them should interview the three shortlisted women for the position of Magrete's personal maid. After all, Magrete had done the shortlisting of the candidates in consultation with Gertrude, so Elfi wondered about her sudden inclusion. Were there two applicants that were splitting Gertrude and Magrete? She read the résumés. Two of the applicants were women in their early thirties who lived locally. The third was an interesting selection, a sixteen-year-old girl who was the daughter of Eva and Hans' non-residential housekeeper. So that's why I've been included in the decision-making process, thought Elfi.

After six months in the house, Magrete made no secret of the fact that she was embarrassed to give Gertrude orders, since Gertrude was just seven years younger than her mother. Elfi noted that Magrete did appear uncomfortable in the presence of Gertrude and Tomas, whereas she took no nonsense from Lotte, who was in her early thirties.

Elfi and Magrete sat at a dining room table. Elfi tugged on a cord behind her that silently informed Gertrude to bring in the first person to be interviewed. Gertrude brought in the applicant, introduced her as Frau Frieda Schulze, and then positioned herself behind the applicant's left shoulder. Elfi and Magrete pored over her résumé again. Elfi led the interview, asking a number of clarifying questions about her work experience, marital status, family needs, and housing requirements. Magrete took another pathway of enquiry, focussing on character, demeanour and particularly on the applicant's learning potential. This line of enquiry surprised Elfi, but for Gertrude it was of deep concern – she was uncomfortable with servants who had a more ambitious agenda. Once the interview was over, Gertrude escorted Frau Schulze out of the room and promptly returned. At this point Elfi requested Gertrude to express her opinion regarding the strengths and weaknesses of the applicant with respect to the position at hand.

'My lady,' Gertrude said, addressing Elfi, 'she has some experience and does come across as being very strong-headed. Some of her answers were curt, to say the least. On the positive side, her requirements are few and of the four who applied for the position, she was the most secure, family-wise.'

Elfi was surprised to discover that there had been only four applicants for the position. Unemployment was still very significant in Berlin, especially for women seeking work. Perhaps, Elfi mused, Magrete might have shown Gertrude only four applications rather than all the applications. Then she told herself not to be cynical. 'Thank you, Gertrude. Please bring in the next applicant.'

The second applicant, Frau Erika Heinz, was physically much sturdier than Frau Schulze. After Elfi's probing it was clear she was the favourite thus far. Her service records were excellent. Her last employer noted that if it had not been for the Great Depression, she would have remained in their employ. In 1933, when she was let go, some six million Germans were unemployed. She was also trained as a midwife, and Elfi reasoned that this might come in handy for Magrete in the not-too-distant future.

Magrete started her enquiries in a similar vein to the previous applicant, and then veered slightly, but pointedly away from her previous script.

She asked, 'Have you taught children how to read or write or do arithmetic operations?'

'No, ma'am,' Frau Heinz answered nervously.

'Is that because you find reading, writing and doing arithmetic difficult?'

'Yes, ma'am,' Frau Heinz answered, lowering her eyes.

'Can you read and write?'

'No, ma'am,' Frau Heinz answered honestly.

Sheeting home her line of enquiry Magrete asked, 'Then who put this résumé together?'

'Tomas, ma'am! He's my uncle on my mother's side,' Frau Heinz revealed shyly.

'Thank you,' Magrete replied. She had seen and read a handwritten draft of Frau Heinz's résumé that Tomas had carelessly left on Peter's desk. She was familiar with Tomas' handwriting, because of the notes he would occasionally pass to her. When the application was delivered it was typed, with Frau Heinz's signature at the bottom of the page.

When Gertrude returned, Magrete could see the shock of the revelation still resonating on her face. Elfi spoke directly to Gertrude. 'Having Tomas' niece as an employee could be a strength or then again a weakness. It could change the balance of authority within the household. How do you feel about the situation, Gertrude?'

'Well, my lady, she is the most qualified of the short-listed applicants on paper. I can work with her if she is chosen. Nevertheless, I agree it could be awkward. We already have problems with Emma and Lotte, but they are distant from you and your family. Also, I'm the person who directs them about your concerns and requirements. If we hire Frau Heinz we might have to review the line of authority, with your family solely directing her, because if I rebuke her on some matter, her uncle might not be pleased with me, and as he is the head servant of the household, it could create unease amongst the other servants in your employ.'

'I can see the awkwardness of such a relationship,' Magrete said rephrasing Gertrude's fear. 'I have another concern.' Both women turned to her. 'I would prefer to have a personal maid who is literate and numerate and could double as a governess if need be. Someone who has attended high school, and who has the potential to learn more than just housework; someone who can frame a budget; someone we can groom in the longer term to take over Gertrude's position when Gertrude decides to retire, in decades to come.'

Elfi smiled. Magrete, she felt, was manipulating them. Every idea she expressed made sense – successional planning, generational change, having a governess and framing a budget – and yet there was something a little contrived about all of this. She had shortlisted one candidate who should have never been interviewed, and another who might create disharmony and change the line of authority due to a familial relationship. Elfi decided to see how it played out.

Elfi turned to Gertrude. 'Please bring in Frau Schuster.'

Anna followed Gertrude into the room. Gertrude introduced her and positioned herself as before. Elfi looked up and saw a child.

Everyone is looking far too young these days, she thought. Sixteen, and she barely looks thirteen. She reiterated her line of enquiry and then handed the questioning over to Magrete.

'Frau Schuster, when did you leave high school?'

'When I was fourteen, ma'am,' Anna said confidently.

Magrete hoped that Anna would understand her next question. 'Are you literate and numerate?'

'Yes, ma'am! I can read, write and do arithmetic.'

Ester had tutored Anna well, thought Magrete.

'It says in your résumé that you have babysat young children. Could you please explain what that entailed?'

'Ma'am, when I left school and couldn't find employment, I'd babysit for family members, who needed help because they worked. Most women in my extended family make, mend, iron and wash clothes or are non-residential servants. So I would wash and change nappies, feed and dress children. I'd play with the older ones, and read books to them. My mother, for example, worked for the Deputy Commissioner of the Vienna Police, which gave me an insight into the chores of a non-residential housekeeper-'

'My father is the Deputy Commissioner of the Vienna Police,' interrupted Magrete, 'and yet I have never met you and barely remember your mother.'

'Yes, ma'am. You and your sister Mimi were in boarding school and over the summer and during school vacations your family would not require my mother's services. Apparently your mother, Lady Holweg, wanted the two of you to understand domestic responsibilities – or so my mother said.'

Magrete looked at Elfi to indicate she was done with the interview. Elfi said officiously, 'Thank you, Frau Schuster.' Anna lowered her eyes, curtsied and left the room.

Elfi turned to Gertrude. 'Magrete and I will need to discuss a few private matters. I'll call you when we're finished.' Gertrude nodded, a wry smile on her face. It seemed to Magrete that Elfi and Gertrude had discussed the shortlist and the inclusion of Anna.

Once the room was cleared, Elfi asked, 'Why is she in Berlin?'

'When Papa telephoned,' Magrete answered, 'I told him of this position. He told me that Frau Schuster was visiting her grandmother in Berlin, and he asked me if she could apply for the position.'

Elfi smiled as she enquired, 'Is she pregnant?' Magrete was stunned. 'Come on, Magrete, don't be so naïve,' Elfi said with some dismay. 'She has been in and out of a number of households for two years now. The women of the house are always absent when she works. Most of the children she has babysat are too young to comprehend their surroundings, let alone anything more complicated. She is young, on the cusp of womanhood, and stunning. Many a girl has come to Berlin to visit their relatives, with families masking the real purpose of the visit – they've come here seeking an abortion! She may be in the early stages of her pregnancy. Is she pregnant?' Elfi asked the last question with greater force.

Magrete sat still, her lips slightly parted. Finally, she responded, meekly and distractedly, 'I do not know.'

'This household can't afford a scandal,' Elfi said sternly. 'We'll hire her on probation for three months and if it becomes evident that she's pregnant, her position here will be immediately terminated with consequences. However, first I want you to ask her grandmother directly whether she's pregnant or not. If she is, we'll offer Frau Heinz the position, or re-advertise.' Magrete nodded, still in shock.

Elfi tugged the cord and Gertrude entered. Elfi asked, 'What do you think, Gertrude?'

Gertrude looked at Magrete and could see that the question of pregnancy had really shocked her. Gertrude now needed to navigate a considered course. She knew Magrete wanted to appoint Anna, and so she would give Anna's appointment notional support. Gertrude did not want Tomas' niece on the staff and did not want to be bypassed via another line of authority. 'My lady,' Gertrude addressed Elfi, 'she's young and beautiful and is not as yet in any sort of romantic relationship, or so she told me. She's got a lot of potential. She's bright and quick-witted. However, she has a lot to learn before she reaches Frau Heinz's level of competence. She told me she's ready to start at any time. I believe she'll make a valuable contribution to the household in the long-term.'

'Thank you, Gertrude. I think I can safely say that Frau Schuster is, at the moment, the strongest candidate. However, before she's placed on probation, Magrete needs to make some additional enquiries. Please let all three candidates know that a decision will be made tomorrow.'

A veil had been lifted from Magrete's eyes. She looked at Elfi and understood who was running the household, and how the household was being run.

18

The following day Magrete revisited the house in Rosenthalerstraße. She was nervous and hoped that Anna was not pregnant. She knocked on the door and it was quickly opened. Ester instantly hugged her and asked, 'Did she get the job?'

'Not yet,' Magrete answered. 'I need you to tell me truthfully. Is Anna pregnant?'

Ester stared at her. 'Of course not!'

'Ester, Anna will be on a three-month probation and if there is even a hint of a pregnancy her position will be immediately terminated, and with consequences.'

'Come upstairs,' Ester said. 'Anna is at the market, and we shouldn't talk about this at the front door.'

On entering the large room Ester looked more relaxed. 'Look at this room. We've both been living like two peas in a pod in this one room. Anna had her period last week! Has she got the position?'

'Yes!' Magrete cried. They hugged as Ester wept. Then they heard the front door open and close, footsteps on the stairs, and Anna appeared. She saw Magrete and dropped the groceries on the floor as she ran to them. 'You have got the position,' Magrete said quickly. 'First on a three-month probation, and then permanently.'

Ester and Anna hugged, and Magrete heard Ester whisper in Anna's ear, 'You're safe now. Don't let this chance slip away. Be strong, my love, be strong!' Magrete knew she could not swim against the tide, but so long as she kept Anna safe and alive, this one act of defiance would be a continual reminder of who she wanted to be and not how the German Reich wanted to define her.

Just before Magrete left, and out of view of Anna, Ester handed Magrete Anna's birth certificate and identity papers and said, 'She'll need these one day.'

When Magrete arrived back at the villa with Anna, the household knew who had been appointed to the position. Elfi summoned Gertrude and said in front of Magrete, but not in front of Anna, 'You'll need to take Frau Schuster under your wing, Gertrude. Whenever Magrete is not in the house or not upstairs, Frau Schuster will report to you. Frau Schuster is young and pretty and so you must protect her from the advances of temporary male staff and others who may take advantage of her, until she is old enough to protect herself. She is Emma's age and so the two of them will share a bedroom. I'll go and speak to Tomas and let him know why his niece has been overlooked.'

Magrete felt a little uneasy. Twice Elfi had alluded to the sexual activity of female domestics, first when she had asked if Anna was pregnant, and now this. Was such activity so rife in domestic households?

Suddenly Magrete was brought back to reality. 'This came for you today,' Elfi said, handing Magrete a small addressed envelope. Magrete opened it and read: 'Frau Margarete Himmler requests the pleasure of Frau Magrete von Appen's company for afternoon tea on Friday 5th of June at 3pm.'

Magrete handed it to Elfi, who read it and appeared unimpressed. 'You'd better show this to your husband.'

19

Magrete arrived at the house at five minutes to three. Her dress was casual but stylish. Her brownish blonde hair was cropped in a Jean Harlow style; the elegant waves both accentuated and softened her features. She appeared sensual and very wealthy.

Magrete's husband had told her all he knew about Margarete Himmler. She had trained as a nurse during the Great War and was appointed to a Deutsches Rotes Kreuz (DRK or German Red Cross) hospital near the end of the war. Her first marriage did not last long. It was childless. With her father's support, she operated and directed a private nursing clinic in Berlin. She had married Himmler in July 1928, and was seven years his senior. They had one child of their own, Gudrun, born in 1929, and had adopted a son, Gerhart, in 1933. They had recently occupied a large house in Dalhem (Berlin) – an official residence that came with Himmler's government responsibilities.

Magrete stood at the front door of the Himmlers' residence, waited until exactly 3 pm, and rang the doorbell. A man opened the door, obviously a valet, and ushered her through to the back porch, where she could see Margarete.

When Magrete approached her, Margarete rose, barely remembering Magrete from her wedding day. 'You must be Magrete. Just call me Marga.' The two women kissed one another on each cheek. Marga pointed to a wrought iron chair with a cushion on its seat, indicating that Magrete was to sit there. The two women looked faintly alike, almost as if they were related. Marga was some twenty-five years older than Magrete. Both had brownish blonde hair and a light complexion. Marga's hair was cropped shorter and was becoming darker as she aged. She wore glasses.

'Your name is very similar to my own, but the spelling is significantly different,' Marga observed.

'It is Norwegian in origin,' Magrete said.

'Oh,' Marga sounded disappointed. 'Nevertheless, we're both Aryans.' Magrete hated that description. 'I wanted to get to know you a little better,' Marga continued. 'At your wedding Himmler talked highly of your husband. He also tells me your father is the Deputy Commissioner of the Vienna Police, a job that is not too insignificant.' Magrete could see why people disliked Marga – she had the ability to render a compliment into a veiled criticism.

'Püppi (dolly)!' Marga screamed. 'Stop that!' Magrete looked in direction of the command and saw a young girl, perhaps seven years old, grabbing the tail of a small dog. A stout woman in her middle years ran across the lawn and lifted the child away from dog, which had started snarling and barking. She waved to Marga to indicate all was in control.

'She should lose more weight,' Marga said, referring to the governess. 'If Püppi had been bitten, all hell would've broken loose.' She appears to be obsessed with her own feelings to the exclusion of anyone else's, thought Magrete.

Marga smiled and said, 'I hear you had a profession before you were married.'

'I have a business and accounting diploma. I was employed in 1935 by the Kaiser Wilhelm Institute for Chemistry.'

'In my previous life, I trained as a nurse and operated and directed a medical clinic in Berlin,' Marga informed. A medical clinic, thought Magrete. Herbert told me it was a private nursing clinic. Is she so insecure that she is trying to exaggerate her importance to me? Is she competing with me?

'The clinic was well ahead of its time,' Marga continued. 'We were at the forefront of herbal medicines and homeopathy. Some of our breakthroughs in those areas shocked the medical world. Of course, I had to relinquish my practice when I married the second most important man in the German Reich!'

Just as Marga said this, Himmler appeared. 'Magrete, so glad to see you! Please don't get up.' He picked up Magrete's right hand and kissed it gently on her knuckles. From the look on Marga's face, Magrete gathered that Marga was angry Himmler had paid this much attention to a younger female. Magrete had known women who were far older than their husbands, and these wives shared three common traits: they were insecure when their husbands were in the company of younger women; they completely dominated their husbands and while their husbands complained about it, that was the main reason for the mutual attraction; and they tried to manage their husband's time away from them.

Himmler addressed Marga. 'Hitler is having a meeting at his Berlin apartment in the Reich Chancellery. We're laying down public relation strategies for the Berlin Olympics.'

Marga warned, 'Make sure you home for dinner tonight,' as Himmler walked away feeling embarrassed by the warning. Two out of three, thought Magrete.

When tea and biscuits were served Marga asked, 'Have you ever been to Hitler's apartment?'

Magrete's immediate instinct was to reply, 'Not yet!' but she decided to be wiser and more truthful. 'No,' she said, 'we really are not that important in the scheme of things.'

'Well, I can tell you it's lavish. His office is twice the size of any reception hall. The doors of the Reich Chancellery are grand, but his private rooms have a much more lived-in look, because of his clever use of baroque furniture.'

The conversation proceeded along these lines with Marga telling Magrete about all the important people she had met, about the generals who listened to her every word, and about her knowledge of medicine. Magrete listened but did not take in a single word.

Afternoon tea was over within the hour. 'We must do this again,' Marga said sincerely and then asked the valet to show Magrete the way out. Has she just insulted me, thought Magrete, by not showing me the way to the door?

As soon as she got home, Herbert wanted to know how it had gone. Magrete told him what had occurred and ended by saying, 'In one fell swoop she insulted me, belittled me, made me feel insecure, and treated me as worthless and unimportant.'

Herbert laughed and added, 'That's what Himmler says about her!'

Three out of three, thought Magrete, because she clearly strives to dominate Himmler just as she tried to dominate me.

20

On 17 June 1936 Hitler appointed Himmler as head of the unified police system of the Third Reich, as well as being in charge of the Gestapo. As Reichsführer-SS, he only answered to Hitler. The Gestapo now had the authority to investigate cases of treason, espionage, sabotage and criminal attacks on the Nazi party and, more generally, on the German Reich. They could operate without judicial oversight, placing the organisation above the law. People were unable to take action against them in the administrative courts, so the Nazis could not be legally forced to comply with the German Reich's own laws.

Himmler sent Hans Holweg a telegram informing him of his new responsibility and requesting Holweg not to arrest Austrian Nazis while high-level discussions took place between the Austrian Chancellor Kurt Schuschnigg and the German Reich authorities. In July 1936 the Austrian Chancellor signed an Austro–German Reich Agreement, which, among other concessions, allowed the release of imprisoned July Putsch insurgents, much to the chagrin of Hans Holweg. Himmler was angry that the Nazi party was still banned in Austria.

From 1 August to 16 August 1936 the Summer Olympics dominated Berlin and the world. Every highlight was captured on newsreels and shown in cinemas all over the world. Radio issued live broadcasts of the events. The German Reich dominated every medal count, accumulating thirty-three gold, twenty-six silver and thirty bronze medals, with an accumulated total of eighty-nine medals. The person who spoilt the party for the Nazis was African-American Jesse Owens, who won four gold medals, three individually and one in a team event. His success challenged the doctrine of Aryanism. You only needed one counterexample to render a concept false, and he was it. The three amigos coincidentally watch every one of his victories. Magrete was secretly pleased, George was bemused, and Herbert was livid!

At the beginning of September Elfi, Magrete, and Gertrude reviewed Anna's performance. Elfi wanted to first hear from Gertrude about how Frau Schuster fitted in with the rest of the staff, and whether Tomas had accepted the decision to appoint Frau Schuster over his niece.

'Can I start with Tomas first, my lady? I think he was initially hoping that Frau Schuster would fail so that his niece might be reconsidered. However, to his credit he has accepted that Frau Schuster is very obedient, respectful and a quick learner, and I believe he'll eventually see her as an asset to the household.' Elfi looked pleased as Gertrude continued. 'Frau Schuster really interacts well with the cooks. In fact, Emma and she are getting on well. She has had a beneficial effect on Emma in that Emma is no longer as belligerent as before. Of course, Lotte has taken to Frau Schuster as if she is her second daughter.'

Magrete was glad to hear Anna was making friends.

'Frau Schuster is a good listener and is a not lazy person,' Gertrude continued. 'If she doesn't understand what she has been told to do, she'll question you until she understands what's required of her. She does have one flaw though: she gets emotional on occasions.

When she's in her bedroom alone, I sometimes hear her crying. If I approach her about what's troubling her, she says little and gives you the impression it's because her mother has written her a letter, when no letter has been delivered to her. I think she misses her family.'

Elfi frowned and turned to Magrete. 'It's strange that her mother has never written or enquired after her since her appointment.'

'I should have told you that I take Frau Schuster with me sometimes when I go shopping, and we visit her grandmother,' Magrete lied. 'Her mother writes letters to Frau Schuster and sends them to her grandmother's address. She knows the ins and outs of being in service, and so she does not want to disturb our household.'

Elfi and Gertrude did recall Magrete taking Frau Schuster on shopping trips and so both seemed satisfied with her explanation.

'I know you're happy with her,' Elfi said to Magrete. 'You've told me so at least once every week!' They both smiled.

'As for me,' continued Elfi, 'I'm really pleased with her. I think we can now change her status from probationary to ongoing. We'll now refer to her as Anna rather than Frau Schuster. Could you please write to her mother, Magrete, and inform her of Anna's changed status. If ever Anna's mother is in Berlin, we'd be more than happy for her to visit her daughter here. Just let Gertrude know, and she'll make all the arrangements.'

21

From September 1936 through to February 1937 there was little that was eventful for Magrete. She continued to worry excessively about her health and diet. She visited her doctor and was advised that matters such as pregnancy took time. Magrete was afraid that she and Herbert might not be able to conceive.

Magrete decided to take up yoga to better control her state of mind. In 1936 Eugen Herrigel had delivered a lecture titled 'The

Chivalrous Art of Archery' to the German–Japanese Society in Berlin, and the three amigos had been in the audience. George wondered whether he could apply the same Zen inner thought process to push his fencing onto a higher level. From that point in time Magrete was fascinated with the Orient, and eventually she read an article on yoga. She found a yoga teacher in Berlin, Indira Devi. Indira was an early disciple of Sri Tirumalai Krishnamacharya, whose instruction reflected his conviction that yoga could be both a spiritual practice and a mode of physical healing. Herbert told Magrete that Himmler was fascinated by India, and deeply influenced by the Indologist SS Captain Jakob Wilhelm Hauer of the University of Tübingen, a yoga scholar. In fact, Herbert said that Himmler carried a copy of the Bhagavad Gita in his pocket. This information did not deter Magrete from continuing with her yoga lessons, although she grimaced at the thought that she and Himmler shared a fascination with India and yoga.

For Herbert the lack of a pregnancy was even more distressing. The party propaganda machine of the German Reich emphasised the importance of a large family. The party had set-up an office to deal specifically with mothers and their children: the Mother and Child Welfare Office. Herbert was desperate for Magrete to become pregnant. However, if pregnancy did not eventuate they would foster or adopt at least one child. Herbert suggested this to Magrete after he discovered that in 1933 the Himmlers had become foster parents to a boy named Gerhard von Ahe, the son of an SS officer who had died.

The social side of their life was a different tale – the three amigos were in full swing again. Magrete and Herbert tried hard to matchmake their Hungarian amigo, but he found excuses why this or that woman was not right for him. Occasionally he would bring along a new companion, only for them never to see her again.

On the political front events were starting to shape the future. On 1 November 1936 Mussolini and Hitler agreed to form a military alliance and on 25 November the German Reich and Japan signed an anti-Comintern pact. The German Reich and Italy continued to aid Generalisimo Franco with an abundance of planes, tanks and arms, while the Soviet Union aided the Republican side.

Herbert decided he would join the National Socialist Flyers Korps (NSFK). It had begun as a paramilitary organisation of the Nazi party, founded in the early 1930s, during the years when the Treaty of Versailles forbade a German Air Force. The organisation's structure was based on the Sturmabteilung (SA – Storm Division) and maintained a system of paramilitary ranks. During the early years of its existence, the NSFK conducted military aviation training in gliders and private aeroplanes.

The Luftwaffe was established on 26 February 1935, led by Hermann Göring. Many of the NSFK members joined, giving this branch of the armed service a strong Nazi ideological base. The NSFK continued to exist after the Luftwaffe was founded, but on a much smaller scale.

After one year of part-time training Herbert gained his B2 license and was given the rank of Group Leader on receiving his coveted pilot wings. He progressed quickly because he already had his A2 license before he joined the NSFK. Magrete and his parents were not pleased with his increased focus on flying. His parents particularly missed his total focus on the company.

Magrete, on the other hand, did not approve of his increasing Nazi fever. It started to dawn on her that Herbert was slowly and surely being sucked deeper and deeper into the Nazi quagmire. When she first met him in Vienna, he was a fully fledged businessman. Even if he was a Nazi sympathiser or a party member, in Vienna he had suppressed those feelings at the time, she believed, because the Austrian Nazis were in constant battle with the authorities and most of the Austrian public was not sympathetic or supportive of their battles. Magrete recalled getting the first inkling of his feeling towards the Nazis in 1933, when he had become angry that the Austrian Nazi Party had been banned after a hand grenade attack in Krems.

The first time she knew that Himmler had befriended Herbert was when a carrier had delivered two large framed autographed photographs of Hitler and Himmler. A major row had erupted between Elfi and her son about where to position the photographs. Herbert wanted them in the reception hall, a demand that his mother flatly refused. She suggested that they hang in his bedroom for no one else to see. After much toing and froing Elfi relented and allowed them to be hung in the drawing room, a place she and her friends seldom frequented. With the rearrangement of the villa, the two photographs were now hung, each in one of the empty bedrooms upstairs, much to the delight of Elfi and Peter.

It seemed to Magrete that each time Herbert met Himmler, spoke to him on the telephone, or exchanged letters with him, his soul would slowly shrink before her. The only time he seemed like his old self was when the two of them were in the company of George – Herbert's humanity and humour would come to the fore again. However, the dark shadow of Himmler would always reappear. Magrete was determined that their future children would help immune Herbert from the Nazi influence and return to her the man she fell in love with in Vienna.

In August 1936 Tomas, the gardener and the chauffeur were conscripted into the Wehrmacht (defense force). Gertrude hired a non-residential gardener who was in his late fifties to attend to the property. The residential household domestics were now all females. Gertrude was in charge, and felt confident in her newly found authority.

22

In late February Magrete travelled to Vienna to see her parents and to help Mimi and her mother prepare for Mimi's wedding. The wedding was to be held in a small German Reich village only 17 kilometres from Salzburg called Freilassing. Cattle farming and the timber industry had dominated the village's early economy. However, with the construction of the Munich to Salzburg railway line in 1860, it became a major railway hub and so the village had prospered.

Albert Kuebler had studied for a veterinary science degree at the University of Vienna. His parents were pleased with his choice of degree, because they ran a small cattle farm on the outskirts of Freilassing. His second passion was music and while at university, nearing the end of his degree, he sought piano lessons. Hence, he met Mimi and within six months they announced their engagement and wedding date. Hans and Eva were surprised, but shook their heads, noting that Magrete and Mimi were poles apart – if Magrete became the tortoise then Mini would become the hare, and to complicate matters, Mimi would flip roles, depending on how Magrete reacted to a particular situation.

To assist the engaged couple financially, Albert moved into the Holwegs's household, which was located in Josefstadt, the eighth district of Vienna. It was near the city centre and had been established as a district in 1850. It was heavily populated, with many residential homes and in easy walking distance to the University of Vienna. The Holwegs lived next door to Kurt Gödel, an unpaid mathematics lecturer at the University of Vienna. They got on well, but whenever he talked about his research, the Holwegs tuned out.

Hans was pleased at Magrete's arrival, as he wanted to know how Anna had fared. He had rung Magrete after she returned from her honeymoon and talked about the need for the family to quarantine themselves from Rachel and Anna, due to the rising storm of anti-Semitism both in Austria and in the German Reich. Hans had asked Magrete if she had delivered Anna's new identity papers. She had thought fast and whispered to him, 'Look, Papa, if it was not for Rachel you would be without a wife, and we would be without Mutti. We must do more for Anna than just give her a new identity! When you send me her identity papers, I want you also to include a one-page character reference highlighting that her mother, Frau Schuster, is your non-resident housekeeper still in your employ and that over the years when Frau Schuster brought Anna to your residence, you observed her to be intelligent, polite and obedient. Hence you recommend that she would make an excellent maid one day. You also need to be prepared in case Elfi rings you to enquire about Anna, or to probe you for more detailed information about her.'

'But Schatz,' her father pleaded, 'don't you think one day they might visit us and expect to see Anna's mother?'

Hans could hear Magrete laugh. 'That is the least of our worries!' She rang off on those words. Magrete's logic was simple – you can always hide a bird, but you can never hide a flock. Anna needed to get away from the flock if she was to survive the German Reich.

Magrete was sharing Mimi's bedroom, because Albert was ensconced in her old bedroom. It was clear to Magrete that Albert had been in Mimi's bedroom more than once. She knew Mimi well, and knew she was not an avid reader of books such as How to Treat Common Ailments of Farm Animals (1936 edition), with page 120 earmarked. She placed the book in a more discreet location and started to unpack.

Magrete had noticed that after every evening meal her father would sit near the lounge room window and open the curtain ever so slightly, peering nervously into the street. She had asked him whether he was expecting someone, and he would always reply, 'No, Schatz,' but he would then conduct a full conversation with her without leaving his post or looking at her.

Her mother was also behaving in a mysterious manner. She was wringing her hands a lot, and talking to herself. For example, she would mutter: 'Now let us do the dishes' or 'Are we hungry?' and responded, as if she were two people.

Mimi behaved as if it was normal, and that night when Magrete went to bed she decided to tackle Mimi about it.

'Have you noticed that Papa is always staring into the street after a meal?' Magrete asked. 'He has never done that before. What is going on?'

'Old people do strange things,' Mimi replied. 'I think it started in June 1936 when our next-door neighbour Gödel found out his hero Moritz Schlick was assassinated by one of his former students, Johann Nelboeck. It made Gödel batty and it triggered a severe crisis in Dad later on. As deputy commissioner Dad probably feels he must protect his neighbour and so looks out the window to check for the presence of strangers.'

'I cannot believe that that is the sole reason. He is doing it habitually; he does not even know he is doing it.'

Magrete could see Mimi was not interested in further discussing the topic and so she decided to tackle the other problem that was bothering her.

'Tell me, then,' Magrete demanded, 'when did Mutti start addressing herself as if she was two people rolled into one?'

'I think that's funny, actually,' Mimi said flippantly. 'It started when she agreed you could have a civil marriage. Something snapped! Maybe it was the realisation that you would never live here again. She's including you in all of her conversations with herself.'

'Oh, come on, Mimi, that is the most ridiculous and specious explanation I have ever heard!'

'Your trouble is that you've been away for so long you can't remember their habits anymore, and anyway, whatever I say you'll always find fault with!' Mimi said with asperity. 'Just accept that our parents are getting old, and they're doing strange stuff. God, you should be grateful that they still remember you and that they haven't lost their memories altogether!'

'Mimi!' Magrete protested, but Mimi just shrugged. Magrete continued, 'Can't you see you are normalising their paranoid behaviour? Papa is now peering out of windows and Mutti is talking like a lunatic. Even when Mutti was suicidal, she was not like this!'

Mimi sat up. 'When was Mum suicidal?'

'Oh, forget it,' Magrete said, turning on her side with her back to Mimi.

Mimi got out of bed and went to the light switch. 'I'm turning off the light. We have to be in Freilassing tomorrow for the final wedding preparations. Please make my wedding a joyous affair, Magrete. Goodnight!'

'Goodnight,' Magrete repeated. 'I love you, and I know your wedding will be something for all of us to remember and treasure.'

The room fell silent, but Magrete went over her parents' mannerisms in her mind. Her thoughts took her through a maze of stranger and stranger explanations. Are they really becoming senile? she thought. And with that thought, darkness descended over her mind.

23

Freilassing was a small village of some 10,000 inhabitants in the south-eastern corner of Bavaria. It was originally a peasant village named Salzburghofen, but was renamed Freilassing in 1923. It was in a very picturesque setting, located in the valley of the rivers Salzach and Saalach, which merge close to the northern part of the town. To the south and the east, the Alps rise to altitudes of more than 2,000 metres and to the north and west of the town, rolling hills dominate the landscape. There was a vibrant commercial sector in the middle of town: the railway industry had brought significant employment to the village.

Finding accommodation in the village was difficult for visitors. However, the Holwegs managed to secure accommodation in two hotels, and so were able to accommodate twenty of their guests as well as themselves. Other guests from Vienna preferred to lodge in Salzburg, come by train on the day of the wedding and leave by train that evening. The wedding service was therefore scheduled for

3 pm, with the bridal reception being held in a council reception hall from 4 pm to 8 pm, allowing some of the guests to return to Salzburg on the last train. One of the hotels that lodged the Holwegs' guests catered the reception.

Herbert had flown to Munich, left his biplane at the airport and visited the Munich department store to inspect the books, which showed that the store was still performing poorly. Next day he caught the train to Freilassing, arriving at 1 pm on the day of the wedding.

Magrete was not a maid of honour, nor did she or Herbert have any official role in the wedding or reception ceremonies. They sat in the front row with Magrete's mother in the small Catholic Church, on the right side of the aisle, which was earmarked for the bride's guests, with the groom's guests on the left side. Most of the guests were from Albert's family and friends who lived in or near the village.

The wedding was small compared to Magrete's, and less expensive. It nevertheless had a romantic atmosphere, not only because it was held in a religious setting, but also because of the geographical location of the town. The church's pipe organ music served to uplift the spirits of those present.

Mimi's wedding gown was a dress with lace ruffles, and a princess-style bodice with short petal sleeves. It made her look younger and more vulnerable than she was, and added to the romanticism of the event – here was a young woman, innocent and sweet, on the threshold of marriage.

The reception was simple but effective. Instead of a band, the hotel had installed a large Crosley Console radio and record player in the council reception hall. Its stereo speakers made you feel that a band was in the room. There was a person designated to operate the record player and play the chosen music list. His name was Fritz, and he was also the master of ceremonies.

The order of the speeches and the meals was the only element adopted from Magrete's wedding. Near the end of the reception, Fritz introduced the father of the bride, Hans Holweg, to toast the in-laws.

Hans look tired and slightly dishevelled. He rose and started to search his pockets for his speech. He finally located it and began. 'Father and mother of the groom, Herr Dieter Kuebler and Frau Giselle Kuebler, and the groom, Herr Albert Kuebler, and distinguished guests.' He stopped, stared at Herbert with disdain, then returned to his speech. 'I feel we have known the Kueblers for a lifetime, but in fact we have known each other for just on eighteen months.' He stopped and stared at Herbert again, this time with more venom and for a longer period. Mimi was heard to faintly whisper 'Dad!' Several of the guests turned to look in the direction in which Hans was staring and only saw his son-in-law. He continued: 'What amazes our two families is the love and respect both Mimi and Albert have for each other.' He stopped again and stared pointedly at Herbert, and this time there was an audible murmur among the guests. Hans raised his glass and made a toast – 'To Giselle and Dieter' – and quickly sat down.

'What's wrong with your dad?' Herbert asked Magrete. 'He keeps staring at me as if I'm some sort of Judas!'

Magrete snapped. 'He has not been feeling well lately. It is not always about you, Herbert!'

After saying their goodbyes Mimi, Albert, Magrete and Herbert took the 9 pm train to Munich.

The following day, Mimi and Albert continued their journey to Paris for a week-long honeymoon. Herbert stayed in Munich in order to see the manager of the department store and outline a strategy to improve the store's financial health. Magrete journeyed to Berlin, more worried than ever before about her parents' mental state. She was determined to keep in telephone and letter contact with her father, for her mother never answered the telephone and had not replied to Magrete's letters since her civil wedding.

PART TWO

The Fall

1

On 14 October 1937 Magrete received another invitation from Marga Himmler. It read: 'Frau Margarete Himmler requests the pleasure of Frau Magrete von Appen's company for afternoon tea on Friday 21st of October at 3pm.' Magrete was not pleased, but there was little she could do. Marga Himmler had a reputation of being humourless, and toxic. She also prided herself on having conflicts with most of the wives of the highest-ranking SS leaders. She was not the sort of woman who would entertain a refusal, and if it did occur, she would make that person pay heavily. So Magrete wrote her a reply, accepting the invitation.

Events were unravelling on the eastern front of the German Reich. On Sunday 17 October pro–German Reich riots took place in the Sudeten area of Czechoslovakia. Czechoslovakia had been created in 1918 from territory that had previously been part of the Austro–Hungarian Empire. The country had some three and a half million German-speaking people, most living in the Sudeten region, which bordered the German Reich. The German-speaking people complained that the Czech-dominated government discriminated against them, and felt they would be better served under the Nazi regime. This culminated in the October riots, which were ruthlessly suppressed by the authorities.

Four days later Magrete found herself once again at the Himmlers' residence, ringing the doorbell at 3 pm precisely. She was shocked to be greeted by Marga and was ushered to the back patio, where another woman was already seated. Annelies Ribbontrop looked a few years younger than Marga, who introduced the two women to each other. No children in sight, thought Magrete and so Marga was freed from overseeing their supervision. I wonder if that is the reason she answered the door, Magrete thought.

'I thought I'd bring us all together so Annelies can finally meet my newest friend, my namesake Magrete. Magrete's husband Herbert – I don't think Joachim knows him – is a businessman who has recently joined NSFK.' Marga appeared to have elevated Magrete to the status of friend, based on a single one-on-one social encounter. If that is the case, Magrete concluded, she must not have many female friends.

'As you know,' Annelies said, 'but Magrete may not be aware, ever since Joachim was appointed Ambassador to the Court of St James we've really lost touch with what's going on in the social scene in Berlin.'

'Nonsense, Annelies,' Marga chided her, 'you've always moved in the most social of circles wherever you are. Now, I've an announcement to make that will shock both of you. In 1934 we built a house, which we named Lindenfycht, in a small village named Gmund at the Tegernsee in Bavaria, not that far south of Munich. The children and I've been living there off and on, and so Heinrich and I decided it would be best for their well-being, and education, if we lived there permanently and only occasionally return to Berlin, when social events demand that I accompany my husband. I would love to see the two of you there.'

Magrete was perplexed. Had her first visit impressed Marga so much? Something was not right. She could see that Marga had put on a considerable amount of weight. Magrete wondered if Himmler was having an affair. Herbert had told her Himmler's secretary was slim and good-looking and so Magrete reasoned that Marga was probably moving her children away from Berlin in order to shield herself and them from the affair and the associated gossip. Magrete felt empathy for Marga's situation, and so less inclined to be critical of her.

Meanwhile Annelies said, 'Of course, we'll be back in the German Reich next year. Joachim has been told that Hitler plans to appoint him Foreign Minister of the German Reich.'

Magrete decided to speak. 'We have one of our department stores in Munich. This will give me an excuse to accompany my husband on one of his many business trips there, so a diversion to visit you in Tegernsee is a possibility.' Magrete was polite but non-committal.

'Heinrich is working so hard,' Marga said. 'This crisis in Sudeten is taking all of his time. Hitler wants a report on how we should respond.'

'I know,' Annelies added. 'That's why Joachim was recalled. Hitler wants his opinion on what the British might do if we invade Czechoslovakia.'

The conversation for the next hour moved between Marga and Annelies, with Magrete only adding a few sentences here and there to be polite.

When Magrete returned home, Herbert wanted to know what had transpired. At the end of her debriefing Magrete said, 'Himmler is working extremely long hours with his secretary Frau Potthast. I really feel sorry for Marga. I give Potthast less than two years before she moves in with him.' Herbert shook his head and laughed.

2

In 1938 Kurt Schuschnigg, Chancellor of the Federal State of Austria, visited Hitler at his summer retreat at Berchtesgaden near the Austrian border. Hitler demanded that the Austrian Nazis be given key posts within the Austrian government. Schuschnigg compromised and appointed Seyss-Inquart, an Austrian Nazi, as Minister of the Interior. On 9 March Chancellor Schuschnigg announced a referendum in which the Austrian people would decide if they wanted to be a part of the German Reich. One day later, Hitler ordered Chancellor Schuschnigg to call off the referendum. Chancellor Schuschnigg conceded, knowing that he would not receive help from Italy, and that France and Britain would not interfere with Hitler's plans. He called off the referendum and resigned. Seyss-Inquart was ordered by Hitler to ask the German Reich to help restore order in Austria. On Saturday 12 March, German Reich troops marched into Austria unopposed. Hitler announced he would hold a plebiscite on 10 April to decide if the Anschluss would become a legal reality.

Magrete finally got through to her father on the telephone on 19 March – all telephone communications prior to that date had been disabled by order of the Minister of the Interior. Hans assured Magrete that everything was fine and spoke to her as briefly as he could. Mimi and Albert were in Freilassing. They had no telephone and could not cross the border – only the military were allowed that option. They were anxious, but powerless to do anything. They waited and prayed.

The top commanders of the Vienna police force were stood down. Hans was at home, unsure of his future, unsure of an income, unsure whether he would survive the Anschluss. Day after day as the plebiscite got nearer Eva became more delusional. She spoke to a baby within her body as pregnant women do, but she was not pregnant. Hans was getting more paranoid, watching the street from his post near the window. He swore that if the Nazis came and knocked on his door he would fight them to the end, but he had nothing to fight them with except for his bare hands. His only salvation would be if the Austrian people refused to be united with the German Reich. He was convinced that would happen, and believed if the majority of the people voted 'no' to the Anschluss, Hitler would honour the plebiscite. He waited and waited by the window.

The telephone rang, but Hans decided he was not mentally strong enough to answer it. He had convinced himself that it was Himmler trying to get in contact with him. He hated Himmler and had come to despise Herbert. Why had Magrete married such a despicable man? Magrete, always the more clear-headed child, surely had not married him for his wealth? At least Mimi had married a workingman, not a dilettante, or a no-hoper. Nevertheless, he decided to secrete in Magrete's room a copy of a letter he gave to his solicitor, as an added precaution against the original not being delivered to Magrete, and he hid it in a hiding place known only to them both. He could not trust Mimi with its contents.

Hans and Eva seldom ate or talked to one another. Each was drifting in and out of a private world that the other was excluded from. They navigated around one another, barely washed or slept. They were sleeping apart, each in one of the girls' bedrooms: Hans in Magrete's old room and Eva in Mimi's. When they met in the lounge room, dining room, kitchen or in the corridor, they would meekly smile at one another and move on.

This lasted until the day of the plebiscite. That day they bathed, and in Hans' case shaved, dressed in clean clothes and headed for the polling booth. Each cast a vote against the Anschluss, though there was no discussion between them on the matter. When they returned home, they sat together in the lounge room. For the first time in nearly a month they occupied the same room. Hans put on the radio and by 11 pm that evening it was evident that most of the Austrian people had voted for the Anschluss.

Eva's voice was weak and quavered, but for the first time since Magrete's wedding, she was lucid. 'Darling, you've tried so hard to save us from this evil. The girls are settled, but we aren't. This new era will drive us into madness, and we'll only cause grief to our girls. They'll remember us, not for who we are, but for what we've become. My baby still sits within me. I can feel him kick. He and I want to be released from this unholy union. Darling, let's end our lives with the few drops of dignity that we have left.'

Hans raised himself and went over to her and for the first time in months he held her tenderly and kissed her on her lips. He placed his arm around Eva's waist and slowly they walked into the kitchen. He knelt. She knelt. They hung their heads and said the Lord's Prayer in unison. His voice was two octaves lower than hers and together their voices sounded like a chant. Hans kissed her once again. Eva responded in kind.

The next day their neighbour Kurt Gödel smashed down the kitchen door. He found Eva and Hans' heads buried in the gas oven. He turned off the gas and ran to get help. Himmler heard of their suicide a day later, and he was very pleased for Herbert.

3

Magrete arrived at her parents' home two days after Mimi and Albert. Mimi told her she had found the house in a filthy state. Clothes were strewn everywhere, beds unmade, cans of food half-eaten lying on the floor, cupboards ransacked, toilets in a despicable state, and dirty dishes lying in every sink. What was most disturbing for her was that the rooms reeked of body odour. It was as if the house had not been aired for weeks, if not months.

Magrete thanked Albert and Mimi for restoring the house to a state of cleanliness. What her parents had gone through must have been horrific. It seemed that they had spiralled out of control, emotionally and psychologically. Her father had refused to answer the telephone after 19 March. Mimi and Magrete had not been able to travel to Vienna, because the border was closed to everyone except the military of the German Reich and so communication with their parents had ceased.

Magrete suggested that all three of them visit Herr Gödel, not only to thank him, but also to get first-hand information about the circumstances in which he had found them. Albert asked if he could be excused, as he was expecting a call from Herbert on the arrangements the von Appens were making to reach Vienna.

Mimi and Magrete knocked on Kurt Gödel's front door. He knew the sisters and invited them in, but stayed on the porch for a few seconds longer, looking left and then right to check that the street was clear. Kurt followed them into the lounge room and pointed to the sofa, while he sat in an armchair. A photograph on a side table next to Magrete made her feel uneasy. It was a photograph of a dancer with a scribbled 'Love Adele' at the bottom. Magrete thought Adele looked far too old for him.

Kurt started the conversation. 'I'm sorry that your parents committed suicide. I know that they worried about the Anschluss. Your father was stood down, or so I understood from the newspaper reports-'

'Stood down?' interrupted Magrete. 'Papa never told me that when I rang him on the 19th of March.'

'Oh, yes,' Kurt said. 'The top echelons of the Vienna police force were all stood down! They even did away with my privatdozent position at the University of Vienna. I applied for a different position under the new order, but because of my association with Jewish members of the Vienna Circle, the university turned down my application.'

Trying to redirect the conversation back to the purpose of their visit Magrete asked, 'Why did you visit my parents on the day you discovered them?'

'When you live next door, you get used to the particular rhythm of your neighbours. Certain lights go off at particular times in different rooms. Gardens are attended differently in different seasons. Rubbish bins are put out for collection and letters are collected at similar times. Over past three weeks the rhythm of your parent's house had completely collapsed. It was chaotic! I also noticed your father constantly peering out the window as if he was on guard. From first-hand experience I can tell you this is a sign of paranoia. No one in their household sought help, and so I became even more attentive to what they were doing.'

Mimi, burst into tears on hearing that her parents had not sought help. Magrete placed her arm around Mimi's shoulders and wiped her tears away with a silk handkerchief. 'Do not cry, Mimi,' she said. 'They will always live in our hearts.'

Mimi turned to her and said, 'Magrete you were right and I was wrong. I should've listened to you. I should've sought help when you queried me about their behaviour.' She turned to Kurt and said tearfully, 'Please tell Magrete the rest of the story. I'll let myself out.'

Kurt waited for Mimi to leave before continuing. 'I knew they were home, but they never answered the telephone. It kept ringing and ringing. Late at night on the day of the plebiscite, a strange thing happened – the whole house was pitch black except for the kitchen. I can see the kitchen from my bedroom window. I got up at 3 in the morning and the kitchen light was still on. It was on at 5 am and 6 am, so I got up, dressed and went to their kitchen window. I feared that there might have been an accident. I peered in the window, and all I could see were two pairs of legs side-by-side, not moving. It looked like they were lying on their stomachs. I called out their names, but they didn't respond. I smashed down the door and that's when I smelt the gas. I covered my mouth and nose, ran inside and saw that their heads were buried in the gas oven. I turned off the gas and ran to get help.'

Magrete looked at him, stunned, and said to him mechanically, 'Thank you.'

Kurt looked sadly at her and said softly, 'If the world is rationally constructed and has meaning, then there must be such a thing as an afterlife. Take care, Frau von Appen.' Magrete turned and let herself out of the house.

4

In the Catholic Church suicide had been viewed as a sin since the fourth century, when Saint Thomas Aquinas claimed it was one of the gravest sins. It was prohibited on three grounds: it was contrary to natural self-love, whose aim was to preserve us; it injured the community of which an individual was a part; and it violated our duty to God because God had given us life as a gift and in taking our lives we violate His right to determine the duration of our earthly existence. The Catholic Church prohibited funerals and burials of individuals who committed suicide. The ban was not meant as punishment, but rather as discouragement for individuals contemplating suicide.

This attitude was a problem for Magrete and Mimi. They wanted to hold the funeral service for their two parents at St Stephen's Cathedral and the burial service at Zentralfriedhof cemetery. St Stephen's Cathedral, with its beautiful Giant Gate and the Towers of the Heathens, dated back to the thirteenth century when Vienna was growing in importance and significantly expanding its city limits. Duke Rudolph IV of Hapsburg in 1359 had laid the cornerstone of the Gothic nave with its two aisles. Zentralfriedhof cemetery contained the graves of Austria's most famous musicians such as Ludwig van Beethoven, Johannes Brahms, Franz Schubert and Johann Strauss – just to mention a few.

When Magrete returned to her parent's home, Mimi came rushing to her. 'Your wonderful husband has given our family the biggest honour we could wish for. He has talked to Himmler about our parents' deaths. Himmler has ordered Internal Minister Seyss-Inquart to issue death certificates stating that their deaths were accidental due to leaking gas pipes. We can now have a Catholic funeral and burial.' The sisters cried and hugged one another.

Magrete realized that the funeral could be further delayed because of purgatory, which is associated with a cleansing of the soul by way of temporal punishment. She rang Herbert, who got in contact with Himmler, who then instructed Seyss-Inquart to speak to the Archbishop of Vienna, Theodore Innitzer. On receiving a sizable donation from Herbert, the Archbishop issued an indulgence (a remission before God) to allow the funeral to take place on Saturday 16 April 1938.

The von Appens arrived in Vienna several days before the funeral, bringing Anna Schuster with them. Peter von Appen insisted that all immediate family members – and that included the Kueblers – should stay at the one hotel to give emotional and psychological support to Mimi and Magrete during this traumatic time. He booked and paid for the top floor of the Hotel Stephanie to accommodate the immediate family members. Herbert flew to Vienna the day before the funeral and met them at the hotel. George Nagy and Helmut Gruen stayed at another hotel, the Hotel Imperial.

The beginning of the funeral rites, the Vigil, involved the parish priest and other clergy going to the family home. One cleric carried the cross and another carried a vessel of holy water. Before the coffins were removed from the house, a priest sprinkled holy water onto them. The priest with his assistant recited the psalm 'De profundis' with the antiphon 'Si iniquitates'. The small procession set out for St Stephen's Cathedral. The cross-bearer went first, followed by two clerics carrying lit candles. The priest walked immediately before the coffins, and the friends and family of Eva and Hans Holweg walked behind. The only family members not present were the von Appens, who, being Lutheran, felt this part of the funeral should be limited to baptised Catholics. George and Helmut were present, as was Kurt Gödel.

Few people attended the funeral service. Only the first three rows were mostly filled, despite over 200 notices having been posted, and others published in all major daily newspapers. Those who attended were mostly family members and close family friends. Magrete noticed that Kurt Gödel and a woman who looked like Adele were in the third row of pews. It seemed that many of Hans' work colleagues found it prudent not to attend. They were well aware that Himmler was not pleased with Hans Holweg. Some doubted that a proper investigation had been conducted into the Holwegs' deaths, and believed that the Holwegs had in fact committed suicide and so should not be afforded a church service or burial.

Either way, Magrete was impervious to the way others felt. She was absolutely determined to make the funeral memorable for their immediate families and friends and, moreover, to pay respect to her parents and to show that respect publicly to the whole of the city. Magrete was thick-skinned, as her father had often said, and now she was proud to be so.

The funeral began with the sprinkling of both bodies with holy water, the placing of the pall (a white cloth placed over each casket to recall the white garment of holy baptism), an entrance procession and the placing of Christian symbols - the Bible and the crucifix. There were readings and a sermon, which was of interest in that the priest first talked about Hans' career as the Deputy Commissioner of the Vienna Police and mentioned how devoted he had been to ensuring that justice was not only done fairly and with compassion, but openly documented. With respect to Eva, the preist talked about her devotion to Christianity and to her religiosity. He gave examples of her helping the poor and talked about the deeds of her favourite saint, Francis of Assisi.

Fewer mourners went to the cemetery: Kurt Gödel and his female companion were among twenty who were now absent. The coffins were carried to the graves, laid side-by-side in the cemetery. The burial plots were individually blessed, the coffins sprinkled with holy water and incense. The final petition was made by the priest – 'May their souls and the souls of all the faithful departed through the mercy of God rest in peace.'

Exhausted and emotional, Mimi and Magrete led their party back to Hotel Stephanie. George Nagy and Helmut Gruen bid the party goodbye on the steps of the hotel and made their way to the Hotel Imperial.

On the day of the funeral, Anna visited her parent's grave in Seegasse, in the 9th district of Vienna. There were about 350 gravestones there, and her parents shared one. She removed the weeds from the grave and planted European roses in shades of white.

As she was planting, she reflected on her parents, their love for one another and for her. Her mind drifted to Magrete, and she smiled thinking about how generous Magrete was. Even though Magrete was grieving, as soon as she had seen Anna at the hotel she had taken her into the bathroom, told her she must visit her parent's grave during the funeral service, and thrust two weeks of Anna's salary into her pocket. She told Anna that if Lady Holweg asked about her mother's whereabouts, she must tell Lady Holweg that her mother was in Berlin, visiting her grandmother.

Magrete understood loss, thought Anna. It was Magrete's money that had enabled Anna to freshen her parent's grave. Anna's mind went back to childhood memories of her parents, and tears streamed down her face as she prayed alone. She ended her pray with 'Shalom Aleichem' (peace be upon you) and made sure she was back in the hotel before the funeral party returned.

5

Elfi was determined that Anna should stay behind and assist Magrete in whatever way Magrete needed her. However, Magrete was equally determined that she and Mimi needed to oversee their parents' last will and testament, which meant there was little Anna could do in Vienna. Magrete quickly added that Anna's mother was visiting her grandmother in Berlin and so it would be better for Anna to be there. Elfi, Peter and Anna made their way back to Berlin by train on Monday 18 April, as did George and Helmut. Herbert needed to go to Munich on the morning of that day, and so he flew there in his biplane. Albert and his parents also left by train on the same day.

Mimi, who was always slightly envious of her older sister, while totally trusting her, came to realise what an asset Magrete had been. Not only had she organised all aspects of the funeral that were supposed to be under their shared care, but whenever Mimi had become emotional, Magrete had become cooler, more organised, and stepped into the breach. Mimi was not up to spending hours in the company of a solicitor at this point in time.

'Magrete, you know I've always trusted you, even though we've had our differences.' Magrete turned to look at Mimi, not sure where she was heading. 'I just want to tell you how great you've been with Mum and Dad's funeral. If it wasn't for you, it would have been a mess.'

Magrete hugged her and said, 'Without your love I could not have planned a thing.'

Mimi pulled back from Magrete saying, 'I really don't feel up to dealing with Dad's solicitor this afternoon. We just had the funeral two days ago and I don't feel strong enough. I wonder if you can talk to him for both of us. I shall do whatever you require me to do.'

The Klein law firm was one of the oldest in Vienna, having been founded in 1875. Dieter Klein, the grandson of the founder Conrad Klein, had been Hans' solicitor. Dieter was tall, slim and in his late forties. He was very formal in manner. He greeted Magrete at the door, knowing fully well that she had married into the von Appen wealth, and that she might bring more business to his firm, especially since they had opened a department store in Vienna.

'I'm so sorry about the tragic accident that killed both of your parents,' Klein said, noticing that Magrete flinched at his comment.

'Thank you, Herr Klein,' Magrete said in a matter-of-fact tone.

'Where is Frau Kuebler?'

'She preferred not to come today, as she is not feeling well,' Magrete said, again without emotion.

'You are aware that you are the sole executor of both wills, so her presence is not critical,' Klein informed.

'Yes,' Magrete replied.

'I've gone over the wills of both parties, as they died within a very short time period of one another. I've had to do this because it can't be established who died first. I hope this is not too distressing for you.'

'It is,' Magrete confessed, 'but what else can be done? Please continue.'

'The law is fairly clear on this matter, especially because both of your parents have individually expressed their wish in such a case. All of their belongings, such as the house and its contents, the money in their bank accounts, jewellery and any other possession of theirs that may or may not be of value, will be equally divided between Mimi and yourself.' Klein paused.

'What if I want to gift my entire share to my sister Mimi?'

'Then, Frau von Appen, that would have to be specified in another contract between Mimi and yourself, after this process has been completed.'

Magrete answered him immediately, 'After the wills have been properly processed, my instruction is that you prepare such a contract at my personal expense.'

'I will do as instructed. Oh, I almost forgot! Your father on the 21st of March came to my office and left an envelope with me and said if anything should happen to him, it must be personally delivered to you. He sealed it with wax.'

Dieter disappeared and returned with an envelope, which he handed over to Magrete. He expected Magrete to open it, read its contents in his presence, and if she was perplexed about any matter, to raise the matter with him. Instead, Magrete accepted the envelope and rose to leave. He escorted her out of the building. Rich people, he thought, as she walked away from him, treat everybody like they are servants!

Magrete returned and relayed what had occurred to Mimi, who cried and said she could not accept Magrete's gift. 'I will keep some of Mutti and Papa's jewellery and other things, like their photograph album of my wedding, that we agree that I can have, but Mimi, I am living in a villa, which someday Herbert and I will inherit. You do not have a house, and currently you and Albert live in one room in a dilapidated farmhouse. Albert is a vet. If you live here, it will be easier for him to find work. You will be able to plan a family once you own this house, and you and your family will keep Mutti and Papa's memories alive every time we come to visit you. I will not take no for an answer. If you want to make me happy, you will say yes!' Magrete stared at her sister and marched slowly towards her, stamping her feet, repeating, 'You will say yes!' Mimi, who had been watching her sister with alarm, suddenly remembered that this was a game Magrete had played when they were children. She would continue until Mimi wilted and said yes. This time it took Magrete only four attempts.

6

Magrete knew Dieter Klein was curious about the sealed envelope. Once her father had committed suicide, Klein had been tempted to open it, since it might have had a direct bearing on Hans Holweg's last will and testament, but he had been given strict instructions not to do so, and therefore he had no choice but to obey.

Magrete knew her father well. He had purposely sealed the envelope with wax, because if the seal had been broken she would be aware that an unauthorised person had read its content. He wanted her to read it and no one else. Magrete was hoping that it might shed light on why her parents had committed suicide.

Magrete could not open the envelope in a common place, so she waited until she was in her old bedroom, before she went to sleep. As she stared at the envelope she made an oath that whatever it contained she would not whimper, cry or get angry. Her emotions must be held in check, or Mimi would enter the bedroom.

Magrete broke the seal and pulled out the envelope's contents. The letter was written in her father's beautiful copperplate handwriting. She read the first line, then stopped and said to herself, I can do this. I can do this without crying and then she read on.

20th March 1938

Dear Schatz,

Your mother's and my life has been in turmoil because of the proposed Anschluss. It has triggered in us a paranoid existence that we are both trying to cope with, and which we find incredibly difficult to comprehend and contain. Your mother acts as if she is pregnant with her stillborn. I am seeing shadows of a Nazi surveillance team watching our house and our every movement. I dare not pickup the telephone for I fear that Himmler is calling me. We are praying that the plebiscite on the Anschluss will fail and that Austria will return to its former self. Enough about us!

I want to inform you of some facts that may shock you. Under no circumstances are you to tell Mimi. She wears her emotion on her sleeve and so knowledge of my past will destroy her. I trust you with this knowledge, Schatz, because knowledge has always empowered you rather than diminished you. In these times, you need to be empowered. However, you must burn this letter after you have digested it and never let it be found, otherwise there will be dire consequences for all of our connected families.

My mother, Ilse Schwab, is Jewish! She converted to Catholicism before she married my father Hanse. Her parents Lisa and Herz Schwab had two daughters, Ilse and Ruth. Ruth married Gerhard Braus and had only one daughter, Ester, who in turn married Isaak Bornstein, and they only had one daughter Rachel, who married Joseph Sulzer and had only one daughter Anna. As you can see, the women on my mother's side of our family tree found it difficult giving birth to many healthy children. Some of these women had several miscarriages (e.g. Ester) or died in the delivery of a child (e.g. Ruth). Rachel was murdered at a young age.

Ilse's sister Ruth was disgusted with Ilse's conversion to Catholicism and refused to speak to her ever again. Ilse kept in contact with her parents and so would hear about Ruth's family. Hence, we became aware of Ester and her child Rachel. I am Ester's first cousin. I made contact with Ester, but we wrote to each other sparingly. She lives in Berlin, which made personal visitations rare, although she did visit us in Vienna once with Rachel and Anna during school term. Just before your mother's stillborn pregnancy Rachel got in contact with me when she read I was promoted to the position of deputy commissioner. We had a long conversation, and because she was unemployed at that time and I had been promoted, I offered her a non-residential housekeeper's position. Without Rachel, things would have been most dire for us during that time. You and Mimi are Rachel's second cousins. Your and Mimi's children will be Anna's third cousins.

I felt obliged to help Anna when both of her parents were murdered. I used my position to gain entry into the Department of Births, Deaths and Marriages on the 11th of April 1936 (one week after your wedding). There I stole a copy of Anna Schuster's birth certificate as well as replacing Ilse Schwab's birth certificate with a forgery that pronounced her Catholic at birth. One of the advantages of being a police officer is you know people who work on the wrong side of the law!

The Nazis would claim I am 100% Jewish because I have four grandparents on my mother's side who are Jewish. The irony is that the Zionists would claim I am 100% Jewish because my mother is Jewish. The Nazis would claim that Mimi and you might be Jewish because both of you have only one and not three grandparents on your father's side who are Jewish and further criteria would have to be met for a determination. The Zionists would claim you are not Jewish at all, because your mother is not Jewish. These definitions are just so silly!

Schatz, you need to destroy this document, otherwise the Nazis will send our families to the concentration camps and I definitely do not want that for any of my connected family.

I do not know what will happen to us if the Anschluss is approved by the plebiscite. I will probably go to jail for obeying the law, which the Nazis think I should not have invoked on their people. Alternatively, I might find myself in a lunatic asylum undergoing insulin shock therapy, or I might take my life. Whatever happens to me, take care of your mother and sister.

Love,

Papa

As Magrete read the end of the letter, she let silent tears meander down her cheeks. She was dumbfounded that Anna and she were related, and that her father was officially a Jew. Her Jewish heritage had been diluted, but the Nazis would have still asserted them to be Jewish. She had always assumed that Rachel was the problem for her father because, in his position, hiring a Jew, even as a non-residential housekeeper, automatically rendered him suspect to the Nazis. Now she knew that Rachel was a problem not only because she had been hired, but more importantly because they were related. Rachel and her husband were well known in both Jewish and Austrian Nazi circles. Clearly Ester had known they were related, but did Anna? Magrete vowed that on returning to Berlin she would see Ester and find out what Anna knew. Magrete knew that her father was right, and that Mimi would not recover from such a revelation. The von Appens must be kept in the dark. Herbert would be shocked that he had married a Jew, albeit a watered-down version.

It was clear to Magrete that when her father had written the letter he had not contemplated a suicide pact with her mother. He had expected her mother still to be alive whether he died by his own hand or at the hands of others. It seemed that the trauma they had gone through in the lead-up to the plebiscite had triggered the suicide pact.

The house was deadly silent. Magrete leaned over the bed to the drawer, took out a pen and paper and made a family chart based on the information her father had given her. She used a transposition cipher. First, all the names would be spelt backwards so that a name such as Ruth would become htur, and then she swapped every pair of letters so htur would become urht. It would not fool the experts but it would fool an accidental discovery from a family member or an in-law, or a domestic servant. Once Magrete had completed the chart she stole into the lounge room and burnt the envelope and its contents. Nothing was left of her father's last letter to her, but ashes.

7

Herbert flew into Berlin on Friday at 7 pm on 21 April 1938. His mother was home, his father was visiting the department store in Prague, and Magrete was still in Vienna. He drove out to Wannsee in his 1937 BMW Roadster. Herbert parked the car in the new garage and saw that most of the ground floor lights were off. He decided not to disturb the household and made his way as silently as he could up the backstairs into his quarters. He opened the door quietly, and then froze.

Anna stood holding one of Magrete's dresses at her shoulder and around her waist, looking at her image in a floor-to-ceiling mirror. She could not see him because of the angle of the mirror. He knew Anna was eighteen, from her identity papers. She looked radiant! Her long, flowing hair spread out from beneath her maid's cap. Herbert could imagine her naked body from the flow of her uniform. He could see her cup the left breast of the dress against her own bosom. Her bosom was smaller and rounder than Magrete's. Anna swayed to the left and to the right with the dress pressed tight against her rear.

He stealthily made his way behind her. Anna still could not see him in the mirror. He cupped his left hand over her mouth and as she struggled he pinned her arms with his right arm. Magrete's dress dropped to the floor. Herbert whispered to her menacingly, 'If you continue to struggle, I'll make sure you'll never work for anyone again. Do you understand me?' Anna froze and nodded. Not trusting her Herbert still kept his hand over her mouth as he slowly kissed the nape of her neck. He could feel her crying softly, transfixed with fear.

He slid his right hand from Anna's arms down to the front of her right breast, squeezed her nipple gently and let his hand rest there for a second or two, feeling its shape. Anna was now shaking and sobbing. He whispered, 'Don't cry, and I'll take my hand off your mouth.' Anna nodded. Herbert's right hand meandered down, and he lifted her uniform and slowly massaged her undergarment between her legs, kissing and licking the nape of her neck. He could feel Anna moving her body so as to minimise his touch. He let go of her mouth and heard her sob and beg softly, 'Please don't touch me. Please don't touch me.' Herbert closed his eyes and was licking her neck and about to reach into her undergarment, when Anna was ripped away from him with force!

Gertrude stood between them. Anna pushed herself behind Gertrude, clutching the back of Gertrude's dress.

'Gertrude!' Herbert screamed. 'How dare you come in here without announcing yourself! Get out! You're not allowed to be here when I'm home!'

Gertrude did not move. Anna stood behind her, crying and pleading, 'Please don't leave me alone with him!'

'If you don't leave immediately, Gertrude, I'll sack you! I'll make sure no one, but no one, will ever hire you again!'

'No, you won't!' a voice behind him shouted. He turned and it was his mother.

'Gertrude,' Elfi ordered in a reassuring tone, 'take Anna to her sleeping quarters, and comfort her. Anna, no harm will come to you ever again.'

As Gertrude and Anna left, closing the door behind them, Elfi marched straight up to Herbert and slapped him as hard as she could, not just once, but twice across his face. He was shocked and raised his hand as if to strike her. 'Don't you dare hit your mother, the woman who gave birth to you and reared you,' Elfi said. 'And I've reared you for this? Your wife is mourning in Vienna, and you can't stop your penis from doing the thinking for you?' Herbert had never heard his mother use such foul language before. 'This is the third domestic servant you've tried to have sex with. One left us, and we still don't know if she had your child, and another left after we paid for her abortion, not trusting that you wouldn't try to rape her again! I was too soft on you, not like I was with Simon. He had more integrity than you'll ever have.' Herbert was now moving towards the rear door, and Elfi followed him, screaming, 'It is you that should have died in that car accident, not him!'

Herbert left but Elfi's scream followed him: 'Don't come back unless you can be faithful to your wife!'

Elfi went downstairs and across to the servant quarters to comfort a shaken Anna. 'Anna,' she said, 'I give you my word that you'll never be sexually accosted by my son again. You are never to stay in the upstairs quarters if Lady Magrete is not there. Gertrude, you are to enforce this rule rigorously. I won't tell Magrete what happened tonight. She has had enough grief with the loss of both of her parents.' Elfi looked compassionately at Anna and whispered to her, 'The trouble is you're far too pretty, and so we need to make you a little uglier.' Elfi smiled, and Anna smiled back, wiping away the last vestiges of her tears.

8

Herbert was sitting in his roadster, reflecting on what he had become. He was ashamed of himself and realised that when his older brother Simon died, something had snapped inside of him. His father had been too involved in the business and absent far too often to be a father figure to him, and Simon had taken on the role, although just fourteen months older than Herbert. If he needed protection, Simon would protect him. If he needed advice, Simon would steer him in the right direction. If he ever strayed morally or ethically, Simon would sense it and correct it before it had dire consequences for him. Once Simon died, he had no companion looking after him, and so he strayed often.

When Simon died, Herbert was expected to run the company. He loved being adventurous, flying planes, driving fast cars and being in the company of loose women. Once he was thrust into a business role, little adventure was left open to him. His mother had pushed him to marry, to settle down, to have children and to be a respectable businessman. Herbert loved Magrete, but he felt that his life was becoming humdrum, predictable and moreover, ebbing away slowly and painfully into nothingness. He started his roadster and left the villa, heading for George's residence.

George lived in a ground floor flat in Kaiserswertherstraße Dahlem, within walking distance of the Institute. When George opened the door he was shocked to see Herbert – it was 10 pm and Herbert and Magrete had never visited his apartment.

'Anything wrong?' he enquired.

Herbert asked with a smile, 'Are you good for a bed tonight?'

'Of course, come in,' George said, in a more relaxed manner.

George's apartment contained a number of rooms: a bedroom, kitchen, bathroom, toilet, and a larger dining room. The dining room was cluttered with textbooks, scientific journals and scientific magazines. They were stacked in columns that you had to navigate around in order to reach a sofa, an armchair, and a small dining room table with three chairs. It looked like an internal forest – organised mayhem! George picked a path for Herbert to follow in order to reach the dining room sofa and armchair. George sat in the armchair and Herbert sprawled on the sofa.

'So what happened?'

'I had a huge row with Mum when I told her I was joining the Luftwaffe (air force) tomorrow,' Herbert lied, hoping that the real reason would never be revealed to George.

George stared at Herbert, speechless for a moment. 'I thought you and Himmler were friends and if you didn't want to be enlisted, he'd bail you out. And if he couldn't, I would've expected you to join the SS or some unit he's in control of. After all, promotion would be so much easier.'

Herbert laughed. 'I know people claim I manage upwards, rather than downwards, but I never thought you were one of them. At any rate, as you know I'm a keen airman and when I joined the NSFK I always had in mind that one day I'd join – or be conscripted into – the Luftwaffe. Mum was shocked. She expected me to run the company for them. Instead, I'll be glad to get out of the Arado Ar 96 that I fly for the NSFK and into something more powerful.'

'What about Magrete?'

'She doesn't know yet, but I'll fly to Vienna and tell her on Saturday,' Herbert said.

George sat back, understanding that Magrete was going to be presented with a fait accompli. 'What about your father? This will devastate him! He was grooming you to take over the business. What will he say?'

'What do you think Dad's going to say? He'll try to dissuade me by bringing up Simon and telling me that I'm the last of the von Appens. Mum and Dad will cry and beg me to contact Himmler to veto my conscription on some business grounds. No, George, I don't want my Dad to try to persuade me against something I've already decided on. Now, it's getting late, where do I sleep?'

George pointed to the sofa. 'I'll bring you a pillow and two blankets and after that you're on your own.'

After George had brought in bedding and said goodnight, Herbert found some stationery, a pen and an envelope. He penned a letter to his mother. In the morning, he asked George to hand deliver it to the household. George promised him he would and bade him farewell.

9

Herbert flew into Vienna on Saturday 23 April and immediately made his way to the Holweg's residence. He had engineered his conscription into the Luftwaffe on the previous Friday and was told his training would begin on 28 April at the Kitzingen airbase. Herbert had four days to transition Magrete into accepting his situation, and knew that this might not be enough.

The letter that George had delivered to his mother apologised unreservedly to her, Gertrude and Anna for his unconscionable behaviour. He explained that he had lost his way with Simon's death, attributing his immoral and unethical behaviour to the absence of Simon and to his own lack of self-control. He begged them never to tell Magrete or his father of the incident. He was certain that neither would forgive him if told. He also wrote that he could not see them for the next seven months because he had been conscripted. He was confident that by the time he would return to the villa from training, Anna would have had sufficient time to overcome her fear of him. Herbert wrote that he was flying to Vienna on Saturday and would fly directly to Kitzingen airbase from Vienna. He sealed the envelope feeling that the three women would never tell Magrete or his father.

When Herbert arrived, Magrete was bubbling over with excitement and news. She informed him that Mimi had returned to her in-laws' farm at Freilassing, so they would be alone until he had to leave in four days' time. She told him that her parents' house and its contents had been gifted to Mimi and Albert, and how excited Mimi and Albert were to move from a single room in a farmhouse to Josefstadt, a fashionable suburb in Vienna. Herbert was secretly pleased that Mimi had inherited the house and its contents. He reasoned it would make Magrete more financially reliant on him and so she would find it harder to leave him.

Magrete wanted to hear all the news about his parents, George and Anna. Herbert squirmed when she mentioned Anna. He recomposed himself and told her that, rather than waking up the villa, he had slept overnight in George's apartment. Magrete petitioned him for more details, and Herbert described George's apartment and its furnishings. She laughed when Herbert told her how George had to guide him through a maze of shrub-high columns of books, journals, and magazines to get to the dining room furniture.

Herbert's strategy for telling Magrete about his self-imposed conscription was simple: first he would set-up the political circumstance, then he would wine and dine her, make love to her, and lastly he would tell her that the decision was not his, but had been made for him by law. If they ended up arguing, at least they could do so in private.

Magrete offered him afternoon tea and when she returned from the kitchen, she sat next to him pouring the tea in his cup. He could smell her sweet perfume and for a second it distracted him. Herbert took a sip of his tea and started the conversation on a political tack. 'You know that as a businessman running an important company I have been up until now exempted from conscription, but this cannot last.' Magrete nodded, and Herbert continued. 'Himmler has told me that the European situation is becoming critical and those previously exempt will be called up soon. In fact, Hitler secured the western front by taking back the Rhineland, which should have never been annexed from us in the first place. With the Anschluss, Himmler believes there is now no threat south of Austria through to the Mediterranean Sea, due to our pact with Italy. The problem is that we have shared borders that could be problematic for Hitler: Czechoslovakia and Poland. The German Reich has to support a large army with the capability to protect us. Right now Himmler tells me we have 36 infantry divisions of 600,000 men.'

Magrete looked at him with dismay. 'Darling, why do you listen to Himmler? He is a politician through and through, and you are not!'

'Magrete, we can't bury our heads in the sand and hope that when we resurface the world will have become a Garden of Eden. Reality can be harsh, but we must face it.'

Magrete sighed. 'I know that to be forearmed is to be forewarned, I live by that motto, but Himmler is on a different plane to us.'

'Alright,' Herbert surrendered, 'no more political talk for now. Please let me take my wife out to dinner tonight.' Magrete leaned across and kissed him.

That evening Herbert took her to one of the most exclusive restaurants in Vienna, Zu de drei Husaren (To the Three Hassars). In 1933 the Ziners had rented out the department store's former canteen to three Hungarian noblemen, who turned it into a famous restaurant. In 1938 the owner, Count Paul Pallfy, decided he no longer wanted to operate a restaurant in Nazi Vienna and sold the lease to Otto Horcher, the restaurant tsar of the Third Reich.

Horcher immediately recognised Herbert as a friend of Himmler and ushered him to the finest table in the restaurant. He went into the kitchen to tell the waiters, chefs and other staff that nothing should be spared for Herbert and his wife.

They had a four-course meal in the glow of candlelight. Magrete looked stunning and Herbert was entertaining and humorous. After the meal they walked to Magrete's parents' home, arm in arm.

Magrete was undressing in her old bedroom when Herbert came in, and she was delighted that he stripped the rest of her clothes from her in a sensual manner. They made love and when Herbert slept resting against her naked body, Magrete's parents' suicide seemed to have occurred in a distant place and time. She felt slightly ashamed for forgetting them so quickly as she slid into a deep sleep.

On the following day, Herbert walked hand in hand with Magrete as they toured the Prater. The Prater had just become the property of the City of Vienna. It had been an imperial hunting ground only accessible to the aristocracy until the Austrian Emperor Josef II donated the area to the Viennese in 1766 as a public leisure centre.

Since its donation, the Emperor had allowed the establishment of restaurants, snack bars, coffee brewers, ginger bread bakers, seesaws and merry-go-rounds as well as bowling alleys. Magrete and Herbert played like children and both laughed when Herbert, in an effort to impress Magrete, fell off the merry-go-round.

That evening Herbert took Magrete to the Vienna State Opera. They were seated in a private balcony box and were enthralled by the performance of Wagner's Die Meistersinger (The Master Singer) conducted by Furtwaengler. This opera, only a few days before, had been performed on Hitler's birthday in the presence of Göring. Not surprisingly Richard Wagner was Hitler's favourite composer. Wagner's personal views of Jews were aligned with Hitler's. Often Hitler had Wagner's music played at Nazi party rallies and functions – it was serious and, more importantly, intensely Teutonic. The cultural symbols Wagner used suited Hitler's theory of Aryanism. Magrete was consciously uncomfortable with these associations, whereas Herbert was not.

They arrived back at her parents' home still intoxicated by the operatic performance. Magrete slumped in the armchair and Herbert sat next to her on its arm, caressing her hair and gently massaging her shoulders and the nape of her neck. He kissed her, lifted her, and carried her to their bed. They made love for the second evening in a row, something they had not done since Venice.

On the third day Herbert told Magrete he had been conscripted. Unknown to Magrete, Herbert had seen Himmler and explained that he wanted to join the Luftwaffe, but his parents did not want him to. Himmler was glad that Herbert was finally committing himself and not hiding behind a businessman's exemption. As Göring was in Vienna, Himmler rang Field Marshal Erhard Milch and told the Field Marshal exactly what needed to be done. Herbert and Himmler shook hands, and within two hours a conscription notice came via courier to Himmler's office.

Magrete read the conscription notice. 'But this cannot be. You have a businessman's exemption.'

'I tried to tell you on Saturday about the changing situation in Europe, but you refused to listen. Hitler is trying to secure our borders. He has done so in the west and south, but not yet in the east-'

'I know what you said,' Magrete interrupt him in anger, 'but what has that got to do with revoking your businessman's exemption?'

'The Luftwaffe is the smallest section in the German Reich's defensive power. The army and navy are much larger. Göring is determined that by 1939 Luftwaffe will command a total of 4,000 aircraft and 400,000 personnel. Himmler has told me that a reorganisation of the Luftwaffe will occur in July of this year. They desperately need pilots and for that reason they have emptied the NSFK. As I hold the rank of group leader, they earmarked me for conscription and have waived my exemption on national security grounds. I will be away training until November.' Herbert knew how to lie convincingly.

Magrete sat there dumbfounded, looking at the floor. She had only just rediscovered him; the last two days had felt like Venice all over again. 'November! But that is a lifetime away! What about Himmler? Surely he can negate this,' Magrete pleaded.

Herbert looked at her and gently brushed her hair away from her cheeks. 'Himmler can't interfere. This is Hitler's territory. Himmler helped secure Hitler the leadership of the military by getting rid of General Fritsch, and in February, according to Himmler, Hitler decreed that he would personally take over the command of the whole armed forces. There's no way Himmler would be seen to undermine any of Hitler's military goals. If he did, Göring would have a field day!'

'What about Marga? I know her, maybe she could do something.' Magrete was clutching at straws.

'Himmler is most likely having an affair with Potthast, from what you told me. It won't be long before his wife knows if she doesn't know already. Anyway, she's despised by the wives of most of Himmler's senior staff and if she has no sway over Himmler's world, there's no way she has any influence over Hitler's.'

'I know,' Magrete said in defeat, 'it was a stupid idea. When do you have to report?'

'This Thursday, but I have to go back on Wednesday to pack and make all the final arrangements. We only have today and tomorrow.'

Magrete looked at him through soft tears. Herbert gently wiped them away and they kissed. The rest of the day they spent in each other's arms, talking about themselves, their relationship, their friends, and their most precious memories. Magrete showed him photographs of her parents, Mimi and herself that her mother and father had kept in a number of photograph albums. Herbert was fascinated by the way Magrete's face and body had changed during her short history. They did not make love that evening.

The following morning came and Magrete knew this would be the last day they would have together for the next seven months. It had to be special. Magrete cooked Herbert a wonderful breakfast, and he amused her by saying, 'I've just sacked Emma and Lotte, you're hired!'

She washed the dishes and made Herbert dry them, something he had never done in his life. Herbert asked, pointing to the apron she had made him wear, 'Am I now Tomas or Gertrude?'

It was a beautiful day, not a cloud in the sky. Mid-morning Herbert made a special announcement. 'Today you're going to see Vienna like you have never seen it before. I'm going to blindfold you first and only when I'm ready can you take the blindfold off. I'll have to guide you. Do you agree?' He looked at her with his puppy brown eyes.

Herbert has been so much fun today, she thought, why not? 'I do,' she said, 'but if I fall heaven help you!'

Herbert blindfolded Magrete, then held her shoulders and said, 'Walk straight ahead, no looking.' He guided her to the front door. 'Two steps now.' He gripped her a little more firmly, to steady her. Magrete had lived in this house for most of her life, and so she had no difficulty in walking blindfolded down the front path and through the gate, then into her father's car, which was waiting for them in the driveway. 'When did you move the car? How long have you been planning this, Herbert?'

'Ssh!' Herbert said. 'Just place your two hands on the dashboard so you don't fall about as I'm driving.' Magrete did as she was told, intrigued. Herbert talked to her, warning her so she could brace herself. 'Now I'm turning left; now I'm turning right; I'm coming to a stop; I'm moving again.' They drove for nearly thirty minutes. Herbert got out of the car and helped Magrete out. 'Close your eyes,' he said as he took off the blindfold, and then he commanded, 'Open them!'

'Oh, no!' There in front of her was Herbert's Waco O series biplane.

He pulled her back into his arms and whispered in her ear, 'If you're not scared of the Wiener Riesenrad (Vienna Giant Wheel), and I know you're not, then if I promise to fly below 100 metres, I don't see what's your problem.' Magrete looked at him, afraid.

'Look,' Herbert said, trying to allay her fears, 'if at any time you feel uncomfortable, just tell me and I'll turn back to the airport. After all, it won't be good for either one of us if you start to panic.'

Magrete considered her options. The day had such a wonderful beginning, and it was his last day with her for the next seven months, so she decided against making this day less congenial. After they had climbed into the plane and Herbert had explained what he needed to explain to a novice passenger, he got the all clear from the tower. He knew that once the propellers were in motion, even if she gave it her best scream, he would be unable to hear her.

The take-off was not as bad as Magrete had imagined. Her stomach got a bit queasy, because she felt as if a catapult had hurled her into the sky. She quickly realised that Herbert would never hear her scream over the roar of the engine. When he turned to check on her, she gave him a thumbs-up sign to signify she was okay. Once he got to 100 metres he indicated to her, using his hand that they were flattening out. Herbert then indicated that he was banking, but he did it in such a wide arc that Magrete felt no butterflies in her stomach. He indicated he was flattening out again, then gently lowered the plane to 100 metres and pointed below. Magrete could see the middle of Vienna unfolding before her: St Stephen's Cathedral, parliament house and the Danube. She was in raptures. Oh, if only George could see me now, she mused, he would shudder in his boots!

Herbert followed the Danube until he reached the Donau Auen National Park, which covered some 93 square kilometres of wetlands. Herbert lowered the plane to 70 metres and began circling the park. Magrete loved her bird's eye view. She realised now what flying really meant to him. He had often told her it was like riding on the back of an eagle. She had not understood that description until today. Herbert circled the park for the final time and then retreated along the same flight path that he had previously taken, back to the airport. The only fear Magrete experienced was when he descended to land. She shut eyes tight, held her breath, and prayed to God. Magrete would never tell George about the landing: how the plane hopped and skipped before the wheels finally gripped the tarmac. The rest she would brag about, telling George that this girl was a passenger in a plane, and loving it!

After they taxied back to the car, Herbert shut down the engine and they climbed back to the ground. Magrete's feet wobbled and Herbert quickly lent her support. 'What do think?' He was curious to know.

'Loved it!' Magrete replied. 'But not the landing – that part is truly scary!' Herbert laughed.

That night when they made love, she felt again the freedom of flight.

When morning came, Magrete drove Herbert to the airport and watched him fly off into the clouds. She cried softly as she drove herself back to her parents' place. Mimi and Albert returned on Saturday, and she said farewell to them and took the train back to Berlin.

10

By the time Herbert reached the villa at Wannsee, it was already 8.30 pm. He parked his car away from the property and stealthily walked 300 metres until he reached the back entrance to his living quarters. He opened the door quietly, and noticed that no room was lit. Herbert took off his shoes, walked into the bedroom in the dark and put on the light. He searched underneath his bed for a suitcase, located it, and methodically filled it with clothes. He turned off the light and walked to the bathroom, where he grabbed his shaving gear, toothbrush, toothpaste and hair pomade, which he wrapped in a bath towel. On completing his packing, he went to a drawer, fumbled behind some clothes and took out a wad of money. Herbert retraced his steps to exit, put on his shoes, and headed towards the car.

Unnoticed by him, Elfi was peering through the window when he arrived and when he left. Peter was sleeping in an armchair, snoring loudly. She was desperate to run out, hug her son and kiss him on the cheek, but she instinctively knew, as only mothers know, that this was not the right time for him, because he had lied to her when he wrote that he was flying direct to Kitzingen airbase from Vienna. When the right time came she promised to wash him with her tears and kiss him with affection – all would be forgiven!

Herbert knocked on George's door at 10 pm that night. George opened the door and Herbert said, 'Good for another night?'

'Of course, my friend.' George ushered Herbert inside.

'I flew into Berlin too late, and so I didn't want to disturb my parents. If I get a chance, I'll see them tomorrow before I leave.'

They sat in the same places they had on his previous visit, Herbert on the sofa and George in the armchair.

'Well, amigo, you're on your own now,' Herbert quipped. 'Magrete flew in the biplane around the surrounds of Vienna!'

'I don't believe you!' George noted that Herbert's eyes were fixed on his. 'Really?'

'Yes, amigo,' Herbert confirmed, 'it's true! There's only one person who's scared of heights amongst the amigos and that's you, my friend!' Herbert pointed directly at him and laughed with so much gusto that George started to laugh at himself.

When the laughing subsided George enquired, 'How did Magrete take you being enlisted?'

'Not well at first, in fact she was downright upset. But after I explained to her that it was inevitable, she had to accept it. Anyway, what could she do? These are the times we live in, a time when war is inevitable. A time when people will die.' Herbert stopped, paused, and looked directly into George's eyes. 'My friend, I have a really big favour to ask, and please hear me out and say yes.' Herbert was speaking rapidly now. 'A war is closing in on the German Reich, whether it's of our making or not. When it breaks out, it'll be devastating! The weapons of war are far more sophisticated than what was used in the Great War. You've told me that a fission bomb, if built, would cause immense destruction and the radiation fallout would kill even more people. A war may break out today, tomorrow, or in a year's time. When it does you can always go back to Hungary; you don't have to be a part of a German Reich's war. The front-line soldiers will be the first killed, and the most front-line is the Luftwaffe. This war will not be won on the ground, or on and in the water – this war will be won by whoever controls the skies! America has the flying weapons to control the skies and if they enter the war against the German Reich, we'll be done for! I'm going to ask you to make a solemn oath that if I die you'll marry Magrete.'

George looked at him, stunned. He searched for words. 'But Herbert,' he said, 'Magrete and I love each other as brother and sister. I can't make an oath that Magrete might not want to be a party to.'

'George,' Herbert looked him in the eye, 'at present you're friends, but that's not how it needs to be forever. Friendship can grow into love, amigo. I'll incorporate my wish in a letter that I'll give to my solicitor, which will be released to Magrete three months after my death.'

'Herbert,' George reasoned, 'I might be married by then and have children of my own.'

'I'll make sure that the release of the letter is contingent on Magrete being alive, and available, and you being alive, and available.'

'What if you have children?' George asked. 'They might want a say on who their stepfather is, or, more importantly, not want to diminish the memory of their father because of a second marriage.'

'Look, George, we've been married for two years and Magrete has not been pregnant in that time. I believe she can't conceive while she is my wife.' Herbert looked away. 'If for any reason Magrete doesn't want to marry you, all I ask is that you'll take care of her in my absence, but if she does want to marry you, promise me you will. Can you give me your solemn oath?'

George could see that Herbert was desperate for some assurance, and said reluctantly, 'Considering all the ifs and buts, I give you my solemn oath.'

Herbert hugged him and George felt a few tears fall on his neck.

By the time George got up in the morning, Herbert was gone. A note was left on the dining room table. George opened it and read: 'You're the only one I trust to be Magrete's companion for the rest of her life if I die, and so I'll go to war confident about her future.'

George was not sure if Herbert understood the commitment

he had actually made. And there was a past commitment, Julia, unbeknownst to Herbert entirely. He wondered if the gypsy was blessed with an uncanny foresight. He immediately dismissed the idea as silly.

11

When Magrete returned to the villa, the household was in disarray. Her father-in-law was angry with Herbert, because the heir-apparent had dumped the family business. Her mother-in-law, who was usually mentally strong, was depressed. Lotte was angry with Emma for being romantically linked to Tomas, who was fifteen years her senior. Gertrude seemed to be shielding Anna, but from whom?

What was most disturbing for Magrete was Anna's behaviour. It was as if she had lost all confidence. If Magrete addressed her, she would look at her feet and say 'Yes, ma'am', and then scurry off to do the chore requested. She no longer lingered in Magrete's presence, as Magrete had come to expect. Anna was ashamed of something, thought Magrete. Perhaps she is ashamed that she is a personal maid to a woman who is a second cousin to her mother? Magrete decided to visit Ester the next day to find out if Anna knew that they were related.

On the morning of the day Magrete was going to visit Ester, she had some concerns. She had read in the Berliner Tagblatt that the criminal police had made raids in the Hackescher Market area and arrested a number of Jews because of their links to the Austrian Jewish underground. The article was not specific about who was arrested, but the report made it clear that the criminal police were routing out the Jewish underground network in Berlin. Magrete listened to the morning news bulletins on radio, but they were just as vague. Magrete decided she needed a plausible excuse for being in the area, just in case she was stopped and questioned. She knew that since December 1937 the criminal police had been able to issue a preventative detention order for persons considered to be habitual and professional criminals, or to be engaging in what the regime defined as anti-social behavior, whatever that meant. Neither order was subject to judicial review, nor review by any agency outside of the German Reich Security Police.

Magrete walked along Rosenthalerstraße, entered the alleyway and knocked on the door. No answer. She knocked again, this time a little harder, then she heard a man behind her say, 'She was hospitalised yesterday.'

Magrete turned and faced a SS- und Polizeiführer (SS police leader).

'Why?' she asked, trying to look unafraid.

'She suffered a heart attack. God wanted to rid us of this Jew!' As he said the last word, he spat on Ester's front door step.

'A Jew!' Magrete exclaimed. 'Frau Schuster is not a Jew!'

The SS police leader looked at her, a little rattled. 'You've knocked on the door of Frau Ester Bornstein.'

'Bornstein?' Magrete looked genuinely surprised by the surname. 'Is this alleyway off Kleine Rosenthalerstraße?'

'No, you've missed it. Rosenthalerstraße and Kleine Rosenthalerstraße merge into each other. You've taken the wrong turn.'

'Thank you,' Magrete replied. 'It would have been most embarrassing for me if someone had answered the door.' She turned and walked towards the train station, without once looking over her shoulder.

'Stupid woman,' he muttered to himself, lifting his trousers higher on his waist. 'She doesn't know east from west.'

When Magrete got home, she knew it had been a close call. If the SS police leader had not believed her, she could not have predicted the outcome of her visit.

Over the next two days Magrete scoured every newspaper. Finally, a death notice appeared that reported that Frau Ester Bornstein had died of a heart attack. Magrete would have to tell Anna, but when? Magrete also knew that if she approached Anna about what she knew of her family tree she might expose their familial relationship to a girl who was ignorant of it. Magrete decided she would never mention the familial relationship to Anna - what would be the point - if Anna did not know, Ester would have had good reasons to keep her in the dark, the most obvious based on security.

12

Over the next three months the villa returned to its normal state. Peter was determined to retire, giving Helmut Gruen the leadership of the company, with Peter acting as his adviser. Helmut was given bonuses and allowed to amass a 25 per cent stake in the private firm. Gertrude was becoming less protective of Anna. Anna was gaining more confidence daily, and was staying by Magrete's side whenever she could. Elfi was feeling less depressed, the more letters she wrote to and received from her son. Magrete was exchanging letters with her husband as well. Some she would share with Elfi, as Elfi would share with her. Others she would not share, because of the personal content.

In June 1938 the round-up of Jews began. Thousands were arrested without reason. Magrete decided that she would not tell Anna that her grandmother had passed away, because she did not want them to leave the villa while these street arrests were taking place. More importantly, she wanted Anna to be told away from the household in order to ensure that the conversation between them would be private.

In early July, it was Magrete's custom to take Anna shopping, and after shopping they would usually visit Ester. Magrete decided she would use this outing to tell Anna of her grandmother's death, and that they would then stay away from the household for as long as possible to allow Anna to recover from the shock. Magrete had cut-out the death notice, and because the cost was borne by the government, the date was not contained in the notice itself.

Usually they went to the Wertheim Department store on Leipziger Platz, one of the three largest department stores in Berlin. Here Magrete would be politely served, but at a distance, which she much preferred than being fawned over, which always occurred in the von Appen department stores. However, this time Magrete decided not to go there with Anna, as it was not near the vicinity of a church.

The von Appen's department store in Berlin was near Alexanderplatz in the Mitte district of Berlin. Nearby was St Mary's Church, located in Kaiser-Wilhelmstraße, where Peter von Appen was an elder. Magrete decided to take Anna to a bench near St Mary's and break the news to her there.

They took the train to Alexanderplatz station and walked along Panoramastraße to St Mary's. They found a park bench near the church. 'As you know,' Magrete began, 'the last three months have been very difficult time for Mimi and me, having lost both parents in one night. I cannot image what grief you have been through, first losing your mother Rachel, and then your father Joseph, at such a tender age.'

'Ma'am,' Anna's eyes welled with tears, 'I never did thank you for suggesting that I should visit my parents' grave while you were attending your parent's funeral. That gave me a lot of solace that day. I planted flowers at their shared grave with the money you gave me, and fond memories of both of them flooded back to me.'

'Anna,' Magrete place her arm around Anna's shoulders and drew her closer, 'I have more bad news for you. Your grandmother passed away.' Magrete said it softly and with great empathy. Anna sobbed uncontrollably, her whole body shaking with grief. Magrete kissed her on her head, and said to her, 'She died in hospital from a heart attack. She had an initial attack in the flat. The ambulance took her to the Charité in Mitte Berlin, and she died in her sleep peacefully. I only found out recently.'

Magrete handed Anna the newspaper death notice, which Anna could barely read through her tears. Magrete was now stroking Anna's shoulders, saying, 'Cry as much as you want, Anna. Your grief should not be constrained. Your grandmother did more for you than what most grandmothers need to do. She worked so hard to place you in a safe haven, and she did not care about her own circumstance, only yours. She wanted you to live, and to experience life without unnecessary fear.' Anna looked at Magrete and saw that there were tears in her eyes.

Magrete gave Anna a silk handkerchief, which Anna used to wipe away her tears. Anna said shakily, 'I only got to know her really well when I was sent to Berlin. But in those three to four months, when we both shared that one room off Rosenthalerstraße, I had some of the happiest moments of my life. She showed me how to cook, mend clothes and do all of the things a mother normally teaches her child to do. My grandmother told me that one day we might be imprisoned, not for what we've done, but just because of who we are. She told me that ever since Jesus died on the cross, it was our people who were blamed, persecuted and prosecuted for an event that we don't even believe in!'

Anna stopped talking, because a woman pushing a pram was passing by. The woman looked hard at both of them, but because of the public display of emotion, she appeared to assume that it was associated with a church service honouring some personal event. Once the woman was out of sight Anna continued but more calmly. 'She taught me how to laugh again. She'd walk around the room, mocking the man next door. She'd do this grotesque thing that always made me laugh, tugging at her underwear through her dress to rearrange it, just like he did.' Both Anna and Magrete smiled.

'Anna, let us go into St Mary's Church and pray for your grandmother. After all, their God' – she pointed to the Lutheran Church – 'is my Catholic God and your Jewish God.' Anna nodded. They entered the church and sat side-by-side on pews in the very last row. They both knelt and, clasping their hands, prayed for Ester to a God that spanned all of their religious beliefs.

Afterwards, Magrete and Anna stopped at the department store and shared a pot of tea. Magrete told Anna that the household should know that her grandmother had died from natural causes, a heart attack several days ago, and that she was buried at Friedrichsfelde, which the household would know is a pauper's graveyard, so no funeral service would be conducted.

'Anna,' Magrete said compassionately, 'you should wear a mourning dress to truly show the household how you respected Ester. In an ideal world, the religion that binds your family should be acknowledged and practiced in the open without consequence. However, in our world and in our time, you being Jewish must remain hidden.'

Magrete gave her a gold locket that Anna opened to reveal a photograph of Ester, Rachel and a very young Anna. Magrete's father had taken it when Ester made a rare visit to Vienna and Magrete had found it in one of her parent's photograph albums. Anna kissed Magrete and understood that in Magrete's home she could grieve for her grandmother without fear of persecution.

13

Magrete had been glad that her period had ended prior to Herbert's arrival in Vienna in late April. She bled sparsely at the end of May, but did not get her period at the expected time in June. Her twenty-eight day cycle was regular, so she was concerned that her period had not arrived. She waited a further two weeks, and when nothing occurred she went to see her physician, Dr Zimmerman.

Dr Zimmerman took her temperature and noted that she had a higher basal body temperature than normal. Fidgeting with her chart he asked, 'Frau von Appen, have you noticed lately that you're not eating your normal portions of food?'

Magrete thought about his question and answered, 'I have been so busy lately that I have not really thought about food.'

'Has the sight or smell of food made you experience nausea?'

'Now that I come to think of it, if the food has a very strong odour, it makes me feel a little squeamish, and I have waved it away. Later I might ask for a sandwich.'

'I see,' he said pushing his spectacles higher on the bridge of his nose. 'When did you last have your menses?'

Magrete blushed at the thought of having this discussion with a man. 'At the end of May.'

'Hmm.' The doctor then proceeded on a different tack. 'Your husband is a very important businessman. Has he been home most of May and June?'

'No. He was conscripted into the Luftwaffe in late April and will be away until early November.'

'I see.' Dr Zimmerman scratched his ear with his pencil. 'Other than your husband being absent from the household, have you been under stress? Have you travelled long distances?'

'My parents died in Vienna in April,' Magrete said, feeling her eyes moisten.

'Frau von Appen, there are two possibilities. The first is that the severe stress of your husband being conscripted, together with your parent's death, might be playing havoc with your normal cycle. Medically you're fit, but mental trauma can interfere with physical processes. On the other hand, your basal body temperature is higher than normal, you had no menses in June, you're eating less because the sight and odour of food is making you nauseous – all of this suggests that you are pregnant.' His last phrase did not take hold in

Magrete's consciousness until he added the next observation. 'We'll shall know by the time of your next cycle whether you are pregnant or not.'

Magrete left Dr Zimmerman's surgery stunned, but excited.

On Monday 1 August Dr Zimmerman confirmed that Magrete was three months pregnant. She rushed back to Wannsee. For the first time she entered the upstairs quarters via the rear entrance. She wanted time to herself before announcing her pregnancy to her in-laws. Magrete sat at Herbert's desk and reached into the top drawer for a pen and paper. She wrote him an account of her two consultations with the physician, avoiding any medical details, but relaying the two propositions that Dr Zimmerman had placed before her: was it mental stress that was causing the bodily changes she was experiencing, or was it pregnancy? After delaying the revelation for as long as possible, she wrote: 'I am PREGNANT!' She addressed the letter and went downstairs to see Gertrude.

'I didn't know you'd arrived home, ma'am,' Gertrude said apologetically.

'I came in via the rear entrance. Could you please send this letter to Herbert? Where is Lady von Appen?'

Gertrude noted Magrete's excitement. 'Lady von Appen is in the study with Herr von Appen. Can I get Anna for you?'

'No, that will not be necessary,' Magrete said over her shoulder as she rushed towards the study.

Magrete flung open the study doors and walked up to Elfi, who looked surprised. Magrete hugged her and whispered into Elfi's ear, 'I am pregnant!'

Elfi hugged her tightly but carefully and then over Magrete's shoulder shouted to Peter, 'We're going to be grandparents!'

Peter rose from behind his desk. 'Grandparents?' And then realisation hit, and he shouted, 'Grandparents!' He sped around the desk and hugged both women simultaneously. Magrete regaled to both of them the contents of the letter she had just written to Herbert.

After Magrete had finished, Elfi said to both of them, but in particular to Peter, 'Magrete needs to be looked after every hour of every day, especially since Herbert will not be home until November, when Magrete will be seven months pregnant. I propose we convert the attic into a bedroom for Anna, leaving the three bedrooms on that floor for Magrete and Herbert, and for their growing family. With Anna in her new bedroom, if anything happens during the night, she will always be there to help.' Magrete waved her hand to indicate that such cost was not necessary. 'Ssh,' Elfi said. 'To offset some of the work Anna did for Gertrude, I think we should hire Tomas' niece Erika, as a part-time non-residential domestic, and now that Tomas has been conscripted, there shouldn't be any authority conflict with Gertrude. Also, I suggest that Anna gets some training as a midwife.' Elfi looked at Magrete and said pointedly, 'I know that when I gave birth to Simon, Peter was hopeless. I had to scream at him to get me a midwife and luckily for me it was a long delivery – he even found that difficult!' Magrete could see Peter smiling as he was recalling the incident.

'You really should not spend so much money-' Magrete began.

'Nonsense!' interrupted Peter, touching Magrete gently on her wrist. 'What Elfi is suggesting makes a lot of sense to me. There'll be times at night you'll need assistance, and so I'll arrange to have a cord near your bed so that Anna can be alerted in her bedroom when you need her. Elfi is also right about giving Anna midwife training. She can do that in the mornings when Erika can look after-'

'Not necessary,' Elfi interrupted. 'Erika has already trained as a midwife. She can train Anna here in the upstairs quarters in front of Magrete.'

'Then we should hire Erika as a full-time non-residential domestic,' Peter advised. The conversation between Elfi and Peter continued for another half hour, with Magrete a non-influential observer. She understood more than ever how important her baby was not only to Herbert and her, but also to Elfi and Peter.

At the end of their conversations Elfi summoned Gertrude, told her that Magrete was pregnant and gave her instructions about hiring Erika and telling her about the plan to convert the attic into Anna's sleeping quarters. Gertrude was pleased with the first instruction, but not with Anna's new sleeping arrangements. Peter was reinvigorated for he always enjoyed overseeing tradesmen.

By the start of September the attic had been converted into Anna's bedroom. Without alluding to the past, Elfi told Anna in front of Gertrude that when Herbert was at home, Anna would move back to the servants' quarters, as Magrete would then be in Herbert's care. Elfi was unsure how long Herbert's training was going to take, but she was absolutely certain that once it was completed, Magrete and her child would live at Wannsee, no matter where the Luftwaffe might station Herbert.

Anna was pleased with her new bedroom. Magrete would finally be in her care 24 hours a day. Anna loved the idea of gaining special skills and, in particular, she was thrilled that she would be learning the trade of midwife. Her knowledge of sex and childbirth was minimal and so the lessons would not only be invaluable to her professionally, but also personally.

Even though Magrete was three months pregnant, she continued her private yoga instruction with Indira Devi. The most important intervention Indira did was to mitigate Magrete's morning sickness. She adjusted Magrete's diet and taught her a series of yoga poses that were most beneficial in terms of the physicality of Magrete's pregnancy. Just as the wrong food odours made Magrete queasy, the right odours soothed her symptoms. Hence, Indira suggested that Magrete sniff ginger, mint, cinnamon or lavender and grate fresh ginger into hot water for a calming tea.

The letters between Magrete and Herbert increased in volume, as did the letters between Herbert and Elfi. With this significant event ahead of them, the family became more focussed on itself. Elfi and Magrete, who moved in different social circles, stopped seeing their friends. Peter was less interested in the business, giving more responsibility to Helmut Gruen.

Magrete had suddenly remembered that George was ignorant of her pregnancy. She immediately wrote him a letter telling him the news. George wrote back expressing his happiness over the new addition to her family. He wrote that the addition of a mini-amigo would do wonders for their sobriety. Secretly George was relieved that his vow to Herbert would be further tempered and so might not impact on a previous commitment he had with Julia.

Anti-Jewish sentiment was becoming more hysterical in the German Reich. In August a law was enacted that would come into force on 1 January 1939. It required Jewish men and women with first names that were non-Jewish in origin to add Israel in the case of a male and Sara in the case of a female to their given names. All German Reich Jews were obliged to carry identity cards that indicated their heritage, and in the autumn of 1938 all passports of German Reich Jews were stamped with an identifying red letter J. As the Nazi leadership stepped up their war preparations, anti-Semitic legislation paved the way for more radical persecution of Jews. The government intended to permanently separate Jews from the rest of the population, for reasons that would surface later. Of course, Magrete consciously ignored the law, and made sure Anna was ignorant of it, whereas Mimi was not aware that it should apply to her.

14

Herbert arrived at Kitzingen airfield confident that within six months he would have his C licence. Over that period of time he was given ground training in advanced aeronautical subjects, and flew obsolescent operational planes such as early versions of the Dorneir Do 17. When he qualified in September at C School and received his advanced pilot's license, he was now able to fly his aircraft by day or night with reasonable proficiency. He had limited training in instrument flying, but could perform simple cross-country navigational flights under fair weather conditions.

The dive-bomber or Stuka pilot school was operating at the airfield, and so he joined the Geschwader (squadron) in order to acquire training in tactics. The initial training focused on dive-bombing rather than ground attack. He wrote to Elfi and Magrete, that he was hoping to be home by 12 November.

The Junkers Ju 87 or Stuka, the plane Herbert was scheduled to fly, was a dive-bomber and ground-attack aircraft. It had made its combat debut in 1937, during the Spanish Civil War. It was a single-engine plane with a two-man crew (pilot and rear gunner) with iconic gull wings and a spatted undercarriage. The plane was instantly recognisable because of its wailing siren. It had the ability to deliver bombs with previously unheard-of precision.

Herbert flew the Ju 87 many times with his trainer in the rear giving him instructions, where the gunner would have normally sat. On 9 November a new group tactic was being trialled. Each Stuka was fitted with a 50-kilogram bomb, the usual size of a wing bomb, under the fuselage. The chief instructor, Oberst (Colonel) Kurt Hofman, briefed his five student pilots. 'Today,' he said dryly, 'you'll be flying solo. After take-off, you'll form the squadron into a swarm formation.' He handed each student a chart showing him his position in the swarm formation. 'You'll fly at 4,600 metres, and locate the target, an old farmhouse near the airfield, through a bombsight window in the cockpit floor. After you've opened the dive brakes and eased back on the throttle, you must roll the aircraft 180 degrees, automatically nosing the aircraft into a dive. As you know, the red tabs protruding from the upper surfaces of the wing will act as your visual indicator. In case of a g-force induced blackout, the automatic dive recovery system will be activated.'

He paused and then with a pointer he proceeded to highlight aspects of chalked diagrams he had drawn on the blackboard. 'You must dive at a 60 to 90 degree angle, and you'll need to accelerate to 600 kilometres per hour. When your aircraft is reasonably close to the target, a light on the contact altimeter will come on to indicate the bomb-release point, which should be at a minimum height of 450 metres. You must release the bomb by depressing the knob on the control column to release the weapon and to initiate the automatic pull-out mechanism. As you know, the clutch located under the fuselage will swing the bomb out of the way of the propeller, and the aircraft should automatically begin a 6-g pull-out. Once the nose is above the horizon, the dive brakes need to be retracted, the throttle opened, and the propeller set to climb. At that point you should have regained control and resumed normal flight. The remaining bombs under the wings will not be fitted today. I'll be positioned at 12 o'clock to observe you in action. Are there any questions?'

Flying Officer Karl Hauptman quipped, 'Who'll clean up the mess we make of that farm house?' They all smiled.

The five pilots took off sequentially, with Oberst Hofman following. Within minutes, they were in the swarm formation and heading to the farmhouse location, with Oberst taking the 12 o'clock position. Once near the target, the first Stuka peeled off from the formation and struck the farmhouse perfectly. The second Stuka then peeled off and missed the centre of the target. The third Stuka peeled off from the formation and dived at a 90-degree angle, accelerating to 600 km/hr and, with no bomb released, smashed and exploded on impact, demolishing what little was left of the farmhouse. The Oberst immediately called off the exercise. The four training pilots could hear the Oberst cursing the pilot for this disaster.

15

Three days before Herbert was to arrive back on leave, the villa at Wannsee was put in lock-down mode – no one was allowed in or out. The household was frightened and shocked by the events taking place in Berlin. Peter von Appen was one of the few Berliners who hung his head in shame thinking that they must have emptied insane asylums to find people who could do things like that. It had begun in Paris, when Herschel Grünspan, a seventeen-year-old Jewish refugee from Hanover, shot German Reich diplomat Ernst von Rath in an act of protest against Hitler's policies regarding the Jews. After Rath's death on 9 November the anti-Jewish riots spread throughout the German Reich. The Sturmabteilung (SA – Storm Detachment) paramilitary, with the unofficial support of the government and with the support of a sizeable faction of the German Reich population, went on a killing rampage. Almost 100 Jewish residents in the German Reich lost their lives in the violence. Jewish homes, hospitals and schools were ransacked as the attackers demolished buildings with sledgehammers. Over a thousand synagogues were burnt. Some 7,000 Jewish businesses were damaged and plundered. Jewish schools were destroyed. It was called Krystallnacht (Crystal Night), because so many shop windows were smashed.

Reinhard Heydrich instructed the police not to interfere with the riots unless his guidelines with respect to guarding foreign and German Reich properties were violated. Police were also instructed to seize Jewish archives from synagogues and community offices, and to arrest and detain healthy male Jews for eventual transfer to concentration camps.

Fourteen hours after the violence began Dr Paul Joseph Goebbels, Minister of Propaganda, ordered that the destruction be stopped, and addressed the nation on a radio news bulletin about the events. 'The justified and comprehensible indignation of the German Reich at the cowardly Jew murder of a German Reich diplomat in Paris extensively manifested itself last night. Reprisals have been taken in numerous towns and cities of the German Reich against Jewish buildings and shops. At present, however, the entire population is earnestly warned immediately to abstain from any further demonstrations against Jewry, no matter what kind. The final and correct answer to the Jewish outrage in Paris will be given to the Jewry through laws and decrees.'

The gates of the von Appen's villa at Wannsee were reopened for the return of their son. At 10 am there was a knock on the door. Peter was on his way out, and he opened the door, to be confronted by Luftwaffe Oberst. 'My name is Oberst Kurt Hofman. I'm your son's flying instructor. A terrible accident has happened. Your son's plane crashed in training and I'm very sorry to inform you that he has died. Here is a letter explaining the circumstances of his death and a death card. If I can do anything for you, please do not hesitate to ask.'

Peter was mute. Oberst Kurt Hofman handed over the package to a shocked father, gave a Nazi salute and retreated to a chauffeur-driven car. Peter followed the car with his eyes as it left his property, and he heard Elfi behind him ask, 'What's the matter, Peter?'

On hearing the news of the death of her son, Elfi collapsed and was taken to hospital with Gertrude in assistance. When Magrete was informed of Herbert's death she cried hysterically and was comforted by Peter and Anna in the upstairs quarters. When Magrete became calm through sheer exhaustion, Peter retreated to his study, slowly unfolded the letter and read it in utter disbelief. The letter informed him that Herbert's plane had crashed with force and, because it was carrying a 50-kilogram bomb, the explosion had completely disintegrated the plane and the pilot. None of Herbert's remains could be found.

My son, thought Peter, completely evaporated. Two sons, both killed in accidents. The letter went on to say that there would be a complete investigation as to what might have gone wrong, but because all planes in the squadron had been mechanically checked prior to the accident, and four of them had been re-examined after the accident, the initial finding was that it was due to pilot error. Oh Herbert, Peter thought, you always loved to live on the edge of excitement.

Peter pulled out the death card and read it.

The unavoidable fate of death presses us down,
only the hope of coming resurrection lifts us up.
For the ones, who believe in you, oh Lord,
life can never be robbed,
it will be only transformed.

A pilot's life suffered a hero's death of your son, husband, brother or colleague on 8th November 1938 at Kitzingen Airfied.

Herbert Otto von Appen

Oberleutnant (first lieutenant) at the age of 29 years died
Kitzingen Airfied, on 8th November 1938
Wilhelm Reuss, Chaplain, presently in the armed forces.

The phone rang and Peter was told Elfi had collapsed again in the emergency ward of the hospital. He rushed to the hospital, knowing that his family was slowly unravelling because of Herbert's death.

16

The Lutheran service for Herbert von Appen was held in St Mary's Church. It was not strictly a funeral service, because Herbert's remains were never found. However, as Peter was an elder of the church, Pastor Gerhard Ebling was more than willing to accommodate this unusual situation. Unlike Catholics, Lutherans do not believe in purgatory and so there was no conflict in allowing a service to be held as soon as practicable. It was held within a week of Peter receiving notice of Herbert's death. Gertrude took on most of the responsibility for the organisation, with Peter signing off, showing little interest in what was put before him. Elfi had returned home, but was heavily sedated most of the time. Magrete did not leave left her upstairs quarters before the funeral. Gertrude had daily meetings with Anna downstairs, to be informed of Magrete's condition. Anna told Gertrude that Magrete was terribly distressed and crying continuously until fatigue set in.

The Lutherans do not have a prescribed formula for liturgy. An empty casket was displayed and, in the Lutheran tradition, it remained closed throughout the liturgy. Magrete saw the coffin and thought it a meaningless symbol of loss – there was no body in it! A candle was lit nearby signifying death and resurrection with Christ. The pall was placed over the empty casket to recall the white garment of holy baptism.

There were about sixty people at the service. Magrete, and Peter sat in the front pew, all in a daze. Peter was now using a cane, and Elfi was in a wheelchair, guided by Gertrude. The wheelchair was positioned between Peter and Magrete. Anna placed a small blanket around Magrete's knees and lap. Both servants walked to the end pew of the front row. George sat on one side of Magrete. Helmut sat on the other side of Peter. Himmler was sitting next to Helmut, which completely terrified him.

The congregation stood while the processional hymn was sung, but Magrete, Elfi and Peter remained seated. The pastor and acolytes processed into the sanctuary, and the pastor stopped at the foot of the altar steps.

'In the name of the Father, and of the Son, and of the Holy Spirit', he began, and even Himmler made the sign of the cross on his chess. Magrete, Elfi, and Peter remained motionless.

'In Confession,' the pastor said, 'we kneel humbly before our God, acknowledging our sin and seeking purification of our Spirit.

In the declaration that follows, we receive from God Himself the assurance of God's mercy, and grace that enables us to focus on our loving God.' The congregation and the pastor knelt as he intoned, 'If we say we have no sin, we deceive ourselves, and the truth is not in us.'

The congregation replied, 'But if we confess our sins, God who is faithful and just will forgive our sins and cleanse us from all unrighteousness.'

There was a moment of silence as the congregation stared at the three principals, each sat motionless and expressionless.

The pastor said, 'Let us confess our sins to God our Father', and the service proceeded. It included four hymns and a tribute that was a brief summary of Herbert's life in Christ and emphasised the hope and faith he had in life. The tribute had been prepared by Gertrude, but was handed to the pastor by Peter von Appen. The funeral service ended with the pastor commending the deceased to the Lord's care and keeping, and then giving a benediction. Magrete kept thinking - but there is no corpse in the coffin!

After the service, Himmler walked over to Peter and Elfi, giving them his condolences. To Magrete he said, 'I'm so sorry for your loss. Herbert was unique. Hopefully one day you'll come and have morning tea with us.' Magrete nodded and looked at his companion, Hedwig Potthast, a slim young woman. For the first time since Herbert's death Magrete spoke without a tremor in her voice, saying to Hedwig, 'So nice to finally meet you.' Hedwig smiled at Magrete and nodded as a sign of respect, then steered Himmler away and out of the church as quickly as she could.

17

Elfi was incapacitated and making a slow recovery, so Peter decided that Erika should take some of the load from Gertrude and be Elfi's full-time maid. Peter's leg was giving him so much trouble that he found walking difficult, and impossible without a cane. He stopped visiting the upstairs quarters. He still had meetings with Helmut, who was running the business on a day-to-day basis, but at Peter's request, they were meeting fortnightly instead of weekly. Peter was extremely worried about Magrete and the effect of Herbert's death on her pregnancy. Dr Zimmerman was visiting Magrete weekly. He assured Peter that Magrete was emotionally fatigued, but in good health. Her years of yoga had made her lithe, and surprisingly physically fit. Anna was looking after Magrete full-time and taking daily midwifery lessons from Erika, when both of their charges were asleep. Peter wanted Magrete to become more mentally engaged, and hit upon an idea. He instructed Gertrude to ask Magrete to visit him in his study.

Magrete knocked on the door and entered. She looked weary and listless, but her eight-month pregnancy suited her in that it made her body look far more substantial. Peter was seated behind the desk. She walked up beside him and gave him a soft kiss on his head. 'I was about to sleep, Peter, when Gertrude told me you wanted to see me.' She sat down in an armchair near to his desk.

Peter got up and, with some difficulty, drew his chair nearer to her. He leaned towards her. 'Magrete, in about a month or so you'll be a mother, and down the track I'll need to put in place an orderly business successional plan. As you know, Helmut Gruen is running the company and has a 25 per cent stake in it, and we own the rest. I've been training him but lately he no longer needs me.' He paused and looked reassuringly at her.

'What I want you to do is become more involved in the family business,' Peter continued, 'especially later, as your child gets older. I know you have a Diploma in Business and Accounting and so you'll be a real asset to the company. Helmut is coming today to give me a final briefing for the year, and I'd like you to be present. Usually our December meeting is not so lengthy. It'll give you a glimpse into the sorts of matters we discuss. If at any time during the meeting you feel too tired or sick, or you've had enough, don't hesitate to leave. After all, your health is the most important business for all of us.' Peter paused.

Magrete looked at him, suddenly feeling more responsible than ever, not only in terms of the well-being of her child, but also in assisting Peter to care for the financial well-being of the household at large. She knew that women in the German Reich were considered homemakers, but Peter was taking a bolder approach in asking her to become a business associate. Magrete looked at him fondly and asked, 'When is Helmut meeting you?'

'Oh,' Peter said nonchalantly, 'in about five minutes.'

Right on time, Gertrude ushered Helmut into the study. 'Peter, Magrete,' Helmut greeted them, expecting Magrete to leave, but she remained seated.

'Helmut, I've asked Magrete to sit in on our meetings, because I want her to get more involved in the business as time goes on,' Peter explained. 'Magrete and I both understand she has a child to birth, and of course to rear in its younger years, but sooner or later she needs to become more aware of what we're doing.' Hmm, thought Helmut, successional planning but with a twist. Peter continued. 'You mightn't be aware that Magrete has a Diploma in Business and Accounting, and so she'll be familiar with some aspects of the business, but definitely not with other aspects.'

The next hour was filled with profits, losses, margins, investments, liabilities, and lastly bonuses for executive staff. Peter and Helmut observed that Magrete, while not offering any comments, listened intently. Nearing the end of Helmut's account Magrete thought it appropriate to leave, because the next item of business was Helmut's yearly bonus, and she reasoned that was a subject better for her to be informed about, when Helmut was absent.

While Christmas and New Year were sad events, Peter noticed that Magrete was far more robust than he thought. Elfi's health was slowly improving, and the business was doing well, because the economy was being fuelled by the militarisation of the German Reich.

18

At around 8 am on Sunday 15 January, Magrete desperately rang the cord to summon Anna. Her water had broken and she was having contractions, clearly in the early stages of labour. At this point Magrete's contractions did not last long, and there were lengthy gaps between them. She asked Anna to get Erika. Anna reminded Magrete that both Emma and Erika were visiting Tomas in Saarbruecken.

When Gertrude told Peter von Appen that Magrete was in labour, he asked that Elfi not be woken and rang Dr Zimmerman. The butler who picked up the telephone informed Peter that Dr Zimmerman was in Munich and so was unavailable. Gertrude was a spinster and knew little about children or childbirth. She decided to leave it to Anna.

Magrete's contractions stopped for a while, but just as she felt it might have been a false alarm, they started again, this time more actively. The contractions were lasting longer, and becoming more frequent and more powerful. Magrete was gripping Anna's hand more and more tightly. Towards the end of the first stage of Magrete's labour the contractions became extremely intense and as much as she tried to resist screaming, on occasions her agony was so great it forced her to whimper.

In the next stage of Magrete's labour, Anna became more involved, shouting 'Push! Push, ma'am, push!' Magrete could feel the pressure of her baby's head low down in her pelvis. With each contraction, she pushed in response to Anna's urging, gasping between each push. With every push, her baby moved further down the birth canal, but at the end of each contraction, Magrete felt her child retreating back up the canal. It felt to Magrete like two steps forward and one step back.

Anna then saw the child's head crowning, and this time it stayed stationary when the contraction had ended. She told Magrete that she could see the baby's head, and asked her to stop pushing. She said, 'Blow or sigh out your breaths. That will help you resist the urge to bear down for two or three contractions, so your baby can be born gently and slowly. Do you understand me, ma'am?' Magrete nodded. She felt a stinging sensation as her vagina started to stretch around her baby's head. Anna used warm compresses in order to prevent tearing.

When the child's shoulders appeared, Anna slid the child out. She placed a clamp on the umbilical cord and cut it. She washed and dried the baby off with a clean towel, wrapped a soft woollen blanket around the child's body and placed the child on Magrete's chest.

At 1 am on Monday 16 January 1939 Magrete's child was born, some 17 hours after she felt the first contraction. Gertrude informed the household it was a baby girl. Anna was proud that she had assisted in birthing the child. Magrete named her baby girl Ilse Elfriede von Appen, Ilse after her father's mother. Elfi and Peter were proud that they had a grandchild, although both had secretly wished for a boy.

19

Magrete got in contact with George Nagy and asked him to meet her at Café Buchwald on Saturday 22 April at 10 am for morning tea. She had not seen George since Herbert's funeral, and felt it would be nice for him to meet baby Ilse. George, though, feared that the oath he had made to Herbert might be the reason for the meeting.

For the past three months the household had been completely taken over by Magrete's child. Everybody was thankful that Ilse was not a screamer, slept well, and had a happy disposition. She was constantly smiling and giggling, to whoever held her in their arms. Baby Ilse was a wonderful health tonic for Elfi. Although she was still wheelchair-bound, the improvement in Elfi's health was directly related to the time she spent with baby Ilse, or so it seemed to Magrete. If Elfi napped, then Peter monopolised the child's time. Ilse had spent more time with her grandparents than with Magrete, who also had to compete with Anna for time with her own child. Breastfeeding gave Magrete some respite from sharing her child with the household.

Magrete was late and George busied himself by reading the newspaper. He was concerned that Hungary had left the League of Nations, paving the way for the Hungarian government to aggressively support the German Reich. The paper also had news about Italy's invasion of Albania. He remembered a conversation he had with Herbert, who had predicted that the German Reich would focus on its eastern flank eventually. Not only had the German Reich secured Sudetenland on 30 September 1938 unopposed, due to English and French appeasement, by 15 March 1939 the Czech president had signed a document stating that he had confidently placed the fate of the Czech people and country in the hands of the Führer of the German Reich. Two hours later, amid a late winter snowstorm, the German Reich Army rolled into the first non-Germanic territory to be taken by the Nazis. Hitler announced to the people later that day, just before departing for Prague, that 'Czechoslovakia has ceased to exist!' Poland is next, thought George.

As Magrete and Anna entered, Magrete noted that the café was almost empty except for George and a few couples. George rose and kissed her on both cheeks, and she responded in kind. 'Anna, show George baby Ilse,' Magrete said beaming with pride. Anna swooped the baby out of the pram and presented the child to George, who tickled Ilse on her stomach. Ilse giggled back at him.

Anna placed the child back in the pram and sat down at the table, gently rocking the pram to and fro. She stared at George and when he responded with a smile, she immediately turned her attention to the baby, straightening the blanket in the pram. He really is gorgeous, Anna said to herself. Beautiful brown eyes, black hair, pale skin, pearly white teeth, an engaging smile, and a slim body, but with some muscle. At every opportunity, when he was not watching, Anna would steal another glance, and then another. She tried to gauge his age – perhaps late twenties, she thought. Magrete noticed that Anna was closely observing George and smiled.

'How are you, Magrete?'

'I'm well, considering. It has been six months, but it feels like a lifetime. I often cry at night; that is when I miss Herbert the most.' She smiled and looked at the pram. 'The baby is just three months old. Both Elfi and Peter dominate her time, as does Anna.' Magrete smiled at Anna, who smiled back. Then, as if to prove to George that Magrete's concerns were well founded, Anna placed the dummy back into Ilse's mouth, as a mother would do, and in doing so increased Ilse's sleepiness.

'I've been thinking about Herbert a lot as well,' George confessed. 'He was like my younger brother. We used to meet here often, when you were not available, and of course he would talk about politics and I had little to offer him in return. Everything he's predicted is slowly coming to pass. I'm worried we're heading towards a war.' If Magrete was going to discuss my oath to Herbert, George wondered, why had she brought Anna along?

Magrete asked in a matter-of-fact tone, 'If the German Reich goes to war will you return to Hungary?'

'No, I won't go back,' George said thinking of past commitments. 'Once the farm was sold, I knew that I had to create my own future elsewhere. Anyway, being a scientist is what I do best! Hahn is a wonderful director and the team members I'm leading are a close-knit group. The Nazis are putting a lot of pressure to incorporate our activities within the industrial-military complex, and so take it away from pure research. Whatever happens with the Institute, I'll still remain there – it's my life!'

The waiter came to take their orders. Magrete ordered a dobos torte and espresso, as did George, who then turned to Anna and said, 'Madam, what would you like to order?' Anna did not answer, and George repeated his question. In the von Appen household Anna was not considered an equal, and so was invisible to all except Magrete. Guests could talk about private matters in her company; she had the same status as a piece of furniture. Anna blushed and looked at Magrete, who nodded toward George as if to say - answer him!

'I'll have the same,' Anna stammered, not knowing what she had just ordered.

Magrete saw George hand the waiter a wad of Reichsmarks. The waiter nodded and disappeared. Magrete remembered that coffee and cacao beans were now a rarity and said, 'George, how much is this costing you?'

He dismissed her concern with a wave of his hand, and whispered, 'Shh! We've just committed a criminal act', and laughed.

When the cake and coffee came, Anna loved the cake but hated the coffee – it was so bitter. George and Magrete were now making her feel part of the conversation. At seventeen Anna was on the verge of womanhood and so mature handsome men were of great interest to her. She leaned forward to listen to the conversation, a posture she was convinced would make her look far more interesting, and older than her age.

'Peter wants me to get more involved with the business now that Herbert and Simon are gone,' Magrete said. 'He thinks my Diploma in Business and Accounting might come in handy.'

'That makes a lot of sense to me Magrete. After all, there needs to be some continuity. How does Helmut feel?'

'I am not sure,' Magrete answered, with a tinge of anxiousness. 'I will get a better idea at our September meeting. I have told Peter that I would like to defer being present at their fortnightly meetings until Ilse gets a little older.'

After they had spoken for some time, Anna interrupted. 'Ma'am,' she said, 'we need to return to the villa for lunch.' Magrete understood that it was breastfeeding time.

'We must do this more often,' Magrete suggested and George responded that he would love to.

As Anna got up, she lost her balance and George quickly supported her. What a wonderful man, Anna thought, as she followed Magrete out the door, pushing the pram.

George realised that Magrete had really wanted him to see her child, and had no intention of raising the oath he had given to Herbert. He wondered whether she had received Herbert's letter, and if she had, why hadn't she mentioned it?

20

Peter and Helmut rescheduled the meeting of 3 September to 10 September, because France and England had declared war on the German Reich on that day. To neutralise the possibility that the USSR might come to Poland's aid, on 23 August the German Reich signed a nonaggression pact with the Soviet Union. On 1 September, one and a half million German Reich troops invaded Poland along its 1750-mile border. Simultaneously, the Luftwaffe bombed Polish airfields, and German Reich warships and Unterseeboots (Under sea boats or U-boats) attacked Polish naval forces in the Baltic Sea. Adolf Hitler claimed that the massive invasion was a defensive action. His claim was rejected by France and Britain, and so on 3 September 1939 those nations declared war on the German Reich; on that day, appeasement towards the German Reich had ended. One week after the declarations of war, the atmosphere in Berlin remained the same as before – tranquil.

Although Magrete only had few memories of the Great War, she remembered that once Germany surrendered, food became scarce because of hyperinflation in 1919 – one trillion paper Marks could buy you a single gold Mark! She was worried about her family, as women and children always bore the brunt of a brutal life. Magrete was glad that she had weaned baby Ilse very recently; although that tie was an important sensual link to her child, it made Ilse too dependent on her, and the more independent a child, she thought, the greater the probability of survival in a war-torn society.

Magrete, Helmut and Peter met in Peter's study. It was clear that Helmut was not comfortable with her presence. Helmut gave them both a complete financial breakdown of each department store, starting with Berlin and then Frankfurt, Munich, Leipzig, Dresden, Magdeberg, Vienna, Prague and Budapest. He then moved on to the financial health of the company as a whole – where it was financially vulnerable, and where it was financially strong. His detailed and lengthy presentation was predicated on non-turbulent times. It was at this point that Magrete intervened.

'I know you may think of me as being naïve, but the atmosphere in the German Reich at the moment is as if there had been no declarations of war issued – and yet there were! There are three aspects of war we must urgently think about. The first has to do with supply. All materials will be channelled towards the war effort. Also, many of the goods we are currently selling are not produced within the German Reich, and if they are produced elsewhere, like Spain or Switzerland, getting the products to a department store might be problematic, due to the military intervention of the enemy or the closing of borders. The second is staff. We will have severe staffing shortages due to the war effort. The third is property. Most of our department stores are in central locations, which normally are the hardest hit. For example, in Madrid during the Spanish Civil war, German Reich warplanes decimated shops, although they were targeting important government offices. The most important consideration is what happens to us financially if we lose the war. Look at what happened to us after the Great War – hyperinflation!'

As Magrete was talking, Helmut sat down and listened. Peter was proud of her. Not even I, thought Peter, and I'm most astute, have thought about this as clearly as Magrete. Now he spoke. 'I think Magrete has hit the nail on the head. I was fooled by talk of a phoney war. We need to safeguard some of the properties as soon as possible, and make contingencies for lack of staff and goods, as well as for the loss of property, and we need to somehow safeguard our wealth against a possible defeat.'

Helmut ventured, 'We could make some of our department stores available to the Deutsches Rotes Kreuz (DRK or German Red Cross) in order to convert them into hospitals. With a DRK sign on the roof, the enemy will not purposely target the building, and what's more, the goods in those stores could be redistributed to the stores that we wish to keep open, to maintain cash flow. In some cases we might be able to shift female staff to the open stores as well, therefore mitigating male staff losses.'

'Brilliant!' Peter and Magrete said simultaneously.

Peter floated another idea. 'We need to take some money out of the German Reich as soon as possible to safer havens. Countries that might not get involved and who will probably stay neutral are Switzerland, Sweden, Norway and America. Shifting money to these countries will be illegal shortly, if it's not already.'

'Let me look into that,' Helmut said.

'So,' summarised Peter, 'this will be our strategy. I'll spend most of my time on which stores we should close and which stores we should leave open. Helmut, you look at how we can move money to safe havens, legally or illegally, and Magrete …' Peter hesitated.

'I will go and see Marga Himmler,' Magrete said, 'who is not far from Munich and who I understand has good connections with the DRK.'

Helmut and Peter looked at her with appreciation. They agreed to meet in a fortnight's time, each to make a presentation to the other two on their assigned responsibilities. As Magrete was leaving,

Helmut stopped and said to her most sincerely, 'Welcome aboard!'

Magrete knew he had accepted her and smiled as she replied, 'Thank you.'

When Magrete and Helmut had departed, Peter smiled to himself and thought, I have a son, and he is called Magrete! The tomboy in Magrete had survived and Peter, like her father before him, loved it.

21

Magrete decided she would travel to Munich and visit Marga Himmler alone, and then travel to Vienna and visit Mimi for three days. She would spend one week away from baby Ilse. Anna and Elfi loved the idea that Magrete was travelling without her baby. Both women could bottle-feed Ilse and spend lots of time with her – Elfi during the day, and Anna whenever Elfi was napping and especially at night, when Elfi was sleeping. Peter relinquished his time with the child on most days. He would now accompany Helmut into the company offices, where he needed access to information. Only before and immediately after dinner would he spend time with his granddaughter.

Magrete found herself in Munich during what was known as the sitting war – the period between September 1939 and the spring of 1940, where little occurred in terms of armed conflict. The Americans had coined it the phoney war. On 3 September alone, 6 million copies of a 'Note to the German People' were dropped in just one night by the Royal Air Force (RAF) – the equivalent of thirteen tons of paper – the idea being that the German people would learn about the evils of the German Reich. It was also intended to show the leaders of the German Reich how vulnerable their country was to bombing raids. The result of these initial intrusions was that the German Reich stepped up the preparation of its anti-aircraft batteries and the production of its fighter aeroplanes.

Magrete was in Munich on 17 September 1939, the day Poland was invaded from the east by Russia. She made contact with Marga Himmler, who was living in Gmund am Tegersee in Bavaria, not far from Munich. Marga invited her for morning tea at 10 am on the same day.

Magrete arrived on time. Marga's house was a two-storey home, with bay windows and a balcony on the second floor. It was Bavarian in style, with large pine trees obscuring its view from the road. Marga opened the door and greeted Magrete by kissing her lightly on each cheek. She took Magrete into the living room, where tea and cakes were waiting. The children were not to be seen.

'How are you, Magrete? I'm so sorry to hear about the loss of your husband. Heinrich didn't tell me about the funeral.' She gestured to a chair and Magrete sat down.

'I am well, but you know how it is when you lose someone close,' Magrete replied. 'I miss Herbert so much that sometimes I feel empty inside.'

'These emotions will subside in time,' Marga reflected, coldly thinking of Himmler. 'How's your child?'

'She is fine and is being totally spoilt by my in-laws. Now that Ilse is bottle-fed my mother-in-law is happier, because she can spend more time with my baby,' Magrete said, sadly reflecting on her lack of interaction with Ilse.

'I can well imagine. I don't go to Berlin anymore. Heinrich and that gold-digger Hedwig Potthast are having an affair. It's so embarrassing for me, but I have to tolerate it for the sake of Gudrun. What is it with these secretaries that bosses just can't get enough of them? I'll never trust a female secretary again!' Magrete was surprised at how open Marga was about Himmler's love affair. She understood how humiliating it would be to have a younger, slimmer and more ruthless woman take your husband away from you.

'If it wasn't for Püppi,' Marga continued, 'I wouldn't talk to her father, but she's our child, and she needs to feel the love of each parent.

Anyway, Potthast squirms whenever Heinrich is in the company of his daughter.' Marga paused and then sighed. 'Since I saw you last, I've been languishing out here.'

With Marga seemingly directionless, it seemed the perfect time to enlist her assistance. 'Marga, I remember you telling me, when we first met, that you trained as a nurse and near the end of the Great War you worked for the DRK.'

'Yes, and it gave me a great deal of satisfaction,' Marga said smiling at the memory.

"The family business is now being run by Helmut Gruen, because Herbert's father, Peter von Appen, intends to retire from the business in the not-too-distant future. Do you know Helmut?'

'I don't know him well.'

'The business, from what Peter tells me, needs to undergo a significant restructure and so the company wants to mothball some of the department stores that it owns. However, the company wants to help the war effort and so would offer some of these premises to the DRK to be converted into hospitals. I wonder if you could approach the DRK on the company's behalf?' Magrete paused as if trying to recall a fact. 'Is the secretary Herr von Rotenham, and the president von Winterfeldt-Menkin?'

'Darling,' Marga said condescendingly, 'you're a decade behind. The president is Carl-Eduard Herzog von Sachsen-Coburg & Gotha and the secretary is Ernst-Robert Grawitz. You really do need my help.'

Magrete knew that Marga loved to correct people because it made her feel superior – and was, in fact, counting on it in order to ensnare Marga's assistance.

'Could you please sort this out with Helmut and Peter? I would be forever in your debt!' The last sentence Magrete knew would also appeal to Marga, and she quickly added, 'Of course, once in Berlin you would be chauffeured to whoever you needed to approach in the company of Peter and Helmut.'

Marga smiled because she now had a legitimate excuse to return to Berlin, and she knew that Potthast would hate it. She also saw an advantage that she could secure for herself in Berlin. 'Gudrun and I will stay with Heinrich in Berlin. I think on this occasion it would be wiser for Heinrich to approach the President of the DRK.'

Magrete sat back with a small sigh of relief. She knew that with Marga and Himmler on the company's side, the DRK could hardly refuse, and moreover, the German Reich would assist to reconfigure each department store into a hospital. Magrete would recommend that the architectural talents of Albert Speer, who was prominent in Hitler's inner circle, should be enlisted for these conversions.

When Magrete travelled to the Munich department store, she telephoned Peter and Helmut separately and told them that Margarete Himmler would be staying in Berlin with Himmler from 30 September. Himmler would be representing the company to the DRK, and she herself would be back in Berlin on 23 September.

For the last few days of her trip Magrete visited Mimi and Albert at her family home, which was now their home. Albert was working as a vet for the local infantry division, which employed hundreds of horses since the German Reich lacked natural oil resources. Mimi was three months pregnant. The two sisters were excited that there would be another addition to the family.

Her parent's bedroom was now Mimi and Albert's bedroom. Mimi's old bedroom was being converted into a baby room. It was currently sparse and without furniture. Magrete took Mimi to the von Appen's Vienna department store, and introduced her to the store's executive team. In front of the director of the store she rang Helmut, who immediately responded to her call, demonstrating her importance to the store's director. Helmut gave her authorisation to choose from the store any gifts she wished for the baby. Magrete and Mimi took an entire day to select a cot, a pram, some baby clothes suitable for a girl or boy, and functional items such as towels, dummies and nappies. Magrete left for Berlin on the third day, with Mimi and Albert grateful for her visit.

When Magrete returned to the villa, Gertrude told her that Peter had convened a meeting for 24 September. Magrete, who had greatly missed her baby, refused to share Ilse with anybody including Anna, and so she gave Anna the day off.

22

Peter, Helmut and Magrete met in Peter's study on the 24 September. Peter gave a presentation on which stores should remain open and which should be offered to the DRK. He based his analysis not just on economic grounds, but also on political and military arguments. On economic grounds alone Berlin, Frankfurt and Vienna were making the most profit. Politically, the Berlin department store had to remain open, no matter what the circumstances. Also, as Hungary had not entered the war, Peter advised that the Budapest store should also remain open. Munich had not been performing well even in Herbert's day, and so he suggested it should be closed. Prague should be closed because it was too close to the Russian border and if the German Reich was ever invaded by Russia, this store would be at high risk. Magdeberg's aircraft industry would make the department store in that city extremely vulnerable, and Leipzig was one of the German Reich's busiest railway stations and, since the department store was in the station precinct, it would not survive an aerial attack.

After much discussion, it was decided that Magdeberg, Prague, Munich and Leipzig would be closed and offered to the DRK, and that Berlin, Frankfurt, Dresden, Vienna and Budapest would remain operating. All the stock in the Munich store would be shipped to the Frankfurt store; all the stock in Prague would be shipped to Berlin; all the stock in Leipzig would be shipped to Dresden; and all the stock in the Magdeberg store would be shipped to Vienna and Budapest.

Staff would have to go and female staff that could be relocated would reinforce diminishing male staff in the remaining stores.

Magrete then presented the result of her discussions with Marga Himmler. She began by outlining her meeting and then presented them with her analysis. 'Marga at this moment is extremely vulnerable emotionally. She is heavily overweight and still smarts that Himmler is having an affair with his secretary, Hedwig Potthast, who is younger, slimmer, and more attractive than her. She is using her daughter's presence in Berlin to annoy Hedwig. Marga wants to move back to Berlin so that her daughter can be close to Himmler. So we should demand that our offer is contingent on Marga managing a DRK hospital in Berlin of her own choosing. It will also be favourable to Himmler if Marga has a reason, other than himself, for moving back to Berlin. He really does love his daughter and wants to spend more time with her.'

Magrete paused and then added as an after thought, 'We should further suggest to Marga that the DRK must use Albert Speer as the architect to convert our department stores into hospitals. Speer is in Hitler's inner circle, and so it will be easier to secure German Reich money for such conversions if Speer is involved. After all, the German Reich has significantly bolstered its coffers by looting assets from annexed Austria, occupied Czechoslovakia, and Nazi-governed Danzig. Both of you need to meet with Marga and Himmler in Berlin – Helmut as head of the company and Peter as the major owner of the company.'

'I would prefer, Magrete, if you were with us,' Peter said.

'I do not think that will work,' Magrete asserted. 'My presence would be a distraction for everybody. What I could do is prepare a dossier for both of you so that you know the main elements of the offer and the contingencies that need to be put before Himmler.'

'Now, that would work,' Helmut said. 'Now for my project! Most of what I'm going to talk about is illegal. There is no legal way to buy currencies on the open market and bank it in a foreign country.

The German Reich can obviously do it, but if we do it, we must do it illegally. Let me start in reverse. The best currency to have is gold. In times of crisis, gold is the currency of choice not only for countries but also for us. The demand for gold will get stronger on the black market as the war progresses. One troy ounce of gold at the moment is worth officially about 90 Marks or US$35.'

Peter asked, 'Helmut, is the price of gold fixed and where should we house it?'

'It is fixed on the international market, but not on the black market. The best place for us to bank gold is in Switzerland, for a number of reasons. We can smuggle gold across one border more easily than several. Switzerland will remain neutral and will be allowed to stay neutral because all the warring nations will need a neutral country in their midst to conduct secret negotiations. More importantly, the Swiss Banking Act of 1934 clearly states that bank secrecy falls within the criminal domain, meaning any banker who divulges bank–client information is punishable by imprisonment.'

Magrete enquired, 'Helmut, who do you know in Switzerland that can handle such deposits?'

'I've connections with the law firm Meier and Schmidt in Basel. The law firm will open up a Swiss bank safety deposit box account with the Swiss Credit Institution, also located in Basel. We shall smuggle to the law firm a shipment of gold bars via a diplomatic pouch, from a corrupted German Reich diplomat, who will remain nameless to both of you. The law firm will place the gold bars in our safe deposit box. They will send me an audit of what's in the account four times a year, which I will pass on to you-'

'How will you know if the diplomat delivers?' interrupted Magrete. 'And if the law firm is telling you the truth about what is in the safe deposit box?'

'If our diplomat doesn't deliver the gold, or delivers less than the amount expected, we can expose him via a third party, and he'll be executed. As for the law firm, I'll be going to Switzerland twice a year, if the war permits, sourcing products for our stores such as watches and clocks. I've an apartment in Basel that I visit now and then, and so I can check on the gold stored in the Swiss Bank safe deposit box. Remember, the law firm can put gold in but they can't take it out. Only I can do that.'

'What happens if you die,' Peter said, 'because of this blasted war?'

'My last will and testament will bequeath you an envelope that contains the number of the account and its password.'

Magrete queried, 'Where is the money coming from to buy the gold?'

'The money to purchase the gold is coming from two sources,' Helmut propositioned, 'from our personal bank accounts and from the sale of our properties. Let's start with our personal bank accounts. We shall run these down gradually over a three-month period, leaving only a small amount in our accounts. Now for the properties! Peter, you have the villa in Wannsee, a house in Tailfingen, a chalet in St Moritz, and Magrete, Herbert has left you an apartment in Vienna. I have a flat in Berlin, an apartment in Basel and a house in Beelitz. The company is going to purchase all these properties at highly inflated prices. In doing so, this will create some liquidity problems for the company that I have to solve.'

'But where are we going to live?' Peter asked.

'In exactly the same places,' Helmut replied. 'You and Magrete at the villa, and I'll move to my place in Beelitz. The accommodation will now be part of our salary packages. Since I'll be busy putting all of this in place, I'll divide all the assets into two divisions: the German division – Berlin, Frankfurt and Dresden department stores and the properties in Berlin, Beelitz, and Tailfingen; the non-German division - Vienna and Hungary department stores and properties in Switzerland and Vienna. The manager of the Leipzig store will run the German division and the manager of the Prague store will run the non-German division. Each will oversee one division and report to me in Beelitz once a fortnight. As part of their salary packages, each division manager will be given a company apartment: one in Berlin (my ex-apartment) and one in Vienna (Magrete's ex-apartment). The property in Tailfingen will be used by our managers when securing textiles for the company and the one in Basel for purchasing clocks and watches. The ownership of the department stores we have gifted to DRK will be similarly divided.'

'That accounts for all the properties except St Moritz,' Peter observed. 'How can we justify the company purchasing it?'

'Well, Peter,' Helmut said searching for an explanation, 'the argument for St Moritz, which will belong to the non-German Division, is a little thin, but the company will claim it's a business retreat for our executive team – a place where the company executives can get together to discuss the future direction of the company in a relaxed atmosphere.'

Magrete admired Helmut's common sense approach. She asked, 'How much commission do we need to pay on top of the price of gold?'

'That's difficult to say at present,' Helmut said. 'My initial enquiries to the bank, lawyers, my jeweller, who's assessing the gold bars, and my gofer who has to locate, purchase and melt the gold into bars and then pass it to the diplomat for delivery, suggest anywhere between 15 to 40 per cent.'

'Where will the gold be sourced?' Magrete asked, with concern. 'I hope not from prison guards of concentration camps such as Gusen and Mauthausen.'

'I'll be frank with you, Magrete,' Helmut said forcibly, 'no matter what I say to my gofer about where the gold should be sourced, I'll never be in a position to check where it was actually sourced. She could tell me anything she wants and I would have to believe her, because if I probe, it will put this whole operation at risk.'

With that the meeting ended. Both Magrete and Peter were shocked that the gofer was a woman. Who would suspect a woman dealing on the black market, thought Magrete, admiring Helmut's cleverness!

23

Before they left the villa, Magrete handed her dossier over to Helmut and Peter. In the dossier, Magrete noted that it was important to stress that the DRK would be receiving four well maintained but empty premises in centralised locations in the four cities: Munich, Prague, Leipzig and Magdeberg. Each was in a location that had ready access to public transport, making working there, and delivering patients there, far easier.

Peter and Helmut arrived at the Himmlers' residence at Dalhem (Berlin) in a 1938 Daimler ElS24 saloon, with Helmut at the wheel. As they approached the front door they could hear a woman and a man in a heated argument. Helmut looked at Peter, unsure if they should ring the doorbell. Peter shrugged his shoulders, as if to say who knows, and rang the doorbell. The shouting ceased as a valet opened the door and, after being told who they were, the valet ushered them into a living room, where Herr and Frau Himmler warmly greeted them.

When Helmut had met Himmler at Herbert's funeral he was terrified of him, and Himmler sensed it. Himmler could always sense when people were frightened of him, and when they were not. The latter he never trusted and the former he treated with a passionate menace. However, Himmler could never pick if a person was disinterested in him, and Peter was just that, disinterested in both Herr and Frau Himmler. They both greeted Peter as the father of a close friend and Helmut as an acquaintance.

'Well, gentleman,' Himmler said slowly, observing them as if they were soldiers to be inspected, 'I hear from my dear wife that you intend to make available four of your stores to be converted into hospitals for the DRK.'

'Yes, my Reichsführer,' Helmut answered, sweating profusely. 'Munich, Prague, Leipzig and Magdeberg.'

Himmler, walking closer to Helmut, asked, 'Why are you reducing the size of your company?'

'My Reichsführer,' Helmut said, with Himmler now standing only centimetres away, 'we need to take into account the lack of staff numbers due to conscription and the availability of stock due to diminishing access to international markets.' Helmut's voice was trembling.

'Shouldn't you have confidence that the war will be a Blitzkrieg (lightening war) and that your customer base will be the whole of Europe and not just the German Reich and, who knows, one day even Russia?' Himmler spoke softly, and in doing so sounded even more menacing.

'War is not so predictable for business,' Peter countered.

Himmler turned and asked in a friendlier tone, 'Ah, Peter, why so?' He did not move from Helmut's side, which made Helmut feel even more uncomfortable.

'Business relies heavily on cash flow – that is, liquidity. If people are under threat, they hoard their money, protecting themselves against the worst. Even though the greater German Reich may one day stretch from Norway to the Mediterranean Sea and from France to Poland-'

'From Britain to Poland, Peter,' Himmler corrected him in a chiding tone.

'From Britain to Poland,' conceded Peter. 'Nevertheless, even if the war ends quickly, it's only when people start to open their wallets that we'll reclaim each store from the DRK and, at our own expense, revert them back to commercial enterprises. In the meantime, why leave them empty? Better to have the DRK use them to bring our soldiers back into good health than leave them as empty stores only to further depress the surrounding population. What's more, all of these premises are in central places, located near transport hubs, making it easier for workers to travel there and for injured soldiers to be delivered there.'

'Good,' Himmler replied. 'If only we'd more companies like yours, Peter, the war would be won in seconds, not minutes. Perhaps one day you'll be awarded the Order of the German Cross, Silver Class, for a significant performance in aiding and supplying the military war effort. Now, what's this about Marga?'

Helmut looked at Peter and it was clear Helmut wanted to remain silent. 'Marga,' Peter said, 'has worked for the DRK before, and we're seeking her assistance in making this transition from empty department stores to DRK hospitals. As part of our gift, we'd like Marga to decide which present facility of the DRK in Berlin she would like to manage. In fact, we would make her choice contingent on our offer to the transfer the stores to the DRK.'

Himmler was especially pleased with this response on two accounts: firstly, Marga would be busy and out of his hair, and secondly, he would see Gudrun more often. 'This is very generous of you, Peter,' he said.

'It was Magrete's idea, Herbert's wife, who's really fond of Marga. She made us realise what an asset Marga would be for us and for the DRK.'

Marga stood up and walked over to stand beside Himmler, allowing Helmut to retreat closer to Peter without being noticed. 'See, I told you not to worry about me,' Marga said, smiling at Himmler. 'Gentleman,' she said, turning to Helmut and Peter, 'Himmler will be seeing Herzog von Sachsen-Coburg & Gotha and the secretary Ernst-Robert Grawitz on your behalf. I feel certain that they'll be grateful to accept your offer and as I wish to stay in Berlin, undoubtedly they'll suggest that I manage their hospital in the Military District III (Berlin-Brandenburg). Who do you suggest should convert your empty department stores into hospitals?'

'Albert Speer,' Helmut answered, remembering Magrete's brief.

'Albert Speer,' Himmler repeated slowly, looking intensely at Helmut. 'A sensible choice!'

When they returned to their Daimler, Helmut looked towards the sky as if in prayer and said, 'Thank you, Magrete, for that dossier!' He looked toward the house. 'That man terrifies me!'

'Thank god you've never met Hitler,' Peter replied, smiling at him.

24

By March 1940 they had sold all their properties to the company at highly inflated prices. Helmut held a senior executive meeting in St Moritz about the next phase and direction of the company. On his way home he visited his lawyers in Basel and the Swiss Credit Institution and confirmed that they had amassed 24,000 troy ounces of gold in sixty gold bars at market value US$840,000. They had agreed from the outset that Helmut would get 25 per cent of it, making his net worth US$210,000. They had paid a 30 per cent commission to amass this quantity of gold. When he returned he called a meeting at Beelitz for 7 April 1940.

Beelitz is a historic town in the Potsdam–Mittelmark district in Brandenburg. It had a small population of some 10,000 people. Its main industry was farming and it had a sanatorium. Its main claim to fame was that Adolf Hitler had recuperated there during October and November in 1916, after being wounded in the leg at the Battle of the Somme.

Helmut's house was near the St Mary and St Nicholas parish. Magrete and Peter arrived in Herbert's roadster at 10 am, with Magrete at the wheel. Helmut assembled them in the lounge room where tea, coffee, cake and biscuits had been laid out.

'What a lovely house and what a lovely small village! I have never been to Beelitz and yet it is so close to Berlin,' Magrete observed.

'Hitler recovered here from wounds during the Great War,' Helmut said. 'You can smell him from here!' All three of them laughed. Helmut handed each of them a report on the content and value of their safe deposit box in Basel, and they were shocked that within six months they had accumulated so much wealth.

'Well,' Helmut said, 'that's with all of the properties sold and with all of the personal bank accounts depleted. In the end we paid a 30 per cent commission, which is reflected in the account as a liability. Any questions?'

Magrete looked at the balance sheet. 'That is a lot of gold you have amassed in such a short period, Helmut. I am surprised that it has not caused a bit of a stir, and we have not been arrested. I would have expected that the pace of disposal would have been much slower.'

'True, it has been fast and furious,' Helmut conceded, 'but it needed to be because the sitting war won't last, and once the war begins in earnest, half of what we did would not have gone unnoticed. My gofer is smart. She operates a pyramid business. Think of it like a triangle, with the base larger than the apex. She sits on the apex and the base filters the gold upward. That's why her premium is so high, but it also acts as a safeguard for the apex: if a person at or near the base is arrested for black market racketeering she's physically well removed from them and unknown to them. The only way you can reach the apex in her pyramid scheme is if you plant an infiltrator who works his or her way up the pyramid, and that takes time. That's why we had to move so fast.'

'She is very clever,' Magrete said, emphasising the word 'she'.

Helmut noted that Peter and Magrete seemed extremely pleased with his work. 'Once you're happy, you'd better give me back the balance sheets, because I have to destroy them,' he said. 'I want to talk to you about the next phase of the operation.'

Peter queried, 'The next phase?'

'That's right, Peter. Currently, I've got a 25 per cent stake in the private firm and you've got 75 per cent. We need to dilute this down significantly. We need to transform the company from a private firm into a propriety limited company and so sell off our shares. I believe you need to bring your shareholding down to 40 per cent and mine has to come down to 15 per cent. If the company becomes insolvent, then the risk to us is mitigated. Also we'll still retain 55 per cent of the company to effectively own it.'

Peter thought about this new proposal and asked, 'Will we still have a 75 per cent and 25 per cent stake of the safe deposit holdings once we've converted the money from our shares into gold?' Helmut could see where Peter was coming from – Peter was underwriting an extra profit for Helmut.

Magrete suddenly spoke up. 'Dad! Helmut is taking all the risks and is implementing all the ideas to safeguard our family against financial hardship or ruin. I see this as a bonus for him. Neither you nor I would have been so creative or so adventurous.'

'Of course,' Peter conceded, 'an old businessman always thinks in terms of profit or loss. I hope you weren't offended.'

'Not in the least,' Helmut said. 'You've given me my first job in the company and undoubtedly you'll give me my last! We will maintain the 3 to 1 split.' Magrete looked annoyed that Helmut had made this concession to Peter.

From 6 to 9 April 1940 the Germany Reich used the Blitzkrieg tactic on Greece, Yugoslavia, Denmark and Norway. On 10 May they used the same tactic on Belgium, the Netherlands, Luxembourg and France. The Blitzkrieg tactic required the concentration of offensive weapons, such as tanks, planes, and artillery, along a narrow front. These forces would drive a breach into enemy defences, permitting armoured tank divisions to penetrate rapidly and roam freely behind enemy lines, causing disorganisation amongst the enemy. German Reich air power prevented the enemy from adequately resupplying or redeploying forces, and from sending reinforcements to seal breaches on the front. The German Reich forces could also encircle opposing troops and force surrender.

By 4 June Great Britain was saved from the Blitzkrieg, due to the English Channel. Now Helmut had to move faster – the sitting war had just evaporated into a full-blown European war.

25

Helmut Gruen was in Basel in late July 1940. He had just returned from the safety deposit box at Swiss Credit Institution and confirmed that they had now amassed 200 gold bars. He had already incorporated the company into a propriety limited company, and he had sold shares to a significant number of brokering houses based mostly on the value of their property portfolio and partly on the profit margins of the company. The brokers liked the fact that four of the major premises were centrally located in significant cities in Germany and Czechoslovakia and, moreover, were DRK hospitals, which should be immune from destruction, and that the other properties were based in neutral Switzerland. They were impressed at the management restructuring, which created a separation between German and non-German divisions and assets.

Helmut gave a seminar to speculators in Switzerland who had bought shares in the company and while he was in Basel he visited the Union Bank of Switzerland (UBS). The three central planks that the UBS rested upon were confidence, security and discretion, all three of which he approved. He talked to senior investment managers of the company and left a prospectus for UBS to consider.

Helmut's old apartment, which now belonged to Appen Pty Ltd non-German division, was near Münsterplatz, where stood one of the most impressive cathedrals in Switzerland. The promontory on the riverside commanded a panoramic view that swept over the city and the Rhine. While not religious, Helmut always liked living near churches. They somehow made him feel more secure. His mother used to say to him, 'Always keep your enemy as close to you as possible, so they have no room to move; give them freedom, and they'll cut you down in pieces.' Helmut thought his mother was very shrewd.

As Helmut was meandering towards Münsterplatz he was thinking of Himmler and how terrified he was of him. Here in Switzerland he felt safe. He enjoyed the dance scene and occasionally would go to Zürich to the Amicitia Ladies Club. His favourite magazine was Human Rights, which he would read religiously whenever he landed in Basel. Those in his outer circle thought Helmut was a born bachelor. Occasionally, when he was young he had been associated with film stars such as Marlene Dietrich, but he had never featured in any of the society pages of newspapers and magazines, since nothing ever came of it.

He had really enjoyed his conversations with George Nagy, when both of them were staying at the Hotel Imperial in Vienna. George was a handsome man, and he and Magrete would make a very attractive couple, Helmut thought. His mind wandered to the funeral service of Eva and Hans Holweg – such a tragic loss, this suicide pact that Himmler had covered up as deaths caused by a gas leak.

Thinking of Himmler made him reflect once more on their meeting, and he literally shivered at the thought. Being homosexual made him extremely vulnerable. By the beginning of 1933 homosexual societies similar to the Amicitia Ladies Club had been banned in the German Reich. Homosexuals within the Nazi Party were murdered, or arrested and sent to concentration camps and murdered there. Since homosexuality was generally considered ungodly, their victimisation at the hands of the German Reich was never acknowledged in the press or elsewhere. Like the Romani, who were considered lower than dogs, they became the German Reich's invisible victims.

During the night of the long knives, Hitler used Röhm's homosexuality as a justification to suppress outrage within the ranks of the SA, because of Röhm's execution. Himmler, who had been a supporter of Röhm, initially argued that Jews had manufactured the charges of homosexuality against Röhm. Himmler changed his mind when Hitler elevated his status. He suddenly became very active in the suppression of homosexuality: 'We must exterminate these people root and branch ... the homosexual must be eliminated,' he proclaimed. In 1933 Himmler created a Reich Central Office for Combating of Homosexuality and Abortion.

Helmut had been in the presence of evil that day, and he shivered once more just thinking of it. He knocked on the company's apartment door, and heard a reassuring voice: 'Coming.' When the door opened, there stood his lover, actor Karl Meier.

26

Helmut called for a meeting in Beelitz on Wednesday 11 September. The Battle of Britain was well underway and four days before the meeting, the Luftwaffe had attacked London. German Reich planes had dropped 337 tons of bombs on London. Even though the civilian population was not targeted, London slum areas such as the East End suffered direct hits due to their proximity to targets of interest. Fires broke out and spread throughout the district. While carnage was occurring in England, Beelitz was tranquil, cold, and sunny.

The meetings between Helmut, Peter and Magrete were becoming less frequent. Helmut heard the 1938 Daimler ElS24 saloon pull-up. He went to the window and saw Peter being helped out of the car by Magrete. Gertrude was rebuilding a folded wheelchair she had extracted from the boot of the car. Helmut immediately went out to assist them.

'Helmut,' greeted Peter.

Helmut looked at Peter concerned. 'What happened?'

'Sciatica,' Peter said. Gertrude grasped the handles of the wheelchair and pushed Peter towards the house.

'Magrete, with Peter in the condition that he's in, why did you come?'

'Peter insisted,' Magrete said, raising her hands in a gesture of surrender. 'His health has deteriorated severely. Ever since I had Ilse, his health has worsened, whereas Elfi's has greatly improved.'

'How is Ilse?' Helmut asked, since he had not seen her for some time.

Magrete looked dismayed. 'You would think Anna was Ilse's mother and Elfi was Anna's. I am lucky to get ten minutes alone with my baby girl.'

They moved into the living room but as they did, Gertrude put her index finger to her lips and looked down at Peter, who was fast asleep. Helmut pointed to Magrete and himself and to the door. Gertrude nodded.

Once outside the house, Helmut said, 'Let's go over to the church. There shouldn't be anyone there this early in the morning. I've some news for you. It's not all bad,' he quickly added, seeing her look of concern.

In the church they sat in pews in the back row. The church appeared empty. Helmut said quietly to Magrete, 'We've now 200 gold bars in the safety deposit box.' She shook her head in amazement. 'I have sold 48 per cent of the shares to German and Swiss brokers and investors. Your family has a 39 per cent stake and I've got a 13 per cent stake in Appen Pty Ltd.'

Magrete looked at Helmut, embarrassed. 'You did not have to keep the 3:1 ratio intact. For all of your creative input, my family was more than happy with your previous strategy. Peter was just being Peter!'

'Thanks for your vote of confidence. It's really appreciated,' Helmut replied. 'However, my contract is with Peter.' Magrete patted the back of his hand in a gesture of thanks.

‘My gofer was murdered three weeks ago,’ Helmut whispered. Magrete gripped his forearm. ‘It’s okay at the moment,’ he continued. ‘Himmler’s Gestapo have been here and asked the parish priest two weeks ago if a rich blonde man lived in Beelitz. Of course, the house is modest and people know I work in Berlin, but they really don’t know what I do. I’m not blonde either. The priest told them he knew no one who fits that description in Beelitz. The Gestapo told him that another lead indicated that the suspect might live in Potsdam, and so they left. As soon as the priest told me, I went back to the office and rang our lawyers in Switzerland, Meier and Schmidt, who I know well, and informed them of the situation. I told them that sooner or later foreign agents would approach them for information or raid their premises. I asked them to close our account and gave them authority to handover our file to a friend of mine in Basel, who would finalise our account with them. My friend burnt the file. Hence, there’s no record anywhere that we ever were clients of theirs.’

‘But our lawyers know our safety deposit box account and what we have placed in the safe deposit boxes,’ Magrete said slightly annoyed at the thought.

‘They know the account number only, not the password,’ Helmut replied. ‘They can put stuff in, but can’t take stuff out. They were given diplomatic satchels that they placed in our safety deposit boxes. We must assume whoever handled the satchels, both at the law office and at the bank end, had a peek at what they contained. However, when I was there not so long ago, everything tallied. This phase of the operation is now complete, and so we’ve no reason to go to Basel at this stage. No more deposits need to be made.’

‘So what happened with the Gestapo?’ Magrete asked, anxious about what might occur in the future.

‘Eight days ago,’ Helmut began, ‘the newspapers reported that the husband of my gofer had been charged with murdering her. They had located the murder weapon and found fingerprints, which matched the fingerprints of her husband. When they interrogated him, the husband confessed to the murder, and told them he had killed her for her money, in order to satisfy his gambling debt. They located some large satchels of money hidden in a sealed compartment under the floorboards. No doubt his confession was extracted using physical means. It tallied to the Gestapo that they were involved in black market racketeering, because of the amount of money they recovered. The paper was vague on how they found out who our courier was, but my guess is that the satchels gave him away. They arrested a low-grade German Reich diplomat who works in the German Reich embassy in Switzerland. Of course, when my gofer hired him, she showed me a photograph of him and I could see he was blonde. We must also assume that the diplomat knew he was delivering gold bars, and that the Gestapo knows this now as well. That's why it was so important to quickly sever our ties with Meier and Schmidt. At any rate I only dealt with the gofer and with no one else, not even with her husband, and so with her death the link to me is now hopefully buried.'

'You have been through a lot,' Magrete said, 'and you have carried this burden on your own.' She gently kissed him on the cheek and held his hand in hers.

Helmut felt uneasy that Magrete appeared to be displaying a romantic attachment towards him. He was convinced he could trust her with a revelation that ordinarily would put him in harms way. 'I've something that I need to confess to you,' Helmut said, 'that I've never told anyone in Germany.'

Helmut was about to reveal his secret when she whispered in his ear, 'That you are homosexual.' Helmut gasped, and it was at this moment that he noticed the priest at prayer, who he had not noticed before. The priest turned and stared at them, and Helmut greeted him with a friendly wave.

Magrete rose, and Helmut followed her out of the church. They sat on a bench in the church garden. Helmut asked, 'How did you know? Am I so obvious?'

'No, you are not obvious at all. Lately, Anna has been pressing me to have morning tea with George in a place not far from his Institute. One day, when Anna was not there, I was talking to George about how much I admired your intelligence, integrity and decency. George may have been feeling a little insecure that you had replaced him as my closest amigo, because he then said to me, "Did you know Helmut is a homosexual?" I was shocked, but I said to George that I could not careless if you are.'

Helmut queried, 'But how did he know?'

'He then told me this story: that in 1929, just before Simon's death, he and Simon were involved in a fencing tournament at ETH in Zürich, which George won. The person who came second was a Swiss national, and Simon came third. All three of them decided to go out and celebrate, and they found themselves drunk in the red-light district. That is when Simon spotted you standing with another man outside the Amicitia Ladies Club. George suggested to the other two that they all go in. The Swiss fellow turned to them and said, "Are you mad? Only homosexual men go there." Simon asked the Swiss competitor, who was the man who had his arm around your waist. The Swiss guy said that he was a famous homosexual actor – I have forgotten his name. When George met you, the day he was returning the épée, he recognized you and then recalled the incident.'

Helmut looked concerned. 'Has George told anyone else?'

'He has not, nor will he! He knows what the Nazis do to homosexuals, and he is very protective of you. He was just jealous!'

Yes, thought Helmut, he was jealous, but not because of the amigo thing. He was jealous because he thought you really fancied me romantically – as I did!

When they returned, Gertrude woke Peter, and they put him into the car and drove off. Sitting next to Magrete, who was driving, Peter tiredly asked, 'Was it a good meeting?'

'It was the best meeting we have ever had, and you missed it,'

Magrete replied. They both laughed, and even Gertrude had to smiled.

27

Late afternoon on 21 December Magrete, Anna, baby Ilse and Gertrude went to Alexanderplatz. Magrete drove the Daimler along Panoramastraße to St Mary's and parked the car in the church grounds. Normally, Elfi and Gertrude would go shopping for Christmas, but as Elfi was not feeling well, and because it was cold and wet, she was happy for Magrete to take on the responsibility this year, accompanied by Gertrude.

Magrete wanted to buy clothes for Ilse and because she was growing rapidly, she decided to bring her along, so Anna came as well. Gertrude felt uneasy about this, but was somewhat placated when Magrete asked her to sit in the front passenger seat, relegating Anna and Ilse to the back seats. Anna preferred this arrangement anyway – she could lay a sleepy baby Ilse on the back seat. Anna had also brought with her nappies and a bottle of milk.

Once the car was parked, they headed for the shopping centre with Anna pushing baby Ilse's pram. As they were initially shopping for the adult presents, Anna remained with baby Ilse in the foyer of the von Appen's department store, which pleased Gertrude even more.

The Christmas tradition in the von Appen household was that each person would receive a single gift on behalf of the entire household. Elfi had already chosen Peter, Gertrude and Magrete's gifts, and Gertrude would choose gifts for Anna, Erika, Lotte, Emma and the part-time gardener Werner, as well as for Tomas, who was visiting the household over the Christmas period. Magrete would choose presents for Ilse, Elfi, Helmut and George. As the von Appen's company was now a public listed company, cash and rations were needed for each purchase, making the choice of gifts price-sensitive.

As Magrete and Gertrude made their final adult purchases, air-raid sirens began blaring. Magrete dropped the presents and ran to the foyer as Anna, baby in her arms, ran towards her. They both ran to Gertrude, who had picked up Magrete's dropped presents, and all three made their way down the stairs into the basement that served as an air-raid shelter. As it was early evening, there were approximately a hundred people in an area that could hold three times that many. Ilse was crying. Anna initially comforted her and then gave her to Magrete. Gertrude took it the hardest. This was the first air raid they had experienced since bombing first began in Berlin on 25 August 1940. She was shaking, trembling, and praying for her survival.

'Gertrude,' Magrete summoned her considerable presence, 'do not think about the bad that might happen, think about the good that has happened! We have not heard an explosion as yet.' As Magrete finished her last sentence, an explosion rocked the room. Bad timing, she thought. Magrete handed Ilse to Anna and hugged Gertrude, who was now whimpering. The explosion was followed by ferocious anti-aircraft fire, forcing the RAF planes to increase their altitude in order to prevent the bombs being targeted accurately.

'Put down the presents,' Magrete commanded Gertrude, 'and think of something pleasant that might calm your nerves. Close your eyes and think about the Wannsee garden, about those wonderful roses that you planted last year.' Another explosion rocked the building, followed by fierce anti-aircraft fire.

Gertrude closed her eyes, mumbling and crying. She suddenly shouted, 'I don't want to die! Please God, send them away!' This caused an audible murmur of annoyance within the shelter.

Magrete was now holding Gertrude, and gently rubbing her back. They could hear distant explosions. Slowly Magrete lowered Gertrude until they were both sitting on the floor. She looked to Anna, indicating she should join them. Anna gave Magrete Ilse, sat, and then retrieved the child from her. The basement was dank and at first the smell was unpleasant, but Magrete gradually became accustomed to its odour. Some people were quietly weeping, others were whispering to each other, some were restless and agitated, and many were praying, but none showed the same degree of anxiety as Gertrude. Many in the basement were now staring at Gertrude and listening to Magrete as she talked to Gertrude to calm her down.

They heard anti-aircraft guns blazing and another deafening explosion. It was close to the building, and so the building rocked. Magrete hugged Gertrude even tighter. 'We're safe here,' Magrete said reassuringly. 'The anti-aircraft guns and our fighter planes are protecting us from the enemy. We will be fine, we will be fine, you will see!'

Gertrude was listening to Magrete's soothing voice, still whimpering. Anna was rocking baby Ilse to and fro in her arms and softly singing her a lullaby. Slowly the loud bangs were diminishing in frequency and ferocity, but never disappearing, returning back in waves; it was as if thunder and lightning had passed overhead and, after causing local havoc retreated to a distant place, only to return. The cyclic pattern of local and distant explosions, followed by local and distant anti-aircraft fire retaliating, seemed endless, hour upon hour, with Magrete constantly speaking to Gertrude to soothe her. Throughout the ordeal, Magrete was determined to shift Gertrude's focus from the bombing raid and possible death to the protective action of the German Reich's anti-aircraft fire and fighter planes, but to no avail.

Suddenly there was silence, which amplified the sounds within the bunker. Tension grew among the dwellers – for Gertrude the silence signalled the stillness before death. Air sirens then sounded indicating the air raid was over. Gertrude burst into tears, shaking in relief. They had been in the basement for three hours.

They walked to where Anna had left the pram, and it was gone. They knew their world had changed forever – people were taking advantage of this awful situation. They walked towards the car and could see people entering the church. Magrete walked Gertrude to the church, giving the car keys to Anna, so Anna could lay baby Ilse on the back seat. In the church Gertrude knelt and prayed as Magrete took charge of the presents. Magrete placed a small gift of money in the offering plate as they exited the church.

28

On the drive home they were all too exhausted and emotionally drained to speak. They were a half a kilometre from their villa when a police cordon stopped them. It was dark. They could smell smoke, and could see little else. Magrete opened the driver's side window. The police officer was polite but officious. 'Ma'am, the road is closed and you had better turn around and make your way via another route.'

Magrete was polite and engaging. 'My name is Frau von Appen and I live in a Wannsee villa. I have a small child in the back, and we are very tired. We were stuck in an air-raid shelter in the von Appen department store for over three hours. Is there any chance we can drive through?'

'Wait here, ma'am,' the officer said.

Magrete could see the first policeman talking to a senior officer, who approached the car holding a torch. When he was near the car he examined the people in the front and back seats with his torch. He immediately recognized Magrete von Appen. 'Lady von Appen,' the Senior Officer said sadly, 'there's been a serious incident, and so I'd like you and your family to go immediately to Martin Luther Hospital, 27-31 Caspar-TheyssStraße.'

Magrete parked the Daimler near the entrance of the hospital. Over her shoulder she said to Anna, 'As baby Ilse is sleeping, please sit in the front with Gertrude.' She then turned to Gertrude, who was still upset. 'You are not to get out of this car until I get back. Do you understand me?' As Magrete got out of the car she whispered to Anna, 'Keep all the doors locked until I come back.' Anna nodded.

Magrete introduced herself at the reception desk. The receptionists seemed to recognise her and immediately went to summon Dr Schwarzer.

'Frau von Appen, could you please come into my office.' Dr Schwarzer guided her into his office and pulled up a chair to sit beside her. 'Frau von Appen, I've been Elfi and Peter's doctor for over forty years. As you know, there was an air raid today. From what I've been told they were targeting Tempelhof Airport.' He placed his hand on her forearm. 'I've been informed that the anti-aircraft fire was ferocious and as a result a lone wolf RAF bomber dropped its entire payload onto your in-laws' villa.'

'Are they hurt?' Magrete said, with her hand in front of her mouth.

'I'm afraid, Madam, they're dead,' Dr Schwarzer said, his voice breaking.

Magrete let out a cry and tears streamed from her eyes. She was voiceless. Dr Schwarzer watched her carefully, holding her hands in his. 'They died in their bedroom,' he continued. 'Your part-time gardener, who was on the property when the bombs fell, identified them. He hid in the servants' quarters during the raid. Is there anything I can do for you? Are there any questions that you want me to address?'

Magrete was in shock. 'Were the domestic staff also in the servant quarters?'

'I'm afraid they were huddled in the cellar of the villa and were directly hit. We've confirmed that Tomas, Emma, Lotte and Erika have perished,' he said slowly with compassion.

Magrete bent over, placed her face in her cupped hands, and sobbed uncontrollably. Even Tomas, who had only been there for a short visit, had died, she thought. Dr Schwarzer brought his chair closer and placed his arm across her shoulders and whispered, 'It's hard for all of us.' She looked at him through her tears, and could see that he was upset. His cheeks were wet with tears, and she knew he had lost not only two of his patients, but two friends. Dr Schwarzer's touch, compassion, and his own grief comforted her.

Magrete asked, 'Can I see their bodies?'

On his way to the morgue Dr Schwarzer, still appearing distressed, said, 'They took the domestic staff to another hospital, which is not open this late. I'll get in contact with them and ask if you can see them early tomorrow.' He pulled the sheets back so Magrete could see Elfi and Peter's faces. Each looked serene, as if they were without pain. Their appearance comforted her in a strange manner. She kissed each of them on their cheeks, said a prayer, and turned around to go – but to where? She decided to take Ilse, Anna and Gertrude to Helmut's place in Beelitz.

Magrete stood up straighter, wiping her eyes as she returned to the car. She had been gone for over an hour. Anna immediately moved to the back seat. Magrete told them both compassionately and with tears in her eyes that Elfi, Peter, Tomas, Erika, Emma and Lotte had died in the air raid. Gertrude and Anna became hysterical, but Gertrude could not be calmed. Magrete took Gertrude to the hospital, where she was sedated by Dr Schwarzer and given a bed for the night. He gave Magrete a sleeping draught for Anna. Anna swallowed the draught and was asleep within minutes in the back seat of the car. Magrete took baby Ilse, who was sleeping, placed Ilse next to her, and drove carefully to Helmut's place.

Helmut greeted Magrete at the door, shocked to see them in Beelitz this late at night. Magrete asked, 'Can we stay here tonight?' Helmut nodded; he could sense that a tragedy had befallen them. 'Could you please carry Anna to a bedroom? She was given a sleeping draught and is sleeping on the back seat of the car.'

It was a three-bedroom house and so Anna was placed in one bedroom. Magrete took baby Ilse to a bed in another room. When Anna and Ilse were bedded down for the night, Magrete told Helmut what had transpired and they both cried softly so as not to wake the household. Neither slept very well that night. In the morning Helmut rang the hospital where the domestic staff's bodies lay. He was told that the cellar had taken a direct hit and so little remained of the bodies of those who had perished.

The death of her husband, her parents, her in-laws and the domestic staff was an enormous emotional blow to Magrete. For the whole of January and February 1941, Helmut, George, Anna, and Magrete were attending funerals. Gertrude was too ill to attend any of them. The last funeral was that of Elfi and Peter. Himmler brought Hedwig Potthast with him, as well as Peter's next-door neighbour, Reinhard Heydrich. Helmut was terrified of Himmler, but sensed he had the measure of Heydrich.

29

At the outbreak of the war there was no desire for large-scale evacuations. From early 1940 KLV (Kinderlandverschickung – children's country mailing) was extended to children under the age of ten, but participation was voluntary. By the start of 1941, some 382,616 children and young people, including 180,000 from Berlin and Hamburg, had been sent to country areas. Magrete convinced Helmut to let her stay in Beelitz, because she was desperate to be close to Berlin. Helmut decided that he needed to leave Beelitz so that she could have the house to herself. The Beelitz house belonged to Appen Pty Ltd, German division.

With the destruction of the villa, the company had a cash flow problem: the banks downgraded the worth of the villa and demanded a cash injection to offset the loss. Helmut also needed to find an apartment in Berlin, but to do so he needed temporary accommodation, because the manager of the German division of the company occupied the company's Berlin apartment. He met with

George, who readily agreed Helmut could stay in his lounge room for as long as it was convenient for him.

Magrete was more cashed strapped than she had realised. Helmut needed to form a board of directors, and because Magrete and he held 52 per cent of the shares, Helmut appointed Magrete chairperson of the board of directors. She would receive a stipend to chair the board and as part of her salary package the accommodation in Beelitz would be rent-free. She was the first woman chair in the German Reich's history. Magrete and Helmut appointed members of the board, who looked favourably upon them and their company. Initially the board members found a woman as chairperson strange, but, they reasoned, more and more men were needed in the war effort and so more and more women were forced into the workplace to do men's work.

Gertrude had not recovered well from the von Appen household's deaths. She had moved into the Beelitz home, and was comforted that there was a church nearby. Magrete overheard the priest telling Gertrude that Lady Magrete von Appen was not cursed and that it was only God who could determine Gertrude's life and death. This hurt Magrete, for the last thing she wished was for Gertrude not to trust or love her. She told Helmut about Gertrude's paranoia and asked him whether he could use her as a residential housekeeper once he found an apartment. Helmut said he liked the idea so long as Gertrude was amenable and did not mind living in Berlin, a city where air raids were far more frequent.

On 13 May 1941, Magrete, Anna and Gertrude sat in the lounge room of the Beelitz house, with Anna holding baby Ilse. The RAF had bombed Berlin the day before, making Gertrude extremely nervous. Magrete did not realise that the RAF would never consider Beelitz a target, because the main business of the village was the hospital.

'I know what I am about to say will be difficult for all three of us, but the destruction of the villa has left my financial situation precarious,' Magrete said. 'I can still afford to keep both of you in my employ, but it may get a bit more difficult as the war progresses. Gertrude, you have been with the family longest, and so I would like your opinion first. Helmut needs a residential housekeeper, and he has agreed that as soon as he finds an apartment in Berlin, he will temporarily take one of you to lighten the pressure on my finances. However, if both of you want to stay with me, we will struggle, but we will survive. What do you say, Gertrude?'

Anna already knew what the end result would be: Gertrude had said to her many times that their lives were doomed because Magrete was living with a curse that was responsible for the deaths of those associated with her. She knew that Gertrude liked Helmut Gruen, and that she would be a good housekeeper for him.

Gertrude looked at Anna as if in pity. She understood that her grief was starting to cloud the household and, for the first time in a long time, she was determined to sound rational and unemotional. 'Ma'am, I'm the longest-standing employee of the family, but the war is beyond anyone's control. I think at this juncture we need to be as practical as possible. Baby Ilse will need more financial support the older she gets and so taking the pressure off your purse is a sensible approach. Also, I'm a housekeeper and overseeing the staff was one of my most important responsibilities, and-' Gertrude started to cry, thinking of the loss of her staff and her two wonderful employers, Elfi and Peter.

Magrete immediately knelt in front of Gertrude to wipe away her tears with her silk handkerchief. She whispered, 'You and I have lost our world, but our lives will be livable one day – stay, please stay.'

Gertrude steadied herself and said, 'Ma'am, we need to be practical about this. Anna is a natural governess and midwife – one gift of hers you already need, and the other may become useful to you again in the future. I work best with adults and so it saddens me to say I should go to Herr Gruen and Anna should stay here with you.'

'You know you will need to go to Berlin, and Berlin is a natural target for enemy warplanes,' Magrete said gently, taking Gertrude's hands in hers. 'Have you considered this? Can you cope Gertrude?'

'Ma'am, I really don't know. However, knowing that our separation is not forever will help. I'll do the best I can.'

Magrete asked, 'Anna, do you also want to go?'

'Ma'am, I don't want Gertrude to go – she has been my protector, so to speak. But if it's only temporary - '

'It is definitely only temporary, Anna,' interrupted Magrete. 'When the war ends our family will be reunited. I will make certain of it.'

'I know you're her mother,' Anna said holding Ilse across her shoulder, and patting Ilse on her back, 'but I love her so much that to leave her would tear me apart. Please let me stay!'

'You do not need to ask. I will make us a cup of tea.'

Both Gertrude and Anna exclaimed, 'No! No, ma'am!'

'Ladies,' Magrete said, 'Mutti would never allow our non-residential housekeeper to be there during school holidays. She was determined to make us understand our responsibilities in the home, and domestic duties was one of them.'

As the war progressed, communications became unreliable. A letter posted one day after the birth of Mimi's child, but received six weeks later, informed Magrete that Mimi had given birth to a boy named after Albert's grandfather, Dieter. Magrete sent Mimi's son a present – a wooden carved piece that was a Buddhist symbol for inner peace. Mimi did not understand the present and concluded that its inexpensiveness was a sign that the war had significantly diminished her sister's wealth.

30

Helmut, George and Magrete decided to meet at Café Buchwald on 23 June, the day after the German Reich invaded Russia. In the two years leading up to the invasion, the German Reich and Russia had signed political and economic pacts, the former in order to grab parts of Poland for themselves. Nevertheless, the German Reich always saw communism, religious and ethnic groups as their natural enemies, irrespective of whether the individuals involved were men, women or children. Aryanism demanded a religious and political cleansing as well as a racial one.

In 1938 Himmler established the Ravensbrück concentration camp, which typified the German Reich mentality towards these groups. It was a concentration camp with Polish women as the largest national component. Soviet prisoners of war and German and Austrian communists had to wear red triangles; common criminals wore green triangles; and Jehovah's Witnesses wore lavender triangles. Prostitutes, Romani, lesbians and women who refused to marry were classified separately, with black triangles. Jewish women always wore yellow triangles, but sometimes they wore a second triangle for another category. More than 132,000 women and children were incarcerated in Ravensbrück.

George and Helmut arrived on time, whereas Magrete was late, because she had a much longer path to travel. Café Buchwald was nearly empty. Coffee and cake were becoming prohibitively expensive for people who relied solely on rations and food stamps. In fact, you could only buy coffee and cake with cash. Both men knew Helmut would foot the bill. George whispered, 'If America enters the war on the British side, sourcing coffee and cacao beans will be a nightmare. I don't think this café can survive it. In fact, I'm surprised that it's still open today.'

'Not good for business,' Helmut whispered, not sure who might be listening. 'Hitler's Napoleonic adventures may overstretch the economy so significantly that he won't be able to fund his own war. The whole tenet of a Blitzkrieg is to subdue the enemy quickly, capturing all the weaponry and wealth. For example, in the March 1939 invasion of Czechoslovakia, the German Reich gained over 2,000 field cannons and nearly 500 tanks, not to mention the anti-aircraft artillery pieces, machine guns, military rifles, pistols, plus rounds of ammunition and anti-aircraft grenades. They didn't have to pay for a single piece, because the annexation was so quick. The annexation of Austria, Czechoslovakia, and Danzig boosted the German Reich's gold reserves by US$71 million. If the German Reich is slowed by Britain on the western front and by Russia on the eastern front, with the economic rubber band overstretched in two opposite directions, once the Reich's economic structure falters, it will hurtle back to the source of the stretch – Berlin! God, the Nazis are stupid!'

'Hmm – interesting,' George said. 'We've a similar dilemma in science called the big bang theory. The Universe started as a singularity that exploded, creating matter that is accelerating radially outward, like the surface of an expanded balloon. Some have speculated that gravity will be the key factor in slowing most of the matter, not all of it, but most of it and so the expansion of the bulk of matter will be greatly slowed. Once the expansion of most of the matter is sufficiently slowed, gravity will force the bulk of the matter to retreat to a new epi-centre that is displaced from the original point of explosion, causing a never-ending cycle of explosion, expansion, contraction, and displaced epi-centres until the Universe finally becomes totally chaotic. It'll take us a hundred years to understand gravity – it's the only macro force that no one at present has been able to quantize and so without its integration, and without the knowledge of evident or non-evident matter in the universe, modern postulates of an ever expanding universe are just that – postulates!'

'Macro force, quantization, what are you two talking about?' said a women's voice. They both looked up and there stood Magrete. She sat down, looked at them, shaking her head at the tenet of their conversation. 'Are you at it again George? First you gave me a lecture on special relativity and now you are giving Helmut a lecture on the big bang theory. The whole universe is talking about the invasion of Russia by the German Reich. Seriously gentlemen!' Changing her tone completely she turned to Helmut and said, 'Oh, by the way, Helmut, this telegram came for you at Beelitz. It appears that Reinhard Heydrich still thinks you live there, and yes, I have read it!' She beamed at him.

The telegram read: 'PLEASE MEET ME AT MY VILLA STOP 12 NOON 28 JUNE STOP FOR LUNCH STOP HEYDRICH'.

PART THREE

The Survival

1

Helmut had done his homework on Heydrich and knew of the rumours accusing him of having a familial Jewish connection. After Heydrich's father was born, his grandmother had married a man with a Jewish-sounding name. Although Heydrich was not blood related to his father's stepfather, there was guilt by association.

When the Nazis took control of Germany in January 1933, Heydrich and Himmler were placed in charge of the mass arrests of anyone who might resist, including all anti-Nazi elements. There were so many arrests that the authorities ran out of prison space, and converted an abandoned munitions' factory at Dachau, a town near Munich, to a concentration camp for enemies of the Nazis. In April 1934, Himmler took control of the Gestapo and Heydrich was his second in command. In 1939, when the German Reich invaded Poland, Heydrich was given control of the combined police forces of the SS, Gestapo, criminal police and foreign intelligence services of Poland.

Helmut was interested in the Nordhav Foundation, which had been created by Heydrich. The Foundation's official purpose was to obtain real estate to be used as rest and recreation centres for members of the SS, Reich Security Police, and their families; its initial endowment was 150,000 Reichsmarks. The most important financial transaction of the Nordhav Foundation occurred in November 1940 with the acquisition of the Wannsee villa at Am Grossen Wannsee

56–58 in Berlin. The industrialist Friedrich Minoux, owner of the villa, had been jailed for defrauding the Berlin Gasworks, the largest financial crime of the Nazi pre-war era. From his jail cell in Berlin, Minoux sold the villa to the Nordhav Foundation for 1.95 million Reichsmarks. Heydrich's intention was to use the villa as an SS guesthouse and vacation lodging, with part of the villa reserved for his personal use.

In June 1941 Hitler recalled Heydrich to Berlin. Discussions between Hitler, Himmler and Heydrich centred on Reich Protector Konstantin von Neurath, whom they believed ruled too mildly, especially since he tried to restrain the excesses of his police chief, Karl Hermann Frank. They needed an excuse to strip him of his day-to-day powers. His initial appointment was intended to assuage international outrage at the German Reich's occupation of Czechoslovakia, and this was no longer relevant now that war had been declared on the German Reich. While these discussions were taking place, Heydrich entrenched himself at Wannsee.

Helmut arrived at Wannsee, knocked, and was ushered into a small dining room, which had been especially prepared for the meeting. Interesting, thought Helmut, he wants us to eat in private.

'Cognac?' Heydrich asked.

'Sounds good,' Helmut said. They sat in two armchairs, side-by-side, separated by a small round table, not far from the dining table. Reinhard Heydrich reminded Helmut of an eel – slippery and venomous. Helmut understood why Heydrich hated Jews so badly: he was tainted, and to be tainted in the Aryan world could lead first to exclusion and then to death.

The cognac arrived and Helmut swirled it to warm its contents, release its fragrance and enrich its taste. Heydrich tossed his cognac into the back of his throat. 'Himmler tells me that you've never joined the party,' Heydrich mused. 'Rather, you're a fellow traveller.'

'Oh!' Helmut was surprised that Himmler even remembered him. 'My forte is business. I find little time for anything else. Politics makes the world go round, but money underpins its spin.'

'Well put,' Heydrich said. 'Himmler also tells me that your company has given on loan, so to speak, four centrally located premises to the DRK, which have successfully been converted into hospitals, designed by Albert Speer. He spoke in glowing terms about your company's support for Marga as well.'

'Every German Reich company wants the German Reich to be victorious in these battles we find ourselves being pushed into. Anything we can do to help the war effort, we'll do. But we still have to make money for our shareholders – companies like ours are walking on a tightrope.'

'I see,' Heydrich said. He stood, indicating that Helmut should follow, and they moved to the dining room table, where the entrée, gazpacho, had been served.

'Interesting,' Helmut remarked, who had never tasted the dish before.

'Our chef learnt the recipe during the Spanish campaign. It originates from the region of Andalusia.'

'It's delicious.' Helmut changed the direction of the conversation in order to pursue another line of enquiry. 'I'm interested in the Nordhav Foundation. How did it begin?'

'The Foundation's principal purpose is to obtain real estate in order to build rest and recreation centres for members of the SS, Reich Security Police, and their families. Our little villa in Wannsee is one of our acquisitions.'

'I see,' Helmut replied. Lunch was served: roast duck, potato dumplings and red cabbage.

'What do you intend to do, Helmut, with the bombed property next door that your company owns?'

It took him until lunch was on the table, thought Helmut. 'Our company has demolished the villa,' he said, 'and we've removed the debris. The square hole you see will be the foundation for a new villa.'

'When do you plan construction?'

'Not until after the war has ended,' Helmut said firmly.

'How many square metres of land is it?'

'Seven and a half thousand square metres,' Helmut replied. 'And how many square metres is your property?'

'Approximately the same,' Heydrich said. Moving his body closer, Heydrich lowered his voice as he said, 'What I'm about to tell you is top secret, not to be repeated to anyone. Within one month Hermann Göring will give me written authorisation to prepare and submit a plan for a final solution of the Jewish question in lands under German Reich control, and to coordinate all government organisations to put the plan into action. I want to hold a conference at Wannsee. However, I want to buy your company's property in order to do so. How much will you sell it for?'

Helmut feigned surprise, and was about to reply when espresso and chocolate torte were served. He dug his spoon into the torte, took a bite, and washed its sweetness away with the coffee. 'We've already had a bid for the property from Ursula Lindgens, which we've knocked back.' Lindgens had approached him with a ridiculous offer of 750,000 Reichsmarks.

'Isn't that the former wife of that Jew, Georg Wertheim?'

'She is,' Helmut answered, unperturbed by the revelation. 'The property is worth well in excess of 2 million Reichsmarks and as her offer fell a little short of that, we had to knock it back.'

'But we paid 1.95 million Reichsmarks for this property and our property is the size of your land, plus a villa of some 1,500 square metres,' Heydrich said.

'Yes, but you bought it from Minoux in 1940, when he was arrested for fraud and embezzlement. He signed the property over to your company when he was in jail - hardly a strong negotiating position. I'm interested in a fair price. Let's take a walk and inspect the property.'

They rose and Helmut took Heydrich on a tour of his company's property. He pointed out its spectacular gardens, which had been unaffected by the bombing. He walked over to the hole in the ground that had been the old villa. 'If I was in your shoes,' Helmut said, 'this is where I would build an air-raid shelter; that is, a concrete bunker. It's not too far from your villa; it's located in a stretch of beautiful grounds and if you placed soil and a herb garden on the concrete roof, from the sky it would meld into the rest of the garden. The protection of your guests during an air raid is a very important consideration. Over there is a garage that houses six cars, and with a little alteration you can make it easily house a dozen, without it being too obvious from the air.'

Helmut took Heydrich to the servant's quarters, which had also survived the bombing. 'This could be your servants' quarters and as you see, they're well away from your villa. By providing them with their own space you significantly increase the guest capacity of your villa.' Heydrich was now impressed, and beginning to understand why Helmut was asking for more than just what the land was worth.

'How many rooms?' he asked.

'Let's go in,' Helmut suggested. 'It has four bedrooms, one bathroom, two toilets – one for women servants and another for the men – and a kitchen and lounge room.'

'These bedrooms are small,' Heydrich observed.

'We would fit two servants per bedroom and so eight servants occupied this space.'

'I'll offer you 1.4 million.' Heydrich eyed Helmut as if this were a poker game. Helmut had a perfect poker face – expressionless!

'That's what Lindgen's offered,' Helmut lied.

'Okay, my final offer is 1.6 million.' Helmut looked at his shoes, then looked Heydrich in the eye, then back at his shoes. Heydrich could sense he was tempted, but something was holding him back. 'Okay, final offer: 1.8 million, and I promise you this is as high as I can go.'

‘Deal,’ Helmut said reluctantly, ‘and now I’ve some real explaining to do to the board.’

‘Himmler was right,’ Heydrich said, ‘you’re a fellow traveller.’ They shook hands to cement the deal.

Both men walked away pleased. Heydrich was now in possession of a 15,000 square-metre property containing beautiful gardens, a bunker location, a large garage and servants’ quarters, with the latter well away from his villa. Helmut had solved his company’s liquidity problems, and could lower his company’s debt levels – much to the amazement of his bankers.

One week later Helmut received a letter from Heydrich inviting him to become a property and business consultant to the board of directors of the Nordhav Foundation. Helmut wrote back and accepted the consultancy. Being on the inside would benefit von Appen Pty Ltd for any future sell-off, he reasoned.

On 27 September 1941, the Reich Protector Konstantin von Neurath had fallen ill, and Hitler named Reinhard Heydrich as Reichsprotektor of Bohemia and Moravia.

2

The board of directors meeting was held on the top floor of the Berlin von Appen Pty Ltd department store in Alexanderplatz. Magrete and Helmut had decided there would be four board meetings a year, in February, May, August and November. The exact day of the meetings was at the discretion of the chairperson of the board. Magrete generally liked having the board meetings on the last Friday of the appointed month. There were five appointed directors – Felix Grönemeyer, Franz Segwick, Ernst von Papen, Adolph Langer, and Wilhelm Bebel – as well as Magrete and Helmut.

Before the first board meeting, Magrete decided that the night drive from Berlin to Beelitz might be problematic if something went wrong with her car, and so she was determined to stay overnight in Berlin. She could not afford hotels and did not want to stay with Helmut because of Gertrude. Helmut had overcome Gertrude's initial fear of air raids by purchasing a set of DT-48 earphones; she would wear them and listen to the radio to drown out the sounds of bomb bursts and the ferocious fire of the anti-aircraft guns. However, if Magrete was present during an air raid this strategy might become ineffective, because Gertrude was convinced that Magrete's curse would bring bad luck to the household. Magrete's only option was George, and when she approached him he had to say yes, remembering the oath he had sworn to Herbert.

Magrete laughed when she saw the state of his lounge room and the state of the sofa she would be using as her bed. George immediately told her she could use his bedroom and refused to listen to any other proposal. The first night Magrete slept in his bed, she slept well. His room had an aroma of 4711 cologne, a perfume that the Wehrmacht soldiers proudly wore, and a scent that she fancied for herself.

Her second directors' meeting was in November 1941. She arranged for the directors to tour the department store on a Saturday; she would stay at George's place for two nights. The first thing she noticed on her second visit was that the lounge had been completely cleared of books, journals and scientific magazines; it looked and felt like a lounge room again. She also noticed that a great effort had been made to clean the whole apartment. His bedroom no longer had the scent of the 4711 cologne, which she missed, but the vase in the bedroom was filled with flowers, whose aroma dominated the room.

Sharing the same bathroom and toilet with a man who was not her husband brought her into areas of mutual exposure. On one occasion when she forgot to shut the bathroom door, she had placed one foot on a stool to rub cream into her leg. She was wearing a dressing gown, but her upper thigh and calf were exposed. George went to the bathroom thinking it was unoccupied, saw her rubbing cream into her thigh and gave a wolf whistle. Magrete looked up, smiled at him, then slammed the door shut! As Magrete had already experienced the love of a man, such glimpses of his or her body were more humorous than embarrassing.

On the second visit, Magrete found herself feeling guilty because George always did the cooking. She asked him several times if she could cook. Each time, he tried to look offended. When she tried to drag him out of the kitchen he made himself ten times heavier, and Magrete tripped and fell on top of him. For a split second she could feel her bosom on his chest as he held her. George tickled her, and she shrieked with laughter, falling onto the floor next to him. He kept on tickling her until Magrete begged him to stop, and did so only after she promised that he could cook.

Magrete had discovered something in George that appealed to her, something she had not noticed when he was her amigo. George, she thought, is a natural flirt. He makes himself available without being offensive in the process. Then she chastised herself: your husband died only two years ago, what on earth are you thinking!

3

By 20 February 1942 nearly every continent contained countries that had declared war on the German Reich. Following the Japanese attacks on Pearl Harbour on 11 December 1941 the German Reich declared war on the United States and the United States reciprocated hours later. By 19 February distant cities such as Darwin in Australia had experienced acts of war, with the Japanese bombing the city.

On this day, Magrete had arrived at George's apartment and let herself in, because he was at work. She seated herself at the dining room table and wrote down the agenda for the board of directors meeting: 'Board Members (Present, Absent); Quorum Present; Others Present; Proceedings: Meeting called to order, Welcoming

New Director, Last Month's Minutes, Chief Executive Report, Finance Committee Report, Development Committee Report, Other Business, Assessment of the Meeting, Meeting Adjourned, Minutes submitted by the Secretary.'

Magrete had been concerned that Helmut wanted to appoint Werner Best as a director. She had strongly argued against his appointment, for she feared that he would be a bridgehead for a Nazi takeover of the board. Helmut assured her that such a takeover was impossible, because between them they held 52 per cent of the company's shares. Magrete finally relented when he told her that Herr Best could not attend every board meeting due to the position he held in Occupied France.

Magrete decided she needed to check on Herr Best's background. She could see why Helmut liked him. Werner Best had studied law and in 1927 obtained his doctorate from the University of Heidelberg. He had been a deputy to Reinhard Heydrich, and was currently serving as a civilian under Military Commander General von Stülpnagel in Occupied France.

Magrete went into the kitchen, made herself a cup of tea and brought it into the dining room. It was twenty-seven months since Herbert had passed away. It was hard for Magrete to get the sense of loss that so many wives and husbands experienced when they visit the grave of their loved one. Herbert had a grave head to mark a plot of ground where no body or spirit lay. She had visited the farm where he died – there was nothing there except air and dirt! No feeling of loss at either site.

Magrete would look at her photograph albums to try to regain a sense of him. The photographs showed happiness. It was as if all her grieving had taken place in the months of mourning after his funeral, when loss was directly related to actual physical pain. Now his loss was more like a memory than a reality. His absence during her pregnancy and Ilse being born after his death meant there was not the living connection to him that children could often provide. Move on, Magrete said to herself, just move on.

4

All the men on the company board enjoyed Magrete holding the position of chairperson of the board of directors. Magrete would purposely come late, and they knew it, so they could drink and smoke their cigars in the atmosphere of men.

Helmut excelled in these conditions; he loved to be in the company of men. He quickly introduced the newest member of the board, Werner Best, to Ernst von Papen, Adolph Langer, August Bebel, Felix Grönemeyer, and Franz Segwick. They each shook hands with him. He was known to all of them, not only as a lawyer of talent, but also as an effective administrator. They were also seduced by his lineage to power: Heydrich first and foremost, and through Heydrich to Himmler, and through Himmler to Hitler – powerful links in the German Reich chain.

Magrete walked in just as they were putting away the beer glasses and butting out their cigars. As usual, she looked professional, but stunning. Herr Best had heard about Magrete and knew she was the widower of Herbert von Appen, but he could not work out why she did not marry again and so stay at home with her child.

Magrete walked straight to him with the back of her hand outstretched. He took her hand and gently kissed her knuckles. He saw no rings.

'Herr Best, so good of you to accept our invitation to join the board of directors of our company. Your legal and administrative expertise will be a valuable asset.'

Smiling in Helmut's direction, Werner replied, 'Thank you Frau von Appen, but I'm afraid my legal skills, with respect to business, are not as valuable as Helmut's.'

'You are far too modest,' Magrete said. 'I understand you have a position in Occupied France with General von Stülpnagel. How is Paris?'

'The Parisians love their food. Because of the food shortage, restaurants a serve noodles, turnips and beets in exchange for certain number of tickets. However, I've heard that for 500 francs, suddenly a pork chop can be found hidden under cabbage and served along with a litre of Beaujolais and some real coffee.' Everybody smiled, including Magrete.

'Gentleman, we best start the meeting,' Magrete said. It was 1 pm, and the meeting was over by 4 pm. It was clear that under the stewardship of Helmut Gruen the company was on track to report an increase in its profit and, therefore, a greater dividend for its shareholders, as well as reducing its debt levels to the banks. Hidden in the report, but not unnoticed by Magrete, was the sale of the property at Wannsee – the prime reason for both the increased profit and reduced debt.

Magrete returned to George's flat by 5 pm, giving Helmut the impression she was heading back to Beelitz. She knew that Anna liked to have a weekend alone with Ilse, who was not a baby anymore, being just over three-years-old. Magrete did wonder if Anna was seeing a man in Beelitz. She noticed that Anna was occasionally using her oils and perfumes, though not to excessive amounts. It would not shock Magrete to know that Anna had a man in her life, since Anna was now twenty.

Magrete went into the bathroom, undid her bun and let her hair out so it spread onto her shoulders. She heard a familiar knock on the bathroom door, opened it and there stood George.

'I'm taking you out for dinner tonight.' Magrete held her hands towards him, wiggling her fingers as if she was going to tickle him, and George took one step back, raising both hands in a gesture of surrender. 'Seriously,' George said, 'dinner will be served at restaurant Nagy at 7.30 pm. I want you to dress up. I've got a rabbit, vegetables, potatoes, herbs – don't ask me how or where I got them! I've also managed to find us a bottle of Egri Bikavér red wine.'

'George, I will only agree to this if you dress up while I look after the rabbit.'

'Agreed,' George said, knowing when to retreat.

It took one hour for Magrete to wash, put on make-up and dress. She wore the same long black dress she had worn at the board of directors meeting. However, this time she did not wear the formal lace jacket that hid her shoulders and bodice. She turned to the side to check herself in the mirror. The dress hugged her body appropriately.

When Magrete returned to the kitchen, George whistled, and she waved him out. George was cooking a Hungarian paprikash rabbit. She could see some brown onion he had already cooked on the kitchen table. The roasted vegetables needed more cooking time. Magrete took out the rabbit and saw that it had browned. She added the brown onion back into the pot, and searched the table for a white wine. She saw a jar of what looked like white wine, and when she smelt it, she knew she was right. She added enough to cover the rabbit and onions and simmered it until the meat felt tender when she probed it with a fork. She removed the rabbit from the pan and looked for a serving plate.

When she checked again, the roasted vegetables were ready. Perfect, she said to herself.

Now she looked for the sour cream, which was impossible to buy with rations in the German Reich – and found it. She added it to the wine mixture left in the pan, heated it gently, and whisked the mixture together. When the sauce was ready, she added the rabbit back into the pan. She garnished it, and it was ready to serve.

Magrete placed the vegetables and rabbit on the dining room table. She called George, and he entered, wearing a tuxedo and carrying two glasses and one bottle of red wine.

'It smells delicious. I'm amazed you knew the recipe,' George said bringing his nose closer to the serving plate.

'I think you have forgotten I come from Vienna. The Hapsburg Empire was all about Vienna. You Hungarians were just our poor imitations. We took from you what you knew best: red wine and paprikash rabbit!'

George turned out the lounge room light, but the open kitchen door spread an indirect light throughout the room. He served Magrete and poured red wine into her glass.

Magrete leaned forward, the knuckles of her right hand under her chin, looking directly into his eyes, and asked, 'So why are we celebrating, and why at this expense?'

'It's a long story. Basically, Werner Koester wanted me to work for the Reich Research Council on non-ferrous metals research, because of my PhD research. But Otto Hahn, the director where I work, told Koester that my research in trying to purify radioactive uranium from its other isotopes had far more important consequences for the war effort than making materials to build faster planes. Then Hahn made a personal plea to Albert Speer, who's now Minister of Armaments. Speer had heard of me and knew I was a friend of Herbert's, and that Herbert's company had recommended him to redesign four of your department stores into hospitals. Speer apparently vetoed Koester and gave Hahn his wish. To Herbert!' They toasted him.

Magrete smiled at George, thinking, if only you knew it was my suggestion to use Albert Speer. She wonderd – how interconnected is the world of the German Reich?

'Do you know Magrete that I gave an oath to Herbert about you?'

Magrete washed down the rabbit with some of his red wine. 'I got a strange letter from him, three months after his death.'

'You've never referred to it – why? Were you angry?'

George and Magrete's eyes locked. Her eyes are so blue tonight, he thought.

Magrete placed her fork and knife down. 'No matter what was in Herbert's mind, and what were his protective intentions, wives cannot be gifted from a husband to a friend. You should want to woo a woman on your own terms rather than because of an oath, right?'

George raised his glass and drank the last of his wine while Magrete sipped the last of hers; she rarely drank wine. She rose to collect the dishes, but felt his hand on her arm as he took her from the dinner table to his Brunswick Panatrope record player. He put on Johann Strauss, Tales from The Vienna Woods. She smiled, accepted his arm, and danced with him. The more her body brushed against his as they waltzed, the more she liked it, and the more he responded to her touch.

That night they made love, slept together, and Magrete dreamt of a new beginning.

In the morning Magrete woke and saw George's arm across her chest. She felt a great weight had been lifted from her – she was no longer a von Appen! George woke five minutes later. He never thought about his oath to Herbert again, but he remembered his previous commitment to Julia. He shook his head and smiled and deemed that his commitment to Julia was now dead and buried. He frowned – the gypsy had predicted her loss!

Magrete had loved Herbert. She had also loved his family, and his lifestyle. She had been young, and he was dashing, daring, adventurous. When Herbert and she made love, he would take her under his wing, because he was experienced and she was not. Making love with George was a different experience. Magrete was now a mature woman. Making love with George had a depth of feeling and tenderness that she had never experienced before; each was responding to the other's emotional needs. She felt liberated for the first time in her life.

By midday, Magrete had kissed him goodbye. She was late getting back to Beelitz. Anna sensed something had changed in Magrete; it was as if some kind of radiance emanated from her inner core.

5

Rationing had been introduced in the German Reich in late August 1939, shortly before the invasion of Poland. Initially most foods were rationed, together with clothing, shoes, leather and toiletries. Although rations were sufficient to live off, citizens could not purchase luxury foodstuffs such as whipped cream, chocolates or cakes laden with cocoa. Meat was too expensive to be eaten on a daily basis. Other items simply were not available, because they had to be imported from overseas. Coffee was in that category and so the coffee taste was mimicked using roasted barley, oats, chicory and acorns. Vegetables and local fruit were not rationed, but imported fruits such as bananas became unavailable. Various imitation foods were produced. Cooked rice was mashed into patties and fried in mutton fat and called ersatz (substitute) meat. Rice mixed with onions and the oil reserved from tinned fish was called ersatz fish. Flour for bread was created using ground horse chestnuts, pea meal, potato meal and barley. Salad spreads were made using chopped herbs mixed with salt and red wine vinegar. Nettles and goat's rue were used in soups or were cooked and mixed together as spinach substitutes.

Ration stamps were issued to all civilians. These stamps were colour-coded and covered such basics as sugar, meat, fruit, nuts, eggs, dairy products, margarine, cooking oil, grains, bread, jams and fruit jellies. Ration stamps did not entitle civilians to free handouts; items still had to be paid for. Food stamps were also needed to eat in restaurants. The waiter would remove all the stamps needed to produce the meal in addition to taking a monetary payment. Theft of stamps or counterfeiting was a criminal offence and typically resulted in a spell of detention in a forced labour camp. As the war wore on, a death penalty sentence was not uncommon for such thefts.

In April 1942 bread, meat and fat rations were reduced. The German Reich explained that this was due to poor harvest, lack of manpower for farming, and the increased need to feed the armed forces and the millions of forced labourers and refugees that had fled to the German Reich. All of which had some basis in truth, but none of which explained the increasing difficulty the German Reich had in accessing worldwide markets.

When Gertrude left Magrete's household, Anna and Magrete had a meeting to reorganise the household chores. It was agreed that Anna's main focus should be looking after Ilse and her secondary jobs would be ironing, washing and mending. Magrete would take on cooking and purchasing food and household items. They would both share the house cleaning – Magrete would wash the dishes and Anna would dry them, and so on. They paid an elderly gardener from the local church a small sum of money to keep the garden tidy.

Anna was shocked at how well Magrete could cook, and that she was a great vegetarian cook. Gertrude had loved hearty Germanic food and would use fats and oils in all her meals; Anna got a bit heavier eating from Gertrude's kitchen. However, with Magrete doing the cooking, Anna started to lose weight. She was slimmer around the waist than ever before.

Magrete did most of her shopping in the village using money, rations and food coupons. Once a month she would drive Anna and Ilse into the surrounding countryside to get food on the black market, directly from local farmers. Most farmers had small vegetable gardens, livestock and, in one case, a fish hatchery set aside for their own needs as well as for the black market.

Magrete's four-point strategy to obtain food on the black market was simple. She would visit one farm on the third Monday of the month and barter with the farmer for a fair price for the produce. When she first started, she would knock on the farmhouse door and ask the farmer's wife if she could speak to her husband to make a trade. Magrete wanted to make certain that the farmer's wife was not threatened by her physical presence. After Magrete had done several rounds over many months, the wives would simply point or tell her where their husbands were.

Her second strategy was to bring Anna and Ilse along. She wanted the farmers to know she was also shopping for her child, and the governess of her child. Although having a governess could have given the impression Magrete was wealthy, she told the farmers that her governess was an orphan, which aided the perception that Anna's employ was one of necessity for both women, rather than one of choice. Magrete purposely elevated the status of Anna; she wanted the professional class, such as bachelor male doctors who worked in the local hospital, to be attracted to Anna for future male companionships. Magrete did not want Anna to become a spinster like Gertrude. Anna was naturally bright and so she fitted the governess role perfectly. Anna would often stand beside Ilse or have Ilse in her arms or on her hip while she watched the banter between Magrete and the farmer.

Magrete's third strategy was to overcome the general perception of wealth. The problem for her was the Daimler. Very few women could drive, and even fewer women owned a car; she could not hide the fact of the car from the village. Her tactic was to rarely wash it. She would only wash it when she was travelling to Berlin to chair the board meetings. The dirt that clung to the body of the car, made it appear older and more dilapidated than it actually was.

Magrete's last strategy was to let the village know that her husband, Herbert, had died while flying for the Luftwaffe. The villagers assumed that he had died in battle. She never corrected the misconception and everyone tiptoed around his death, just in case the subject was still too raw for her.

Magrete quickly established herself as a fair but hard barterer. Her company gave dividends to shareholders twice yearly. On 20 April Magrete was cashed up, and placed Anna with Ilse in the back of the Daimler. They would shop on the black market from a farm in the surrounds of Beelitz.

Anna asked, as she positioned Ilse on her lap in the back seat, 'Where to, Magrete?'

Ilse, aping her governess, also asked, 'Where to?' and both women smiled at her.

'Today we will visit farmer Joe Fasch and his lovely wife Suzanna.'

The Beelitz area was famous for its asparagus, and by 1939 1,000 hectares of farmland was dedicated to asparagus alone. Joe Fasch's farm dedicated 50 hectares to it; it was the first fresh vegetable of spring. His other 5 hectares were ostensibly dedicated to farming household produce, although in reality it was partly dedicated to his soft trade, as he liked to call it. Joe Fasch was familiar with dealing with women on a working basis, since in the 1930s the Nazis had sent girls to farms for compulsory service.

Joe saw the Daimler pull-up near his home. His wife went to the door to see who it was and immediately retreated inside the house. He groaned. 'Magrete, why come to me when you've got so many other choices in Beelitz?'

Magrete approached him, with Anna and Ilse in tow, and said, 'Long time no see, Joe. I hear you are heading for a bumper crop of asparagus this year. Do not worry, I have not come for the first crop of spring.' She stood in front of him, legs fashionably apart and hands on her hips.

Joe tried very hard from that point not to be putty in this beautiful woman's hands. 'I heard Freddie copped it in the neck last month,' Joe replied in an unflattering manner.

Magrete was unimpressed. 'Now, Anna, can you remember a man, a farmer I think, so drunk that he was crawling on his hands and knees and collapsed on my doorstep? I can, can you Anna?' Magrete never took her intense blue eyes off Joe.

'Yes, ma'am, I remember him well, because I had to clean-up the vomit he threw up all over you as you bent down to take his pulse.' Anna was enjoying this as much as Magrete.

'I thought this farmer friend of mine might have had a heart attack,' Magrete continued. 'Can you remember us dragging him all the way to this old car? Was he a light-weighted man?'

'No, ma'am, he was very heavy.'

'Do you remember that the vomit contained carrots, and also peas?'

'Yes, ma'am! I remember saying to you that, unlike us, this man eats well. It look like he'd also had meat for dinner.'

'Anna, did I not retrieve his bicycle from the pub and put it in our backyard for safekeeping?'

'Yes, ma'am, I thought that was so brave of you,' Anna added.

'When I brought him to his home in this old Daimler, I remember his lovely wife yelling at him that he was not worth a pinch of-'

'Alright! Alright! I get the picture,' Joe interrupted. He knew she would have said 'shit', and he knew she would have said it with style. He sighed, 'Let's have a look at your list.' Magrete had been helpful to him in times of need and now it was his turn.

Magrete gave him a list that included rabbit, chicken, pork, some herbs, and fresh milk. Joe automatically gave her a family price rather than a black market price. The next time he was in the pub he would tell his friends how 'Magrete the Terrible' had stung him. They would all laugh and pat him on the back, a sign that he was another notch on Magrete's belt. What a girl, they would beam!

Magrete was well known in the district, even among the farmers' wives. If they were in financial strife, especially in the winter months, Magrete would provide the farmer's families with the cash they desperately needed to survive. She would buy fewer goods, but pay more, and so she became part of their extended family. What the farmers loved was the battle of wits, which Magrete always seemed destined to win.

6

For Magrete, the war seemed to speed-up her life and to contract her personal space. Holidays in foreign places became a dream of the past. Travelling became more dangerous as the military dominated all transport corridors. Magrete thought of what George had told her about special relativity, a theory a German-Jewish scientist named Albert Einstein had taught him: the closer you got to the speed of light, the more space contracts. Magrete was determined to slow down her life to regain more personal space. She decided to go back to her yoga exercises. On 22 June 1942 she decided to teach Anna yoga. Anna was secretly hoping that yoga might help her further reduce her figure, especially around her backside and upper thighs.

Magrete's yoga instructor, Indira Devi, had left the German Reich in 1939 prior to the invasion of Poland to teach yoga classes in China. Before she left, she advised Magrete to become a yoga teacher. In just a few months, Magrete had mastered ten different sequences of postures, each on average containing twenty-five asanas. In total, she had mastered two hundred and fifty postures. Mindfulness was an important ingredient in every posture.

Magrete and Anna entered the lounge room before breakfast, hoping Ilse would not wake. Magrete placed a soft blanket on the floor. They sat facing each other, wearing only underwear and a loose-fitting top. Magrete showed Anna some loosening-up and stretching exercises. Anna mimicked Magrete, enjoying this extra time with her. Anna treated Magrete more like an older sister than the lady of the house, and that was made easier with Gertrude no longer living with them. Anna still addressed Magrete as 'ma'am' in company, though, because she did not want their familiarity to be witnessed by guests or the village folk.

'The starting point is to cool your brain down,' Magrete began, moving from the lounge room to the kitchen. 'To do this we inhale saltwater through our nose and exhale the water from our mouths into the sink. There is a thin membrane that sits between your nose and your brain. The Egyptians used to extract the brain through the nose, when they mummified a corpse.'

Magrete showed Anna the technique. Anna did one cycle and exclaimed, 'Yuck!'

'No, Anna,' Magrete said softly chastising her. 'You must be respectful and mindful. Mindful means you are consciously aware of what you are doing. You are not doing exercises for the sake of doing exercises and thinking about something else; you are doing the exercise as an avenue and an awareness to become more spiritually enlightened.'

This time Anna did it with a greater concentration. They went back to the lounge room and sat on the blanket facing each other. 'There are eight steps in yoga,' Magrete began, lowering her voice. 'Yama (universal mortality); Niyama (personal observances); Asanas (body postures); Pranayama (breathing exercises and control of prana); Pratyahara (control of sense); Dharana (concentration and cultivating inner perceptual awareness); Dhyanan (devotion, meditation on the divine); Samadhi (union with the divine)-'

'Ma'am,' Anna interrupted, 'why do I need to know all this stuff? I thought we were doing yoga exercises.'

'Anna, if you do not understand this stuff, as you put it, the exercises will be meaningless since they will not awake a meditative seat within you. I will write all of this down, but I want you to promise me that you will read it, study it and if you do not understand it, you will come back and question me, time and time again until you do. Okay?' Magrete was determined for Anna to experience not just a physical exercise, but a mindful and spiritual one as well.

'Yes, ma'am,' Anna replied automatically.

'I mean it, Anna,' Magrete phrased it as a soft warning.

'I promise, ma'am,' Anna replied, with greater conviction.

'Today we will start our Pranayama or breath control. Pranayama is the measuring, control, and directing of your breath. Pranayama controls the energy (prana) within you, in order to restore and maintain health and to promote evolution. When the in-flowing breath is neutralised or joined with the out-flowing breath, perfect relaxation and balance of body activities are realised. Now, this how I want you to sit. I want your right foot placed on top of your left thigh with its sole facing upward and heel close to your stomach. The other foot is lifted up slowly and placed on the opposite thigh in a symmetrical way. The knees are in contact with the ground. That is good, Anna. The torso is placed in balance and alignment such that the spinal column supports it with minimal muscular effort. Your body is centred above your hips, like so. To relax the head and neck, allow your jaw to fall towards the neck and the back of the neck.'

Anna started to giggle. 'Anna,' Magrete warned her softly.

'Sorry, ma'am, please go on,' Anna said, who was finding the posture difficult to reproduce.

'Move your shoulders backwards,' Magrete continued in a soft meditative voice, 'letting your ribcage lift. Rest your tongue on the roof of the mouth. Rest your hands on your knees with the palms of your wrists pointing upwards. Let your arms relax with the elbows slightly bent. Close your eyes. This is called the Lotus position. It allows your body to be held completely steady for long periods of time. Remember what our Master said – Master your breath, let the self be in bliss, contemplate on the sublime within you.'

Magrete appeared to Anna to be completely relaxed and in a blissful but mindful state. 'My inner thigh muscles feel tight,' Anna whispered, trying to imitate Magrete's meditative voice.

Magrete flickered her eyes open, viewed the way Anna was positioned, and then her eyelids fluttered down slowly, shutting out the world. 'Do not put so much pressure on them,' Magrete said softly, returning to her state of bliss mindfulness. 'Do not overlap your thighs so tightly.'

Anna moved the position of her feet and whispered, 'Ma'am, that's much better.'

'Now we will do rhythmic breathing,' Magrete instructed. 'You need to breathe in a fixed rhythmic pattern where you inhale to the count of four, you pause your breath in your lungs on the count of 5 and 6, exhale on the count of 7, 8, 9, 10, and pause on the count of 11 and 12, and then repeat. Stop counting out loud when you can do the rhythm intuitively.' Magrete's breathing was barely discernible.

It took Anna at least another thirty minutes before she was relaxed enough and confident enough to breathe without counting.

Magrete re-entered the now from her blissful but mindful retreat, as her eyelids fluttered open. 'We are going to do this one exercise every morning this week, until you can do it without thinking and until it becomes a natural part of your psyche.'

Anna opened her eyes and then she closed them again. She could not believe how slowly paced yoga was, but she really felt relaxed. Anna thought to herself, when am I going to lose these thick upper thighs?

Thanks to Magrete, Anna was one of a handful of Jews who had completely and successfully melded into the backdrop of life inside the German Reich.

7

On 29 May 1942 Reinhard Heydrich, the Reichsprotektor of Bohemia and Moravia, lay dying in the Bulovka hospital in Prague from wounds sustained during an ambush by Czech partisans as his car travelled through the city outskirts at Holesovice, on the Rude Armady VII Kobylisky. He suffered copious wounds, and shrapnel from an exploded hand grenade, which gave him blood poisoning. He developed a fever, and on 2 June suddenly went into shock, quickly lapsing into a deep coma from which he never recovered. He died at 4.30 am on 4 June 1942.

Helmut Gruen sent his condolences to the directors of the Nordhav Foundation – Karl Albert, Herbert Mehlhorn, Kurt Pomme, Walter Schellenberg and Werner Best – and attended Reinhard's funeral in Berlin.

Since the day Reinhard Heydrich asked him to be a consultant on the Foundation board, Helmut had expected to receive some communication from the Foundation confirming the offer. It never arrived. As he had not met any of the other directors, Werner was the obvious point of contact. Helmut's plan was simple: in order to retire more company debt to the banks, he needed to convert some of the properties into cash and, in order to do so, he needed to on-sell some of them to the Nordhav Foundation, at a good profit.

Helmut had a simple plan but it relied on Werner Best making an offer to him and the rest of the Foundation agreeing with Werner. He made an appointment to meet Werner Best in Paris on Monday 27 July. That would give the Foundation directors nearly two months to get over the death of the chairperson of the Foundation – Reinhard Heydrich.

Helmut decided to take Gertrude with him, and let Magrete know that his flat would be available for her use while Gertrude and he were absent. He had heard Magrete had been travelling to Berlin at least once a fortnight and was staying there over the weekend. He was intrigued, not knowing where she was staying.

Helmut, with Gertrude in tow, booked into the executive suite of the Champs-Élysées Plaza Hotel on 25 July, one of the most expensive hotels in Paris. It had been built in 1909 in the purest Haussmann style of the age, and was 50 metres from the Avenue des Champs-Élysées, in the heart of Paris. He hired a private lunchroom for Monday at 12.30 pm.

Werner Best arrived promptly at the allotted time, and was immediately ushered into a small private dining room. Helmut rose and the two men shook hands. Helmut said, 'I still can't believe what happened to Reinhard Heydrich. I attended his funeral in Berlin in the new Reich Chancellery. I thought Himmler's eulogy was moving and Hitler's gesture of placing all of Heinrich's medals on his funeral pillow was important – it was a reminder to all of us what a loss Heinrich was to the German Reich.'

'I understand Hitler plans to build a monumental tomb designed by Wilhelm Kreis,' Werner said, 'and that he'll commission Arno Breker to design an appropriate sculpture for the monument. The reprisals surrounding Heinrich's death have been measured and appropriate. Hopefully, it will dissuade any further attempts by partisans to take the lives of high-ranking German Reich officials. They know the price they'll pay, and it's not a small price!'

It was clear to Helmut that Werner was still angered by Reinhard Heydrich's death. But surely as a lawyer, Helmut reasoned, Werner should have been more tempered. Measured and appropriate, thought Helmut, you Nazis are dangerous and crazy! Tens of thousands of innocent lives will evaporate to avenge this one man's death. 'It's only fitting that he has a monument,' Helmut replied.

The waiter arrived with a lunch menu and a wine list. There was no price given for any item. You made a choice based on taste alone, Helmut thought. Werner looked sternly at the menu and said, 'I'll have the rabbit with Swiss chard and truffles. No wine for me, just a glass of cold water. And after the meal, coffee with no milk and sugar. Thank you.'

Helmut rarely ate in such expensive places, so he decided to have the most exotic meal the menu could offer. 'I'll have the pan-fried pigeon breasts with mushrooms and the brandy and red currant sauce. No wine for me, just a glass of water. And an espresso after the meal. Thank you.' Both men knew that food stamps and rations were not paying for this meal.

'What brings you to Paris?' Werner asked.

'The Swiss Bank Corporation,' Helmut said. 'The president was supposed to meet me here, but he had to call it off, and as I'd already booked this place I decided to come anyway. All is not lost, though!

The proposal he's offering will be delivered to me today.'

'He applied for business entry and then withdrew his application,' Werner revealed. 'It came across my desk. What's the proposal?'

As this question was asked, one waiter poured the glasses of water, while another served lunch.

'That rabbit smells amazing!' Helmut said.

'You're not having one morsel,' Werner joked. 'It does smell delicious.'

'As I was saying,' Helmut continued, 'the SBC wants to get a better return for their investors and so what they're offering is to buy our four department stores: Frankfurt, Dresden, Vienna and Budapest. The idea is for us to lease back those same stores over a ten-year period, with the yearly increases or decreases of rents tied to the long-term bond market of the country in which those stores are resident.'

Werner looked confused. 'How can that possibly be sensible for your company? I can see why the SBC might want that deal, but your company will lose out. You're going from no rent to rental payment – short-term gain for long-term loss!'

This pigeon is too good for this conversation, Helmut thought. 'For it to work, the SBC investors debt levels need to be low. In our case the banks want us to reduce debt, because they believe our debt levels are too high. Hence, we need to sell off properties, substantially decrease our debt level, and increase our profits in the short term. On top of that, once we sell our properties, we'll lower our cost of doing business: for example, maintenance of the buildings will no longer be our concern.'

'But how can this be a win-win situation? In any business transaction someone always loses in the long-term,' Werner observed.

Helmut looked as if he was seriously considering the question; really, he was hoping for a stronger nibble. 'So long as interest rates are low, SBC is ahead. Their investors can afford a shared debt level that is low per investor, but the rent returns, when all costs are accounted for, are triple the money they would be receiving from interest rates, and that does not even take into account the value of the properties. Our company loses the value of the sold properties, we must service the rents, and so borrowing will be more difficult for the company-'

'But,' Werner interrupted, 'you don't want to borrow, because you have to reduce your level of debt.'

'Precisely,' Helmut said. 'In ten years' time, when contracts need renegotiation, we might go elsewhere.'

'But wouldn't that seriously hurt the SBC investors?'

'Not at all,' Helmut said. 'The SBC investors might not even want us there, and that's the risk we're taking for the short-term gain. All of our department stores are in central locations in wonderful cities: Frankfurt, Dresden, Vienna and Budapest. Who wouldn't want to see the opera in Vienna and Budapest? These stores can be easily converted into apartment blocks and sold, or SBC investors could sell the apartments to Foundations such as yours, who might wish to use them as rest and recreation centres for members of the SS, Reich Security Police and their families.'

The waiters entered again. One cleared the glasses, cutlery and plates while the other brought in the coffee. This is real coffee, Werner thought. The meal would cost Helmut a fortune. Clearly von Appen Pty Ltd was making a lot of money.

Suddenly Gertrude appeared at the table. 'Herr Gruen, I'm sorry to disturb you, but a courier has delivered this dossier, and he tells me it's urgent that you receive it.'

'Thank you, Gertrude.' Helmut opened the dossier and laid it on the table, fumbling for his glasses. 'My glasses,' he said. 'Gertrude must have them. I'll be back in a minute.' He left the room and, as he did, turned ever so slightly and could see from the corner of his eye Werner Best glancing down at the front page. It read: 'Confidential: SBC Proposal for the Purchase and Lease Back Arrangements of von Appen Pty Ltd Department Stores'. Of course, it was Helmut who had written the proposal, and not SBC.

Werner Best was not a businessman, but he knew without Reinhard Heydrich the Nordhav Foundation would find it difficult to survive. He wanted to see the SBC proposal and to hand it over to the Deutsche Bank investment section. He knew that at present they were dealing in victim or Jewish gold in the course of the so-called Reinhard Operation, but, due to the Foundation's importance to Heydrich, he knew they would jump at his demand to determine whether the Nordhav Foundation should get involved. And if Helmut's modelling was correct, why should the Nordhav Foundation buy from the SBC? Would it not be more prudent for the Foundation to buy direct from von Appen Pty Ltd, using loans secured from Deutsche Bank, rather than eventually buying the properties from the SBC? Provided that the interest rate on the loans was much less than the rent paid by von Appen Pty Ltd, the Foundation could receive a sizeable income stream from these investment properties. He waited for Helmut's return.

Helmut sat down, wearing his spectacles, and began to read the front page.

'Helmut,' Werner said, 'as I'm a director of von Appen Pty Ltd, shouldn't I see this proposal?'

'I'm sorry to say, no. This proposal is commercial-in-confidence at present. When my finance team has fully vetted it, and if we propose to accept it, then it'll go to the finance committee of the board of directors for review and recommendation. It's up to the board to approve or not approve the finance committee's recommendations, and at that point you'll see it.'

'What if this dossier gets waylaid? As a friend of Reinhard Heydrich, say you leave it on the table, and because I'm a very busy man I'll return it to you in a month's time.'

Helmut looked at him seriously. 'You know if the Foundation accepts any part of this written proposal I cannot be a consultant to the Foundation's Board, nor you a director of von Appen Pty Ltd.'

'You being a consultant of the Foundation is easily fixed – Reinhard was murdered before he had time to put it in place. As for me, I'll resign from your board, because my duties are in Occupied France, and so I'll be unable to attend most of the board meetings.'

'My friend,' Helmut said as he stood to leave, 'all I ask is that you beat the SBC offer by 2 to 5 per cent and that the SBC never know that this took place, or that you've sighted their document. If they do, I'm done for.'

'Don't worry, Helmut, not even the other directors of the Foundation will know how or where I sourced this document,' assured Werner. They shook hands and Helmut left the dining room, leaving the dossier on the table. He hoped they would take the bait.

On 28 August 1942 Magrete von Appen, as chairperson of the board of directors, accepted the resignation of Werner Best, since his duties in Occupied France made it impossible for him to attend most board meetings. Von Papen humorously pointed out that this was the shortest appointment in the history of the German Reich. His comments did not make the minutes of the board meeting. The finance committee of the board of directors unanimously accepted the proposal of the Nordhav Foundation to purchase the properties in Frankfurt, Dresden, Vienna, and Budapest on a leaseback arrangement, as well as the outright purchase of the chalet in St Moritz. The finance committee's recommendations and formula – which split the income between lowering the company's debt levels and dividend returns to the shareholders – were unanimously accepted.

When Helmut cheekily placed the chalet in the proposal, to be sold outright back to the SBC Swiss investors, he did not expect the Foundation to accept this component. They did so because Himmler decreed they needed a non-public foothold in neutral Switzerland for future negotiations, as he was concerned about Hitler's growing addiction to the opioids supplied to him by his doctor, Theodor

Morell, who mixed them with a cocktail of vitamins to alleviate Hitler's physical and emotional ailments.

8

Early in the morning of 20 November 1942 Magrete left Beelitz for Berlin to chair the board of directors meeting at Alexanderplatz. Anna was getting used to Magrete staying in Berlin once a fortnight on a Friday and returning late Sunday morning, a routine she had adopted from February of that year. At first Anna was given the impression that Magrete was heading a special committee of the board of directors and staying at Helmut's place. But when Anna asked who she should ring if something went wrong, Magrete told her she no longer resided with Helmut, but had secured accommodation elsewhere in Berlin that did not have a telephone, and so could not be contacted directly. She gave Anna an address to which she could send a telegram. Anna suspected that Magrete was having an affair and the address she was given was the address of Magrete's lover.

Anna enjoyed cooking for Ilse and herself. On Magrete's instructions, every Friday evening was a meat meal. She cooked small portions for herself and smaller portions for Ilse. On a Friday they would play games such as hide-and-seek or catch-me-if-you-can, all designed to tire Ilse. Every night Anna or Ilse would read a segment of a book – the Brothers Grimm were their favourites – with Anna animating her voice as much as possible to play-act a werewolf or a princess. As Ilse was nearly four, she was also made to read passages of the book and Anna would correct her on a word here and there, and tell Ilse the meanings of words she did not understand as well as the meaning of the text she was reading.

After Ilse had read her Brothers Grimm passage, and was tucked into bed, she would say to Anna, 'I love you, Anna. You're beautiful. I want to be just like you when I grow up.' Anna would look at her, smile, give her the biggest hug of the day, and kiss her goodnight. Even when Magrete was home, Ilse would say exactly the same words to Anna in front of her mother. Magrete would look at Anna and hug her saying, 'Let's say goodnight to your young admirer.' Magrete never seemed dismayed that Ilse never said that to her.

On Saturday mornings they would promenade down the main street of Beelitz. Anna would take the pram, but Ilse would always want to walk beside her. They would walk slowly along the main street, saying hello to as many people as possible, stopping in front of shop windows and sometimes entering a shop and buying an item or two using their ration coupons. Most of the rural women would acknowledge Anna, as the governess, and most of the older men would tip their hat at their approach. There was also a teenage boy, Franz Stopper, who always stared at her. Some mothers would stop and ask her questions about what they should teach their preschool children. Anna was listened to and her advice was always respected.

When Magrete was home, Anna felt that the village gaze shifted away from her and onto Magrete. Everybody in the village loved to talk about Magrete and her exploits. They knew she was Viennese and automatically assumed she was cultured, with a happy disposition. She would often tease and joke with the village people, and they enjoyed that because life in wartime was mostly grim; she took those dark clouds away from them. Anna was never jealous or envious of Magrete; rather, she accepted that she was a different person. She was a far more passionate person, for example, than Magrete.

Not every Saturday night when Magrete was not home, but on some Saturdays, Anna, who was now approaching twenty-one, would go into her room and quietly lock the bedroom door. She would place a pillow on her bed and cover it with a towel. She would undress completely and inspect herself in the mirror, noting her small, rounded breasts, then her stomach and thighs. She was losing weight because of the yoga lessons, and also because of Magrete's vegetarian cooking. She needed to lose a fraction more weight, she thought, around the tops of her thighs.

Anna would then cross the floor and turn-off the light and quietly place her backside onto a towel. She would ever so gently stroke her neck, once, twice, until she felt her nipples tinge. Anna would place both index fingers in her mouth and wet them. Her fingers descended to her nipples, and she pinched them softly. When Anna felt her nipples harden she placed her fingers under her two breasts and cupped her breasts lightly, playing with her nipples with her thumbs. Her backside was digging into the towelled pillow as if her back lay on top of a man.

Slowly Anna raised her knees and opened her legs as her fingers drifted between them. As Anna's fingers rhythmically massaged the region between her legs her breathing was synchronous with her play. Occasionally Anna would lift one hand to come back to her nipples. She raised and lowered her rear into the pillow in a rhythmic pulse. Her pace was getting quicker, her breathing heavier. A sudden flash of pleasure extracted a groan and as she pressed her thighs tightly together, love began issuing from her body. Slowly, all sensations started to spiral downward. She relaxed completely as the last vestiges of her excitement ebbed away.

Anna always slept well on such a night. She liked it best when she was ovulating and when she could clearly keep in her mind's eye the image of the man she imagined being with - George Nagy.

The next morning Anna always felt a little ashamed, a little embarrassed, a little vulnerable and a little excited. She would put Magrete's oil in the bath and bath herself to wash off her womanly scent. She would wash the towel and any sheeting that might have been compromised by the previous night's excursions. Then Anna would wake-up Ilse, bathe her, and clothe her in the prettiest dress. They would have breakfast together, and she would do her yoga exercises while Ilse was copying out words she did not understand from the book she was reading. When Magrete returned, she would pester them to know every detail of their weekend.

On 19 November the Soviet forces on the northern flank of the Axis forces at Stalingrad began their offensive; forces in the south began theirs on 20 November. Although Romanian units were able to repel the first attacks, by the end of 20 November the Third and Fourth Romanian armies were in headlong retreat, as the Red Army bypassed several German Reich infantry divisions. The tide had turned for the German Reich.

9

In the first three months of 1943 the Allies were strengthening their positions: in the South Pacific, American and Australian troops recaptured Borneo and New Guinea; to the European East, Soviet troops recaptured Stalingrad and Leningrad; to the South, Rommel was embattled in Tunisia and the first Greek city, Kardista, fell to the Allies. The German Reich and its allies were starting to teeter under these sustained assaults by their enemies.

As the head of a company, Helmut Gruen was concerned that the Allies, and in particular the Americans, were bombing Berlin, Vienna and Munich, cities where von Appen Pty Ltd had valuable assets. On 10 March it was the hospital in Munich that was slightly damaged, even though it was displaying a large Red Cross symbol on its roof. At the beginning of the war, Peter, Magrete and he had been certain that the DRK hospitals would be safer than the department stores. But both sides were finding it easier to bomb population centres rather than military targets, and in some cases the incendiary bombs that they deployed were designed to maximise a firestorm in cities that could not be controlled. German Reich manpower and the economy were stretched to its limits, so that few buildings were repaired if damaged. With respect to the Munich hospital, DRK used forced labour to repair the premise.

Helmut needed to shift these hospitals off the company books, as he had with most of the department stores. He knew that he could not sell them to the Foundation, because on 4 February 1943 the Reichssicherheitshauptamt (RSHA known as the Reich Security Main Office) had acquired all the Foundation's holdings. He was searching for another avenue, and he did not have long to wait.

Helmut detested Martin Bormann and the power that he exerted over Hitler. When you run a company, as Helmut did, there is a certain type of person you do not hire: one who wishes to isolate the CEO from the executive team. A CEO needs the executive team to be forceful individuals in their own right and to fearlessly express their opinions at executive meetings. However, once a decision has been made, the executive team must unite and bring their considerable talents to the fore in order to successfully implement and execute the decision.

Martin Bormann was totally untalented, but knew his influence on Hitler depended on who had access to him. On 12 April 1943, when Hess flew solo to Britain on his Don Quixote mission, Hitler officially appointed Bormann as the personal secretary to the Führer. By this time Bormann had de facto control over all domestic matters, and this new appointment gave him the power to act in an official capacity on any matter. Hitler's executive team could no longer have direct access to him.

Helmut was surprised when Hitler's aide-de-camp Hans Junge invited him to lunch at 1 pm on Monday 12 April 1943 at the Hotel Kaiserhof. The Kaiserhof was a luxury Hotel in Wilhemplatz, next to the Reich Chancellery. It was Berlin's first grand hotel, replete with the most modern features of its day, including gas cookers and electric power. Helmut realised this meeting had been set-up by Martin Bormann and not by Hitler.

Helmut knew that people like Bormann were psychopaths – notorious for their lack of fear, and blaming others for events that were actually their fault. In his lifetime, he had met many top executives who suffered from this mental condition. They were smart enough to know how to protect themselves from future threats. Hence, Helmut reasoned, Bormann would want to put in place an exit strategy; that is, a strategy that would ensure a German Reich afterlife, which would resurface in the future from a distant land and that would be sufficiently resourced to plant the Nazi seed back into its homeland soil. He suspected that Bormann wanted technical business advice that not even Hitler would contemplate – how to safeguard stolen wealth if defeated by the Allies. Hitler, Helmut reasoned, was delusional. He was still convinced of a German Reich victory, and at any rate he would die on German Reich soil rather than leave it.

Hans Junge and Helmut Gruen met in the Hotel Kaiserhof dining room. It was a sizeable room, but they were the only two people there. It was clear to Helmut no one else would dine there for lunch that day. He was impressed with Bormann's power. Hans and Helmut shook hands and seated themselves at the only table that was set for a meal. They were given a lunch menu. Helmut ordered spätzle noodles with stir-fry and Hans ordered chicken schnitzel with buttered vegetables.

Hans immediately went to the point of the meeting. 'Himmler has told us you are completely trustworthy. Our conversation must be strictly confidential and can never be retold to anybody. Is that clear?'

'Of course,' Helmut answered in a somewhat relaxed fashion, 'commercial-in-confidence is my stock-in-trade.'

'I'm not representing anyone, Hitler or Bormann or anybody else for that matter,' Hans whispered.

'I understand, this is your personal enquiry,' Helmut replied in a conversational voice, smiling and knowing fully well that Bormann would shoot him tomorrow if any parts of their conversation were leaked.

'We'll certainly win the war, but in the meantime there'll be a lot of toing and froing going on,' Hans said unconvincingly, but returning to a conversational voice. 'We may lose the odd Greek city to the Allies today, and recapture the same city tomorrow, and so on. What we've done is centralised our wealth and that might in future pose some problems.'

'Problems? Surely you don't expect Berlin to be overrun?'

'No, but-' Hans paused, searching for a way to fill the hole that he had dug for himself.

Helmut came to his rescue. 'Oh, I see! You mean that if the Allies accidentally bombed one of your warehouses in Berlin that contained some of your concentrated wealth, then you would be that little bit poorer.'

'Exactly,' Hans said, looking relieved. 'We want to get some technical advice from you about how we could take some of our wealth and secure it more safely.' The waiters brought out their lunch, reset the table and left.

'The first thing to do is not necessarily to transfer money out of the country, but rather to reinvest money into the country from a foreign place,' Helmut advised. He paused as he saw Hans groping for a pen and paper. 'That won't be necessary, Hans. What I'll tell you will be typed and sent to your office.'

Hans looked a little perplexed and then blurted out, 'No! I'll pick it up from your office.'

Helmut smiled. 'The best place to set-up a bogus company is in Argentina. A business associate I have known through mutual friends, Johann Leo Harisch, is a long-term resident in Buenos Aires. He's the perfect person and in the perfect place to set-up companies for you. It just so happens that our company owns four DRK hospitals. They're centrally located in Magdeberg, Prague, Munich and Leipzig. As they display a red cross on their roofs, they should be safe from getting damaged. After the German Reich wins the war, these hospitals can readily be converted into nursing homes. Herr Harisch can set-up a company in Argentina called Cuidado de los ancianos (Elderly Care) which will purchase these hospitals from von Appen Pty Ltd for a fair price and-'

Hans interrupted, looking baffled. 'I don't understand how this can work?'

'What don't you understand?'

'Why we should send money to Argentina only for it to return to the German Reich?'

'You don't,' Helmut said. 'You pay my company directly from the accumulated wealth stored in your warehouses. You fake a money transfer document at the Argentinian end.'

'That makes sense. But why nursing homes?'

'I can answer best in Martin Bormann's words. He stated last year that National Socialism and Christianity are irreconcilable. Most nurses in the German Reich are denominational nurses. As you know, in 1936 the German Reich formed its own nursing order and so these nurses took an oath of allegiance to Hitler and not to God. Under the Hereditary Health Law, nuns are forbidden to assist in operations conducted in hospitals, thereby forcing an increase in non-denominational nurses. At the moment, the Catholic church dominates apartment residences for the elderly and so this would put in place a futuristic structural displacement of the religious orders that currently dominate the field.'

Hans enquired, 'But what happens if we lose the war?'

'The DRK hospitals would not belong to a German Reich citizen or to a German Reich company or to the German Reich, for that matter. They would belong to an Argentinian company called Elderly Care. No conquering nation would confiscate the property of a company from a country that was not a party to the war. More importantly, as these are DRK hospitals they could hardly be accused of being involved in any war crimes. Hence, all the grime that might normally be associated with a German Reich company would not be associated with this Argentinian company.'

Hans looked unconvinced. 'This is just one company, hardly the size and scale of the wealth transfer we were looking for.'

'Of course not,' Helmut said. 'This is merely a template. If we can work together, set this up and make a successful transfer, you can apply this template hundreds of times to a host of different businesses.'

Hans finally understood the transfer model. 'Brilliant! When can I pickup your written proposal?'

'It will be ready next Monday,' Helmut answered. They shook hands and left.

Helmut gave Hans Junge the proposal on 17 April. Two days later the Warsaw ghetto uprising began after German Reich troops and police entered the ghetto to deport its surviving inhabitants. Seven hundred and fifty people fought the heavily armed and well-trained troops.

On 24 April Hans Junge agreed to a price for the three DRK hospitals, with Prague not sold. The May meeting of the board of directors agreed to the sale of the three hospitals to Elderly Care and the apartment in Basel, Switzerland to a law firm, Meier and Schmidt. Magrete was surprised with the last sale, but did not raise the matter with Helmut, as she trusted him implicitly. The company property portfolio was shrinking fast, now containing one department store (Berlin), two apartments (Vienna, Berlin), two houses (Beelitz and Tailfingen), and a DRK hospital (Prague). On the grapevine Helmut heard that Bormann used his template to generate many more Latin American companies holding German Reich assets.

10

On Sunday 30 May Magrete was about to return from Berlin to Beelitz. She had chaired the board of directors meeting on the previous Friday and had another wonderful weekend with George.

She loved the conversations, the meals, the dancing, the occasional wine and lovemaking. Magrete knew that sooner or later Helmut and Anna would have to be told of her relationship with George, if they did not know already. Ilse, nearly three and a half years old, was too young to be of any concern.

Magrete had bought Ilse a cowgirl hat and used the hat strap to position it on the nape of her neck before she drove off in her Daimler. As Magrete was nearing Potsdamer Wald (Potsdam Forest) she saw a British spitfire peel off from a squadron and head straight towards her. Magrete immediately stopped the car and bolted towards the forest. The fighter plane was spitting bullets, making potholes in the road as it moved closer to her car, while Magrete was running at right angles to the line between car and plane. Suddenly the aftershock of an explosion threw Magrete to the ground. She quickly got up, and ran as fast as she could towards the densest part of the forest. She could hear the plane banking sharply then levelling out as it moved towards her. She knew that the pilot was determined to kill her. She could not have run any faster, but at the last minute she dived to the right. The bullets from the plane followed Magrete's original line.

She picked herself up and continued running toward the forest. She was 50 meteres from the safety of the forest canopy when she heard the plane sharply banking again, and heading in her direction. She was 1 metre from the forest when she heard bullets flying. Magrete ducked her head as the bullets rained closer and over her. She was under the canopy and in a split second she needed to make a choice – left, right or straight. Magrete ran straight ahead, and suddenly fell headlong into a ravine that saved her life as the bullets passed overhead. She pushed herself up against a leafy bank. She could see that both of her legs were badly scratched and bruised, her left ankle sprained and starting to swell. The plane made one last sortie, causing a small tree limb to snap and hurtle down the ravine not far from her. She took Ilse's hat off her neck and saw a bullet hole; she had escaped death by millimetres. The reality of her lucky escape from certain death made her start to panic, and so she began her yoga breathing exercises in the ravine.

After 30 minutes, Magrete grabbed the limb that had been severed by the bullets and used it as a makeshift cane as she hobbled out of the forest and saw that there were no planes in the sky. She inspected the Daimler, but there was nothing that could be retrieved from its twisted frame. She hobbled towards Beelitz and after struggling on for twenty minutes she heard a horse and cart. It was farmer Joe Fasch.

'I see you've escaped death, Magrete.' Joe jumped down and helped her into the cart, then clicked his tongue. The horse moved forward towards Beelitz.

Magrete smiled and said, 'I was thinking of visiting your lovely wife and your farm this Monday. But since that spitfire blew up my car, I think you had better visit me.' She hugged his arm as he whipped his horse to move faster.

'Just come to the pub, where there are many more of us who can satisfy your needs.' Joe smiled and winked at her.

Magrete got the double entendre and said with tenderness, 'Joseph Fasch, you are a dirty old man!'

When she got home Magrete told Anna of her near-death experience and the loss of the Daimler which could not be replaced. She also told Anna that she was seeing George; that in the future she would be staying at George's place, and on some weekends he would be staying in Beelitz with them. It confirmed for Anna that Magrete had been seeing George for some time.

Magrete's near-death experience had awakened her from the cosy relationship she was having with George. In the future, she would take Ilse with her when she was in Berlin. Anna would have to remain in Beelitz, because George only had one bedroom. Anna was saddened by this news, but covered it well. Anna realised that she could die before making love to a man, a thought that greatly disturbed her.

11

It was already foreseeable in June 1943 that the Institute would probably need to leave Berlin. The plan was to find a new place well away from large military–industrial complexes and as far away as possible from the eastern border of the German Reich, because the Russians were brutal in their reprisals in captured territory.

On 18 June George made his way to Beelitz to stay with Magrete for the weekend. The railway was sometimes temporarily out of service due to bombing raids. However, on this day the line was operating. Anna and Ilse would greet George at the station when he visited. All three would walk from the station to the house, talking continuously. When George first visited Beelitz, Anna appeared to be distant to him, but the more he visited the more relaxed she was in his company. Ilse just adored George, as he was the only man in her life that she could remember. He was special to her and he adored her as well. She would dance for him, like a little girl does: twirling her body around and around, lifting her arms and interlocking them in an arch above her head. If she tried some complicated move and fell, George would scoop her into his arms and all three of them would laugh. At first Anna was a tinge jealous of the attention Ilse received from George, but because Ilse was happy that ill feeling quickly evaporated.

George had a way with Anna. He could simply disarm her of any shield that she might put between them. Anna had always liked his good looks, but the relationship between them became much more mature, now that he was with Magrete. He treated her like an equal, as Magrete did, and so in their presence Anna would never address Magrete as 'ma'am'. The only distinction between Magrete and she was that he loved Magrete, whereas Anna was his young adult friend. George was always amazed when Anna would reveal to him a quintessential trait of her generation or the next. He would look at her in disbelief and say to her, 'Really! I have never read "The

35 May" and this little tyke Ilse has read it?' Ilse and Anna would look at each other and laugh. His presence energised the females in the house. When George came to the front door, he would always ask, 'Can I come in?' Anna would say yes, but Ilse would say no, until he produced a lolly and gave it to her in order to gain entry.

Magrete was always cooking when they entered. George would help her in the kitchen, while Anna and Ilse would go into the lounge room and read. Magrete and Anna would never listen to the radio, as most families did during the war years. George tried a few times to interest them, but he always failed. Both women liked talking to him and did so, after Ilse was seen off to bed by all three of them. Ilse would still tell Anna that Anna was beautiful, and she wanted to grow up to be exactly like her. Anna was secretly pleased that not only did Magrete hear it, but George as well. After tucking Ilse into bed, all three of them would adjourn to the lounge room.

This time George led the conversation because he had news. 'Hahn is concerned about the bombing raids in Berlin. He's asked the team leaders to think about where we should relocate.'

'Why not here in Beelitz?' Magrete said. 'It would suit me fine.'

'And me,' Anna agreed.

'There are no buildings that are suitable here, and there would be no place we could store dangerous materials such as radioactive uranium,' George said. 'Anyway, it's too close to Berlin and so the Russians might pose a problem in the not too distant future.'

Anna enquired, 'What's uranium?'

'It's a substance that can be radioactive and so highly toxic to humans if not properly handled,' George said in a matter-of-fact tone.

Magrete enquired, 'What are the other criteria?'

'Hahn is scared of the Russians. They're brutal. If we're going to get captured, he'd rather we be captured by the western armies than those from the east.'

Anna asked, glancing at Magrete, 'Does this mean if we want to be near you we might have to move from Beelitz?'

'That'll be a decision for Magrete and you, but I hope you'll allow me to be a part of your conversation.'

Magrete asked, 'Are there any other criteria we should factor in?'

George was beginning to feel he was being cross-examined by two clever barristers. 'Hahn doesn't want the Institute to be anywhere near a military complex or an industrial–military complex.'

Magrete laughed. 'That is the whole of the German Reich! Does he want the Institute to be shipped off to Paris?'

'Ha, ha, laugh all you like, but no is the short answer. It has to be in Germany, and not even in Austria.'

'I have an idea and it might work best for all of us, if Anna agrees,' Magrete said, looking at Anna, who smiled in response, thinking - that's my Magrete. 'Recently Helmut has been offloading all of our properties to keep the company afloat and also to make sure dividends are being paid to shareholders. I have done a complete audit of our current holdings: we have two houses, one in Beelitz and Tailfingen; a DRK hospital in Prague; an apartment in Vienna and one in Berlin; and a department store in Berlin. The reason we have a house in Tailfingen is that it is a textile town, where our company sourced clothing. It would be a perfect location for the Institute.'

George queried, 'But doesn't that mean it would be bombed?'

'No!' Magrete had to laugh at George's idea of what constituted a military threat. 'Making underwear, dresses and even soldiers' uniforms will not kill anybody and so it would hardly be on the top of a bombing priority list. As a matter of fact, many of the mills had to shut down, as wool is impossible to import and only the local fleece is available. Hence, the building infrastructure for the Institute is available there. Secondly, it has a good railway infrastructure and access to Berlin would be possible. It is close to the Swiss border and so it is most likely that the British or the Americans will capture it.

There is no military or industrial–military complex anywhere near the village, and because it is largely a farming area, if food shortages occur, we can always make excursions into the countryside.'

Anna was surprised that Magrete was already conceding the war to the Allies. A suspicion took hold in her mind that Anna immediately dismissed.

'What about the weather?' George queried. 'I mean it's near the Swiss Alps.'

'A new criterion, George?' Anna asked. George smiled back at her.

'It gets cold in the winter,' Magrete said. 'But the area's elevation ranges between approximately 600 metres above sea level to 1,000 metres, so it is hardly the Swiss Alps. If I could convince Helmut, we could move into the company's house at Number 1 Neuweilerstraße, Tailfingen. The company used it for its senior management, who stayed there while securing contracts for a whole range of clothing and textiles for our department stores.'

'That does sound exactly like what Hahn is looking for,' George conceded.

Magrete looked at Anna apprehensively. 'If you do not want to move, Anna, we will stay here, but what do you say about Tailfingen?'

Anna knew she could tease, but decided against it. 'I see myself wearing lederhosen (leather pants) and yodelling.' Magrete move over to her and kissed her on the cheek. Anna knew how much it meant for Magrete to be near George.

That night Anna was certain she heard them making love. She was pleased that Magrete loved George, a man so different in so many ways to that pervert Herbert.

On the following Monday at an Institute team leaders' meeting, George briefed them on Tailfingen, and why it would be the best place for the Institute. Hahn and his staff member Göttel promised to inspect Tailfingen and the local empty woollen mills. When they returned, they were delighted with George's recommendation, and started to make preparations for the Institute to move there early in 1944.

The following fortnight Magrete stayed in George's apartment in Berlin for the weekend, and saw Helmut, who agreed she could stay in the house in Tailfingen. He was delighted with the outcome, as was Gertrude, because Berlin was no longer a safe place. Both were pleased that they would once again be living near a church. Gertrude was delighted that Magrete would be far from Beelitz.

12

On 27 August Ilse, Anna and Magrete travelled to Berlin by train. Ilse and Magrete stayed with George. As he only had one bedroom, Anna stayed with Helmut and Gertrude. The latter arrangement was Gertrude's suggestion, for she had not seen Anna for a long time. Helmut was pleased that Magrete and George were finally a couple. The board of directors meeting was to be held at 4 pm that afternoon, so Magrete could spend all the rest of the weekend with George and Ilse.

The von Appen stores were managing to bring in a small profit, but the hospital in Prague and the department stores in Berlin and Dresden were in immediate danger. After the victory at Stalingrad, the Soviet army remained on the offensive, liberating most of the Ukraine, and virtually all of Russia and eastern Belorussia during 1943. In the summer of 1943 at Kursk Russia, the German Reich attempted one more offensive, but were badly beaten by the Soviet army in what Helmut believed could be the turning point on the eastern front.

The board of directors eventually decided to mothball Dresden, and send the stock to their most successful department store in Berlin. They reasoned that while the German Reich would throw every resource at protecting Berlin, it would not protect Dresden with the same degree of vigour. They would still have to pay the Reich Security Main Office rent on the Dresden department store, because of the ten-year lease, but Helmut argued the cost could be partly offset by selling their remaining apartment in Vienna to the Argentinian company Elderly Care. The board charged Helmut to investigate such a sell-off. They suspended all dividend payments to shareholders. The property portfolio would now be significantly reduced: one apartment in Berlin; two houses, in Beelitz and Tailfingen; a department store in Berlin; and a DRK hospital in Prague.

When Magrete returned to George's apartment, she was exhausted. The board meeting had been very tiring. The board members were not in full agreement with the sell-off and the mothball strategy Helmut had proposed. Three directors had voiced opposition for this strategy and three directors, including Helmut, concurred. This made for a lively debate and Magrete had to use her considerable reserves of patience and humour to ensure that the debate did not get personal or heated. In the end, they turned to Magrete, who initially had delayed her vote to enable the debate to continue and when the debate had ended, she voted in favour of Helmut's strategy.

Magrete was determined that the meeting would not end on a sour note. She pointed out to the board that she owned 39 per cent of the company and Helmut 13 per cent. It was her suggestion that the strategy be adopted only if dividends to shareholders were suspended. Magrete noted that this strategy was costing her the most, and then Helmut, who had put forward the strategy. In the heat of the argument the board members had forgotten that Magrete and Helmut were financially taking the biggest hit. All of them understood that Magrete and Helmut had cast their votes with integrity.

George cooked dinner and afterwards he stayed up and listened to the radio, while Magrete and Ilse slept in his bed. At 11 pm he sidled in next to her on the opposite side to Ilse. He tucked his legs in behind hers and placed his arm around her waist. She patted his arm to acknowledge his presence, and they both slid into a deep sleep.

The next day they decided to go to the von Appen store in Alexanderplatz. Wherever they walked, Ilse was between them, and they each held one of her hands. Ilse would sometimes skip or jump in the air, and they would support her, as if they were the supports of a swing. They walked, talked, played, shopped and had a wonderful family day. On the way home, George carried Ilse on his shoulders, and when Ilse was sleepy he placed her thumb in her mouth to mimic a dummy.

George cooked dinner that night and after dinner Ilse went to bed. George and Magrete sat on his sofa. Magrete stroked the hair on the nape of George's neck, and kissed him tenderly. He undressed her and she undressed him. They consummated their family day together on the sofa, then lay naked side-by-side. It was nearly five years since Herbert had died, and Magrete realised that she and George had been romantically linked for the last eighteen months. As he stroked her breast with one hand, giving her the tingling sensation that hardened her nipples, he raised his head and said, 'Will you marry me?'

Magrete sat up quickly, nearly pushing him off the couch. He repeated: 'Will you marry me?'

'George,' she said, 'do you think this is the right time for us?'

'Magrete,' he replied, 'there's never a wrong time. When you nearly died, my soul shuddered. The times we live in are tragic enough with so much death around. To marry will mean that we can live under the one roof, and share the company of Anna and Ilse together. I want more days like today. Will you marry me? Say yes or I'll-' and Magrete started screeching softly because he was tickling her.

'Shh! Ilse!' Magrete pleaded and he stopped. 'Before I answer, you need to know more about me and after you know, I will not hold it against you if you withdraw that question. Will you promise to keep what I am about to tell you in strict confidence?'

He had never seen Magrete so serious. 'Of course,' George said, curious.

'I mean it, George, because it could badly affect the life of my child.'

'I promise. What is it?'

'I named my child Ilse after my grandmother, who was Jewish.' Magrete watched George closely, hoping the trust she placed in him was warranted.

'What's it with you Austrians – Aryan, non-Aryan, master race and all that! Will you marry me?'

Magrete kissed him and said yes and laid her head on his chest, very pleased with the outcome. She did not tell George about Anna or the fact they were related; that was not information he needed to know at this point in time.

'My favourite philosopher is Baruch Spinoza, a Jew,' George said. 'My favourite scientist is Albert Einstein, a Jew. My favourite composer is Franz Liszt, who had no qualms about teaching Hermann Cohen, a Jew. My favourite writer is Franz Kafka, a Jew. My favourite lover is Magrete, who has a grandmother who was Jewish. Lastly, my favourite child is Ilse-'

'I get it,' Magrete interrupted him. George made love to his favourite Jewess.

The next day Magrete, George and Ilse caught up with Helmut, Anna and Gertrude, who had been persuaded by Helmut to come.

'Magrete and I are getting married,' George said to the group.

'It's about time,' Helmut said. 'We were afraid that the war would be over before you two came to your senses.'

'All of you will have a role,' George informed. 'Helmut, I want you to be my best man. Anna, Magrete wants you to be her bridesmaid. Ilse is the flower girl and Gertrude, you'll give Magrete away. We'll have a civil wedding in a fortnight's time in Berlin.'

A fortnight later Magrete and George were married and George moved to Beelitz. To enable them to have a honeymoon together, Anna and Ilse stayed in George's apartment for a week. When they were reunited, Ilse was delighted she had a father, and Anna was pleased that they were married, and never thought of George again in a romantic sense.

Magrete looked radiant – but her period was late. She had been using the rhythm method in order to avoid pregnancy. She knew for it to be effective, they had to practice abstinence when she ovulated. Sometimes she lost count of the days, and she had been late on one previous occasion, that had not eventuated in a pregnancy, but this time Magrete was afraid that it would.

George, on the other hand, was concerned that the gypsy's prophecy was starting to be fulfilled – was he moving into Magrete's reality and away from Julia's? He scoffed at the idea, but a tinge of uncertainty lingered in his subconsciousness.

13

On Monday 11 October, Helmut took the train to Beelitz. Magrete was three months pregnant with a baby bump already evident. She met Helmut at the train station. 'Magrete.' Helmut greeted her as he always did, with a kiss on each cheek, and she responded in kind. 'How's the pregnancy going?'

Magrete locked her arm into his as they walked towards the house. 'Fine, but if anyone does the counting they will know I was pregnant one month before I married.'

'In today's age that's very disciplined!' Helmut laughed. 'A lot of women I know, aren't sure who the father is.'

Magrete smiled at him and hugged his arm a little harder. 'Let's not go to the house,' Helmut said. 'I need to talk to you alone. Let's have a chat on the park bench near the church – you know the one.

I need to speak to you about the company. Last week was a bad week. Both the Vienna and the Frankfurt stores were bombed out of existence.'

Magrete was shocked. 'How many died?' she enquired, turning to him with her eyes welling. She knew that Mimi would write to her and give her a full account of the Vienna store, as they were trying to be in monthly contact.

'At last count, 150 people died in Frankfurt and 40 in Vienna. Most of the people in the Frankfurt store died because of the subsequent fire. Apparently the Vienna store had a much better air raid shelter and so fewer people died. Nevertheless, this will have an enormous impact on the company, although we won't have to pay rent to the Reich Security Main Office for these premises, as our lease agreement states that they must provide workable premises. We'll still have to pay rent for Dresden.'

They had arrived at the park bench, and Magrete sat down with him. Helmut loved the church, which he had not seen for a while. He sat silent for a moment, and Magrete broke his reverie. 'With this pregnancy you know I have to resign as chairperson of the board of directors.'

'I figured you would,' Helmut said distractedly. 'I'll take your resignation back with me. And I'll appoint von Papen to the post.'

'Are you sure you want to do that? He argued against your strategy at the last meeting.'

'My mother used to say, keep your enemy as close to you as possible, so they have no room to move; give them freedom, and they'll cut you down in pieces.'

Magrete smiled. 'Your mother was a very wise woman.'

'She was,' Helmut said, reflecting on a past life. 'Anyway, von Papen won't be pleased that I intend in the not too distant future to sell all the company's properties, except for the department store in Berlin.'

'But Helmut, we are moving to Tailfingen and you are moving to Beelitz.'

Helmut took Magrete's shoulders in his hands and looked at her very seriously. 'Do you trust me?'

'You know I do,' Magrete said, looking back at him a little apprehensively.

'I want you to sell your shareholding in von Appen Pty Ltd to me.' Helmut gripped her shoulders harder.

Magrete could see he was under enormous strain. 'But-'

'What I'm about to do I really don't want you to know,' Helmut said, 'because sooner or later the authorities are going to come to you and ask you where I am.' Magrete had never seen him so intense. 'You cannot know any details at all. I'm dealing with one of the most dangerous and ruthless Nazis in the German Reich. Not even Himmler can gain access to Hitler without this man's approval. If I disappear, see that rock over there?' Magrete nodded. 'If I'm still alive, I'll try to leave a message under that rock letting you know.'

'I have a family, Helmut – people I do not want murdered for something you might do.' Magrete had tears in her eyes. Helmut wiped them gently away using his handkerchief.

'Please trust me,' Helmut said, this time more gently. 'Once you're no longer chairperson and have sold me all your shares in the company, anything that the company does is beyond your knowledge and control. Do you understand me?' Magrete nodded. 'So if you're asked, you'll say time and time again that you relinquished all of your shares and the chairperson position on the 11th of October 1943. Do you understand me?' Again, Magrete nodded. 'I've organised with von Appen Pty Ltd a three-year lease of the Tailfingen house for you in your name. That lease will be covered by part of the sale of your shares to me. Here is the lease. Sign it here and date it today.' He gave her a pen. 'I've also leased the house in Beelitz from von Appen Pty Ltd, in my name, for three years. In two months' time I'll give you a satchel containing a large sum of money from the sale of your shares.

It'll help you and your family in times of need. Here's the spare key for the satchel. Once you get the satchel, make sure you hide it and the key in different places. With George's salary, you should be able to live comfortably. If at any time you need money, you'll send me this envelope.'

Magrete fingered the envelope and looked at the address – it was Helmut's apartment, the one that had been sold to his Swiss lawyers. 'But this is just an empty envelope,' she said.

'If for some reason the letter is intercepted by Swiss or German Reich authorities or their agents, they'll understand it is a signal of some sort, but they won't know what the signal is, or who it came from since it has no return address. But I'm telling you too much. If you hear that Gertrude and I have disappeared, that must come as a shock to you. Under no circumstances – and I mean no circumstances – are you to write to the Swiss bank safety deposit company. Ever!'

They walked back to the house. Helmut saw Anna and greeted her. 'Anna, so glad to see you. Magrete is pregnant again, you must be pleased.'

Anna answered very politely, 'Yes, I am, Herr Gruen.'

'Can I stay the night?' Helmut asked Magrete.

'Of course! Anna, could you please put Ilse in your room tonight, and make-up the bedroom for Helmut.'

'Yes, ma'am.' Anna turned and left them.

'It's been a most taxing day for the two of us,' Helmut said, looking like a huge weight had been lifted from his shoulders. 'When will George be home?'

'Usually at 7.30 pm, if the line is operating,' Magrete replied, pleased at the return of the Helmut she knew.

'I'd put that key in a very secure place,' Helmut softly advised her. Magrete placed the key in her bodice and he smiled.

'I trust you with my life, Helmut. Thank you for what you are doing for my family. Take care, for I need to see you again.'

Helmut came closer, kissed her on her lips and whispered, 'If I was so inclined, and I'm not, I would have married you!' He could have not given Magrete a nicer compliment, and she beamed at him.

When George came home he was surprised and delighted that Helmut was staying the night. They talked about the current state of the war, which bored Anna and Magrete. Later that night Magrete slipped into Helmut's bedroom and left her resignation on his bed. When she woke in the morning both George and Helmut had left for Berlin.

14

George approached Otto Hahn and requested that his group be allowed to spearhead the preparation of the woollen textile mill in Tailfingen for the eventual shift of the Institute from Berlin to Tailfingen. He informed Hahn that his wife had signed a three-year lease in October 1943 for a house in Tailfingen, which he would like to take up in early December. His wife would be four months pregnant at that time and so the journey would be far easier for her. Also, it would mean they could have Christmas and New Year celebrations in a safer environment for the family, as Tailfingen had never been subjected to an air raid. Hahn agreed that 12 December would be ideal. It was also agreed that members of his group would stay in rented accommodation until the Institute could secure long-term leases.

Magrete was delighted that they were making the move before Christmas. She contacted Helmut, who invited them to stay in his accommodation with Gertrude from 10 to 12 December. However, he made one unusual request – he wanted Anna to remain in Beelitz until the morning of 11 December, so she could personally hand over the keys of the Beelitz house to him and deliver to Magrete a satchel. Anna could travel to Berlin on the morning of the 11th, and they all could travel to Tailfingen on the 12th. George thought this arrangement unsuitable, but Magrete overruled him and said that one more day in Beelitz would not harm Anna.

Anna said goodbye to Magrete, George and Ilse at the Beelitz railway station as they headed to Berlin. On the way back from the station she recognised Franz Stopper. Franz was nearly five years younger than her. Whenever Anna promenaded with Ilse on the main street of Beelitz, Franz would stare at her unabashedly. He would turn seventeen in January and so be conscripted. She knew his family history: they were poor; his father had died when Franz was ten and his mother when he was fourteen; he had worked on local farms from the time he was thirteen; he lived in an isolated room behind the hotel. Anna looked over her shoulder, directly at him, and he blushed. Anna loved the power she had over that boy!

Anna arrived to an empty house. She had a long bath then walked naked to her bedroom to inspect her body. Anna liked the way yoga was shaping her. She decided to wear a long dress, no underwear, socks and flat shoes. The dress made her look respectable, because the bodice was not too tight.

At lunchtime Anna was not hungry, and so she ate little. She made herself tea and thought about Tailfingen, and about how living there might alter her life. She sat in front of the mirror brushing her hair slowly. She could see that her face and her body were slowly making the transition into womanhood. Magrete's close call with death had had a considerable impact on her – it sheeted home to her that life was fragile and temporary. She plucked and applied a pencil to her eyebrows, and shaded her lips ever so lightly. The day disappeared quickly due to Anna's total concentration on herself. She lightly perfumed behind each ear and the nape of her neck. She placed three large boiling pots of hot water in the bathroom. Anna was ready, but how it would end she did not know.

It was dark outside as winter descended on the village, and she was cold because of the lack of clothes she was wearing. She rode her bicycle to the hotel and knocked on Franz Stopper's door. He opened it, and she stumbled forward clutching her knee. 'I fell off the bike!'

'Miss Schuster! My name is Franz. Can I fetch you a doctor?'

'No, it wasn't that severe. It was slippery, because of the black ice, and I fell off my bike and hurt my knee.'

Anna hobbled inside the room. Franz was clearly on his way to bed, and was shirtless. Anna looked at his stomach muscles and knew how hard this boy worked on the farms. 'Could you please shut the door for a moment? The breeze is making me very cold.' Franz immediately closed the door. 'Can I sit somewhere?' Anna asked. 'My knee hurts.' Franz immediately bent down and lifted her as if she was weightless and placed her on his bed, as there was no other furniture in the room. 'Could you wet this handkerchief and bring it back to me?' Franz immediately took her silk handkerchief, wet it in a tub and gave it to her.

Anna could see his pants starting to bulge. She slowly raised her dress and carefully wiped her knee with her handkerchief. From Franz's view her leg was perfectly shaped. She tried to stand-up but fell back onto the bed. 'Could you lift me, so I can try to see if my other leg can support me?'

Franz placed his arm around her waist to lift her. He could feel her hardened nipple on his bare chest – it made him feel weak. Anna hopped once, then twice, and Franz felt with each hop her nipple rubbing up and down against his bare chest, which made him feel weaker still. Then she unexpectedly lurched back and both fell on the bed.

Anna immediately kissed him, opened the fly of his pants and gently massaged the bulge in his underwear. He was so dizzy with desire he could not remember how he became naked. She rolled him on his back, lifted her dress and straddled him, still wearing her socks and shoes. She moved herself up and down the length of his penis to sense its thickness and size. As she brought her lips to his, he responded by frantically kissing her. She felt the top of his penis with her hand and gently guided it into her. He felt her hardened nipples and groaned as he broke through her membrane. She gasped and now moved up and down, with Franz supporting her with his hands under her rear.

Just as Franz was beginning to become more frenzied, Anna pulled free of him, wiped his penis with her wet handkerchief and placed his hand on it. His eyes were tightly shut and his past habits were now controlling him. She withdrew without him noticing, as he was now fixated on his own climax. Anna quietly moved to the door, pulling her dress down, her eyes never leaving him. Franz, pumping himself harder and faster, fascinated her. She reached the door and witnessed his eruption, which splattered and cascaded over his bloodied pelvis. Anna quietly let herself out, and cycled home as fast as she could.

Anna hid her bike in the hallway, and in complete darkness placed the hot water from the three pots into a bath. She shed her dress, socks and shoes; she could feel that her upper thighs were bloodied. She ignored the soft knocks on her door. As she washed her soiled dress in the bath she could hear a boy's voice whispering at the bathroom window: 'Anna! Anna! It's Franz.'

As Anna lay in bed, she recycled the events of the night in her mind at least a dozen times. She was glad she understood the mechanics of love before her death.

In the morning Anna saw Franz at her front door, but refused to answer his pleas to see her. She ironed her cleansed dress and smiled – not a spot of blood – and put her clean handkerchief inside her dress pocket for safekeeping.

At 9 am Helmut came, and she gave him the keys to the house. 'Anna,' Helmut said seriously, 'I want you to give this satchel to Magrete. It contains valuable company documents, so it's heavy. It's locked and Magrete has the key. Do not leave this satchel for one second. Guard it carefully. Do you understand me?' Anna nodded. 'Have a good trip,' he added.

Helmut watched as she got on the train, thinking, she has made the transition from a teenager to womanhood seamlessly.

15

The war had decimated Tailfingen's local textile industry, as raw materials were impossible to source from markets outside of the German Reich. The mills were now mostly abandoned, but their previous existence had left a mark on the town: it was covered with a thin film of coal dust, as coal had been the major source of energy. A train line connected Tailfingen to Ebingen, and from there to the rest of the world.

They arrived at number 1 Neuweilerstraße in mid-afternoon, exhausted and pulling a baggage cart from the train station. At the door Magrete said, 'Let us enter the Nagy family residence.' She placed the key in the lock and opened the door. Anna clapped as Magrete entered. They explored the house as a family unit. The downstairs featured a lounge room, dining room and kitchen, with a washing tub on the back porch and a clothesline stretched across the porch. The backyard was small, with an outside toilet, but big enough for Ilse to play in. Magrete noted that the stairs to the top rooms would be difficult for a pregnant woman. There were three large bedrooms, and a bathroom. The house could easily fit a family of six or seven, although only one bedroom was furnished. Magrete announced, 'Tonight George will sleep in the lounge room. Anna, Ilse and I will share the bed.'

Magrete then said to George, 'While I unpack, could you, Anna and Ilse go to the shops and buy some food for tonight?' Magrete opened several cupboards and added, 'We will also need three plates and three cups.' She watched them from the front window as they walked down the main street to the shops, Ilse in the middle, George on the roadside kerb holding Ilse's right hand and Anna on the other side holding Ilse's left.

Magrete quickly went into the lounge room. It has been definitely decorated by Helmut, she thought, because it has his signature all over it. The sofa faced the radio, with a small table in between. Beneath the lounge room window was a planter's box that would get direct sunlight and so could be used to grow herbs. In the left-hand corner was a 1930 Bosendorfer timber upright piano. She went over and fingered its keys. Helmut was a wonderful pianist, and his choice of piano showed not only musicality, but style. She opened the lid and carefully placed the satchel onto the muffler felt. She saw that Helmut had left the key on the music rack. Magrete closed the piano's keyboard cover and locked it. She believed the satchel was safe, because no one could play the piano without her knowledge.

The fireplace was small and there was a small-framed picture of Helmut on the mantelpiece. It was slightly dusty, as was the whole house. Anna and she would rectify that situation in the coming weeks. As Magrete was unpacking the case containing all of their books, she reflected on the German Reich's education system. Under the Nazis, biology centred on the study of the different races to prove racial superiority was scientifically valid. Such instruction began with the first class in primary school. Hitler had decreed that no boy or girl should leave school without complete knowledge of the necessity and meaning of blood purity. How sad, she thought, that the minds of the innocent were contaminated by the thoughts of the demented few! What disgusted her further was that young girls were groomed for a life of servitude, limited to the roles of wife and mother. In the subject of Eugenics, the focus was to teach girls the characteristics to look for in a perfect husband, and to never entertain the concept of an interracial marriage. Magrete was determined to delay Ilse's formal education for as long as she could.

'We're back!' George announced. 'I love this town. If you just look at the scenery and not at the filth on the buildings, it's prettier than Beelitz-'

'Mummy, mummy!' Ilse interrupted her stepfather, 'I saw a lion!'

Magrete enquired, 'A lion?'

'She saw a rough collie,' Anna explained.

'A Scottish dog in Tailfingen! I love this village already,' Magrete said.

On this same day Hitler sent General Rommel to mobilise forces along the French coast, in order to defend it against the anticipated Allied invasion.

16

Since they arrived in Tailfingen, George and his team had been exceptionally busy cleaning out the Grotz textile mill, the new home for the Kaiser Wilhelm Institute for Chemistry. They were restructuring various rooms into offices and research laboratories in preparation for the Institute's relocation. George's day began at 7 am and ended at 9 pm, so he rarely ate with his family, eating with his colleagues instead.

Anna and Magrete were forensically cleaning every room as well as receiving furniture that had been shipped from Beelitz and Berlin. Magrete was especially happy to receive George's Brunswick Panatrope record player and long-playing records. She placed the record player beside the radio cabinet, then glanced at the mantlepiece: Helmut's photograph might be problematic, she thought, and so she destroyed it. While Magrete and Anna were busy, Ilse would play in the backyard on her own whenever the weather permitted.

The week before Christmas, George decided to invite his three scientific colleagues to Christmas Eve celebrations in their house. He did so because those who were married had families living in Berlin, waiting for more appropriate accommodation than the present housing: a single room in a boarding house.

Magrete spoke to Anna alone in Anna's bedroom. 'Anna, George wants a Christmas celebration. I will cancel it, if you feel uncomfortable. You are so important to me that this celebration is really meaningless without your blessing.'

'We Jews get blamed for an event we don't even believe in,' Anna whispered, 'and yet for you Christians, Christmas seems to be a happy and festive event. I've never experienced it and I'm intrigued. Please let me be a part of the celebration.' Hmm, Magrete thought, maybe Ester did not tell her that we are related?

Christmas Eve in 1943 landed on a Friday. The celebration meant extra food had to be sourced as well as Christmas items such as tinsel, a Tannenbaum (Christmas tree), candles, confectionery and small gifts. George's salary and the family rations were insufficient for these extra goods, so Magrete took some money from the satchel. She knew that the piano would be used on Christmas Eve, so she removed the satchel and placed it under Ilse's bed, just for this one occasion.

George always seemed to be able to source bottles of Egri Bikavér red wine when needed. Magrete wondered whether George was getting regular wine supplies as a kickback for the farm he had sold to his extended family. She suddenly realised that George never talked about his extended family at all – a subject for another day, she mused.

It was decided that Magrete and George would do the cooking on the morning of Christmas Eve, and Anna and Ilse would be responsible for decorating the Christmas tree and the wrapping of all presents, except their own.

George led a Hungarian team of three: Dr Frank Bacskay, Dr Attila Pulay and Dr Mark Czár. The latter two were close in age to George, and married with children. Only Frank Bacskay was close to Anna's age, being five years older than Anna's real age, and single.

Magrete thought him attractive. There was never any intention to try to match-make the pair, but the thought had crossed the minds of both George and Magrete, without it getting close to a conversation between them.

The Christmas tree was delivered on the morning of their celebration, and was placed in a tub and positioned near the record player. Anna was showing Ilse how to make small white packages containing sweets. She cut a crepe paper sheet into small rectangles, then cut the crepe at the ends of each into a wide fringe. She'd roll a sweet up in the paper, and twist both ends. It would then be hung by one end from the Christmas tree, using a loop of white woollen string. Ilse loved these decorations. She realised she would be the major beneficiary of their work.

In preparation for cooking the meals, Magrete had started to make contacts with the local farmers and, in particular, with a woman name Julianna Gross, whose husband Michael Gross was the ex-mayor of Tailfingen. Once the Nazis seized power they had dismissed the mayor from his office, because he was deeply involved with the Social Democrats and therefore supported the Weimar Republic. Magrete had sourced a large goose and other items for the Christmas Eve dinner from Julianna Gross for a fair price.

George rubbed the goose inside and out with salt, pepper and mugwort. He stuffed it with one pound of chopped apples and one pound of peeled and chopped onions and a good portion of sagebrush. He placed the goose in a large saucepan, added some water, placed the covered pot in the oven on high heat and regularly checked the roast. After one hour, he carefully took out the goose and put it aside, and drained and kept the broth with the extruded goose fat. Next, he put the rest of the finely cut apples, chopped onion, peeled carrot and chopped celery into the pot. He added half of the meat broth, and red wine, placed the goose back into the pot, covered it, and placed it in the oven again. He left it for three hours on a low heat, regularly checking and basting the goose with broth from the bottom of the pot. After three hours, it was nearly done.

George carefully put the goose aside, strained the liquid from the pot through a sieve and put it in a smaller pot on the stove. He put the goose back into the large roasting pan in a moderate oven, to crisp its skin. Meanwhile, he used the liquid to make a sauce.

Magrete had made simple salzkartoffeln (salted potatoes) and rotkraut (red cabbage) packed with chestnuts. The goose was ready to be served on a big plate; George would carve it at the table. The potatoes, red cabbage and chestnut sauce would be served on the side of each plate.

On the previous night Magrete had begun making lebkuchen, a gingerbread containing molasses, spices, almonds and peel. She covered the dough and chilled it overnight. On Christmas Eve she rolled the dough out, cut it into rectangles and baked it. She brushed each one with a lemon glaze while they were still warm.

As Magrete was setting the table, Ilse called out, 'Mum, Mum, come quick! Dad's putting the decoration on top of the tree.' Magrete grabbed Ilse's hand as they reached into the lounge room, there stood the most beautiful Christmas tree she had ever seen: candles lit in safe places on branches, white crepe pocket lollies with the tops and tails slit to give the tree a dusted snowflake feel, and silver tinsels dripping down like vertical striations punctuating the vision with a droplet sensation of winter. It was Christmas in snow but with a difference - it had a spiritual undercurrent that Magrete immediately detected - the holistic view of the tree embedded in the spirit of a holy night.

'I sat the crucifixion decoration on the crown of that tree, so without me this tree would be nothing,' George bragged.

Magrete ignored him. She went to Anna and said, 'You have given us a glimpse into your soul.' Then she looked at Ilse and said, 'Anna has taught you a lot.'

'That's why I think Anna is beautiful, Mum,' Ilse said without hesitation.

Magrete said to Ilse, 'I know you will be just like Anna when you grow older!' Anna beamed at Magrete and lifted Ilse, hugged her, kissed her and then put her down. Magrete hugged Anna and gave her a cheeky slap on the rear. 'There is one last job for the two of you: bring down the presents and put them under the tree. You will find both of your wrapped presents in my room – no peeking!' Ilse, with Anna in the rear, bolted up the stairs.

The doorbell rang. George answered it and ushered the three guests into the lounge room. 'Of course, you know Magrete,' George said to his colleagues. 'Where's Anna?'

'Upstairs with Ilse,' Magrete answered.

'This is a magnificently decorated Christmas tree,' Frank said. 'War or no war, it's the best Christmas tree I've seen in a long time.' The other two guests agreed.

At that point Anna and Ilse entered the room, nodded to the guests and placed the presents under the tree. 'Let me introduce you to the creators of the tree,' George said. 'Ilse and her teacher Anna.' Both Anna and Ilse nodded to each person as they were introduced to them individually. Frank, in particular, was attracted to Anna, finding her very beautiful. Anna noted his fascination, but tried not to acknowledge it.

'Today I'd like to sing a few Christmas songs before we eat,' George informed his guests. 'Magrete will accompany us on the upright.' George organised them into a semi-circle with Anna and Ilse in the middle. Magrete began with 'Stille Nacht (Silent Night)'. All of them sang except for Anna. She just looked at the Christmas tree, hoping that no one would notice. They sang 'O Tannenbaum (Oh Christmas Tree)', followed by 'Weiße Weihnacht (White Christmas)' and ending with 'Alle Jahre Wieder (Every Year Again)'. Magrete ran her finger from one end of the keyboard to the other to announce the end of the singing session and the start of dinner. All the men cheered: 'Bravo, Magrete! Bravo!'

'Magrete,' George instructed, 'you sit at head of the table and Ilse, you sit beside your Mum. Anna, you sit at the opposite end. Frank and I'll sit on either side of Anna, and Attila and Mark on either side of Magrete. This is the year of the female!' They all laughed. You are clever George, Magrete thought, wondering if this was a matchmaking attempt.

George and Magrete disappeared into the kitchen. Magrete appeared first with the vegetable platter and George followed her with the goose sitting high on the platter. The three guests gasped and broke into applause. As Magrete sat down, George carved the goose expertly and in generous proportions and served each guest. He left the table to go to the kitchen and returned with a crystal decanter containing red wine.

Frank immediately asked, 'George, this is not your Egri Bikavér red wine?'

'Nothing but the best for my fellow Hungarians!' George poured each guest a glass of red wine. Magrete stroked her stomach to remind him she was pregnant and so not interested, and Anna politely shook her head. Both had a glass of water by the side of their plate.

George stood up, raising his glass to the ceiling, and made a toast. 'To Christmas of 1943!' Everyone stood up and raised their glasses, echoing his words, with Ilse making the loudest toast.

The conversations ranged from Magrete's pregnancy to the fate of the Institute. However, what captured everybody's attention was a revelation from Mark Czár. 'My cousin wrote to me the other day about a comrade of his, Luftwaffe Oberleutnant Franz Stigler. He's a fighter ace with some twenty-two victories. On December 20th he was engaged in a dogfight and downed a spitfire and was about to attack an American B-17 bomber when he noticed that it was severely damaged. He declined to shoot it down and instead escorted it until it left German Reich airspace. His other comrades were shocked and reported it to their commander. The commander commended him on his chivalrous action. It's wonderful that amongst the many barbarous acts of war, there still can be acts of decency near Christmas.' They all agreed.

After dinner, Magrete and Anna brought in the lebkuchen and ersatz coffee. All praised the cake, which was delicious. Then each guest was given a small present, a unique fountain pen. The guests were shocked and apologetic because George had made it clear to them that they were not allowed to bring presents. Ilse and Anna received beautiful dresses, George a new wallet and Magrete a special maternity dress.

After coffee Ilse said goodnight, as did Anna. After five minutes, Magrete said she needed to go upstairs to say goodnight to Ilse. George asked Magrete to say goodnight to Ilse for him.

As Magrete approached Anna's bedroom she could hear Ilse plead, 'Please don't cry, Anna. Please don't cry. Why are you upset?'

'Anna,' Magrete said softly, 'what is wrong?'

'Nothing, ma'am. Really, nothing. I'll be alright in a minute or two.' Anna was sitting on the side of her bed, her face cupped in her hands.

'Ilse, please sleep in my bed tonight,' Magrete said. 'Anna and I need to talk.' Ilse grabbed her pillow and ran to her mother's bed. Magrete knelt in front of Anna. She placed one hand on Anna's shoulders and gently lifted Anna's chin so their faces were aligned. 'You miss your family?'

Anna nodded. 'We don't celebrate Christmas as such,' she said, very quietly, knowing it was important for her not to be overheard. 'At this time of year we celebrate Hanukkah. We light one candle on the menorah each night. We play games and exchange gifts-' Here she dissolved into quiet sobs.

Magrete sat on the bed beside her, hugged her, allowing Anna's tears to fall on her. 'Anna,' Magrete said softly in her ear, 'I will make this promise to you. I want you to listen to me carefully. I do not make promises lightly but when I do, neither heaven nor hell will move me from my promise. This war will be over and when the Allies win I promise you that George, Ilse, this new one and me will celebrate Hanukkah with you. Do you hear me?' Magrete drew back slightly, and her blue eyes locked deeply into Anna's hazel ones. Anna hugged her, still crying.

Magrete helped Anna to undress and tucked her into bed, saying, 'Do not worry about the guests. I will tell them you have a migraine. And Anna, never address me as "ma'am" again. From now, no matter who is in the room, you will address me as Magrete.' As Magrete turned off the light and shut the door, Anna silently sobbed for her vanquished family. When she was calmer, she realised that this was the second time Magrete had mentioned the defeat of the German Reich.

When Magrete entered the lounge room, she saw the four men listening to the news on the radio. The newsreader announced that the British destroyer Hurricane had been torpedoed in the Atlantic Ocean by the German Reich submarine U-415 and the American destroyer USS Leary had been torpedoed and sunk in the Atlantic Ocean by the German Reich submarine U-275. The war was far from over, thought Magrete.

George turned to Magrete. 'Is Anna alright?'

'With all the excitement of decorating the Christmas tree, Anna is suffering a migraine.'

'Sorry to hear that,' Frank said.

After talking for another hour about the war and the future of the Institute, George's colleagues departed. Magrete held onto George's arm and leaned her head on his shoulder as they slowly made their way up the stairway to their bedroom. 'It was a wonderful Christmas celebration,' George said. 'Good food, good company, a beautifully decorated tree. If only we had peace!'

'If only,' Magrete agreed. 'Oh, by the way, we are sharing our bed tonight with Ilse. Anna needs to be on her own.'

'Well, then ... Ilse's arm will be wrapped around my neck, and so, one, I'll be terrified to move; two, I'll have her breathing in my ear all night; and three, you'll be fast asleep, with no cares in the world, snoring!'

'I do not snore!' Magrete declared indignantly.

'Yes, you do,' George assured her. Magrete hit him softly on the back of his shoulders as they entered their bedroom.

On Christmas Day on the eastern front, the 19th Panzer division was fighting for their lives. General Balck who was at his makeshift headquarters and who was responsible for the operation decided he was unable to defend the division, even if it meant its total elimination. After nearly a six-hour wait, he was informed that the Panzer division was withdrawing west, in tolerable order. He was relieved, thanking God for their survival.

17

By early February 1944, Magrete was six months pregnant and feeling it. Anna was looking after the house and Ilse, as well as doing the shopping. George was coming home earlier and having dinner with the family on a more regular basis. Whenever he was home he would do the cooking, with Anna as his assistant. Anna was looking radiant and at twenty-two, her figure was taut and shapely. On occasions when Ilse, Anna and George did the shopping together, Magrete thought Anna and George looked like the perfect couple, even though George was fourteen years Anna's senior. On occasions, all three of them would laugh when some of the town folk addressed Anna as Frau Nagy. Magrete, hearing about these interactions, could see that George was flattered. Ego, thought Magrete, how predictable are men?

One morning, after they had completed their yoga exercises, when Ilse was in the backyard playing, Magrete approached Anna about her future prospects. 'Anna, I know I have said this to you before, but you are twenty-two this year and you have never introduced us to a boyfriend. You should go out a little more on your own.'

'It's a difficult time for women of my age,' Anna said. 'Most of the young men are off to war and when they return they're desperate for love, because they're scared they'll die soon. Other young women are married and pregnant. I don't want to be either.'

'I can understand that, but what about fun and companionship with women of your own age?'

'I've two difficulties,' Anna replied, lowering her voice. 'I'm Jewish and whoever I make friends with needs to know it and not be ashamed of what I am.'

Magrete stopped towelling her hair and smiled at Anna and said, 'How stupid of me? When George asked me to marry him, I refused to give him an answer until he knew all of my secrets.'

Anna immediately enquired, 'And they are?'

'There are some secrets you tell your girlfriends,' Magrete answered, 'and there are others so deeply buried that only a husband deserves to fret over them.'

At midday Anna and Magrete were shocked to find George home. 'The Kaiser Wilhelm Institute has been completely destroyed in a bombing raid, and Magrete, the big news of the day is that the von Appen department store in Alexanderplatz has also been completely destroyed, with over two hundred people dead or missing.'

Magrete collapsed onto a chair. 'What about Helmut?'

Anna sat down on the arm of Magrete's chair, with her arm around Magrete's shoulders. 'Was Gertrude there?'

'I don't know. The reports have only just come in. I'll need to go to Berlin tomorrow and meet with Hahn and after that I'll make enquiries about Helmut and Gertrude. As you can imagine, everything is in great disarray at the moment.'

'That will not do!' Magrete said forcefully. 'I will come with you and while you are with Hahn, I will search for Gertrude and Helmut.'

'But you're six months pregnant, and travel will be difficult,' George pleaded.

'I could not care less George, if I was nine months pregnant. Now, listen to me: I was the chairperson of von Appen Pty Ltd, and I have far more authority with that company than you realise, George. If I demand to know what has happened to Helmut and Gertrude, then the company directors, or what is left of the company management, will jump at my request and give me all the information they have. Anna, pack our bags. George and I will be leaving tomorrow for Berlin.'

The tone of Magrete's voice left no room for argument and Anna automatically said, 'Yes, ma'am.' When Magrete looked at her sharply, Anna corrected herself and said: 'Yes, Magrete.'

George went back to work. Anna packed most of George's suitcase and all of Magrete's. Magrete collected Ilse from the yard and then slumped in the armchair in deep thought.

At dinner Magrete said to Anna, 'It might take us several days to clear up this mess, so George and I will stay in Helmut's accommodation in Beelitz. We should be home in four days at the most.' Anna nodded. Magrete was clearly not in the mood for idle chatter.

18

They arrived at the Berlin Bahnhof two days after the bombing. Magrete left George and immediately proceeded to Alexanderplatz. George headed to Dahlem with their luggage. Magrete's plan was to get in contact with Ernst von Papen, who had taken over the chairmanship of the board of directors. In the meantime, she decided to go to the department store and see first-hand what damage had occurred.

When Magrete arrived she saw that the site had been cordoned off and a retrieval operation was in progress. It would be impossible to gain closer access, because the Berlin Ordnungspolizei (Berlin regular police) were keeping spectators and family members of missing persons at bay. Women were wailing and some older men sat on the pavement in a daze. When a stretcher was brought to the surface, hundreds of spectators would try to find out who had been retrieved, placing the police operation under severe stress.

Magrete saw Ernst von Papen talking to the rescue service personnel. 'Ernst! Ernst!' She shouted so loud that some of the retrieval personnel stopped to search for who was shouting. Ernst von Papen turned and immediately motioned to police to let Magrete through the cordon.

Breathless, Magrete enquired, 'Is Helmut okay?'

'I don't know,' von Papen said, looking baffled. 'He left the office and Berlin a fortnight before the bombing, and so we know he's not a victim of this tragedy. However, a fortnight is a long time for the head of a company to go missing, so the two senior executives who ran the German and non-German divisions got in contact with me two days before the bombing, and asked if I knew of his whereabouts. Both of them died in this tragedy-' Von Papen stumbled and Magrete quickly supported him. He wiped tears from his eyes. 'All of the senior management of the German division are dead, because none made it to the bomb shelter in the basement. They first rescued all those who survived. They're now retrieving the dead bodies.'

Magrete asked, 'Is Helmut or his housekeeper Gertrude in Beelitz?'

'I went to Beelitz two days ago, but the house was locked and the pastor at the local church had not seen him or Gertrude for the past fortnight. By the way, much to the consternation of the board, Helmut elevated Gertrude to be his executive assistant and effectively shifted her salary from his pocket onto the company.'

'Have he or Gertrude been drawing on their salaries?'

'That's a good point, Magrete, which I haven't investigated. With this tragedy evaporating our senior management, and with Helmut missing, the company is in chaos.'

Magrete decided to take another tack. 'What was the last brief that Helmut told the board he was working on?'

'He's been working with Argentinian and Brazilian companies to try to offload the properties we have left. I opposed this strategy, as you know. I thought he was stripping the company of all of its assets. But after this bombing I understand what he was doing. He'd figured out earlier than most of us that, in a war, trading becomes impossible, stock is depleted, and so there's little income. More importantly, one air raid can strip a company of all of its assets: sales, stock, property value and personnel-' As he said 'personnel' he broke down.

Magrete hugged him and whispered, 'Ernst, we are just ants on this battlefield.' He wept softly as she patted his shoulder.

Suddenly von Papen pulled away from her and asked, 'Are you pregnant?'

'I am, six months. My second husband, George Nagy, works for the Kaiser Wilhelm Institute for Chemistry. It was also severely damaged by the same air raid. Is it possible for us to stay in Helmut's place in Beelitz to work out this mess?'

'As a matter of fact ... before Helmut left on his latest assignment for the company he gave me the spare key to his house in Beelitz and said, "If Magrete comes to Berlin and I'm not here, please give her this." Strange, isn't it? It's almost like he had a premonition.' As he handed Magrete the key, she suddenly recalled her last meeting with Helmut.

Once in Beelitz, she went straight to the church grounds. She sat on the bench where they had sat the last time they met. As von Papen handed her the key, Helmut's words came flooding back to her: 'If ever I've disappeared and I'm still alive, see that rock over there...' She saw the rock. She moved off the bench and tried to budge it, but it would not move. Magrete looked around for a stick or anything that she might use as a lever to lift the rock and as she did a hand tapped her on the shoulder. She quickly turned to see a young uniformed soldier – Franz Stopper.

'Oh, you frightened me!'

'Sorry, I didn't mean to. My name is Franz-'

'Stopper,' Magrete interrupted him.

'Yes, ma'am,' Franz said respectfully.

'You look strapping in your uniform. When did you enlist?'

'I was conscripted just after your family left, ma'am, and I'll be leaving for the eastern front tomorrow. As you know, I've got no family. I was about to leave this letter at your old house, ma'am.' He gave Magrete a letter addressed to Anna. 'And as I have no family I was wondering if I can make Anna my next-of-kin so that if anything happens to me during the war, someone on this Earth will know. I need to know her surname and her current address.'

Magrete scrutinised him carefully. Giving Anna's surname and address should not be Magrete's decision … but he should have somebody who cares what might happen to him. 'Her name is Anna Schuster and if you have a pen and paper-' She took the pen and paper he held out to her and wrote down Anna's name and address.

Cupping her earlobe with her right hand Magrete said, 'Now, I have a job for you. I lost my earring and it fell under the edge of that rock over there. As you can see, I am pregnant and cannot shift it. I wonder if you could lift it for me.'

Franz strained and lifted the rock with his eyes closed and Magrete saw a small cloth bag, which she snatched. She quickly tucked it under one armpit.

'Got it!' she said, cupping her right hand to her earlobe once more as if she was reinstating a lost earring. 'Thank you, Franz!' Franz saluted her and moved away, heading toward the station. Magrete transferred the small bag to her handbag.

On reaching her old home, she moved into the lounge room. She turned the letter Franz had written to Anna over in her hands.

She knew it was a love letter, and could not believe Anna had not confided in her a love interest. Magrete placed the unopened letter in her handbag. She retrieved the cloth bag and saw inside it a letter addressed to her. It was not dated.

Dear Magrete,

Both Gertrude and I are safe and in hiding. The company will be in receivership within months if not in days. The debt it owes far exceeds the total income stream. The company has sold all of its property assets (except the Berlin store) to a foreign company, which is not aware of their latest acquisitions. There will be warrants for my arrest!

Remember, what I told you on the 11th of October last year. On that day, you resigned as chairperson of the board of directors and sold all of your shares in von Appen Pty Ltd to me and so you are totally unaware of any transactions past that date. I am relying on you to maintain that line to anyone who might ask about me, or my business activities. Don't make the mistake of trying to protect me by clamming up. Tell them all of the business activities you knew about because of your chairmanship. Forget what transpired between Peter, you and me at Wannsee. Those meetings NEVER happened and so should NEVER be mentioned!

Rumours of Gertrude's and my death will be swirling around. Ignore them! Only when you see both or either one of us in the morgue or in a grave can you believe that we're dead.

Destroy this letter as soon as you have read it.

Love,

Helmut

PS. Don't tell George or Anna about this letter. The more people who know that we are in contact, the more dangerous it will be for everyone.

Magrete put a match to the letter and placed it in an ashtray.

When it had burned to ashes, she emptied the ashtray into the kitchen bin.

George arrived at 7 pm. He told Magrete he needed to stay for at least another two days. There was little in the fridge that was edible and so she bought bread and cheese with little rations and money she had on her.

Magrete told him what von Papen had told her, namely that Gertrude had been made Helmut's executive assistant and that they were working on a commercial-in-confidence project for the company and so were not in Berlin when the store was bombed, but their whereabouts were unknown. She omitted her encounter with Franz Stopper.

'Gertrude is an executive assistant? That's hard to believe. I mean, does she have a formal education?'

'Not that I know of, but she is excellent at taking notes and arranging travel, that sort of thing,' Magrete said trying to shut down his line of enquiry.

Within four days they were back in Tailfingen. George had to source accommodation for Herr Göttel, Professor Strassmann, Dr Wittig and Professor Hahn and their families as well as the families of those already in Tailfingen.

On the morning following their return, Magrete met with Anna in Anna's bedroom. She told Anna that Gertrude and Helmut's whereabouts were unknown, but that they had not been in Berlin at the time of the bombing. Magrete then recounted her meeting in Beelitz.

'I ran into a young soldier, Franz Stopper-'

'Franz Stopper!'

'Yes,' Magrete said. 'Franz has no one, not one relative alive, and he asked me if he could make you his next of kin. He's been conscripted and was on his way to the eastern front.' Anna appeared enthralled with Magrete's account and at the same time anxious. 'I hope you do not mind, Anna, but I had to make a decision on the spot, a decision that was yours and not mine to make. I gave him your name and current address, so he could make you his next of kin. He wrote you this letter.' Anna snatched the letter from Magrete and checked that it was sealed.

'Anna, did I do the right thing?'

'I suppose so,' Anna said. Magrete could not gauge Anna's feelings from her tone.

Magrete left her to read the letter in private. Anna scrambled to open the letter and read it very slowly, several times over. It was the most beautiful letter she had ever read.

When Anna returned to the lounge room, she rushed over to Magrete and kissed and hugged her. 'You did the right thing by giving him my name and address. Thank you!' Seeing how happy Anna was, Magrete knew that Anna had received her first love letter.

19

On 19 March 1944 the German Reich troops Occupied Hungary, and on 22 March a new government was established under Prime Minister Dome Sztojay, formerly the Hungarian Minister in Berlin. When the Nazis Occupied Hungary, the deportation of the Jews to the death camps in Poland began. Adolf Eichmann and a group of SS officers arrived in Budapest to take charge of Jewish matters and ten days later anti-Jewish legislation was enacted, calling for the expropriation of Jewish property. Eichmann set in motion machinery to round-up and deport Hungarian Jews to extermination camps.

The invasion of Hungary had devastating consequences for George Nagy and even more so for Frank Bacskay, Attila Pulay and Mark Czár. All were working in a top scientific institution and on a top secret project – the separation of radioactive uranium from its other isotopes. The Nazis decided that the Hungarian scientists working on secret projects were potential security risks, especially because the Hungarian government had been playing each side – friend and foe alike – in a duplicitous manner. The fear was the Hungarians might leak the German Reich's nuclear program to other countries. Hahn was devastated, as the Hungarians were an integral part of his research program. He liked George in particular, because he had been instrumental in bringing the Institute to Tailfingen, but also his research team was making important inroads into the separation technique: they had decided to use centrifuges to make a gaseous separation of radioactive uranium-235. George alone had built the centrifuges and was now trying to find an appropriate chemical reaction to change the uranium ore into the gas phase. His research suggested fluoride compounds of uranium might be the right direction to take, but before he could test his ideas, the German Reich residencies for Frank Bacskay, Attila Pulay, and Mark Czár were revoked. They were single, or married to Hungarian wives. The German Reich officials wanted to deport George as well, but because Magrete's first husband, Herbert, was well-known to the upper echelons of the German Reich and, in particular, was a friend of Himmler, they decided that George could stay – but not at the Institute. Magrete's Nazi connections had saved them from deportation.

George no longer held a job and, more importantly, he was without a salary. Magrete subtly let it be known that she had an independent income, due to her first marriage to Herbert von Appen, a family well known throughout the district. George was annoyed by these rumours and understood he was now ensconced in Magrete's reality, which the gypsy had foretold.

Magrete was eight months pregnant, had a satchel full of money, but she was not sure how long it would last. She also had the empty, addressed envelope to send off if she was destitute, but she felt that her family at this juncture was not in that predicament.

The longer George was unemployed the more he enjoyed the company of Anna and Ilse, and the less he enjoyed Magrete's company. Magrete did not understand that Anna, George and Ilse had a common thread – Magrete was providing for them financially. George was annoyed by it, Anna accepted it, and Ilse was oblivious of it. Magrete noticed that George had lost all interest in cooking. Anna was a proficient but uninspiring cook, and with access to mainly rations and food stamps, a cook needed to be creative and inspiring. Magrete had to fill this breach and others that George had vacated.

It all came to a head on 24 April when Magrete found George drunk on the lounge room floor after Anna and Ilse had gone to bed. She was nine months pregnant, and angry. It appeared to her that his family had spoilt and pampered him, so that if he faced social hardships he would retreat and sulk rather than endure them or find solutions.

'What is wrong with you? And where are you getting all this alcohol from?' Magrete bent down, slapped him hard on the face to rouse him and then she tried to lift him off the floor. George pushed her away and Magrete lost her balance and fell hard, and felt the beginning of a contraction. Oh no, she thought, my water has broken, and he is drunk and Anna is fast asleep upstairs. George had collapsed back into his original position.

Magrete started to crawl to the staircase, was hit by another contraction, and rolled over, holding her pelvis. It is early days, she thought. But the contractions were not like her first experience of birth – they were happening at a much faster rate. She climbed on her hands and knees up one stair at a time. Another contraction hit, and she steadied herself against the newel, breathing deeply. 'Anna!' she shouted, but there was no response and so she kept on climbing, hoping she would not fall backwards for if she did, she feared for her child. The contractions were getting closer than before. 'Anna!' Magrete screamed and as she looked up Anna suddenly appeared.

'What's wrong?'

'I am having my child!'

Anna flew to her side, lifted her under her arms and supported her as they made their way to her bed. She laid Magrete down, putting a pillow behind her back.

Ilse woke and came into the room rubbing her eyes. 'What's wrong?'

Anna said, 'Your mother is having a baby! Get your father!'

Ilse ran downstairs and saw her Dad slumped on the floor. 'Dad! Dad!' she screamed, shaking him, but he would not wake-up. She ran back upstairs and said, 'Dad's asleep. He won't budge.'

Magrete was trying to regulate her breathing as Anna prepared for the birth. 'Stay with your Mum,' Anna said to Ilse. 'I need to put the kettle on.' As Anna rushed to the kitchen she saw George on the lounge room floor. When she leaned over him she smelt his breath, which stank of alcohol. She knew he was useless for tonight's events. As soon as the kettle boiled, she bolted back upstairs, noting that George was now lying in a puddle of vomit.

Seven hours later, Magrete birthed a baby girl. Ilse was shown into the room and introduced to her baby sister. The baby was cleaned-up, and Anna, Ilse and Magrete admired the new addition to the family. Ilse wanted to carry the baby, but Magrete and Anna told Ilse that the baby needed to sleep. George was still lying drunk on the lounge room floor, not knowing he had fathered a child.

The following morning when Anna went to the kitchen, George was asleep on the lounge room sofa, snoring loudly. She cleaned his vomit from the floor and retreated back to Magrete's bedroom.

Magrete was breastfeeding her child. 'Is George still asleep?'

'Snoring loudly,' Anna replied with a smile.

'You know,' Magrete said with some venom, 'if anything had happened to this child because of his drunkenness, I would never have forgiven him.'

'Nor I,' Anna said, sitting down on the edge of Magrete's bed.

'I'm so sorry!' Magrete and Anna looked up and saw George standing in the doorway. He started to beg Magrete to forgive him.

Anna silently left the room and shut the door behind her. In her bedroom, she found Ilse in a deep sleep with a smile on her face.

After George had been chastised and forgiven by Magrete, the newborn was named Elisabeth Anna Nagy. Her maiden name, Elisabeth, was George's mother's name or so he said. Anna was pleased with the child's middle name, but felt that George had lied that it was his mother's name. Although she could not recall his mother's name, she knew from a previous conversation it definitely was not Elisabeth.

George was now fearing that the past he left behind in Hungary might one day haunt him. The prophecy of the gipsy kept on resurfacing in his memory.

Eighteen days later, Operation Overlord (popularly known as D-day) was put into operation. Over 160,000 allied troops crossed the English Channel. The coastline of Normandy had initially been divided into seventeen sectors, with eight further sectors added when the invasion was extended to include Utah on the Cotentin Peninsula. The battle for Western Europe had now begun in earnest.

20

When Albert Speer publicly promised retribution with a secret weapon against the mass bombing of German Reich cities, the Americans were concerned that the German Reich's nuclear program was ahead of their own. However, what Speer was referring to was the V-2 rocket. On 20 June the Vergeltungswaffe (V-2 rocket – retribution weapon 2) became the first artificial object to cross the boundary of space with the vertical launch of MW 18014.

On that day Anna, Ilse and George went shopping for food staples, leaving Magrete and Elisabeth at home. The arrival of Elisabeth saw the dynamics of the household change significantly. Ilse did not want to move out of Anna's bedroom, but it was not possible to leave Elisabeth in a room on her own and so Elisabeth was placed in Anna's room. Initially, Magrete allowed Ilse to sleep in her bed, but George was getting very little sleep. Magrete put her foot down and left Ilse in Anna's bedroom and moved Elisabeth and Anna into the spare bedroom. That placated Ilse because now and then she could sneak into Anna's bed, unnoticed by Magrete since Magrete's bedroom was furthest from the other two, and at other times Ilse was beginning to accept that she was old enough to sleep alone.

George did not drink from the day of Elisabeth's birth. He was disgusted with himself and became once again the man Magrete had married: hard-working and domesticated. He took up all of his previous chores in the kitchen, and more. He helped clean the house and kept the grounds spotless.

Anna's focus was naturally drawn to Elisabeth, but Ilse rejected that notion and became even more obsessed with Anna. Magrete gladly spent more time with the baby than she had when Ilse was born and felt more motherly because of it.

When George, Anna and Ilse returned from shopping, Anna was very excited. 'I met Professor Hahn today, and he called me "madam". Such a nice person!'

'Mum, he lifted me and gave me a kiss on my forehead,' Ilse said, proud that she had met a very important scientist.

Magrete looked at George, wanting a more detailed explanation. 'I've got some good and bad news,' George said. 'Hahn wants me to lead a team consisting of Wolfgang and Erhardt to search for the uranium ore that was left behind in the rubble of the old Institute site in Dahlem. I shall stay in my old apartment. He's paying me an excellent salary. The downside is that it'll probably take us three to six months-'

'Six months!' Magrete interrupted him. 'That is a long time to be apart.'

'I can come back at least one weekend in every month,' George said.

'What happened to you being a security risk? Hungarian, and all that?'

'Since I won't be at the Institute, I won't know anything about any new developments in Hahn's research. My job is temporary, isolated to a bombed building site in Berlin, and what I'm doing is recovering materials, making the Berlin site safer for the public and providing a valuable resource for Hahn's research.'

'But six *months*!'

'It might end up being less, but that's the maximum time they've allowed for it.' George moved closer to Magrete. 'We can really use the money, especially now that there are five in the family.'

Anna smiled. 'It'd make our budget so much easier.'

'Okay,' Magrete conceded. 'But four women in one house without a man makes life very tedious.'

'Don't worry, Magrete,' Anna said. 'I'll just walk out, grab one of those farmer boys and chuck him in the house for us to devour.' Magrete smiled because she knew Anna was in correspondence with Franz Stopper. She wondered whether Anna had already done that to Franz.

Magrete enquired, 'When do you need to leave?'

'Provided that Anna doesn't lasso a farm boy into the house' – George smiled at Anna – 'in three days' time, on Friday the 23rd of June.'

Magrete looked at Anna and sighed. 'It looks like we are about to become a man-free zone, Anna.'

George left on Friday and the house felt empty without him. The chores were once again divided between Magrete and Anna, with Ilse now old enough to be given some domestic duties as well.

21

The week after George left for Berlin, Magrete, with Elisabeth on her hip, asked Anna to get a pound of butter and gave her their ration book. Ilse wanted to go with Anna, but Magrete knew that would only slow Anna's progress. When Anna left, Ilse watched from the window as Anna walked down the road. After about ten minutes she called out, 'Mum, mum! Here comes Anna! She's got the butter!'

Magrete looked out the window along Goethestraße and saw Anna waving to Ilse. She also saw a man approximately in his fifties cycling behind Anna, who then hopped off his bike and shoved Anna into the shrubs of a vacant block.

Magrete shouted, 'Look after Elisabeth!' and bolted out of the house towards the vacant block. When she reached it she saw that the man had one hand over Anna's mouth, and was trying to pull his penis out with the other hand. Magrete kicked him as hard as she could between his legs. He fell sideways, releasing Anna, and grabbed his crotch with both hands, groaning in pain. Magrete yanked Anna to her feet, grabbed the butter and told her to run back to the house. When she turned back to the man, she recognised him immediately: Michael Gross, ex-mayor of Tailfingen and husband of Julianna Gross. 'You filthy old bastard!' Magrete shouted, and, just for good measure, as he turned away, she placed her foot on his backside and shoved him as hard as she could, propelling him so hard that he hit his head on the base of a tree. She ran back to the house, hurried inside and locked the front door.

'Where is Anna?' she asked Ilse.

'In the bathroom.'

Magrete opened the bathroom door and saw Anna washing the area between her legs with a wet towel. 'Did he touch you, Anna?' she asked, concerned.

'No! Just thinking of that man groping me makes me want to vomit. What's wrong with that man?' Anna put on her underwear and straightened her dress.

'Perhaps he's senile,' Magrete suggested.

'That gives him no right-'

'I know,' Magrete said. 'We have to go to the police and report this. If we let it go, he will do it again to someone else. I know who he is - Michael Gross. He used to be the mayor of Tailfingen.'

'Do you think that's a good idea? I don't want to be the focus of attention,' Anna said and then lowered her voice. 'They might find out I'm Jewish.'

'Rubbish!' Magrete said decisively. 'One day he might do this to Ilse, or Elisabeth, or to you again! No, we must report it.'

Anna acquiesced, but asked Magrete to take the lead. She knew that Magrete's action would embolden her.

Magrete placed the butter in the cupboard, put Elisabeth in the pram and placed George's large rolling pin on top of the blanket. Anna held Ilse's hand, and they walked on the roadside with Magrete on the inside as they passed the vacant block on their way to the police station.

They arrived at the ordnungspolizei (order police) station at 5 pm. The policeman who stood at the front desk had a nameplate informing the public he was Fritz Hauptman. 'Good evening, ma'am,' Fritz said, addressing Magrete. 'How can I help you?' He did not lift his eyes from the report he was reading.

'Officer-'

'Just call me Fritz. This is Tailfingen, not Berlin!' He looked up and smiled at Magrete, then looked back to the report.

'Fritz, at approximately four thirty this afternoon, my governess, Anna Schuster, was sexually assaulted by Herr Michael Gross.'

'And who is Anna Schuster?'

'I am!' Anna said, angrily. 'He attacked me on that vacant block on Goethestraße.'

Fritz looked at her dismissively. 'Impossible, Anna, since he was here celebrating with us.'

'Nonsense!' Magrete said. 'He got off his bike, pushed Anna into the bushes, and physically assaulted her. I saw it! I am a witness!'

'So you say,' Fritz said coldly. His eyes went to Anna. 'If you were attacked, where are your bruises, young lady?'

'If it wasn't for Magrete I would have had plenty of bruises all over my body – if that's what you wanted!'

Fritz looked impassively at Anna. 'There's no evidence to show that you've been attacked, assaulted or hurt in any way. Michael Gross is fifty-six years old, hardly a strapping young man, and you two are accusing him of sexually assaulting a 20 something?'

'Believe me,' Anna said, 'he tried to hurt me! If it wasn't for Magrete, he would have!'

'There's no way Herr Gross-'

'Herr Gross,' Magrete interrupted him with a furious tone, 'is a sexual pervert! You have to arrest him! Look at my children! If you will not arrest him, they might one day be sexually assaulted by this pervert - '

'That's enough!' Fritz interrupted her. 'Frau Nagy-cum-von Appen, we know your type. We're simple alpine folk that you Berliners probably think are a little backward because we speak a little different. You come here and cause trouble. Let me say this to you, you Himmler-loving bitch: all the people here know about the von Appen empire and your place in it. We've read about you in the society pages; we see Peter, Herbert and Helmut promenading around here as if they own the town. Tailfingen is a Social Democrat haven, and you Nazis come here and try to frame the best mayor this city ever had.' Fritz paused trying to calm himself down.

'Let me make this clear to you,' Fritz continued but this time more calmer, 'tomorrow, if your Nazi friends came here and enquire about Michael Gross, there'll be four policemen who'll testify that we were having drinks with him on the eighth anniversary of him becoming mayor at exactly the same time you claim Anna was assaulted. Sure, we might get our hands slapped because your Nazi pals don't want you to lose face, but from that day on in this village no one will talk to you, sell anything to you, or help you. Do you understand me?'

Magrete shouted back at him. 'All I understand is that you are a fool! Come, Anna! This man will one day regret every single word he has uttered today.' Magrete stormed out of the police station with Anna and the children in tow. Fritz Hauptman was left feeling uneasy. Magrete had powerful friends. He hoped she would not destroy him just because he had lost his temper.

As they were walking back to the house Magrete reflected on the many times she had seen Julianna Gross with bruises on her arms or face. 'You know, Anna, I think Herr Gross has been hitting his wife for several months now.'

'That wouldn't surprise me,' Anna said. 'He's a pig of a man!'

'The other day, when I bought that chicken from Julianna, she was wearing a scarf,' Magrete reflected, 'and I could not see her face properly, but now that I think back, her left eye looked as if it was partly closed.'

'When he shoved me into the bushes,' Anna said, 'he did it so brutally that it stunned me.' But something Fritz had said was nagging at her. 'What's all this Nazi stuff?'

'Herbert!" Magrete sighed as she spoke his name. 'He was in the Nazi party and got on well with Himmler.'

'Talk about a pig,' Anna said, reflecting on Herbert, but Magrete thought her remark was directed at Himmler.

Ilse asked, 'Who's Himmler?'

'No one you need to know about,' Anna replied.

'If you ever see Michael Gross again, you need to take charge of the situation,' Magrete instructed her. 'Do not show him any fear and if he does approach you, and if you do not feel strong enough to defend yourself, move away from him confidently but quickly. From now on, Anna, you will never leave the house without taking Ilse with you. Men act differently when they see a woman with a small child.'

'Yes, take me!' Ilse begged, hugging Anna's arm.

The following day Magrete cycled out to the Gross farm, with George's large rolling pin in the front basket of her bike. Julianna was home, but her husband was in town, summoned by the police.

'Magrete, my husband is very angry with you and with the rumours you're spreading about him,' Julianna said, looking distraught.

Magrete saw that Julianna was still wearing her scarf. She put her bike on the stand, walked up to Julianna and whipped off the scarf. Julianna quickly cupped her hand over her face to hide a black eye and bruised cheek.

'If he ever does this to you again, you will come to my place and seek refuge. Do you understand me?' Julianna stood silent and motionless. Magrete moved to hug her and whispered in her ear, 'Your husband is not well. He would never have done this to you when he was the mayor of Tailfingen. You need protection.'

'Ever since our only son died on the eastern front,' Julianna said, 'he has become angry with everyone, but he is especially angry with Eastern European women. My son's death was at the hands of a Polish woman partisan.' Julianna started sobbing. 'He started hitting me six months ago. He gets blind drunk and lashes out. He's a good man but his hatred is eating him up.'

'Julianna, if he ever hurts you again, promise me you will come to my house and seek refuge. I do not want my favourite dealmaker becoming an invalid. Promise me!' Magrete entreated, and Julianna had no choice but to respond.

'I promise,' she said tearfully.

'Good!' Magrete gave her another hug. She rode back to home feeling a little relieved but still concerned about Julianna's well-being.

Between 25 and 30 June 1944 three divisions of the British 8th Corps counted more than 4,000 men killed, wounded, missing or captured. The German Reich losses were also heavy, but the Allied Operation Epsom remained a failure in a strategic sense: the Canadian and British troops progressed only 10 kilometres in five days, so the front was still not open and the situation remained extremely fluid – positions were captured, abandoned and then recaptured again.

22

Magrete had been in contact with her younger sister Mimi. The letters were irregular and often crossed paths. Some letters were not received at all, because the holding depot had been destroyed by Allied air raids. Mimi still had not acknowledged the birth of Elisabeth, but knew Magrete had married George Nagy, a development she welcomed. Though Magrete occasionally mentioned Anna in a letter, Mimi never acknowledged her existence. At first Magrete took it as a sign that Mimi thought servants or even a governess was beneath her. On reflection, Magrete could see a pattern emerging: whenever she mentioned Anna, Mimi's next letter would remind Magrete of the lovely times they had together as children, and how Mimi had adored her older sister – not the childhood Magrete remembered! It seemed that Mimi saw Anna as threat to her relationship with Magrete. Magrete decided to reassure Mimi in the next letter that she treasured their relationship.

Anna, Magrete noted, was also writing letters, not to a relative, but to Franz Stopper. The letters between them were even more irregular. Whenever Magrete handed Anna a letter from Franz, Anna would go to her bedroom for an hour or two. She would not allow even Ilse in the room. When Anna came out she would hand Magrete a letter to Franz Stopper for Magrete to post.

Ilse loved Elisabeth, so long as Anna doted on her and not on her sister. She loved to play with Elisabeth's soft toys, which were hung over the baby basket. Elisabeth would smile and try to grab them, but they were always beyond her reached and Ilse would giggle with delight, which would make Elisabeth giggle in unison with her sister.

George would stay the occasional weekend. When he arrived on a Friday, the whole house was energised. He heard about Michael Gross's attempted assault of Anna, and went to the police station himself to let Fritz Hauptman know in no uncertain terms that Professor Hahn was aware of the situation and if there was a repeat offense, Hahn would bring his considerable weight to bear on Albert Speer to ensure that the spouses of his staff were appropriately protected. Hauptman was feeling the pressure and conveyed this to Michael Gross.

On 1 and 2 July the 5th Division fought a series of intense battles against the Fifth Guards Russian Tank Army northwest of Minsk. The German Reich army was stalling for time so that the wounded and administrative personnel could be evacuated west along the railway lines. By the end of a week's fighting, the 5th Panzer, a supporting Tiger battalion and some smaller reinforcements had knocked out 295 Soviet armoured vehicles. Nevertheless, by 8 July all the Tigers were lost and the division was reduced from 125 tanks to eight. The division was outflanked to the south. The remaining panzers withdrew westward in order to regroup, and in doing so were forced to abandon comrades retiring toward Minsk from the Berezina. When the Fourth Army was permitted to retire west of the Berezina, there was almost nothing left to save. By the end of the operation, the German Reich army had lost 130,000 of its 165,000 men. Franz Stopper was one of them!

Anna received a death card informing her of his death some two weeks later. She was devastated. To give Anna time and space to get over her grief, Magrete moved Elisabeth from Anna's bedroom into her own.

'Anna.' Magrete gently knocked on Anna's bedroom door. 'Anna!' The door slowly opened. Magrete saw Anna going back to her bed and sitting on its edge. Magrete sat next to her and put her arm around Anna's shoulders. Anna leaned her head on Magrete's shoulder.

'I didn't know him for that long,' Anna sobbed, wiping her tears with her silk handkerchief, 'but I really got to know him through our letters. He was more like a younger brother to me than a lover. We both lost so much when we're so young. He had no one. At least I've an aunt in Berlin – if she is still alive. That's what we used to write to each other about, the memories of our families. Why him?' Anna broke down in a torrent of tears.

Magrete was stroking Anna's hair; she felt there was little that she could say. Finally, she said, 'War makes us all powerless, no matter who we are or how important we think we are. Those of us who survive will always feel guilty or lucky because of those we know who have died. But the memory of your connection with Franz will make you stronger and a better person.' Anna cried, clinging to Magrete. 'Lie down, Anna, and rest.' Magrete helped Anna undress and she lay down and was soon asleep, exhausted. Magrete shut the door silently, with tears in her eyes.

23

At 4:30 pm the next day there was a frantic knock on the door. Magrete looked out the window and saw Julianna. She opened the door, let her in and locked the door behind her. Julianna did not have to say a word – she had two black eyes, a bleeding lip and her nose bore traces of blood.

'I will only stay the night,' she said, 'if you promise that you'll not call a doctor nor summon the police. Promise me!'

Magrete looked at Julianna in dismay. Reluctantly, she said, 'I promise.'

She helped Julianna up the stairs and into her bedroom. 'Anna! Anna!' she called, and Anna appeared with Ilse. 'We have a crisis on our hands. Madam has fallen off her bike and hurt herself. Please get me a water basin, a wet towel, some dressings and lotion. Ilse, I will put you in Anna's room for the time being. Elisabeth and I will be sleeping in your room tonight, Ilse. Please sit down on the bed, Julianna.' Magrete helped Julianna remove her dress, shoes and socks, and laid her gently on the bed.

When Anna returned, both of them worked on Julianna, gently washing away the blood, applying the lotion to the cuts and abrasions on her face. Julianna slid into sleep as Magrete closed all the curtains in the room. Magrete shut the door behind her, and carried baby Elisabeth into Ilse's room for her afternoon nap. Ilse was happily transferring some of her clothes from her bedroom to Anna's, trying not to disturb Elisabeth.

When Anna and Magrete were in the bathroom putting away the lotion that Julianna did not require, Anna saw the anger in Magrete's eyes. 'That pig of a man,' Magrete said with venom. 'He is bashing his wife! Something has to be done about him. It is clear the police will do nothing. He needs to know there are dire consequences for his action.' Suddenly she turned to Anna. 'Stay here and look after Julianna and the children. I should be back in an hour or so.'

Anna now knew that Magrete had lied for Julianna's sake, and that Julianna had not fallen off her bike. Anna accompanied Magrete to the kitchen and watched Magrete go to the drawer and take out George's favourite rolling pin. It was solid and lengthy and had large handles. Rolling pin in hand, Magrete walked determinedly out of the house.

It was 6 pm when Magrete reached Gross' property. He was drunk, and she knew that would be to her advantage. He was in his middle fifties and, she reasoned, weaker because of his years. Gross saw a woman approaching him and eventually recognised Magrete. 'Ah, the bitch who's trying to besmirch my character and reputation.

Come here, pretty one, and get what you deserve.' He was shaking his crotch with both his hands over his lederhosen signifying what he had in store for her – a sexual assault.

When Magrete was almost within arm's reach, he heard and felt a whack, and fell to the ground, hurt. Michael Gross saw that Magrete was holding a rolling pin as if it was a baseball bat. Magrete grabbed him by the shoulder straps of his lederhosen and started to drag him along a dirt track. Gross tried to trip her. Whack! Whack! Whack! He sobered up quickly as her blows were hurting him. Gross threw a punch at her calf, and felt her buckle. He stood, so angry that he did not care that she was a woman and rushed at her, fists flying. Whack! Magrete hit him hard across the shoulders as she spun to position herself behind him. Gross collapsed on one knee. Magrete grabbed the shoulder straps again and managed to drag him along for another 10 metres before he regained his senses.

Gross was by now in fear for his life. If only I was twenty years younger, he thought; if only I was sober. He raised his fist and hit her as hard as he could in the stomach. Magrete stumbled to her knees. He rushed at her, hoping to disarm her, but she rolled just as he pounced and as she regained her feet – whack! This time she struck him as hard as she could across the kidney region. Gross was now completely at her mercy. She dragged him along in the same direction and when they had reached the apex of a small mound, she said to him menacingly, 'From now on, every time you hit your wife I will come looking for you.' She sat down behind him then raised her feet and smashed them into his back. He tumbled into a pigsty, and stayed there, too afraid to come out.

'This is where you belong, Herr Michael Gross, ex-mayor of Tailfingen. Even a pigsty is far too good for you!' Magrete placed the rolling pin in the basket of her bike and cycled back home, sore, angry but pleased.

Gross stayed in the pigsty until he could no longer see her. He slowly limped out, one hand to his back. He felt ashamed that a woman had dealt him so many blows and that he had not been able to defend himself. He realised how helpless Julianna must feel when he hit her in a drunken rage.

He walked into the barn, discarded his clothes, washed himself down and walked naked into the house. He decided to round-up the pigs after he had dressed and returned from Tailfingen. Gross wrote a letter to Julianna, signed it, then cycled to Magrete's house and quietly put it in her letterbox. He rode back to his farm.

His friend, Constable Fritz Hauptman, who was instructed by the local Nazi mayor to talk to him about the complaint Magrete and Anna had made, found his body later that day at the foot of a ledge. After noting where the body lay and where the pigs were grazing, Fritz concluded that Michael Gross had accidentally fallen off a ledge while herding pigs.

The funeral was held in the following week. Most of the townsfolk attended, including Magrete but not Anna. Anna resented the fact that Magrete attended.

Julianna wore a heavy black veil throughout the service. The eulogy spoke of Gross' great importance to the town, and to the people that he served as mayor.

After the funeral, Julianna walked back with Magrete to Neuweilerstraße. 'You know he wrote me a letter the night before he died,' she said.

'I did know. I saw him on his bicycle delivering it late on the day you came to our place. Anna told me she handed it to you.'

'He told me you visited him. I don't know what you said to him, but he wrote to me that after you left, he came to the realisation that the war had made him inhuman. In fact, he confessed he'd attacked three local women since our son's death. Two of the three, Hanna and Julia, are Polish women who married German men. Hanna attended the funeral today, possibly to reassure herself that he had died. Julia moved out of the district soon after he attacked her. He attacked Anna because he thought she was Polish.'

'Anna is Austrian. Her surname is Schuster.'

'I can forgive him for assaulting me – he was drunk, after all – but I can't forgive him for raping Hanna and Julia,' Julianna whispered.

'He confessed that he raped them?'

'War does strange things, it made him inhuman because of the lost of our only child,' Julianna said sadly. 'He told me he was going to commit suicide and make it look like an accident.'

'Suicide? I thought he slipped off a ledge while he was rounding up his pigs.'

'He wanted to be remembered for what he did for Tailfingen and not what he did to those Polish women. If it was known that he had committed suicide, the whole town would not have forgiven him, and we would not have had a church service.'

'Oh, I see.' They moved to the lounge room. Anna had made a pot of tea and sat with them as she served them.

Magrete enquired, 'Where are the girls, Anna?'

'Ilse is doing her reading and spelling exercises and Elisabeth is still sleeping. I call her the sleeping beauty, because she's the most docile child I've ever seen.'

Magrete turned to Julianna. 'What are you going to do now?'

'I've decided to live in Ebingen, where my sister lives. I'd feel guilty every time I see Hanna if I stay here. I hope to sell the farm, and the person who's expressed a firm interest in buying it is Fritz Hauptman. I don't trust him, even though he was a good friend of my husband. It might take a couple of weeks or so to sort it out.' Julianna paused, then seemed to suddenly have an idea. 'Could you look after the farm in the meantime? I can't pay you, but if you feed the horse, hens and pigs and milk the two cows, as payment you can take all the eggs the hens lay, keep the milk, and slaughter a pig. Will you do this for me?'

'It sounds like a fair deal. Although, Anna and I cannot stay there overnight, and so I cannot guarantee your animals will not be stolen, or that your home will not be broken into.'

'It's a risk that Fritz and I will have to take. Be careful of Fritz,' Julianna warned. 'He's getting pressure from above to leave the police force, and he blames you and your husband for it. He's got a lot of influence in this town. It wouldn't surprise me if you find certain shopkeepers telling you they're out of an item you need, even though they've ample in the back. This is a small town and everybody is into everyone else's business. People knew that Michael was hitting me, but they preferred to turn a blind eye. You're the only person who didn't. Thank you.'

Julianna stayed one more night and the next day, suitcase in hand, she left Tailfingen for Ebingen, never to return.

24

Three weeks after Magrete took possession of the farm, an attempt was made to assassinate Adolf Hitler by Claus von Stauffenberg and others within the German Reich military. At 12.42 pm on 20 July 1944, during a conference at the Wolf's Lair, a bomb that Stauffenberg had concealed inside a briefcase went off, killing a stenographer and leaving three officers near death. The others in the room, including Hitler himself, were wounded but survived. Stauffenberg flew to Berlin to carry out the next step of the military coup, but the plan stalled when he was unable to get confirmation that Hitler was dead. A radio broadcast at 6.30 pm reported that Hitler had survived and by the end of the day the coups d'état had failed and Hitler loyalists began arresting the conspirators.

At 9 pm that night, Magrete heard a knock on her front door – late for a visitor. She approached the front door apprehensively and asked, 'Who is it?'

The reply was not one she anticipated: 'Gertrude!' Magrete flung open the door and there stood Gertrude, propping up Helmut. She was about to help Gertrude by taking Helmut's other side when

Gertrude said, 'Don't, ma'am! He's been shot on that side.'

Magrete helped lay Helmut on the couch. He was semi-conscious. 'Wait here,' Magrete said. 'I need to get Anna.' She raced upstairs and knocked softly on Anna's door. 'Anna, come quick! Helmut's been shot, and he is downstairs with Gertrude.'

Anna followed Magrete to the lounge room, saw Gertrude and ran to give her a hug. Gertrude said, 'Not now, Anna, later!' She no longer seemed like the woman who had been terrified during a Berlin air raid.

Magrete asked, 'Where was he shot?'

'Right shoulder,' Gertrude answered without emotion.

Anna asked, 'What type of gun?'

'A Luger P.08 side-arm – one of these!' Gertrude pulled out the sidearm – too confidently, thought Magrete.

'We need to get him to a doctor, and quick,' Anna said.

'Anna, if we do, he'll be dead within a day or two at most,' Gertrude reasoned, 'and I will be shot even before then!'

'Anna,' Magrete said, 'get me a towel, hot water, a basin, some bandages, safety pins, balm, tweezers, scissors, a needle, a magnifying glass, thermometer, a bottle of gin, Elisabeth's rubber stick toy and animal twine.' Anna scribbled down what she remembered and showed the list to Magrete, who checked it and said, 'You have forgotten the magnifying glass.'

Magrete turned her attention to Helmut. 'Can you hear me?' There was no response. She took his pulse and noted it was weak. He now seemed unconscious.

'Gertrude, that gun is making me nervous. Put it on the table over there. Let us take off his coat and suit jacket. Now, help me roll him on his side so that his right shoulder is exposed. On the count of three: one, two, three!' Both women groaned as they moved Helmut into position. Helmut moaned, his eyes partially opened.

'Helmut, can you hear me? It is Magrete!' Helmut nodded weakly. 'Now, I am going to remove the bullet from your shoulder and as I am not a doctor, I will be probing far more than I should, which is going to hurt you a lot. We do not have sedatives or painkillers, so I am going to give you a rubber stick that you can bite into whenever you feel extreme pain.'

Anna brought over a box containing all the items Magrete had requested. 'Helmut, here is the stick. Grip it! Good!' Magrete gave Gertrude the scissors and asked her to cut away all clothing from the wound. She took the magnifying glass and inspected the wound. Slowly she opened up the entry point with the tweezers. Helmut groaned and bit savagely on the rubber stick. Magrete could only see two bullet fragments.

'Anna, clean the wound using only a wet towel,' Magrete advised, 'and make sure it is not too hot.'

She turned to Gertrude. 'For the safety of all of us, I do not want to know why Helmut was shot.' Gertrude looked relieved because those had been Helmut's instructions. 'But I do need to know whether he was directly hit or hit by fragments that ricocheted off a wall.'

'I'm not sure,' Gertrude said. 'We were firing back as the SS were firing at us, but they stopped when we ran into a crowd at the train station.'

'When did you first know he was shot?'

'Just as we were rounding a corner, he turned and fired. We ran and jumped onto the train and that's when I knew because of the blood seeping through is suit coat,' Gertrude replied, trying to recount the event as accurately as possible. 'I immediately placed my silk handkerchief in between his coat and shirt in order for the bleeding to be less obvious. Luckily it was the last train and so there were few people in our carriage.'

Magrete lifted Helmut's shoulder gently and inspected the back of it. Helmut bit hard into the rubber stick. 'The bullet fragments have entered only in the right front of his shoulder. I think he has been extremely lucky, for if the bullet had entered his shoulder and then fragmented within his body, I am certain he would have died.'

Magrete said to Helmut, 'I am going to operate now.' She turned to Anna and said softly, 'Bring the candle over here.' Magrete held the tweezers in the flame for a few minutes, until she could feel her fingers burning and she then clean the tweezers using some gin from the bottle.

'He will probably faint, Anna. Make sure his tongue is not blocking his breathing by pushing it forward.' She then turned to Gertrude. 'Keep wiping the blood from the wound, so I can see the fragments clearly.'

With the magnifying glass and tweezers Magrete successfully removed the fragment nearest to the surface. She felt Helmut go limp and saw Anna removing the rubber stick and poking her finger into his mouth to make sure his tongue was not blocking his airway. Gertrude was cleaning blood away from the wound. The second fragment was bigger and more difficult to remove. Magrete had to grab it several times but on the fourth attempt she managed to remove it, tearing some tissue in the process. Helmut was motionless. Magrete inspected the wound with the magnifying glass: it was clear of any fragments. She threaded the needle with animal twine and used a mattress stitch to close the wound. Magrete had no medical training whatsoever; it was a stitch her mother had taught her when repairing a mattress. Magrete took Helmut's pulse and it was slightly weaker than before but not significantly. He was still unconscious.

'Gertrude, please dress his shoulder using the ointments and bandages we have,' Magrete instructed. 'Anna, I need you to monitor his temperature and pulse every few minutes and record it as a graph. I will be back in an hour or so. Do not answer the door to anyone.' Anna and Gertrude looked at one another and nodded.

Magrete rode her bicycle towards the Gross farm. Julianna had entrusted her with the keys to the house, since the farm was still in Magrete's care. Her plan was simple. It would take a day if not two for the police to come to her, looking for Helmut. He had obviously lost them at the railway station, or they would have been caught before they reached her door. Nevertheless, they needed a safe place where Helmut could recuperate. The Gross' farmhouse would do for now, Magrete reasoned, but after that they would need to make other arrangements. She had maybe one or two weeks at most before Fritz Hauptman and family would move in. For food, there was milk, eggs, pork and of course a hen or two could go missing.

Magrete arrived at the farm at 11 pm and immediately went to the stable. She put her bike on a stand and took the horse out of the stable, hitched it to the cart and drove off towards Tailfingen. Once near the centre of the city she hitched the horse in the vacant block at Goethestraße, walked to her house and let herself in, to be confronted by Gertrude pointing a gun at her.

Magrete angrily commanded, 'Put that away!'

'Yes, ma'am,' Gertrude answered.

'How is he?' Magrete asked Anna.

'He's stable. He's stronger, and he woke a few times.'

Anna passed Magrete the graphs. Magrete inspected them like a professional. 'We need to get him into a cart about a hundred metres from here.' She looked at Gertrude, 'Is that doable?'

'Ma'am, he's still weak. He goes in and out of consciousness, and he might be difficult for us to hold upright.'

'Anna,' Magrete commanded, 'get George's shirt and overcoat from our bedroom.'

When Anna returned, Magrete said, 'Anna, dress him but make sure you stay away from his right shoulder as much as possible. I want to wake him soon.'

Magrete left the room and returned carrying smelling salts. 'The salts should wake him,' she explained.

Magrete placed the smelling salts directly under Helmut's nose, and he woke immediately, coughing.

'Helmut, listen to me,' Magrete said urgently. 'We have to walk about a hundred metres and you need to be conscious, because Gertrude and I will not be able to support you unless you are.'

Helmut nodded.

'Now place your left arm around my shoulders for support. Gertrude, you stay on his right side and hold him tight around the waist and not near his right shoulder. No, Anna, I do not want your help, because you will not be with us when we walk to the cart.' They struggled to the front door, having to stop once or twice because Helmut's full weight was on them.

Magrete turned her head to address Anna in a whisper. 'Do not answer the door until I return.' Anna opened the door and the three of them slowly moved towards the vacant block. It was 1 am.

Magrete knew that in a small village like Tailfingen someone would see them, and that they would listen intently to any conversation. 'Fritz Hauptman,' she said, addressing Helmut, 'you should not come to my place so late at night drunk. We can carry you to your cart, but there is no way you can drive home tonight.' Gertrude looked perplexed, but Magrete put a warning finger to her lips.

They placed Helmut between them in the cart and drove off to Gross' farm. On the way, Magrete said to Gertrude, 'When the wound heals you will need to take out the stitches. Just cut them wherever you see a hump outside his flesh and then pull a cut end with a tweezer.' Gertrude nodded.

They reached the farmhouse door and finally, after a further struggle, got Helmut to bed and undressed him. Magrete explained to Gertrude the situation regarding Gross' farm and told her what she could and could not do. 'First and foremost, at night the farmhouse must remain pitch black. If anyone knocks on the door, do not answer it. During the day, you can feed the hens and collect eggs, milk the two cows and feed the horse. Let the pigs look after themselves. You can chop wood and make a fire, but only for cooking. I will come here every day around 11 am, so if you need something else let me know. Tomorrow I will bring you a full medical kit for his bandages. There are some salted chops that I was going to collect from the kitchen that you can cook tomorrow. We have only one or two weeks before Fritz Hauptman takes over the farm. You will need to be gone by then.'

Magrete pointed to the luger in the belt of Gertrude's dress, under her jacket. 'Do you really need to use that thing?'

'Yes, ma'am,' Gertrude answered confidently.

Magrete shook her head in disbelief. 'Put it away. If anyone spots that pistol we are all dead.'

'Yes, ma'am.' Gertrude placed the pistol in the kitchen drawer.

Magrete rode her bicycle back to her house and was greeted by Anna, who anxiously asked, 'How did it go?'

'They are bedded down for the night. I will go there at 11 tomorrow morning. Are the children asleep?'

'Yes,' Anna replied. 'Have you noticed how tough Gertrude has become?'

'Funny you should ask, but yes. From the woman who was falling apart at the seams during an air raid, thinking I was some sort of jinx, to a woman who acts more like a female prison warden – hard, and a little ruthless!'

'When you went out, and I was checking on Helmut's temperature and pulse, she took up a position in the front of the house as if she was an armed guard. I approached her several times to find out what she's been doing with her life since the last time we met, but she brushed me off quite harshly, saying "Can't you see I'm protecting all of you?" She actually frightened me.'

'War does strange things to people,' Magrete observed. 'For a few, a more ruthless side emerges because of their need to survive at any cost.'

Everyone was asleep by 3.30 am, and Magrete was woken at 5 am by Elisabeth, who needed to be fed. She was determined for Elisabeth in future to be only bottle-fed.

25

Over the next three days Magrete was at the Gross' farm promptly at 11 am. She would check with Gertrude about Helmut's condition before going to see him. On the first day he was fast asleep, but on the second day he was awake and tried to talk. Magrete came and sat on his bed. She could see he was very tired, and he fell asleep while she was there. On the third day he was awake, sitting up in bed with his back against the pillow. Gertrude had just finished bandaging his shoulder.

'How are you feeling?' Magrete asked.

'Mostly tired! I didn't know you were a doctor. These stitches look like they came straight out of a medical textbook.'

'You can thank my mother for making me mend a mattress,' Magrete said, laughing.

'That makes sense. My body is shaped like a mattress!' Helmut joked. Then his face took on a worried expression. 'Has anyone come after us?'

'Not yet, but they will. I will tell them exactly what you told me to say last October.'

'Last October feels a lifetime away,' Helmut reflected.

'Helmut, at best you have another four days, no longer,' Magrete said. 'The man who is taking over this farm hates me, and he will march in the minute he is legally able to do so. Have you got anything planned?'

'I have. I want you to deliver this letter I wrote last night to Ebingen personally and, depending on the reply, we may be able to make that date. Please don't read it.'

Magrete placed the envelope in her pocket and said, 'I will take the horse and cart and go now. I should be there within a hour.'

'Before you do, I need to tell you that Gertrude and I will disappear again, but one day, when the world is safe, you'll get a postcard from me, hand delivered. It will contain a single word that will explain where you should be.' Seeing Magrete's confused expression, Helmut patted her hand. 'Trust me, it will all make sense to you when you receive it.'

Magrete hitched the horse to the cart and bid Gertrude goodbye. Within sixty minutes she handed the envelope to the man who opened the door of the house in Ebingen. He asked her to wait and returned with another envelope for Helmut. Magrete returned to Gross' farm and, as Helmut was fast asleep, gave the envelope unopened to Gertrude.

She rode her bicycle home, where Anna informed her that Fritz Hauptman had appeared and ordered that Magrete must report immediately to the police station.

26

On 23 July 1944, as Heinrich Himmler launched a manhunt to catch the conspirators involved in 20 July Bomb Plot, Magrete found herself out the front of the Tailfingen police station. She took a big breath and walked inside.

'Well, well,' Fritz Hauptman said smiling, 'Nicolaus von Below wants to speak to you – or, should I say, interrogate you in room 11, down the corridor. The room is soundproof, so don't bother to scream.'

Magrete walked past him, saying, 'Still sore, are we, about becoming a farmer boy?'

She walked to room 11 and knocked on the door. 'Come in,' said a cultured voice.

As she entered she saw two men, but only one rose to greet her. 'Nicolaus von Below, adjunct to Hitler.'

Magrete looked at the other officer, and then at von Below. 'Frau Magrete Nagy, please take a seat,' von Below said. Magrete took the seat he indicated, on the opposite side of his desk. 'My stenographer will be taking notes.' His stenographer looks like a senior Gestapo officer, thought Magrete. I could be in serious trouble, no matter how polite he is to me.

'You've married again! I must admit I enjoyed your previous surname far more. I knew Elfi and Peter von Appen very well, in another lifetime, of course. I knew your first husband, Herbert, when he was in the NSFK. I trained as a pilot in 1929 at the Deutsche Verkehrsfliegerschule (DVS-German Air Transport School). I understand your father was the Deputy Commissioner of the Vienna Police, is that correct?'

'Yes, sir,' Magrete replied respectfully.

'Please call me Klaus. We're investigating a very serious offence and it concerns a person you are most familiar with, Helmut Gruen.' Magrete felt the intensity of von Below's gaze.

'Helmut?' she asked incredulously. 'What could he possibly have done?'

'We'll come to that in a minute.' von Below paused and then, turning to his stenographer, asked Magrete, 'When was the last time you saw Helmut?'

Magrete posed as if she was pondering his question. 'Early October in 1943.'

'Not more recently than that?'

Magrete paused and then shook her head. 'No, definitely early October.'

'But from interviews we have on record, you stayed in his apartment in Berlin on 10 to 12 December 1943.'

Magrete knew that her answer had to be accurate. 'Yes, that is correct. We stayed there just before we moved to Tailfingen. But if my memory serves me correctly, Helmut was not there, only Gertrude. Helmut might have been in Beelitz, but I am not certain about that.'

'Tell me about Gertrude, his executive assistant … Is there something funny that I'm missing, Magrete?'

'Gertrude was Elfi and Peter's residential housekeeper and when they died, she became mine. But my finances were getting difficult, so Helmut took her on as his residential housekeeper. I have never really thought of her as an executive assistant.'

Ignoring Magrete's remarks von Below asked, 'Had she any gun or rifle training? Shooting ducks for the household, or anything like that?'

'No,' Magrete said, smiling again. 'During one of the first air raids on Berlin, Gertrude and I were in the von Appen's department store bomb shelter, and she howled for hours, terrified – hardly the behaviour of a person familiar with firearms.'

'Really?' von Below paused, then said in a more relaxed manner, 'Tell me something about your association with the von Appen Pty Ltd.'

'I was the chairperson of the board of directors for a while,' Magrete said. 'I was paid, as well as getting the Beelitz house rent-free.'

'What was Helmut's function?' von Below was watching her very carefully.

'He ran the company once Peter withdrew from the day-to-day running of it. Of course, when Herbert died there was no male heir, so Peter needed someone to take over his role, and Helmut was the natural candidate.'

'Have you heard of Elderly Care?' Again, he watched her face closely.

'Only that they purchased the three DRK hospitals – Magdeberg, Munich and Leipzig – from von Appen Pty Ltd, when I was chairperson of the board, and then much later bought the Tailfingen house. They are currently my lessor.'

'They've been lumbered with far more properties than the three DRK hospitals and the house in Tailfingen. As a result, there is a warrant for the arrest of Helmut Gruen for fraud and embezzlement of a large sum of money from a business called Argentina Property Trust (APT), whose subsidiary is Elderly Care. Have you heard of APT?'

‘No,’ Magrete replied, with complete honesty.

‘Magrete, you’re well liked amongst some of Hitler and Martin Bormann’s closest friends and associates. The APT embezzlement is of concern to us. Right now the United States is pressuring Argentina to declare war on us. Last January they broke off diplomatic relations with us. We believe this embezzlement will heighten their resolve to declare war. That’s why we need to find Helmut and bring him to justice. We also need to find Gertrude. She shot and wounded a policeman who was trying to arrest them at the Berlin Bahnhof. They’ve disappeared, and we reasoned they might have come to you seeking help and refuge. If they do, it’s imperative that you inform the police. Your father was a policeman. He would want you to do the right thing, wouldn’t he?’

‘Of course! I will report immediately to you if they dare to make contact,’ Magrete reassured him.

He looked hard at her then said, ‘You may go.’

As Magrete walked out Fritz Hauptman said, ‘I just had a letter from Julianna’s solicitor. I’ll be picking up the keys from you on Monday.’

‘From today on, I am praying for hail and snow, farmer boy,’ Magrete said, smiling as she walked past him.

Magrete walked home and was immediately greeted by Anna, who handed her a note. It was from Helmut, informing her where she could pickup the horse and cart in Ebingen. It was at a different address. ‘Look, Anna, this is dangerous and you can say no to me. The police will probably be tailing me from today. I want you to cycle to Ebingen and pickup the horse and cart from this address. Place the bicycle in the cart and drive back to Gross’ farm. Pickup as many eggs and as much milk as you can and cycle home. You can say no if you want to.’

‘Magrete, I’ll never say no to you!’

‘Thank you! Now I will go shopping for essentials with Ilse and Elisabeth, and when you see me approaching the vacant lot, I want you to leave via the back lane. If you see anyone, just walk your bike, do not ride it. Say hello to them, and when you are out of the lane, ride back along Neuweilerstraße out of the village. Check the mirror of your bike to make sure you are not being followed.'

Thirty minutes later they enacted Magrete's plan. When Magrete got home from shopping, she fed Ilse and Elisabeth, washed them, and put them to bed. She had a long wait for Anna. After three hours, she heard a faint knock at the back door. She ran and opened it, and there stood Anna leaning on her bike, with a basket full of eggs, one dead hen and a flask of milk.

'You need to give this flask to the new owner,' Anna said. 'Oh, by the way, when I was walking the bike out of the lane, Sofie next door told me how disgusted she was with that drunk, Fritz Hauptman. Apparently she overheard you telling the neighbourhood about his drunken ways.' They smiled at the thought of the rumour mill that would be launched about Fritz in the village.

On the following day, Fritz Hauptman picked up the keys to the farmhouse and Magrete's pipeline to fresh produce from Gross' farm ended. She never gave Fritz the milk flask.

27

On 8 August the plotters who tried to kill Hitler were hanged and their bodies hung on meat hooks. Reprisals against their families continued. On the western front, the German Reich army continued their vast counterattack even though they had lost approximately half of the 145 tanks engaged in Operation Luttich. The counterattack had by now lost its element of surprise, and the Americans had seven divisions, including armoured tanks attached to the 7th Corps of General Collins, to counter the troops of the 7th German Reich Army of General Hausser.

Magrete had taken only Elisabeth shopping because Anna wanted Ilse to complete her writing, reading and spelling lessons. Ilse had been avoiding them by escaping into the backyard to play with the cat next door, which she had befriended. When Magrete returned, Anna was frantic. The new police officer Horst Maute wanted to speak to Magrete.

For the second time Magrete took a deep breath before entering the police station.

'Magrete?' a middle-aged man enquired, wearing a swastika on his sleeve, something she had noted Fritz never wore. 'My name is Horst Maude and I've been placed in charge of this police station. The higher authorities believe that this place was the last remnant of the Weimar Republic in the German Reich. I'm particularly interested in Fritz Hauptman. Some of his past actions as a police officer could warrant further investigation, especially his cosy relationship with the last mayor of Tailfingen, Michael Gross, who was a Weimar Republic acolyte.'

'I know Fritz. He has just bought the Gross' farm,' Magrete said.

'We know. We've reason to believe that Michael Gross raped two women, a Hanna Sieben and Julia Roch. Our records also showed you made a charge against Michael Gross, alleging you witnessed him trying to rape your governess, Anna Schuster. Is that correct?'

'Yes, that is correct,' Magrete replied, unsure where this line of enquiry was heading.

'I've been informed by the upper circles of the SS that you have sound judgement on these matters. Do you think he's a danger to the stability of the German Reich in this region?'

Magrete got the hint. One word from her and Fritz Hauptman would be eliminated.

'Herr Maute,' she said, 'Fritz Hauptman is incompetent as a person and, more importantly, was incompetent as a police officer. His dismissal from the force was a good decision. It means that in the future, investigations will be conducted with authority and procedural integrity, and that will give people in this region far more confidence in the German Reich. Incompetent dolts like Fritz Hauptman will never be a threat to the German Reich. He has now found a vocation for which he is better suited.'

'Can I close his file?'

'I think it would be best. Thank you for hearing my opinion on the matter. It is much appreciated.' He gave her a Nazi salute and Magrete left for home, knowing that she had not yielded to temptation as so many Nazis had before her.

As soon as she opened the front door Anna asked, 'What happened?' When Magrete told her what had transpired, Anna was furious. 'You let that ex-policeman off the hook after the way he treated us when we went to him reporting a crime? How could you?'

'Anna, he has lost his job. Unfortunately, he is too old to be called up, so we just have to let bygones be bygones. He has some supporters here, and we need to avoid being hated by the villagers.'

'I don't care about that. What about me? What about my body? Don't I have rights?' Anna ran into her room, asked Ilse to leave, and slammed the door shut.

Ilse walk down the staircase and asked, 'Mum, why is Anna angry with you?'

'She believes that I did the wrong thing by her. Adults are allowed to disagree with one another, but children cannot.' As Magrete said this, she pushed Ilse's nose with her index finger.

'Mum, watch!' Ilse said. 'I'll put a spell on Anna, one she taught me, but now she's forgotten.'

'A spell?'

'Yes, it's a Hebrew spell. A'bra meaning "I shall create from nothing" and k'dabra meaning "as I speak". So "abracadabra" means "I shall create something from nothing as I speak."'

'Is it a good or bad spell?' Magrete asked, not knowing what else to say.

'It only works if your heart is good. Watch! Abracadabra, one, two, three, Anna, you'll do as I please: let me finish my lesson!' The last phrase Ilse said in a soft, but deep and raspy voice.

At this point Anna's bedroom door was flung open, and she appeared at the top of the stairs and yelled, 'Ilse, get up here! You haven't finished your last exercise!'

Magrete asked, smiling at Ilse, 'It only works on Anna, right?'

Ilse, who was running up the stairs, stopped to say over her shoulder, 'Maybe?'

It took Anna two days to forgive Magrete. This was the first falling out they had had since the day they met, and it was much harder on Magrete than on Anna.

28

In December 1943, Göring had appointed Walther Gerlach as the new director of the nuclear physics research, taking effect from 1 January 1944. On 18 October 1944, Hitler ordered a call-up of all men from 16 to 60 years of age for Home Guard duties. When Hitler's directive was issued, Gerlach wrote to Reichsleiter Bormann to prevent scientists such as Heisenberg, von Laue, Hahn and others from being called up. He argued it would seriously hamper the German Reich's nuclear program. Hahn extended that protection to all of his staff and luckily George was within Hahn's realm, and so was exempted from those duties. George was still angered by the fact that the Hungarian regent Miklós Horthy had been overthrown by the German Reich and replaced with Ferenc Szálasi.

By 25 October, Romania had been liberated by Red Army and Romanian troops. On 27 October George returned home to Tailfingen, unemployed but pleased that he and his team had salvaged some 60 tons of uranium ore from the rubble in Berlin. Hahn was delighted with the results of George's team recovery effort.

While Anna had eventually accepted Magrete's inaction against Fritz Hauptman, she raised the matter privately with George, who concurred with Magrete's decision. He did so with such force he easily penetrated Anna's passionate disposition, and she readily accepted his arguments, something Magrete found difficult to achieve. George loved the fact that he was the only male in the household.

Food shortages affected every shop and every household. George's mission was to protect his family from famine. He began by completely reconfiguring the backyard into an advanced greenhouse. He was able to source from the old woollen mill materials that had been discarded when his team was sent by Professor Hahn to refurbish it into offices and research laboratories. George's colleagues at the Institute aided and abetted his efforts, not only because he was their friend, but also because they were angry at the manner of his dismissal.

Magrete was responsible for sourcing the seeds, seedlings and cuttings. She started with potatoes, tomatoes, lettuces and peas. She also suggested keeping hens and rabbits. It was Ilse's chore to look after the animals. Ilse loved this responsibility but now she had to protect them from Sofie's cat, which she had previously befriended.

While Anna and Ilse were in the house doing daily preschool lessons, Magrete approached George. 'Anna will be twenty-five next February and, except for Franz Stopper, she has had no relationships. I think she should get out and socialise a bit more.'

George was shocked that Anna had had a relationship he had not known about. 'Magrete, let Anna do what she wants to do,' he said, preferring to be the only male in their lives. 'Look how well she's schooling Ilse. That child is reading books that I haven't read.'

'I know, but not being involved in relationships will be a problem for her in the future,' Magrete reasoned. 'Whenever we go out, she cannot go anywhere, because she has to look after Elisabeth and Ilse. Yesterday I got an invitation from Elisabeth and Robert Ammann to attend their annual youth dance for newly conscripted youths - '

'Who's Robert Ammann?' George queried. He was bewildered by friendships that had occurred in his absence.

'He is the administrator who runs the Mayoral Office in Tailfingen and has been doing so since 1941. Anyway, you can take Anna to the dance and I will stay home and baby sit.'

'Hmm. I'm not sure about me chaperoning Anna. Do you really want an uncle around when you're meeting youths about to be conscripted? I doubt it.' George preferred to the only male in Anna's life, because it made his life less complex.

Magrete immediately left for the backyard and ten minutes later returned. 'It's a done deal, old man!'

The next week Magrete and Anna spent a good deal of time resizing one of Magrete's dresses that Anna liked. It was a black dress with a modest bodice, a fitted waist and a knee-length A-line skirt. Anna was curvier than Magrete, whose body had become more lithe and athletic the older she got, although she still had an ample bosom. Magrete's dress had to be let out at the waist and hips, but brought in at the top. When the dress was completed it fitted Anna perfectly and Magrete gifted it to her.

Shoes were another matter. Anna had none that suited the dress, and Magrete's foot size was larger than Anna's. Magrete decided to source a pair of black high-heeled shoes on the black market. She was smart at bartering, and the shoes only cost her six eggs.

At 6 pm Anna and George were ready to leave and Magrete and Ilse inspected them at the last minute. They looked like a perfect couple, except that George was a tad too old. Magrete told them how wonderful they looked and gave Anna some parting advice. 'Anna, do not let George hold you back. He is there just to chaperone you and not to inhibit you from dancing with whoever wants to dance with you.' George, with Anna on his arm, left for the villa.

After Magrete, Ilse, and Elisabeth had eaten and Elisabeth was put to bed, Magrete said to Ilse, 'Tell me more about your abracadabra spell.'

Ilse looked a little hesitant. 'What do you want to know?'

'Do you always have to say the same three lines: "Abracadabra, one, two, three; Anna, you will do as I please" and then state what you want?'

'Yes.'

'So does it work only on Anna?'

Because the two of them were rarely alone, Ilse decided to share some of her secrets with her mother. 'No,' she said.

'Does it work on your father, for instance?'

'It works on him the best!' Ilse said proudly.

'In what way?'

'With Anna, I've got to be within ten metres, but with Dad, it's double that distance.'

'Does it work on Elisabeth?'

Magrete saw a disappointment look on Ilse's face. 'Elisabeth's too young to understand psychic messages.'

'Does it work on people outside of our family?'

'No! I think it's because they're not that interested in me.'

'Oh, I see,' Magrete said. 'Do you have to say it out loud?'

'Not really! I can put my hand over my mouth, like this, and just whisper it.' Ilse illustrated how she could cast a spell without anyone noticing.

'Ilse, you do realise your spell does not work on me,' Magrete said, with a soft smile.

'How do you know?' Ilse said, looking annoyed.

'There are times when you do not want to do what I ask, and I see you hiding your mouth behind your hand, and yet I still make you do it – like making your bed.'

Ilse looked down at her shoes, knowing what her mother said was true. She recalled how often she had tried to dissuade her mother via a spell and her mother had always got her way. 'Mothers are different,' Ilse conceded. 'They're too bossy to listen to psychic messages.'

'Bossy!'

'Yes, bossy!' Ilse said, then she changed the subject before she gave too much away. 'Mum, what's hypnosis? Is it a more powerful spell?'

'Why do you want to know about hypnosis?' Magrete asked, thinking, she must ask Anna where Ilse is getting this stuff.

'It was in one of my books that I've read, and when I looked it up in the dictionary it made no sense to me,' Ilse confessed. 'It sounds like a spell, but it isn't.'

'Hypnosis is not a spell rather it is a state of mind. Some people, like mothers, cannot be hypnotised.' Magrete noted a disappointed look on Ilse's face. 'However, those mothers who want to be hypnotised, do so willingly. Now that you are thinking about these things,' Magrete continued, 'I think you are old enough to join our yoga classes. Would you like that?'

Ilse beamed. 'Can I? Can I?'

'I will talk to Anna sometime this week about it. Now, look at the time! It is way past your bedtime. Brush your teeth and give yourself a birdbath, and call me when you are in bed. Remember, your spell does not work on me.' Magrete winked. When Ilse called out, Magrete went upstairs and kissed her goodnight and turned off the light, but left the door slightly ajar.

It was 9 pm and Magrete had an hour to kill before she expected Anna and George to return home. She put on the radio for the first time in a long time. The announcer read the news and the main item was that the Hungarian government had fled to the German Reich. Magrete thought it was strange that the Nazis would happily announce such a defeat. She then realised that George had tuned the radio to an overseas broadcast. She knew that the Nazis had made this a treasonable offence and that anyone caught doing so faced a spell in a concentration camp. She quickly turned the radio off, determined to talk to George about him putting the family at risk.

Suddenly George appeared, without Anna. 'A young lad is walking her home,' he said, 'so I left a little early.'

'George, how could you be so irresponsible? First I turn on the radio and hear an overseas broadcast, and now you are telling me you left Anna in the hands of a complete stranger.'

'Oh, the radio! I need to know what's going on and not that propaganda spiel,' George said. 'I'll be more careful in the future.'

'That is not good enough, George! I do not want you putting our family at risk. You do realise that the first year they introduced the ban about 1,500 Germans were sent to a concentration camp for listening to London-based broadcasts. You do not want all of us to be in that situation, do you?'

'I promise I won't do it again.'

Magrete asked in a softer tone, 'Now, tell me what happened for you to let a young man walk Anna home alone.'

'When Elisabeth Ammann started to play music, there were so few single women there that Anna was swept off her feet with request after request. They'd march up and ask me if they could have the next dance with Anna, and she'd tell me whom she wanted to dance with and I'd give that one the nod. Near the end of the night she was dancing with a youth who was maybe a few years younger than her, and he came over to me and said, "Herr Nagy, can I walk your daughter home?"'

'Your daughter!' Magrete laughed loudly. George did not see the funny side of it, and the hurt on his face made Magrete laugh even louder. 'So, daddy, why did you let him walk her home alone?' She was having fun at his expense, and he did not like it.

'He sounded like a nice chap and Anna desperately wanted him to, because she kept on shooing me away when he was there,' George confessed.

Just then Anna walked in. 'I could hear you laughing from halfway down the street, Magrete. What's so funny?'

Magrete was smiling as she looked at George. 'This man's ego was deflated when someone thought he was your father and not your uncle.'

'Oh, you mean pops over there? He was a great chaperone.' Anna giggled and George left for the upstairs bedroom, swearing under his breath about how cruel women could be when they want to be.

'Pops!' Magrete repeated, and then laughed.

'That's what all the lads called him when I was dancing with them. Be careful Magrete, some of the young, desperate women thought that pops was good-looking and asked him for a dance. When I waltzed across and told them he was my pops they realised he was out of their reach.'

Magrete smiled at Anna's protectiveness. 'Tell me about the young man who walked you home.'

'He's young and beautiful, with your colouring – blue-eyed and brownish-blonde hair, muscular and off to war! A perfect but flawed man,' Anna said, with relish.

'Why flawed?'

'He thought he'd win me over with his body, which in normal circumstances might have done the trick, and so he unbuttoned his shirt and showed me his chest and there on his chest he'd tattooed ... the biggest swastika I'd ever seen!' Both women were in fits of laughter now, which intensified when they heard George slam the upstairs bedroom door.

When they had composed themselves, Magrete said, 'If you are going to engage in love-making, Anna, you need to know about the rhythm method of birth control.'

'You're sounding like a Mum,' Anna said.

'Well, then, I will do what my Mutti did. I will slip an explanation of it under the door at midnight.'

'And if you do,' Anna smiled, 'Ilse will be the youngest child in the world to know about the rhythm method!' They laughed unconstrained, much to George's annoyance, as he was certain that he was the cause of their muffled mirth.

29

Inflation in the German Reich was kept in check via three mechanisms: rationing of essential goods and services, a 50 per cent increase in taxation, and the occupied countries bearing the brunt of repatriation. Increasingly, the black market for goods started to focus on gold, silver and diamonds, because the inevitable defeat of the Axis powers might reignite the hyperinflation experienced in Germany in 1919 after it was defeated in the Great War. Magrete now needed to barter with a mix of money and jewellery, the latter either inherited from her mother-in-law or from her first marriage to Herbert von Appen, Helmut having recovered it from the rubble at Wannsee.

The afternoon of 30 November was sunny and Magrete decided to ride her bicycle to Bisingen, to deal with a farmer there, Ernst Bindle. She was taking this risk because their greenhouse had been robbed and many of the vegetables stolen.

When Magrete was one kilometre from her destination she saw a column of men walking very slowly. They were shackled and emaciated. Each step appeared to require more energy than their bodies contained. Magrete tried not to look at them, but she could not resist.

There was a boy who looked about fourteen-years-old walking behind them. He looked like he was from Hitler's Youth Brigade rather than being a fully-fledged soldier. He was holding an FG42 rifle. He ordered the group to halt. They stopped and some sat on the ground. The boy motioned for Magrete to get off her bike, his rifle pointed directly at her head. Magrete, knowing that boy soldiers were easily indoctrinated and so could be extremely cruel and dangerous, got off her bike as he motioned her to come towards him with his rifle, then pointed it at her again. She moved slowly towards him, never taking her eyes off him.

'Where are you from?' His voice was youthful.

‘Tailfingen,’ Magrete answered.

‘What are you doing here?’ He liked her face, her lithe figure and her ample bosom.

‘Visiting my friend Ernst Bindel,’ Magrete answered, with a confident air. The boy soldier felt uncomfortable with her steady gaze, and lowered his eyes for a second. Then he slung his rifle over his shoulder. ‘Black market, eh?’

‘No, I am visiting a friend.’

‘Put your hands behind your head and place your legs apart,’ he ordered as he aimed his rifle at her head with his finger on the trigger once again. All the stick figures refused to watch, because they knew what was coming. He slung his rifle over his back after she did what he commanded, and reached under her jumper, placing one hand inside her left bra cup. He cupped his hand on her breast and pushed her nipple with his thumb. Her nipple did not harden, but her steely gaze did, which unsettled the boy. He then repeated the procedure in the other bra cup, but this time he dared not touch her nipple. Then he lifted her dress and slid his hand between her legs, feeling around her underwear to detect any unusual objects. He looked into the empty basket. Magrete did not take her eyes off his. Her gaze was so piercing that he stepped back and waved her on. When she did not move, he lifted his rifle and aimed it at her head again. ‘Go!’ he shouted.

Magrete looked at him, showing no trace of humiliation but only contempt, as she cycled away. Unbeknownst to the boy, Magrete had George build a false floor in her bicycle basket, where she kept her money and jewellery. She came home that evening with a basket laden with new plants and did not say a word to anyone about the boy. She bathed herself, cleansing her body of the boy’s touch. She thought of the stick figures: the German Reich had defiled life in so many different ways, she thought.

30

By 14 January 1945, Auschwitz had closed, the Russians had liberated Budapest, freeing over 80,000 Jews, and the invasion of East Germany by Russian troops had begun. The German Reich was reeling. Like the pharaohs' ritual of having servants killed after their death in order that they would continue to serve them in the afterlife, Hitler was determined that in his afterlife the German Reich would be present to serve him.

However, Himmler thought otherwise. On 31 August 1944 he organised for his contacts in Switzerland to forward a coded signal to Winston Churchill to start peace negotiations at the chalet in St Moritz, which was owned by RSHA. Churchill ignored this opening gambit. On 12 September Himmler approach Hitler suggesting negotiating peace settlements with either Russia or Britain in order to avoid a pincer defeat. Hitler rejected the strategy. Himmler now understood Hitler's pharaoh mentality. With the failure of the Ardennes offensive in December 1944, Hitler realised defeat was inevitable, but he stated, 'We'll not capitulate – never! We can go down. But we'll take the world with us.' In the same month, a liaison officer under the command of Walter Schellenberg, the head of the SS intelligence service working for Himmler, arranged for a secret meeting with the diplomatic British staff in Switzerland at the chalet in St Moritz. A separate peace deal without Hitler's knowledge was suggested by the German Reich staff, which the British again rejected.

Himmler was increasingly concerned about the medicine Hilter was taking: he feared that Hitler had developed a drug addiction and that Hitler's personal doctor, Dr Theodor Morell, who concocted unusual opioid/vitamim remedies, was to blame.

On 16 January Ilse turned six; her Nazi schooling would begin on 1 August 1945, unless Magrete lied about her age. Magrete had been careful to isolate her children from other children in the neighbourhood, because she did not want any conversations overheard at her home to be retold to other children and, moreover, she did not want her children to be subjected to propaganda she could not vet. George, Anna and Magrete were always polite but distant to their neighbours. Some of their neighbours, such as Sofie, put it down to aloofness; others to a big city mentality; and some just to plain rudeness. Either way, the family's footprint in Tailfingen was minuscule.

Magrete decided she needed to invite neighbourhood children close to Ilse's age to a birthday party, because Ilse needed to build friendships prior to entering school. Of those she sent invitations to, Hilda Haushofer, Elsbeth Streicher and Effie Lutz responded and their daughters Hildegard, Marianne and Hannah, all two years older than Ilse, attended her birthday party, which was held after school. George and Magrete cooked Bratwurst sausages with potatoes and salad for a late lunch and made a special birthday cake, a Bavarian apple strudel, only with apples and no other fruits. Anna made some party hats.

It was decided that only Anna and Magrete would attend – George had chores he wanted to complete in the backyard. After the children had eaten lunch and sung 'Happy Birthday' to Ilse, Ilse had blown out the candles and they had all eaten the birthday strudel, the mothers gathered with Magrete in the kitchen, while Anna stayed with the four girls in the lounge room. Elisabeth was ten months old now and so was put to bed by Magrete for her afternoon nap.

Anna listened, but did not engage in the conversation, while the girls occupied the sofa and the lounge room chairs as if they were adults.

Ilse asked, 'Do all of you go to the same school?'

'Yes,' they replied in unison.

'How does school begin?'

The leader of this pack was Marianne and so she was the first to reply. 'School starts at 8 am every morning, Monday to Saturday.

When the teacher comes in, we stand up and raise our right arms, like this, and after the teacher says, "For the Führer, a triple victory", we answer her by saying, "Sieg Heil", three times. It's fun!'

Ilse asked, 'What is the triple victory?'

The three friends looked at one another and Marianne said, 'I'm not sure.'

Ilse shrugged her shoulders. 'What's the first lesson?'

'German, silly!' Hilde said, as she liked to be known. 'From eight to a quarter to nine every morning, in the first period, we learn German grammar and sometimes we read German literature.'

'Have you read *Heidi* by Johanna Spyri?' Ilse said, wanting to impress. 'I loved it.'

'Oh no,' Hannah said shaking her head, 'that's for much older girls.' Anna listened and smugly smiled.

Ilse enquired, 'What happens in the second period?'

'It depends on what day it is,' Marianne said. 'On Monday and Thursday, it's geography.'

Ilse was fascinated with geography. 'What do they teach you in geography? Do they teach you about Australia or India?'

'No!' Marianne was horrified by Ilse's reply. 'They teach about important stuff, like how they shrunk Germany in 1919 after we lost the war, and why we need to have more babies, and more land so they can have a place to live.' Ilse did not like that answer at all. Surely geography lessons can't be only about Germany, she thought. Had they never seen an atlas?

'In the second period on Tuesday and Friday we learn about history,' Hannah said. 'History is my favourite! We learn about Germany's past glories and how the French and the English betrayed us. Next year Mum said we'll learn about the history of the Nazi party and the evils of the Jews, and the people who are called Marxists, who tried to make our country poor. I think the Marxists disguise themselves as Russians.'

Hilde felt left out. 'In the second period on Wednesday and Saturday,' she said, 'we sing and sing and sing! It's fun! In the third period on Monday to Thursday, we study what makes the German race superior to the others. Last week we learnt why we should not marry people who are of a different race.'

'You mean Germans can't marry Japanese,' Ilse reasoned, 'even though they're our friends?'

'Maybe,' Marianne said, looking confused.

Hannah chimed in. 'On Friday and Saturday in the third period we learn all about the Nazi party.'

Ilse enquired, 'Like what kind of thing?'

Hannah hesitated and Marianne filled the gap. 'Last week we learnt that decisions that are best for the country should be made only by Hitler. He's the only person in the whole wide world who knows everything!'

'In the fourth period,' Hilde offered, 'we play in the schoolyard. I love skipping.'

'So do I,' Hannah agreed. 'We also do exercises, so that our bodies are fit.'

'In the fifth period we get taught how to cook, clean the house and look after the garden,' Hannah boasted. 'Next year we'll learn about sewing, knitting, mending and making clothes. We need to do arithmetic, because if we can't, we won't know how to measure ingredients for cakes or how much change we should get when we do the shopping.'

'Do you know how to divide?' Ilse asked.

Hannah said, 'What does "divide" mean?'

Ilse answered, 'It's the opposite to multiplying.'

'Oh,' Hannah said smiling, 'maybe mothers don't need to know how to divide.'

Anna held in a laugh.

'The sixth period is probably the most important lesson,' Hannah continued. 'We get taught how to choose boys who can make great babies. When we're older, the teacher said we'll be taught how to make babies for ourselves.'

Hilde said, 'We also get taught how to spot a Jew.'

Anna leaned forward, frowning.

Ilse asked, 'How do you know a Jew from a non-Jew?'

'Well,' Marianne said, 'I'm the expert in the class. They have very long noses, big ears and big eyes.'

'Oh,' Ilse said with a giggle, 'I never knew that Pinocchio was a Jew!'

At that Anna laughed out loud.

When the visitors had left, Anna was concerned to challenge what these girls had told Ilse – but Ilse got in first. 'Anna, please don't let Mum send me to their school. They're stupid! They pray to Jesus, who's a Jew, and they're so dumb that if Jesus was here they would send him to prison.'

Anna smiled at Ilse, swept her up in her arms and said very softly, 'What if I was a Jewess?'

Ilse looked at her and said, 'You're a beautiful Jewess.' Anna gave Ilse such a big hug that Ilse went limp with delight.

When Anna repeated the girls' conversation, Magrete said, 'As far as I am concerned Ilse is only five, and we will not be thinking about schooling her until the war is over, when the curriculum will be redesigned within a more sensible framework.' This was the third time Anna had heard Magrete hint that the German Reich might lose the war while seeming happy about it. A suspicion started to take hold in Anna's mind.

31

On 16 January 1945 Hitler took up residence in the Führerbunker, which was located near the Reich Chancellery in Berlin. It was part of a subterranean bunker complex constructed in two phases, the first completed in 1936 and the second in 1944. Up until the last week of the war, it served as the nucleus for the Nazi regime. It was an extensive network of rooms containing a hall, a dining room, kitchen, pantry, bathrooms, toilets, living quarters, visitors' rooms, warehouses, lockers, a medical room and a store as well as barracks, a map room and ventilation facilities. In April 1945, Eva Braun and Joseph Goebbels and his wife Magda and their six children also took up residency there.

While Himmler had been appointed by Hitler in a military capacity to try to stop the Russian advancement, it was clear to him that the German Reich was in its last throes and, through Felix Kersten, an intermediary in Sweden, he indirectly negotiated with Count Folke Bernadotte, head of the Swedish Red Cross. Himmler agreed to release 1,400 Jews a month from Theresienstadt in return for US$250,000. However, no money had been exchanged when 1,200 Jews (523 German Jews, 433 Dutch Jews, 153 Austrian Jews and 91 Protectorate Jews) reached Switzerland on 5 February 1945. When Hitler learnt of the release of the Jews he was furious and banned any further releases.

Himmler's star was on the wane from 25 January 1945, when Hitler appointed him as commander of the hastily formed Army Heeresgruppe Weichsel (Army Group from Vistule region, Poland). It was devised to halt the Soviet Red Army advance. His appointment proved a disaster. He withdrew for much of the time on grounds of illness to an SS hospital north of Berlin. His appointment was rescinded on 20 March, when his planned counterattack failed to stop the Soviet advance. Himmler and Hitler met for the last time in Berlin on 20 April 1945, Hitler's birthday, where Himmler swore total allegiance. At a military briefing on that day, Hitler, after taking his medicine, felt buoyant, and stated that he would not be leaving Berlin despite Soviet advances. Along with Göring, Himmler quickly left Berlin after the briefing, both realised that Hitler's mood was now determined by what his doctor, Dr Theodor Morell, was prescribing for him.

On 23 April 1945 the administrator of Tailfingen, Robert Ammann, called for all the citizens of Tailfingen to meet at 1 pm in the village square. He wanted the women and children to be there so that the men over sixty would understand why they needed to protect their village against the French, who were slowly advancing towards them. He asked Magrete to speak at the event. Ammann knew that she was a friend of Marga Himmler, and that Himmler was positioning himself as the most important Nazi in pursuing a peace agreement with the Allies. Anna stood beside Ilse, holding her hand, with Elisabeth on her hip. George had been asked to meet Hahn at the Institute, so he could not attend.

Robert Ammann introduced Magrete as Frau Nagy cum von Appen.

'Ladies and gentlemen,' Magrete began, 'I have only been in Tailfingen since December 1943. Nevertheless, my child Elisabeth was born in this village and as my family is living here, I do have a stake in wanting to protect them.' She heard a few jeers from some women. 'What I am about to say, Herr Ammann might not agree with, but I lived in Berlin from 1936 to 1943, and at one time was the heir to the von Appen fortune.' Everyone knew that the von Appen family supported the textile mills in Tailfingen, and had immense power in the village. 'I have seen Berlin become a bombed-out skeleton of itself. We lost our department store in Alexanderplatz. There were hundreds of deaths – children, women and men – in just one air raid.' Magrete paused and she could see the audience was now attentive.

'The Führer can no longer save the German Reich – it is crumbling before our very eyes. We cannot send shopkeepers, farmers, grandfathers, old men and young boys to certain death by asking them to fight against a professional army. What will this pointless resistance bring? More deaths, the destruction of homes, and the death of scores of children, boys, women and old men!' A number of women in the audience started applauding in appreciation of her comments.

'No Tailfingers, this is the time to capitulate! This is the time to work with the French so that the lads and men that have left our village to fight elsewhere will come home not to ashes, graves and funerals but to loved ones!' She stood down to cheers and a rousing applause.

Robert Ammann pulled her aside, saying, 'Magrete, the French are our enemy and Hitler has ordered every village to resist to the end.'

'Robert,' she said, 'if you save the village you will be praised by all Tailfingers, as well as by the French.' He understood that it was useless to resist.

He mounted the platform and said to all those assembled, 'Ladies and gentleman, Magrete von Appen is right – let's work with the French!' He got a rousing cheer.

Anna whispered to Magrete, 'This war will end for some of these people quickly, but for Jews like myself it won't end for a long time.' Magrete detected a steely anger within Anna that she had not detected before.

32

In September 1942 Brigadier General Leslie Richard Groves took charge of the Manhattan Project: America's top secret war effort to build a nuclear bomb. In 1943, he became responsible for collecting military intelligence on atomic research and created operation Alsos – special intelligence teams that would follow in the wake of the advancing armies, rounding up enemy scientists and collecting what technical information and technology they possessed. Rumours that the German Reich had an atomic bomb persisted as late as March 1945. On 30 March the Alsos Mission reached Heidelberg, where, on interrogation of important German scientists, they discovered that the two most important nuclear scientists, Otto Hahn and

Werner Heisenberg, had their institutes in Tailfingen and Hechingen respectively. Both these villages lay in the path of the French army's advance, but they were also in the French occupation zone. Groves tried desperately to alter the boundaries, but he failed to convince Eisenhower.

On 20 April the French First Army captured an intact bridge over the Neckar River at Horb, establishing a bridgehead. On the same day, the Alsos Mission rendezvoused with the 1269th Engineer Combat Battalion at Freudenstadt. They pushed on to Bisingen and then on to Hechingen, where twenty-five scientists were captured. On 25 April, at Tailfingen, they took Otto Hahn and nine members of his staff into custody. Professor Hahn looked thin and ill, and when asked about his secret work and reports about his research he simply said, 'I have them all here.' The uranium was removed from the mill, and then transported to England. All the captured scientists were sent to Farm Hall in England. George Nagy was not amongst them. He was not an employee of the Institute and, moreover, he was not present at the Institute on 25 April. When he was dismissed, all of his research reports on the possible use of centrifuges to separate radioactive uranium from its other isotopes had been sent to Walther Gerlach, and so they were not in Hahn's possession. Gerlach destroyed these reports before he was captured.

The Tailfingers were expecting the arrival of the French First Army, and were shocked when the American 1269th Engineer Combat Battalion captured Professor Hahn and his colleagues. The township offered no resistance and waited to see what would eventuate.

On 28 April Hitler was given the news, via a BBC broadcast, that Himmler had proposed unconditional surrender to Britain and America. He exploded, calling it '...the most shameful betrayal in human history'. Himmler was stripped of all his offices. Hitler began preparations to take his own life. On 30 April 1945, in his Führerbunker in Berlin, Hitler and his wife Eva (née Braun) committed suicide by taking cyanide. Admiral Dönitz inherited the shreds of power of the Third Reich for a few days. On 7 May 1945, the German Reich signed an unconditional surrender at Allied headquarters in Reims, France, to take effect the following day, ending the European conflict of World War II. Finally, on 8 May 1945 the French 5th Armoured Division, under the command of General Jean de Lattre de Tassigny, rolled into Tailfingen on a cold and windy day. The village turned out en masse to witness the event. There was no waving of banners or a welcome as such; rather, a stoic acceptance that the lives of the villagers would significantly change.

German women's opinions of the French had been lowered by rumours of atrocities supposedly committed by French troops. Nazi propaganda in the closing days of the war focused on alleged cruelties of French African troops in 1944. When the March 1945 invasion of the German Reich occurred, a rumour had begun circulating that French soldiers had raped thousands of girls from Stuttgart in a tunnel, over several days. The British tabloid press printed a story about the incident, and although there was no evidence to confirm that it had actually occurred, German women tended to believe the rumour and felt that they might become victims of French aggression. It was therefore with great apprehension that Magrete and Anna awaited the French occupation of Tailfingen.

George, Magrete, Ilse and Anna, with Elisabeth on her hip, stood in front of the Tailfingen Rathaus (Mayoral Chambers) to watch the convoy make its way from Bisingen along Hauptstraße to the Rathaus. Standing in front of the Rathaus were Elisabeth and Robert Ammann, who greeted the Colonel of the French 5th Armoured Division and handed over the keys to the city. The French command escorted the couple into the Mayoral Offices.

On their way back, when they were nearly home, Magrete and Anna turned quickly when they heard a loud car horn and saw two American jeeps making a left turn from Hechingarstraße into Neuweilerstraße. For Magrete, the presence of American troops in a French zone was a bad omen, but Anna thought the captain in the front passenger seat of the first jeep was better-looking than George, and so a wonderful addition to Tailfingen.

PART FOUR

The Redemption

1

The French zone was directly adjacent to France, linking it with their zone of occupation in Austria, Württemburg, Baden, the Saar, Rhineland-Pfalz and the Palatinate. It consisted of 42,000 square kilometres and 5.8 million Germans, making the French zone of occupation the smallest of the four zones, with respect to both size and population. As in the other zones of occupation, women were the majority of the population, standing at 58 per cent of the total population.

The French command left a First Lieutenant with twenty soldiers (one squad) in Tailfingen, because the major commitment in the area was in Ebingen, where they had headquartered a major with three platoons of 200 men. Some fifteen women and men soon followed, to bolster the Tailfingen administration. The French headquarters in Occupied Germany was at Baden-Baden, a spa town located on the northwestern border of the Black Forest mountain range, about 40 kilometres northeast of Strasbourg, France.

The French were the only occupying power that had capitulated, and were effectively ruled by the German Reich. Although they were appreciative that at the Yalta conference the Americans had insisted on their inclusion as an occupying force, they were extremely sensitive to their relatively weak position within the Allied structure. Therefore, they were not pleased that the US high command had implemented the clause: 'The final directive to implement French participation in military government required the inclusion of French officers in the G-5 staff of the Sixth Army Group, and of American officers in the headquarters of the First French Army and lower echelons if deemed necessary.' The purpose of the clause was to ensure that the American Arm forces could retain a degree of oversight within the French zone.

The Americans insisted that Captain Eugene Gould, a sergeant, a corporal and three privates be stationed in Tailfingen, and gave the French three reasons for their presence: (i) to vet the background of people who are applying for immigration to the United States; (ii) to assist the French in ensuring that all fissionable material from the Kaiser Wilhelm Institute for Chemistry had been located and made safe; (iii) to liaise with the French in the Württemberg–Hohenzollern region on any matters of practical importance to both armies.

The French made three stipulations in order to agree to Eugene's presence in their occupation zone: (i) any uranium recovered must be handed over to the French authorities and the recovery team must be jointly supervised by both countries; (ii) people of interest to the United States can only be interviewed with French permission, and only if a designated French officer was available for the interview; (iii) the American officer and his men were restricted to Tailfingen, and can only travel outside of Tailfingen with the permission of the French officer stationed there. The Americans agreed to these conditions. The French installed the American unit in the villa that previously housed Herr Robert Ammann and his family, at 50 Leimenhäulestraße. Robert Ammann was sent to Baden-Baden for interrogation and his family was permitted to accompany him.

First Lieutenant Pierre Thomas and Captain Eugene Gould got on exceptionally well. What greatly assisted their relationship was Eugene's fluency in French, and while Eugene was younger and had a higher rank, he treated Pierre as his superior officer. Pierre was also flattered that Eugene had hired a German cook who specialised in French cuisine. Eugene invited Pierre to dine at the villa every

Saturday evening under the pretence of it being a French–American consultation session in order to ensure that collaboration between the Allies in the region was effective.

Eugene was relieved that it took him only a month to gain Pierre's confidence. The Americans had a number of reasons for wanting Eugene Gould, an operative of the Office of Strategic Services (OSS) to be stationed in Tailfingen. The OSS had discovered that the Russians had forced three Hungarian scientists – Dr Frank Bacskay, Dr Attila Pulay and Dr Mark Czár – to leave Budapest for Moscow. The Russians were now enquiring as to the whereabouts of Dr George Nagy. The OSS asked Groves to investigate Dr Nagy's scientific qualifications and why he had been a casual employee with the Kaiser Wilhelm Institute for Chemistry. On contacting Farm House in England, Hahn had explained to the British that Dr Nagy and his group were material technicians, responsible for the safe handling and stockpiling of uranium ore. They had been full-time employees of the Institute, but after the German Reich invaded Hungary they had been deemed a security risk and dismissed. Hahn also explained that he had hired Dr Nagy to oversee the recovery of uranium ore from the Institute's building in Berlin after it was bombed. After checking the qualifications of the Hungarians, Groves conveyed to the OSS that the qualifications of all four would have been better suited for positions in the Kaiser Wilhelm Institute for Metals Research rather than for research conducted in Hahn's Institution. None of it made sense to Groves, or to the OSS.

The OSS also secured evidence that Magrete Nagy was a friend of Marga Himmler, who had been arrested by the US army in May 1945 after the invasion of Bolzano, Italy. They wanted evidence of Magrete's possible connection to the top Nazi echelon and in particular, her possible associations with Hitler or Bormann. They were hampered by the fact that Himmler had committed suicide on 23 May 1945. There was also some evidence that Marga, his wife, might have aided and abetted Himmler to commit war crimes and Magrete might be able to enlighten them on this matter.

The OSS was interested in locating all of the Nazi hierarchy. The top man on their list was Martin Bormann. OSS knew that von Appen Pty Ltd had sold a significant number of properties to an Argentinian company, Elderly Care, which they believed was in fact a Nazi front designed to transfer wealth from the German Reich to Argentina and so underwrote a future Nazi resurgence in Occupied Germany. They had temporarily seized all the property holdings of the RSHA in the western zone, except for the chalet in St Moritz, which they were monitoring closely. This was the venue Himmler had proposed to use in brokering a peace agreement with Britain. The OSS believed that investigating Elderly Care and its links with von Appen Pty Ltd might lead them to high-ranking Nazi officers and officials hiding in Occupied Germany or Latin America.

The last reason why Eugene Gould wanted to be in Tailfingen was personal and not known to the OSS. He had Jewish relatives in Occupied Germany, and he desperately wanted to know their whereabouts. More importantly, he was a member of the International Jewish Advocacy Group (IJAG), a clandestine operation seeking information about Jewish property or wealth that had been stolen or forcibly appropriated in the German Reich under laws that had been constructed for that purpose. He was interested in von Appen Pty Ltd because it was rumoured that they had secured gold via an underground criminal network and that some of the gold might have been fenced from desperate Jewish families wanting to flee the German Reich. A person of prime interest was the man running the day-to-day operations of the company, Helmut Gruen, who had not been located. Helmut Gruen had been last sighted near the German–Switzerland border in the Württemberg–Hohenzollern region. It was well known that Magrete Nagy (also known under the name von Appen) was chairperson of the board of directors of the company in which Helmut held the position of CEO, and she was living in Tailfingen at the time Helmut Gruen was sighted in the region.

Eugene decided his first interview would be Dr Nagy, and after that he would seek to vet the most mundane and boring DP applicants in the hope that Pierre would find better things to do than attend future interviews. He sent Pierre a note asking him to make Dr George Nagy available at the villa at 10 am on Tuesday 5 June.

2

On Monday 4 June at 9 am a French private knocked on the door of 1 Neuweilerstraße and handed Anna a letter in French, and a translated version in German, requesting that Dr Nagy present himself at 10 am at 50 Leimenhäulestraße, to be interviewed by First Lieutenant Pierre Thomas and Eugene Gould. Pierre's non-inclusion of Eugene Gould's rank was not an accident.

Magrete became severely depressed by this request, whereas George seemed unconcerned. Whenever Magrete was depressed, she used yoga as an avenue to relieve her anxiety and so Anna and Ilse joined her in an additional session during George's absence.

George recalled that the last discussion he had had with Hahn was on 23 April, the day Robert Ammann called for a town meeting. Hahn had not looked well. He had told George that he was grateful that he was in the French zone, because a French scientific friend of his, Joliot-Curie, had been appointed scientific commissar. When the Nazis occupied Paris, Hahn had refused to inspect Joliot-Curie's laboratory as a sign of respect, and he was sure Joliot-Curie would show him the same level of respect. What Hahn feared was an American raid before the French arrival. He surmised that they would extract all resources – scientists, research reports and materials – relocate them to England or America and purposely destroy the infrastructure of the Institute so that the French would have little to capture. 'If you want to stay with your family,' he had said to George, 'remember that there are no records of your research in this Institute or elsewhere. If I'm captured I'll always claim you were a mere technician, responsible for the storage, maintenance and safe handling of fissionable material. Stick to that story and your life will be in your hands, not in theirs.'

George knocked on the door at 50 Leimenhäulestraße at exactly 10 am, unsure of his future, with an American private by his side.

'Come in,' Eugene instructed. 'Would you like us to talk in French or in English, because I'm afraid I can't speak German.'

George replied, 'English would be fine.'

'Let me introduce myself. My name is Eugene Gould and this is First Lieutenant Pierre Thomas, Tailfingen's administrator.' All three men moved into a study. Lieutenant Pierre Thomas sat down behind a large oak desk, Eugene Gould sat to his left, and George was seated in front of the desk, at the focal point between his two interrogators.

'George, we're having difficulty locating your qualifications,' Eugene said. 'Berlin is in a mess at the moment. Perhaps you could just give us a brief outline.'

'I was awarded a PhD from the Technical University of Berlin in 1934 in material science, under the supervision of Professor Dr Wilhelm Heinrich Westphal.'

Eugene enquired, 'Without going into too much detail, what was the topic of your thesis?'

George looked at Eugene and wondered if he was a prosecutor-cum-scientist. 'My PhD centred on developing nickel-based superalloys that are extremely resistant to high temperatures, pressures, centrifugal force, fatigue and oxidation.'

Eugene looked relieved at the succinctness of George's answer. 'Now, this is our dilemma,' he said. 'Your PhD study is more in line with metal research and less in the area of radioactivity. Why did Hahn hire you? Why didn't the Kaiser Wilhelm Institute for Metals Research hire you? Surely Werner Koester would have made a play for you when the war was not going well for the German Reich?' Pierre looked impressed by Eugene's knowledge of the German

Reich's institutions and research. The information Eugene extracted clearly might be useful to the French authorities in Baden-Baden, he thought.

'Koester did make a play for me early in 1942, if memory serves me right. However, Hahn's Institute was amassing large amounts of uranium ore, and so he needed a team to maintain, store and manage it. Frank Bacskay, Attila Pulay, Mark Czár and myself were given that task. Besides, we were all material scientists, and so we were interested in designing and using lead-lined containers to store the unrefined uranium. It suited us not to be involved in pure research anyway, because security clearances might not have been issued to Hungarian nationals.'

This answer fitted with Hahn's description of the four, but Eugene persisted, hoping that George might slip up. 'Why were you in Tailfingen in December 1943 when the Institute was still in Berlin?'

'That was Hahn's decision,' George answered. 'He was worried about the air raids over Berlin, and he knew it would only be a matter of time before the Institute was bombed, so he sent my team here to prepare for the Institute's eventual move to Tailfingen. We were four technicians, so our absence wouldn't have a significant impact on the Institute's research.'

Clever, thought Eugene, but it appeared to him too well rehearsed. In contrast, Pierre looked bored now that he realised Eugene was talking to a mere technician rather than to an internationally renowned scientist.

'Why do you think the Russians moved your three former colleagues from Budapest to Moscow, and why do you think they're making enquiries about you?' George was visibly unnerved by Eugene's question, which Eugene detected. Good, thought Eugene, he may falter yet.

George knew the real answer. He could give the Russians the process needed to enrich radioactive U-235 or plutonium in order to build an atomic bomb. 'Perhaps the Russians are amassing large amounts of uranium ore for their nuclear program, so they need a team to maintain, store and manage it.'

Without giving Eugene a chance to ask why three scientists with PhDs were needed just to store and maintain uranium ore, Pierre broke in. 'Why did you leave the Institute, George?'

'My team and myself were fired because we were Hungarian nationals.'

'Why did they let you stay when the other three left?' Pierre asked.

'Frank was single, and Attila and Mark were married to Hungarian women. I was the only one who was married to a German national. And Magrete, through her first husband, Herbert, had considerable weight within the high echelons of the German Reich, so it would have been problematic for a low-ranking administrative official to issue us with an order to leave. Her first husband was a friend of Himmler.' George knew that to deny the Himmler connection would be foolish.

'When I talked to people around here,' Pierre continued, 'they told me you worked part-time for the Institute. Why did that not pose a security threat?'

'Hahn hired me from late June 1944 to late October 1944 to oversee the recovery of uranium oxide from the bombed Berlin Institute, thereby recovering a valuable resource for his research as well as making the site safer for the public at large. My team managed to recover some 60 tons of it. Since the mission was in Berlin, it didn't require access to sensitive German Reich research done in Tailfingen.'

Pierre whistled in appreciation and asked, to Eugene's astonishment, 'If I make tools and men available, will you supervise a similar uranium recovery operation with respect to the destroyed Institute here in Tailfingen?'

'Of course I will,' George said.

Pierre stood, as did George, and they shook hands across the desk. Then Pierre walked around the desk and placed his arm across George's shoulders. Eugene could see a relieved George Nagy and a happy First Lieutenant Pierre Thomas. As the men were leaving the study, Pierre looked over his shoulder and said to Eugene in French, 'Thanks Eugene, most informative! Please send me a transcript of the interview in French.'

Baden-Baden approved the project, and sent Joliot-Curie a transcript of the interview. Joliot-Curie replied that Hahn and Westphal were well known to him, but George Nagy was not. His short report was handed to Pierre, who, at dinner on the following Saturday, handed it to Eugene, who read it and knew his opportunity to question George further was lost. He thought long and hard about the situation and decided that the one weak link in the Nagy family structure was the governess, Anna Schuster. He needed to isolate her from the family in order to get inside information that he needed about George and, more importantly, Magrete.

By the end of June, after attending ten of the most boring interviews, Pierre decided that as long as Eugene provided him with a transcript of each interview in French, his life as the only officer in Tailfingen was far too busy for him to be present at the interviews themselves. Pierre also reasoned since Eugene had to give him a written notification of whom he wished to interview, if Pierre thought that person was of interest to the French authorities he would attend those interviews. In the meantime, he was getting plenty of kudos for initiating a uranium recovery program in Tailfingen from the French headquarters in Baden-Baden. However, Eugene knew long before he reached Tailfingen, the Americans who had captured Hahn had removed most of the uranium from the Institute. The recovery program was a distraction he decided not to engage in, much to the delight of the French.

3

The French were determined that the mandatory second language in their zone would be French, in order that the Germans would better understand French culture. The lack of a strong central government in the French zone allowed each sector to make autonomous policies in all areas of German life. For the Germans, these inconsistencies in French policies across the various sectors in the French zone were seen as verging on incompetence. Despite the inconsistencies in such areas as public housing and rations, some Germans in the French zone did learn to appreciate French culture, and Magrete was one of them. She was pleased for Ilse to enrol in the local Catholic primary school in August 1945, as the curriculum had been revamped by the French authorities, and was completely cleansed of the Nazi curriculum. Both Magrete and Ilse were tutored in French by the wife of an administrator, paid with one piece of jewellery. Anna did not care to learn the language, nor was she interested in French culture.

What concerned Magrete was that the Reichsmarks she had in her satchel were now worthless. All new banknotes had Allied occupation marks, and the new coins were minted without swastikas. In actual fact, massive inflation dating back to the latter stages of the war had rendered the Allied Reichsmark not that much more valuable than the old Reichsmark. For all intents and purposes, money had been supplanted by a barter economy. The von Appen's jewellery was the most important transactional currency Magrete had, and she was worried it would not last long. George helped, having secured a position with the French authorities in Tailfingen, but there was little work available for women, even though German women in the French zone had made modest gains with regard to equal pay for equal work. Magrete was looking for paid employment, but the only opportunities available for her rested with the French and the small American delegation in Tailfingen, neither of which were interested in her services.

On 5 July a French private knocked on the door of 1 Neuweilerstraße and handed Anna a letter addressed to her. She was to attend a meeting at 50 Leimenhäulestraße, to be interviewed by First Lieutenant Pierre Thomas and Eugene Gould. The wording was identical to that of the letter George had received. Magrete and Anna had debriefed George when he returned from his interrogation and were pleased and relieved he was now working for the French authorities searching for uranium ore in the rubble of the Tailfingen Institute. Magrete was also troubled by the fact that she had missed her period last month, and was praying that she was not pregnant.

George and Magrete, in private conversations, had reasoned that Anna might be used as an informant about George's activities at the Institute. George questioned Anna lightly at dinner that night about her knowledge of his work. It was clear she had no knowledge of his research, and only knew his team members vaguely, because they had celebrated Christmas together in 1943. She did know that George had been sacked from the Institute and then reinstated, albeit in a casual capacity. They were both satisfied that Anna would reinforce George's testimony rather than discrediting it on any substantial point.

On the following morning, after Anna, Ilse and Magrete had completed their yoga exercises, Magrete saw Anna preparing to leave, wearing the black dress and shoes she had worn at the Ammann's dance.

'Anna, your clothes are inappropriate for an interview. I mean, you look stunning, but your dress and shoes are really for an evening out, not for a conversation with French and American officials.'

'Magrete,' Anna said in her most mature voice, 'I'm twenty-three, and you know how aloof the French are. I'm allowed to have a bit of fun.' The French had a policy of non-fraternisation; citizens of Occupied Germany and the French military and government officials were ordered to be kept separate, in order to help the French maintain control. It was the first time since Anna had been in Magrete's employ that she could claim her correct age without fear and she decided to do so since she wanted to impress the American captain, whom she judged would view her comparative youthfulness as an added bonus.

'Anna, this is serious. I will walk with you to Leimenhäulestraße and wait until they release you and walk you back home. There is no way you are going there alone wearing those clothes.'

'What about Ilse and Elisabeth?' Anna hoped that the difficulty of involving the children would dissuade Magrete from escorting her.

'I will carry Elisabeth and Ilse can walk with you. I will not take no for an answer.'

Anna knew Magrete well enough not to test her mettle, and they arrived at the villa near 10 am. The private knocked on the door and Eugene opened it to see two beautiful women. 'Which of you is Anna Schuster?'

The smaller, curvaceous one said, 'I am!'

Eugene looked at the blue-eyed brownish-blonde and asked, 'And who might you be?'

'Magrete,' she said, and thrust out the hand that was not supporting her baby.

Shaking her hand brought Eugene back to reality. 'Sergeant!' Eugene commanded over his shoulder.

A large man appeared and saluted him. 'Yes, sir!'

'Please drive madam and her children home.' As Magrete was about to protest Eugene added, 'Don't worry, madam, I'll make certain Anna arrives at your place safe and sound.'

Anna entered the villa as the sergeant escorted Magrete and her children to his jeep.

Eugene and Anna settled in the study, with Eugene behind the desk and Anna opposite him. Anna crossed one leg over the other so that Eugene could appreciate the shape of her legs. She wore no make-up and had no stockings to wear. Eugene knew that it would take a considerable amount of willpower and character to focus on the interview and not on her.

'May I call you Anna?'

Anna nodded and then straightened her dress so that it just covered her knees.

'Do you understand English?' Anna nodded again.

'My name is Eugene,' he said politely.

Anna enquired, 'Where is First Lieutenant Pierre Thomas?' While pleased in one way that he was not there, in another way she felt slighted – was she not important enough for him to be there? Typical French, she thought, so arrogant!

'Unfortunately, he intends to be with George Nagy today,' Eugene said. In fact, when he had written to Pierre to notify him of this interview, he had made it sound so mundane that he knew that Pierre would choose not to be present.

'Tell me about George Nagy,' he said. 'What do you know of his work?'

Anna had expected that question, but felt she needed to be protective of George. 'Why do you ask?' She adjusted her dress again to bring Eugene's attention back to her body.

'Because we're interested in his work at the Institute. Please just answer my questions! What do you know of his work?' Feeling he had overreacted, Eugene smiled briefly at Anna and she smiled back at him.

'Nothing much, really,' Anna replied, noting how good-looking Eugene was. 'I'm not a scientist I'm a governess! I know he headed a team at the Institute, and that's about it.' She had used the word 'governess' in order to impress him, and now she placed her hands under her knees, and noticed his eyes followed her movement.

Trying to keep his eyes on her face, though it was another distraction for him, Eugene asked, 'Have you met the members of his team?'

'Only once and that was … let me see … oh yes, Christmas 1943. I can't remember any of their names.' Anna looked at him smiling, and he found himself smiling back at her.

Changing tack, since he realised there was little she could tell him about George's scientific work, he said, 'When did Magrete first employ you?'

Anna thought long and hard and finally said, 'I think it was May 1936. I was hired as Magrete's personal maid.'

'How old were you then?'

'Fourteen.'

That sounded wrong to Eugene – her papers suggested she had been sixteen in 1936. 'Are you sure?'

'Of course I'm sure of my age.' Anna saw him frown.

Eugene asked quickly, 'The date you were born?'

'The 28th of February 1922.' She saw Eugene write it down on a pad in front of him.

Eugene knew it would be easier to locate her through her father's side of the family. 'And your father's name?'

'Joseph Schuster. He died before the war.' Anna's voice had an emotional edge.

That was all he needed to know about her personal details for the time being. He would check with the Berlin Document Centre, a repository for Nazi-era documents, to ascertain whether her or her father had been a card-carrying Nazi. He had been surprised to find that neither George nor Magrete were, and this placed the focus on Anna's father as the possible subordinate Nazi link to Herbert.

'When was the last time you saw Helmut Gruen?' Eugene closely scrutinised Anna's reaction.

Anna hesitated. 'Just before Christmas of 1943 in Beelitz.' She understood that if she mentioned Helmut's last visit in Tailfingen she might seriously jeopardise Helmut and, more importantly, Gertrude and the Nagy family.

'You never met him in Tailfingen?'

'No, never!' Anna looked at him and was sure he believed her.

'Tell me about Magrete's first husband, Herbert? What was he like as a person?' Eugene wanted to gauge her relationship to the only identified card-carrying Nazi in the household.

It was the first time in a long time that Anna had heard his name, and she recoiled. She had vivid memories of him groping her; Gertrude saving her; Elfi protecting her from him. She had never told Magrete what he had done to her. She suddenly blurted, 'Herbert was a filthy Nazi who should have been locked up! Thank goodness he died when he did! Magrete deserved better than that filthy swine of a man, and she got it. Herbert molested young women in the household, and the household hated him! I hated him!'

Then she put her hand to her mouth and started crying. She knew that if any of this got back to Magrete it would devastate her completely, and their relationship would be tarnished because Magrete would feel guilty for making Anna return to Berlin without her and so unintentionally subjecting Anna to a vile act.

Eugene quickly went to Anna and held her as she sobbed. 'Please don't tell Magrete what I've said,' she begged him through her tears. 'Please don't tell her! She would never forgive herself.' Eugene promised. He left the room and came back five minutes later with coffee and biscuits. Anna began to calm down as she drank her coffee, still sniffling.

Eugene drove Anna to the front door of the house. She looked totally vulnerable. 'It would be nice to see you again,' Eugene said, 'but in a friendlier atmosphere.'

Anna wiped away vestiges of her tears, smiled back at him and, as she left the car, said playfully, 'I take Elisabeth for a walk every day. It's up to you to find out where.' Driving off, Eugene knew he had a plan.

When Anna came into the house, Magrete wanted to know what had transpired during the interview. 'It was all about George,' Anna said. Magrete was relieved and pleased – and she had news.

'Anna, I'm pregnant.'

Anna laughed. 'That rhythm method of yours is definitely not working.'

When George got home, he also enquired about Anna's interview and was relieved it had gone as expected. He was shocked when Magrete told him she was pregnant again.

4

After Anna's interview, Eugene had determined that Anna's father was not listed as a Nazi in the Berlin Document Centre. He was surprised that the only confirmed Nazi in the von Appen household was Herbert, and so he concluded that Magrete was at best a fellow traveller.

From 6 July Anna had been meeting with Eugene at 9 am on the corner of Eisenbahnstraße (Railroad Street) and an alleyway that linked the villa to that street. She took Elisabeth with her, but not Ilse, as Ilse was preparing herself for school, which would start on 1 August.

Anna noticed that lots of women took a keen interest in Eugene, and to her delight he was completely oblivious of their attention. These women would hypocritically despise her as if she was a traitor or even a prostitute, since the war was too fresh in their memories and so Americans and the French were still viewed as enemies.

Anna and Eugene would walk for an hour or so. If it rained, Anna had an umbrella and if it was hot she used her umbrella for shade. Eugene asked about her life with Magrete and in doing so he gleaned facts about Herbert, Helmut, George, Ilse and Elisabeth as well.

Eugene was slowly falling in love with Anna and felt his deception was unworthy of her, but he was duty bound. By the end of July, because of Anna's reminiscences, he was convinced that George was just a technician, not a researcher, and that the Russians had got it wrong. Pierre, who reported that George had built a Geiger counter and located 10 tons of uranium ore, supported Eugene's conclusion. What Eugene did not know was that George knew the location of his research laboratory in the Institute rubble, and so had easily located the uranium ore that the Americans, relying on Hahn's memory, had overlooked. Eugene reasoned that Frank Bacskay, Attila Pulay and Mark Czár must have overstated the importance of their work at the Institute in order to get to Moscow, where their standard of living was far higher than in Budapest. He wrote a lengthy report to his commanding officer in the OSS, detailing why George was not worth further investigation at present. He put a caveat on his assessment, which depended on further information that could only be extracted from within Moscow itself. As this was not likely to be obtained at this point in time, he considered his first assignment to be partially complete.

Early in the morning on 3 August, George's work for the French authorities had come to an end. While he was walking home he saw Eugene pushing Elisabeth's pram, with Anna walking next to him. When George arrived home he immediately went to Magrete to give her the news.

'George, you really do not understand women, do you? That affair has been going on since early July.'

'When did she tell you?'

'She has not said a word. Anna is twenty-three and by that age I was married. She does not need my permission, or yours. Are you jealous that she has found herself a good-looking man?'

'Of course not!' George said. He liked being the only man in both of their lives and loved the company of younger women. 'She's dating a man who might be dangerous to this family,' he added.

'You mean she is dating the enemy?' Magrete laughed, shaking her head. 'Look, I married a Nazi who was a friend of Himmler's and he was a friend of yours too, amigo. This man is no Himmler; not even a Herbert.'

'He might turn her against us!'

'That is a risk I am prepared to take if it means she marries a man she loves. Look at Gertrude – a lifetime of servitude. Is that you want for Anna, to look after our children, to attend to our needs and put her life, her loves and her wants on hold forever?'

'I'm worried about her, that's all. I don't want her to get hurt. This man will one day fly back to America, leave her behind, and then what?'

'Then we will pickup the pieces and start again, pops!'

Baden-Baden headquarters shipped off the 10 tons of uranium ore recovered by George to Joliot-Curie's laboratory for analysis. Joliot-Curie was shocked to discover that the uranium ore he received did not contain 0.71 per cent of the radioactive isotope U-235, as he had expected, but ten times that amount. He was now convinced that Hahn had a secret research team, who were exploring the enrichment of radioactive U-235. He decided not to tell the authorities, due to the respect Hahn had shown him when the German Reich controlled France.

On 6 and 9 August 1945 the Japanese cities of Hiroshima and Nagasaki were bombed using nuclear weapons. It was the first time atomic bombs had been used in warfare. The first nuclear attacks killed approximately 130,000 men, women and children. The British officer in charge at Farm Hall gave Hahn the news. It completely shattered him; he felt that his discovery of fission had made the construction of nuclear weapons possible, and that he was personally responsible for the thousands of deaths in Japan. He contemplated suicide as the only way to escape from his deep depression. Fearing this, Max von Laue remained with him until he had weathered this personal crisis.

Later, when Heisenberg reviewed his calculations, he realised that he had embedded into them the fact that uranium would be always highly impure. Critical mass, he reasoned, could have been quickly realised if the scientists of the German Reich had access to pure or enriched U-235 or enriched radioactive plutonium. He thanked his gods that he was a theoretician and not an experimentalist.

Hahn recovered, and took solace in the fact that the German Reich had invaded Hungary, which had put an end to the enrichment program within his Institute that was headed by Dr George Nagy.

5

On 15 September Pierre arrived at the villa for the weekly dinner and informal updates on Eugene's work in Tailfingen. Typically, Pierre would receive one of Eugene's reports, sign off on it or include a few pages of his own as an addendum, then send it to Baden-Baden. He never sent his reports to his superior officer in Ebingen, nor was he expected to.

In September 1945, General Eisenhower rescinded all previous non-fraternisation orders with respect to the American zone. It also applied to Americans in other zones. Nevertheless, Pierre was concerned by reports that were filtering to him, through French female bureaucrats, who were jealous of Anna, that Eugene had been seen walking with Anna Schuster, the governess of George Nagy's children. He planned to raise this concern with Eugene at tonight's weekly dinner.

Eugene was also concerned about his relationship with Anna. At first, he had seen her as a possible source of information about Magrete, George, Helmut Gruen, and, more importantly, Magrete's relationship with Margarete Himmler and the top echelon of the Nazi government. At the same time, he was attracted to her looks and curvaceous body. Anna was not worldly, having been closeted in the von Appen and then in the Nagy households for most of her formative years. It was her naivety that started his fall, but her passion that cemented his love for her.

Eugene understood that his relationship with Anna had compromised his investigations. Under the current American directives he was banned from marrying her, but not from seeing her.

After the two men greeted each other they were left alone in the dining area, as the five non-commissioned soldiers had dined earlier.

After the entrée was served and the waiter had retreated, Eugene said to Pierre quite unexpectedly, 'Magrete's governess Anna and I are seeing each other on a regular basis, and I fear she might have compromised some of the my objectives for being here.'

'You two have been the talk of the village, I must confess,' Pierre said, and smiled. 'My female bureaucrats aren't happy, because of our non-fraternisation directive. How is it compromising your investigations?'

'Magrete is the obvious problem,' Eugene said, leaving his other concerns aside for the moment. 'Anna and she get on well and Magrete is a friend of Marga Himmler and is also thought to have connections with the top echelon of the Nazi party. I've been asked to interview Magrete by the US chief prosecutor, Supreme Court Justice Robert Jackson. Even before Himmler committed suicide, a lot of people believed that Marga was well aware of the Holocaust and may have even encouraged her husband to commit some of the anti-Jewish atrocities. We've collected evidence to suggest that in 1941 she and her daughter, in the company of Heinrich, visited Dachau concentration camp near Munich.'

They had finished their entrée and were drinking a glass of Hungarian red wine that Pierre had brought to the dinner, courtesy of George Nagy. Pierre swirled his glass, looked at the colour of the wine and enquired, 'Didn't Marga end up working for the German Red Cross, or DRK as they called it?'

‘She did,’ Eugene said. ‘By December 1939, she was supervising the Red Cross hospitals in Military District III (Berlin–Brandenburg). For her efforts, she reached the rank of colonel in the DRK.’

They stopped talking business while dinner was being served. Eugene took a sip of wine. ‘Nice,’ he observed. ‘Where did you get it?’

‘It’s Bikavér and it came from the husband of your worst enemy in Tailfingen.’ Pierre smiled.

‘I wouldn’t call Magrete my worst enemy,’ Eugene said. ‘She’s just a problem. Anyway, we have Marga Himmler’s diaries and in one of her entries she wrote …’ Eugene flipped open a notebook and read aloud: ‘Then I was in Posen, Łódź and Warsaw. This Jewish rabble, Polacks most of them don’t look like human beings and the dirt is indescribable. It’s an incredible job trying to create order there.’

‘Hardly incriminating,’ Pierre observed. ‘Even in today’s world we allow bigots and racists to roam the streets of France so long as they don’t incite violence or put their ideas into action. I’m sure it’s the same in America.’

‘I know,’ Eugene agreed. ‘I wonder if you could question Magrete in the municipal offices. I could give you a list of questions that I’d like you to ask her on my behalf, which of course you can edit as well as incorporate your own questions. It would be handy if I could hear her answers, so that I could give you follow-up questions.’

‘You could sit in the room next door with my secretary,’ Pierre suggested, ‘and now and then she could walk in and give me one of your notes.’

‘Perfect!’ Eugene exclaimed, looking relieved.

‘Lucky you’re in the French zone,’ Pierre said. ‘A Frenchman will do a lot to let love flourish.’

‘And thank goodness General Eisenhower has rescinded all the non-fraternisation orders with respect to us,’ Eugene replied.

‘To love!’ Pierre toasted, and they clinked glasses.

On 20 September 1945, President Truman signed an executive

order terminating the OSS. His order would become effective from 1 October 1945. Eugene was assigned to the Secret Intelligence and Counter-Espionage branches, which were housed in the Strategic Services Unit (SSU). The Secretary of War appointed Brigadier General John Magruder (formerly Donovan's deputy director for intelligence in OSS) as the new SSU director. The brigadier instructed Eugene to remain in Tailfingen, to gather any intelligence on the whereabouts of Martin Bormann, and to obey his predecessor's instructions.

6

The French bureaucrats were not prepared to help German women engage in any social or political activity; rather they came armed to de-Nazify the German bureaucracy, to re-educate German citizens, and to build a democratic German satellite territory on the Rhine, administered by the French and within the reach of France.

On 15 October Magrete was notified that she was going to be interviewed by First Lieutenant Pierre Thomas in the Mayoral Offices of Tailfingen. There was no mention of Captain Eugene Gould. Magrete and George, in bedroom discussions that night, reasoned that the captain's absence was more than likely a direct consequence of his growing relationship with Anna. They decided not to tell Anna about the interview unless they had to. Anna was becoming very sensitive to any criticisms George made of Americans when he listened to his shortwave radio.

At 10 am on 16 October Magrete went to the Mayoral Offices. The administrator's secretary was female, and not too different in age to Magrete. The secretary, who spoke only French, told Magrete to be seated. Thanks to her French lessons, Magrete could follow the secretary's instructions without difficulty.

After thirty minutes, the secretary showed Magrete into an empty office and told her to sit in front of a large desk, and she left the door open as if to keep an eye on her. Thirty minutes later a small man wearing a French uniform walked into the room. Magrete stood and he sat in the chair behind the desk, motioning in a contemptuous manner for Magrete to be seated as he rifled through a number of papers that he had brought with him. Magrete noticed the door behind her remained slightly ajar.

He spoke to her in French. 'My name is First Lieutenant Pierre Thomas. Do you prefer French or English?'

Magrete spoke to him in French but said, 'Anglais', much to his disappointment.

'Madam,' Pierre began in English, 'we've a series of questions we need to put to you. We've reviewed your past, and hold a number of documents about you, so please, for your own sake, speak truthfully.' Magrete nodded.

'You were born in Vienna on the 8th of February 1914 and baptised in a Catholic church. Your father and mother died on the 10th of April 1938 because of a leaking gas pipe. You have a sister, Wilhelmina, who lives with a husband and one child in your former parents' home in Vienna. Your father was the Deputy Commissioner of the Vienna Police and your mother was a homemaker. You married Herbert von Appen on the 4th April 1936. He was killed on the 8th November 1938 at Kitzingen Airfield in a plane crash while being trained as a pilot by the Luftwaffe. You married George Nagy on the 10th of September 1943. You have two children – Ilse von Appen and Elisabeth Nagy. Have I missed anything so far?' He raised his eyes from the document to look directly at her.

'No, sir, except that Ilse has the legal surname Nagy,' Magrete said.

Pierre looked at her stomach and asked, 'Are you pregnant?'

'Four months, First Lieutenant,' Magrete replied. She noted that he had the opportunity here to ask her to call him by his first name, but he didn't.

'When did your first husband, Herbert, join the Nazi party?'

Pierre did not hide his disgust when asking the question.

'I really don't know. It could have been anytime from when I first met him in 1931 to 1936, when I was staying in the von Appen household.'

'When did you join the Nazi party?'

Magrete looked surprised, smiled at Pierre and replied, 'I have never-'.

Pierre interrupted her, saying with contempt, 'You're a fellow traveller - I take it!'

Magrete thought before she answered. She knew that if she tried to defend her position it would not be believable. She needed to be consistent with the paper trail that he obviously had access to. 'When I was engaged to Herbert, I was considered a fellow traveller,' she said. It was clearly not an admission he expected, and he did not pickup the nuance of her answer, suggesting to her that his command of the English language was not particularly strong.

As Pierre rifled again through the papers his secretary stepped in and said, in French, 'For you, sir.' He read the paper handed to him, then asked, 'When did you first meet Himmler and his wife Marga?'

'At my wedding reception.'

'And at your husband's and your in-laws' funerals?'

'Himmler was there, but he had another woman escorting him, Frau Potthast, his then secretary.'

'Tell me about your relationship with Marga Himmler.'

'We eventually got on well,' Magrete said, glancing at the door, which was still ajar. 'We had morning tea together several times. In fact, in September 1939 when I was on my way to my sister's place in Vienna, I paid her a visit at Gmund am Tegersee in Bavaria, not far from Munich.'

'Did she ever talk to you about the war, her husband's duties and her many visits to concentration camps?'

'No,' Magrete said honestly. 'She was more interested in the DRK and her contribution to it. As a matter of fact, it was because of her interest that Peter von Appen asked me to write a dossier for him on how his company could get her involved in gifting to the DRK four of its department stores – Magdeberg, Prague, Munich and Leipzig – to be rebuilt as hospitals. Albert Speer designed the conversions. If memory serves me right, Peter made the transfer of the stores contingent on Marga choosing which DRK hospital she wanted to manage. She chose one in Berlin so that her daughter Gudrun could be closer to her father. As a mother myself, I can understand why she made such a choice.'

Pierre frowned. Magrete was making Marga sound normal, and she did not seem to fear her association with Marga. 'Tell me about Wannsee and the sale of the von Appen's villa to the Nordhav Foundation.'

'I was the chair of the board of directors of von Appen Pty Ltd-'

Pierre interrupted, 'A woman as the chair of the board of directors of a company – unbelievable!'

'Yes, many people said a woman should be a homemaker and not in business – it's view that the Nazis and Catholics have in common. But as to your question, Helmut Gruen sold von Appen's villa to the owners of our neighbouring property, the Nordhav Foundation. The board of directors approved of the sale on the 20th of February 1942. When I ceased being the chair, on the 11th of October 1943, I sold all my shares to Helmut Gruen. It is all there in the company records.'

'The company records were destroyed when Alexanderplatz was erased in February 1944,' Pierre said. Magrete heard a soft male groan from the direction of the secretary's office.

Pierre decided to end the interview, because the next five questions that Eugene proposed did not make sense to him. 'Thank you for coming. My secretary will see you out. We may decide to interview you again at a future date.'

Magrete walked to the door and thought she heard someone

scrambling to leave as the secretary held her there temporarily before showing her the exit.

Eugene was disappointed that Pierre had stopped when he did, but he knew that asking questions about Helmut Gruen was not in the brief he had given Pierre. When Eugene returned to the office, Pierre immediately asked, 'Who the hell is Helmut Gruen?'

'He is a person of interest to the US government, because of his financial dealings,' Eugene explained. 'I should have warned you, but you did the right thing. You didn't confuse the focus of this session and rightly edited out those questions that weren't relevant.'

'What did you think?' Pierre asked.

'To be truthful, I really didn't think she would be so candid about her Nazi affiliations and her dealings with Marga Himmler. She made her sound almost human. All the answers Marga has given to questions about Magrete and the von Appen company exactly matched what Magrete told us today. The same goes for Albert Speer, who told us he redesigned exactly those four von Appen stores into DRK hospitals. We know Magrete has never visited a concentration camp and, for that matter, she has never been out of the German Reich, except on her honeymoon when she went to Venice. She was not a member of the Nazi party, although she was, as she has reluctantly confessed to you, a fellow traveller. Her only Nazi interactions were with Himmler and his wife, and even those meetings were because of funerals or the odd tea party or two. Politically stupid no doubt, politically naive perhaps, but what can you say? There are lots of people in America who hold similar political views as the Nazis and their fellow travellors.'

'I never knew George had such an attractive wife,' Pierre observed. 'No wonder he's very protective of her.'

It is a pity Pierre told her that all the company records had been destroyed, Eugene thought. That evening he wrote a report to be sent to the SSU and to the office of US chief prosecutor the Supreme Court Justice Robert Jackson in Nuremberg, informing him that Magrete

Nagy (neé Holweg) was not involved in Nazi activities that could be the subject of a prosecution, and that Marga Himmler's version of events was consistent with the Magrete's testimony. He included a record of the interview. Pierre received the latter, but not the report. Eugene was certain that another opportunity would arise for him to grill Magrete about the business activities of Helmut Gruen and her involvement in the company.

7

French resources for the occupation of Germany were scarce – so scarce that the French offered almost no assistance to the German population and demanded that the Germans pay for all aspects of the occupation in the French zone. The French had little sympathy for these people, as they had lived in relative comfort during the war, being mostly rural and without significant industry, in a zone that was only lightly bombed and barely engaged in the war. The German Reich, however, had stripped French resources and forced the French to serve as workers in order to prosecute the war. The French were not interested in leaving Occupied Germany for this reason: they envisioned that their zone should be a permanent buffer between Occupied Germany and France, acting as a more effective Maginot line to contain any future German aggression. The French also had no interest in a German economic recovery; they were the rulers and the Germans in their zone were the ruled.

Magrete was finding it harder and harder to source enough food for her family in the barter economy of the French zone. While the French remained aloof and turned a blind eye to the ways Germans managed to survive, the economic pressure on individual families was severe. The one saving grace was that they were living in a rural district surrounded by farms and not by bombed-out factories. Another advantage her family had was that First Lieutenant Pierre

Thomas and George had got on well ever since George recovered the leftover uranium ore from the bombed Tailfingen Institute. The Tailfingen administrator would sometimes give George casual work in areas where the French lacked access to professional skills. George's higher education centred on material science, but his undergraduate degree centred on electrical engineering, and so from time-to-time he was employed by Pierre to repair and maintain power distribution networks in the Tailfingen district.

Magrete's other asset was Anna. Her relation with Eugene Gould was worrying, but fruitful. He would often invite Anna to his villa. He would park the jeep in front of their house and toot the horn to announce his arrival. Anna would fly out the front door, hop in the passenger seat, and he would whisk her away. When they returned, he would stop in front of the house, and they would say their goodbyes. Magrete would hear the front door open and slam shut to announce Anna's return. He never acknowledged the existence of Magrete's family.

Economically, his presence had a twofold effect. Firstly, Anna was no longer home for every meal and secondly, he would often take Anna for country drives over the weekend. Pierre turned a blind eye to these weekend excursions that Anna would exploit in order to make Eugene purchase some food for the household. The American dollar was a very important currency on the black market in the French zone and with his American uniform and Anna's bartering skills – learnt from Magrete – farmers were careful not to overcharge them. This brought into the household some much-needed fresh produce.

Early in November Magrete began to sense that Anna was becoming more distant. It was as if they were the same poles of a magnet – every time Magrete moved closer to Anna, she would feel an equal and opposite force pushing her away. It had begun when George and Anna were listening to a radio report on events that were occurring in Nuremberg.

On 6 October it was announced on the radio that the four chief prosecutors of the International Military Tribunal (IMT) – Robert H. Jackson (United States), Francois de Menthon (France), Roman A. Rudenko (Soviet Union) and Sir Hartley Shawcross (Great Britain) – had made indictments against twenty-four leading Nazi officials. Anna made it known to Magrete she resented Magrete's historical links with the Nazis – something that Magrete was unable to alter.

At other times Anna would be the Anna of old. When she wanted to know why the rhythm method of preventing pregnancy did not work for Magrete, Magrete laughed and told her that it was not the method that was at fault, but rather her inability to count the days since her last period while George was desperately trying to make love to her.

On 23 November Magrete announced that they would be celebrating Hanukkah this year – the festival of lights. Ilse was in particular pleased, George was puzzled and Anna was ecstatic. For the first time since her parents' death, her Jewishness was being celebrated and not cursed. She thought about telling Eugene she was Jewish, but their relationship was in its initial stages, and without documentation what would be the point. For her part, Magrete had decided not to tell Anna they were related until she could source official documentation. After all, there was no urgency, because they were acting as a family unit in any case.

The very next day Anna walked Ilse to the villa. By now the private at the gate knew her well and immediately opened the gate for her. She took Ilse inside the villa for the first time. Eugene was walking down the stairs when he saw Ilse and Anna waiting for him in the foyer. He asked, smiling at them, 'What brings you two beauties to my place?'

Ilse looked up and said, 'Wow! Your stairway is big.'

'Now that I come to think of it, it is big. Ilse, go through the door on your left and ask the cook to bring us some coffee and biscuits,' Eugene instructed. 'Ask her to bring it outside to the back verandah and then come and join us there.' Ilse ran off and did as she was told.

Eugene took Anna by the arm and escorted her to a table on the outside verandah. 'Is this where you take all your girlfriends when you get a bit more serious about them?' Anna said with a smile.

Eugene smiled back, pointed to the path and said, 'That's the path I would run along to get to the alleyway and then to Eisenbahnstraße to meet Elisabeth and you.'

Just then Ilse returned and sat herself down on the seat next to Anna. 'Your cook is really nice. She gave me a piece of chocolate. I've never had chocolate before.'

The cook came and served Anna and Eugene coffee and biscuits and gave Ilse a large glass of milk and two chocolate biscuits. 'Thank you for giving her chocolate,' Anna said to the cook, in a friendly manner. The cook nodded and walked back to the kitchen.

'Oh, by the way,' Eugene said, 'I won't be here for the next six weeks. I'll be leaving tomorrow to go to Nuremberg. Robert Jackson, the American prosecutor, is reviewing Marga Himmler's case, and he wants me there to go over some matters that I raised in my report. We're going to interrogate her again – for the last time, I suspect.'

'I hope that bitch gets life,' Anna said emphatically.

'What's a bitch?' Ilse asked.

'A female dog,' Eugene answered, looking at Anna, who poked her tongue out at him behind Ilse's back.

Anna was pleased that she did not have to make an excuse to Eugene about her absence in the following week.

8

On the evening of the first day of Hanukkah, Kislev 25 Hanukkah 1, Anna had the family in the lounge room, explaining to them the meaning of Hanukkah. They could not celebrate Hanukkah during the day, as Ilse was attending school.

'Hanukkah is about God's protection of the Israelites, and the miracles that occurred on that day. It's not the most important holy day of the Jewish year, but it should be! The holiday celebrates the triumph over military might, when a band of Israelites stood up for their right to be Jewish. They were prohibited under the penalty of death from studying their sacred texts or performing important commandments. Their holy Temple had been defiled, and they were ordered to worship other gods. But a small band of faithful Israelites, known as the Maccabees, rose up and defeated the invaders, reclaimed the Temple, and rededicated it to God - '

'I get it!' Ilse interrupted. 'The invaders are the Nazis and the Mac-, Maccabees, are like us.'

'I never thought about it like that,' Anna said, 'but you've got a point, Ilse.'

'Ilse,' Magrete said, more sternly, 'let Anna finish.'

Anna lowered her voice, which invited them to huddle closer together. 'The eternal flame in the Temple's great menorah (lamp stand) had to be lit. But the sacred olive oil that needed to burn in the lamp, took eight days to press and purify. The Jews only had a day's supply of oil. They decided, in faith, to light the flame anyway and then a great miracle occurred – the jug of oil refilled itself each day and so the Temple's great menorah was relit. This continued for seven days, the exact time it took to prepare the new oil. Since that time, Hanukkah has been celebrated for eight days to recall the miracle of when the menorah burned for eight days at the Temple. The main miracle of Hanukkah is the victory of the Maccabees against the most powerful army in the world.'

'They beat the Nazis!' Ilse could not contain herself and they all smiled.

Anna continued to whisper. 'The most basic thing you need to celebrate Hanukkah is a Hanukkiah and candles.'

Ilse enquired, 'What's a Hanukkiah?'

'It's a special candle holder that George will build tomorrow,' Anna replied grinning at George.

'Mum, do we have candles?'

Magrete said, 'We do Ilse, but let Anna talk.'

'The eight branches represent the eight nights,' Anna explained, 'and the last one is usually higher than the rest, and is called the shamash (helper candle) and is used to light the rest of the candles.'

'Shamash,' Ilse repeated.

'The Hanukkiah is usually lit after sunset. On the first night, the shamash is lit, and a blessing is recited as the first candle is lit.'

Ilse asked, 'What's the blessing?'

'I won't say it in Yiddish, but on the first night this is what we'd recite. "Blessed are You, O Lord Our God, Ruler of the Universe, Who has sanctified us with Your commandments and commanded us to kindle the lights of Hanukkah. Blessed are You, O Lord our God, Ruler of the Universe, Who made miracles for our forefathers in those days at this time. Blessed are You, O Lord Our God, Ruler of the Universe, Who has kept us alive, sustained us and brought us to this season."'

Ilse could not remain silent. 'Which one is the first candle and how do you light it?'

'You're a Miss Curiosity, aren't you? The first candle is the one on the far right. The candles are placed in the Hanukkiah from right to left, but they're lit from left to right. So the candle that you light first is the last candle you placed in the Hanukkiah, and the candle you light last is the first one you placed on it.'

Anna then showed them how to make potato pancakes, known as latkes in Yiddish. George, under Anna's instruction, repainted Elisabeth's spinning top. On each of the four sides of the top he imprinted a Hebrew letter. Together the letters formed an acronym for the Hebrew words meaning - 'A great miracle happened there' - referring to the miracle of the oil. Anna showed Magrete, George,

Ilse and Elisabeth how she played with the top with her father and mother.

The following day, with Anna supervising, George nailed a piece of dowelling between two flat pieces of wood, the top piece 30 by 5 cm, and the bottom piece 40 by 5 cm. He then cut nine holes into the 30 cm piece. Anna gave him nine candles, and he shaved the end of each one with a razor blade so that the bottom was tapered, and placed the tapered end in one of the holes. He had built a nine-branch candelabra of sorts.

That evening they sat in the lounge room listening to Anna. 'Today is the 1st of December: Kislev 26 Hanukkah II. It's called Kislev. Since tonight is the second night of Hanukkah, the shamash and two other candles are lit. The lit Hanukkiah is usually placed near a window, so that people passing by are reminded of the miracle of Hanukkah. But I don't want us to do that here – it might make us unsafe, and I don't want anything to happen to my family.'

Magrete was proud that Anna considered them as her family. She wondered if Ester had told Anna that they were related. She would pursue the matter once she could prove to Anna that they were.

'Tonight the blessing we recite is a bit different,' Anna continued, 'but we say it every night from tonight onward. It goes: "Blessed are You, O Lord Our God, Ruler of the Universe, Who has sanctified us with Your commandments and commanded us to kindle the lights of Hanukkah. Blessed are You, O Lord our God, Ruler of the Universe, Who made miracles for our forefathers in those days at this time."'

Not only did they eat latkes that evening, but also, with Anna's instructions, Magrete cooked small powdered sugar donuts called sufganiyot, which they devoured.

On the evening of 2 December, Kislev 26 Hanukkah III, they repeated the previous night's ritual, the only difference being that each person was given a small gift from Anna. She gave George a Jewish cookbook that she had hidden away; to Ilse and Elisabeth, Marie-Teresa coins that her parents had given her; and to Magrete a beautiful silk scarf, which she placed on Magrete's head. Magrete immediately recognised it as the scarf Ester had worn on the first day they met.

'No! You cannot give me your grandmother's scarf,' Magrete protested. 'You must have something of Ester's when you want to honour her.'

'Magrete,' Anna said, 'the scarf is mine to give.'

'Thank you,' Magrete said, showing with her smile how grateful she was for this loving gift.

The dates 3 and 4 December were Kislev 28 Hanukkah IV and Kislev 29 Hanukkah V. Those evenings were spent playing with the dreidel that George had painted.

After dinner on 4 December, when Elisabeth had been put to bed, they broke up into two teams: Anna and Ilse versus George and Magrete. Each team was given ten sufganiyot. The four of them sat in a circle around the dreidel and a pot. They took it in turns to spin the repainted dreidel. The letter the dreidel landed on instructed the team to put a sufganiyot into the pot or take one out. The game ended when someone held all the sufganiyots. By sheer coincidence Ilse and Anna always won. They would share their spoils with Magrete and George, but only after the losing team bowed on hands and knees and sang, 'You're the great ones! The great ones!' Ilse loved the fact that this game gave her power over her mother.

The following two days were Tevet 1 Hanukkah VI (Rosh Chodesh Tevet) and Tevet 2 Hanukkah VII. By now Magrete and George were getting used to Anna and Ilse winning the dreidel game of chance. George and Magrete refused the offers of sufganiyots when they lost on 4 December, because Ilse demanded that they bathe Anna's and her feet. In the end, Ilse agreed to give them sufganiyots if they bowed five times and asked for mercy. Magrete remarked that she would hate to live under the rule of Queen Ilse.

The final day of Hanukkah was 7 December – Tevet 3 Hanukkah VIII. George thought Ilse was old enough to discuss the importance of religious freedom, and after dinner he said, 'You know, Ilse, that Magrete and I were both baptised Catholic and Anna is Jewish. Do you know what I mean by religious freedom?'

'Dad, I'm not dumb,' Ilse said, rolling her eyes at the ceiling. 'I've been taught by one of the best teachers. Isn't that right, Anna?'

Anna hugged her. 'That's right. You tell your father!'

'You're attending a Catholic school,' George continued, 'and they'll probably teach all about Jesus and God. The God they're talking about is the same God that Anna loves.'

'I hope you're not this embarrassing when I bring my first boyfriend home!' Ilse said. Magrete and Anna hid their smiles behind their hands.

George looked at Magrete and said 'I tried.'

'Give it up, pops!' Ilse said, and even George had to laugh.

That night, after Ilse went to bed, Magrete brought out some bread and a piece of Edam. George's eye widened. 'Where did you get the Edam?'

'Don't ask!'

Anna smelt the cheese; the aroma was divine. George left and immediately returned with a bottle of his favourite Hungarian red wine and three glasses. It was the first time Anna had tasted Edam and the first time she had drunk wine. She liked the cheese better than the wine.

'Who taught Ilse to call me "pops"?' George looked at Magrete, who shook her head, and then at Anna, who laughed, not because she was guilty, but because the wine was making her light-headed.

'Watch out, pops!' Anna whispered. 'Ilse is listening from upstairs.'

They did not want to celebrate Christmas that year, but they did so for Elisabeth's sake and so on Christmas Eve carols were sung, presents were exchanged, and a small Christmas tree was sourced and decorated.

9

In January 1946 President Truman created the Central Intelligence Group (CIG). Eugene was still with the SSU. On 3 January 1946 the German scientists at Farm Hall were allowed to return to Occupied Germany. Hahn, Heisenberg and von Laue were brought to the city of Göttingen, which was controlled by the British occupation authorities. In 1946 Fritz Straßmann started the construction of a new Institute of Chemistry on the site of the former Flak-Kaserne barracks in Bretzenheim, in proximity to the newly built university. Repair and renovation work was performed on existing buildings and some new ones were constructed. Hahn automatically assumed that George Nagy had been repatriated to Hungary, and so he made no enquiries as to George's whereabouts.

On 12 January Eugene had returned from Nuremberg and Anna was at the villa to greet him. He unpacked and then joined her on the back verandah in time for coffee and biscuits. In the background a radio was broadcasting the daily news from America. Anna, who had not seen him for some time, saw that he looked tired.

'You should try to get some sleep,' she said. 'You look wrecked! What happened to Marga? Is she behind bars?'

'We interrogated her for the third time. Magrete was right about her. She was not informed of her husband's official business, and so my recommendation not to put her on trial was upheld. She's infuriating to interview, though. She talks endlessly about trivia, gossips about everyone and everything. I don't understand how Magrete could stand her, or call her a friend.'

'Magrete's Nazi friends make me sick! How did the Nazi trials go?'

'Trying those Nazis is fairly daunting. What's so shocking is the systematic way they tried to eradicate the Jewish people in Europe. The Jews have been hated since Christianity birthed, but it reach its peak under Hitler.'

Anna was tempted to reveal that she was Jewish, but at the last minute thought it was pointless without documentation.

'The systematic eradication was really planned at Wannsee,' Eugene said.

'Wannsee!' Anna shouted in disbelief. 'That's impossible! Elfi and Peter von Appen would never do that!'

'Your next-door neighbour, Reinhard Heydrich, was an evil man. After he bought the von Appen property, he held a conference at Wannsee with fifteen top Nazi bureaucrats, to coordinate the "final solution", the idea being to exterminate the entire Jewish population in continental Europe – eleven million or so people.' Eugene suddenly saw an opportunity he should have taken up long before. 'Anna, you were living at Wannsee, can you remember if Magrete or Herbert had any dealings with their next-door neighbour?'

'I wouldn't know. I was her personal maid at the time and nobody would talk politics when I was around.'

'Was Helmut Gruen around much?'

'Only when that filthy Herbert died, and then I was mostly upstairs looking after Ilse, who was a baby then, so I wasn't involved in what was going on downstairs. Look, I can't help you when it comes to Magrete. Her Nazi stuff really frightens me. The friends she had were just evil. When I think about it, I just want to leave her. I get angry and snap at her, and then she looks at me with those big beautiful blue eyes and it's like I'm under her spell again. When I do leave her, though, I'll never want to see her again.'

'That's a bit drastic,' Eugene said.

'Don't worry, I'm not ready to leave right now,' Anna said. 'It's like I'm sitting on the edge of a cliff, and I need something to push me over, and that something hasn't arrived yet.'

They started to walk towards the alleyway on the way to Eisenbahnstraße.

10

On 10 July 1945, the first American Forces Network (AFN) station started broadcasting from Munich. AFN Munich was the station that kept English-speaking Germans informed about what was happening in Occupied Germany, Austria and in Europe in general, but more importantly showcased American politics and its economic might. Every European country that was occupied by the German Reich found that its far-flung colonies were under threat from within, because of the growing realisation that self-rule underpinned America's success. The War of Independence had established a free and prosperous America, and yet there were few free and prosperous colonies, because countries in war-torn Europe extracted colonial wealth back to the homeland. America silently campaigned for colonial independence in order to open up markets that, if not completely closed to them, were difficult for the US to penetrate. The Dutch and the French especially felt this pressure. In its occupied zone, the French were determined to mitigate American influence as much as possible. The problem was that the tongue of wealth was English and the currency that was most valued was the US dollar.

Anna and George would listen to AFN Munich whenever they could, for the news and for music. The big singing stars were Perry Como, Frank Sinatra and Nat King Cole and the jitterbug was the dance craze of the American troops. Magrete did not mind the music, but hearing the news depressed her, and hearing about the Nuremberg trials on the radio made her feel even more insecure. What surprised Magrete was that Anna, who during the war had taken no interest in the news, or listening to the radio, after the war became addicted to it.

It was Magrete's birthday today – 8 February. It fell on a Friday and so all celebrations were put on hold until Ilse came home from school. Elisabeth was nearly two, and Magrete was thirty-two years old and very pregnant. She had not heard from her sister for a while and was pleased that she got a letter from Mimi wishing her a happy birthday. Mimi and Albert were desperately hoping for another child, a girl, but so far without success. Mimi remarked that even though they came from the same parents, Magrete's genes were obviously healthier. Magrete smiled when she remembered how difficult it had been for her to become pregnant with Herbert, whereas with George it was something she could have done without. Why do women always blame themselves, she thought? Why do they never blame the men?

Magrete knew it was only a matter of time before Anna married Eugene, even though at present it was illegal. She mused about the three apexes of the triangle: Anna, Eugene and herself. If only Hitler had not existed, she thought, and if only Eugene had met her in another place and time, she was certain that they would have been friends. She liked his honesty, and she liked the way both Anna and he had grown in their relationship. Anna was passionate and he was more rational. So many people would have let their hate for Marga Himmler swamp them, but in his case, she thought, it was the rule of law that mattered and not his feelings. Anna was lucky to have met such a man.

Magrete looked over to George and Anna. He was leaning towards the radio, and Anna looked angry. They are clearly listening to the news about Nuremberg, she thought. She stood up to go to the kitchen and collapsed back into the armchair. 'Anna! My water has broken!'

The next six hours flashed past. Ilse had arrived home from school and went into the bedroom, only to be ushered out. George was fretting, as if he was birthing the child himself, so Anna instructed him to mind Elisabeth. There were endless shouts of 'Push! Push'; Anna mopping Magrete's forehead; pain, weariness, and more pain.

By 6 o'clock that evening Magrete's face looked scrubbed red, and a child lay asleep on her bosom. Sitting on one side of the bed were George and Elisabeth and on the other side were Anna and Ilse.

In the middle were Magrete and a tiny girl.

'What should we name this child who has the same birthday as me?'

'I've no preference,' George said.

'Ilse, what do you think?'

'I wanted a brother, Mum, so let's call her Robyn,' Ilse answered, with a cheeky smile.

'A bet each way, hey, Ilse? Anna?'

'If she was my child I'd name her after my mother,' Anna said, sadly.

'Raise your right hand for Eva and your left hand for Robyn,' Magrete proposed. 'Three votes for Eva and one for Robyn. Eva it is!'

'Dad cheated!' Ilse shouted. 'He raised Elisabeth's right hand!'

'Your dad has every right to cheat,' Anna said sternly. 'Have pity on him. All night he acted like he was birthing the child!' They all laughed except George.

When Mimi was informed that Magrete had a girl and named her Eva, she was upset; she had wanted to use her mother's Christian name for her own future child. She was mollified, though, by the fact that Eva's middle name was the same as hers, Wilhelmina.

11

In September 1945 General Eisenhower rescinded all previous non-fraternisation orders. In their place was now a more simplified order banning marriages between Americans and Germans. Eugene knew that if he were in the American zone his relationship with Anna would be problematic, due to Anna's connection to Magrete. However, in the French zone as an American soldier he had far more leeway. Furthermore, the sergeant, corporal, and three privates often brought German women into their rooms late at night when they were off duty. Eugene would turn a blind eye to their activities, so they paid him the same respect. In public, he and Anna never held hands, hugged, kissed or showed any other signs of affection. Nevertheless, everyone in Tailfingen knew what was going on, but because of the respect for the von Appen name, it never filtered down to Magrete, George, or their children.

On the morning of Friday 15 March Eugene received a telegram from Berlin. It was from an SI office, informing him that all of his mother's family had died in an Auschwitz gas chamber. His men could hear him crying in the bedroom. The sergeant took the initiative and sent for Anna.

Anna arrived, was ushered into his bedroom, and the door shut behind her. Four soldiers left for a brothel, leaving the youngest private to guard the villa. Anna saw Eugene prostrated on the bed, crying like a child. He had taken off his boots and his uniform jacket, and wore only his army pants. Anna sat down next to him and pulled his head onto her lap, gently stroking his cheek while looking at him with total empathy. 'What's wrong?' she asked. 'What's happened?'

Eugene could not look at her, he felt so ashamed of his tears. But he needed someone to talk to, and she was the perfect person. He regained some composure, hooded his eyes with his hand and handed her the telegram.

Anna read it, then put it down and gently kissed him. She kissed him again, very tenderly. The next time she kissed him he felt totally comforted. She slid her body down next to his, and he automatically placed his arm around her waist. She kissed the side of his neck. He drew her hair back from her eyes and kissed her back, then raised her so she could lower her body on top of his. She slowly slid her hand to his belt and undid the buckle. She kissed his chest, then pushed her entire body along his torso so she could reach his lips, and kissed him again, for longer than before. Eugene could feel her hardened nipples on his chest as he lowered her underwear. He kissed her while pushing down his trousers and underwear, and she could feel his erection.

Very gently, Anna directed him into her. She raised and lowered herself in a rhythmic pulse, kissing him when her face was near his; he cupped her breasts in his hands. Slowly and surely the time between kisses grew shorter, the rhythm increasing in tempo until their movements were frenzied. Eugene climaxed before her, but when Anna climaxed she felt something she never had before. Her body was sensitised to every nuance of delight; her body and mind were electrified and unified with pure emotion. After she climaxed, she rolled off him and hugged him tightly, watching him drift off into sleep. She counted the days from her last period and knew that she was safe.

In the morning Eugene could hear the stir of the other soldiers in the house. He looked at her and said, 'I'm not allowed to marry you right now, due to a directive from General Eisenhower.'

Anna looked at him and smiled. 'This isn't the right time for me either. But it's the right time for me to leave Magrete's household – I cannot live with a Nazi sympathiser anymore, especially because of what they've inflicted on your family and on mine.'

Eugene kissed her and whispered in her ear, 'I love you.'

'There's one more thing you need to know about me. My name is not really Anna Schuster.' Anna looked him in the eye. 'My real name is Anna Sulzer. My mother is Rachel, my grandmother is Ester, and my father is Joseph Sulzer. All have died. I am Jewish. Magrete gave me the identity papers of Miss Schuster, who is two years older than me.'

He was suspicious of her claim of being Jewish. He felt she might be saying it because of her love and sympathy for him, and her sorrow at the loss of his mother's lineage. 'But if you're Jewish,' he reasoned, 'Magrete has saved you from certain death!'

'I've been thinking about this all night,' Anna confessed. 'I remember her saying that the Nazis would lose the war twice before the speech she made to the Tailfingers, and on that day she convinced the villagers not to fight, but to embrace the French. I think Magrete has always known that her Nazi friends would be defeated, and so by hiding a Jew from the Nazis, she was ensuring that if the Allies won as she expected, I was her family's ticket to freedom.'

Eugene could not understand her logic, but if Anna truly loved him, he could understand why she could no longer stay in Magrete's household. 'What can I do?' he asked. 'How can I help you?'

'Make me your residential housekeeper.'

'Now, that I can do!'

That day, Eugene sent his sergeant around to Magrete's house to collect all of Anna's clothes and belongings. Magrete understood Anna's need to have a relationship, and to start her own family. She had always envisaged a process of mutual separation, based on the love and respect she thought they had for one another. She had not expected Anna to discard her family with such disrespect. Ilse cried and both parents accepted that Ilse needed to shed tears at this abrupt separation. George resented Anna for the emotional upheaval and trauma she was causing to his family, after the years of support Magrete had given her.

Magrete was scared to show her family her tears for Anna's loss. She would disappear into the vegetable patch and quietly cry and pray for Anna to forgive her, but that was her biggest hurdle – for what? When she was breastfeeding Eva, she would puzzle over what might have caused Anna to turn against her with such vengeance, but she could not pinpoint the exact nature of her fall from grace. On two occasions she went to the villa determined to speak to Anna, but on each occasion the private at the gate would not allow her entry, saying that the residential housekeeper did not wish to see or speak to her.

Ilse stopped asking after Anna. Her tears dried up as she accepted the situation, as did George. Elisabeth and Eva were too young to understand. Only Magrete was left to grieve, and grieve she did, alone.

12

French women did not have the right to vote in France until after the liberation from the German Reich in 1944. German women had enjoyed the right to vote since 1919. While the French occupiers did not revoke this right, they did not promote political activity for women; they preferred them in their traditional roles.

By 6 August Anna was enjoying her occupation as residential housekeeper. The cook accepted Anna, as did the five enlisted men. She would clean their bedrooms and of course notice female underwear now and then; they loved it when she chastised them about the possibility of catching venereal disease. They had never met a woman who was so open and natural about even the most sensitive of topics. Within months, she was often consulted on romantic matters and asked for advice about women. She would always preface her advice by saying she was not responsible for any of the outcomes that taking her advice might create.

Eugene loved having her there, and often he would steal into her bedroom late at night, as she did into his. At times he felt frustrated, due to Anna's strict adherence to the rhythm method. She would appease him using other means, which he would also do for her. No one within the villa gossiped about the relationship, whereas Tailfingers were not so kind.

Anna did make contact with one member of the Nagy family, Ilse, fairly early in the piece. Anna could not bear the thought of her absence making Ilse suffer. She knew a small child like Ilse would somehow blame her mother, or Anna, or both. Anna did not want her distrust of Magrete infecting Ilse's life. She made contact with Ilse one day after school and would visit her at the school gate several times a week. It was their secret, and of course Ilse put a spell on Anna making Anna visible only to her. The meetings also kept Anna informed about Magrete and the family in general. Ilse loved those secret meetings.

Eugene was collecting a lot of information about Helmut Gruen. He told Anna several times that she was not allowed in his study. His work was extremely confidential and if she became aware of it, he could get court marshalled and both of them could be sent to the electric chair. On occasions when he was not home she would toy with the idea of going into his study. He always locked it, and she would always try to open it. It was a game for her – a game she had to be very careful about, because there were others in the villa on most occasions.

But not today. There was a private guarding the front gate, but the rest were in Ebingen. Anna tried the door and strangley it opened. She looked to the left and right, stepped in and locked it from the inside. She did not touch a thing – she was scared that if she repositioned a single paper, or a pencil, or changed the swivel of the chair, Eugene would notice, and would quickly deduce that it must have been her, and he would be furious. It might even jeopardise their relationship.

Anna clasped her hands behind her back in order to prevent any sudden impulse or temptation. She saw one piece of paper that he was working on, leaned forward and froze. She saw it was a note to himself: 'Check if Magrete was responsible for the murder of Ayelet Gadot (neé Sulzer) in Berlin, 1940.'

She refused to cry – a single shed tear might be enough to let him know she had been in his sacred place. Anna moved to the door, took her handkerchief from her pocket, and wiped the door handle. She unlocked the door and shut it with her hand wrapped in her handkerchief. When she reached her bedroom, she locked the door behind her. She undressed and got into bed with her handkerchief over her mouth, crying silently for the death of the last relative she had, and for the fact that Magrete, who Anna had previously admired, was implicated in her aunt's murder. She cried all night. Anna heard Eugene gently knock on her door and saw he tried to open it, but she did not reply.

At four in the morning she made a promise to herself. 'That bitch Magrete needs to be held accountable for my aunt's death! I have no family left because of her.' From that moment on she prayed for Magrete to be punished. She resolved that once Magrete was convicted she would get back into Ilse's life on a more regular basis and teach her how to love people, not hate them like Magrete hated the Jews and loved the Nazis.

On the same night, Magrete was fretting again about what she might have done to Anna. She found herself once again in the vegetable patch at 3 am, and this time she decided to tell Anna that they were related. She would show her the coded message she had made in 1938 to detail their unified heritage. Then she remembered that it had disappeared when Wannsee was bombed.

She might know that we are related, thought Magrete, and if she already knows then clearly she does not care. And if she does not know, when I tell her we are related she will think it is a callous trick, because I cannot verify it now. And if by chance she does not already know, but believes me, she will still hate me because I have kept it from her before, during and after the war. I have treated her despicably by casting her into a servant role. Why did I not tell her? Why did I make her, a relative of mine, serve me?

Magrete fell asleep near the herb patch. At 6 am she woke and made breakfast for her family – none suspected she had been missing since 3 am.

13

On 1 October 1946 the International Military Tribunal (IMT) announced its verdict. It imposed the death sentence on twelve defendants (Göring, Ribbentrop, Keitel, Kaltenbrunner, Rosenberg, Frank, Frick, Streicher, Sauckel, Jodl, Seyss¬Inquart and Bormann). Three were sentenced to life imprisonment (Hess, Economics Minister Walther Funk and Raeder). Four received prison terms ranging from ten to twenty years (Doenitz, Schirach, Speer and Neurath). The court acquitted three defendants: Hjalmar Schacht (Economics Minister), Franz von Papen (the German politician who had played an important role in Hitler's appointment as Chancellor), and Hans Fritzsche (Head of Press and Radio). The death sentences were carried out on 16 October 1946, with two exceptions: Göring committed suicide shortly before his scheduled execution, and Bormann remained missing. The other ten defendants were hanged, their bodies cremated, and the ashes deposited in the Iser River. The seven major war criminals sentenced to prison terms were remanded to the Spandau Prison in Berlin.

On 16 October at 9 am a French private knocked on the door of 1 Neuweilerstraße and handed George a letter in French and a translation in German requesting that Magrete Nagy present herself at 10 am the following day at 50 Leimenhäulestraße, to be interviewed by First Lieutenant Pierre Thomas and Eugene Gould. George swore and then asked, 'Why are you hounding us?'

On that day Eugene sat in his office and reviewed all the facts he had on Magrete. Every investigator had focused on important Nazis her family had entertained or done business with. Her actual contact with the Nazi echelon was almost non-existent except for Marga Himmler. According to Marga Himmler's diaries, they had only met three times – twice at tea parties at Marga's invitation and once at Gmund am Tegersee, near Munich and had not even met during Magrete's wedding. They had never exchanged letters. Marga always claimed Magrete as a friend, and vice versa, and yet they were barely acquaintances.

Magrete had claimed she was a Nazi fellow traveller. Of course, she had to be, because her first husband was a Nazi who was a friend of Himmler – a man who appeared only three times in Magrete's life, at her wedding and at two funerals. When she married George there were no Nazis in her life, so she was hardly a fellow traveller, Eugene thought.

Then there was the case of Fritz Hauptman. He was an ex-police officer who had botched the investigation of an attempted rape that Magrete claimed she had witnessed. Horst Maute testified in Nuremberg to Eugene that Fritz would have been executed if Magrete had given the go-ahead. Instead, she asked that the case be closed. Magrete had influence, because of Herbert, but in reality she personally was barely involved with the Nazis and the Nazi party. The real issue, Eugene concluded, was the money and not the political trail.

Eugene was fortunate that there had been a falling-out between Anna and Magrete. Anna now bore an ill will towards Magrete and any questions he posed she would freely answer, in detail, in the hope that Magrete would be found guilty of some heinous crime. Anna had recalled that after Herbert's death and the birth of Ilse, Magrete had been spending a lot of time in the company of Peter von Appen and Helmut Gruen, during the sitting war. Surviving Jewish families had told Eugene that this was the time that Ayelet Gadot (neé Ayelet Sulzer), herself a Jewess, had been fencing copious amounts of gold – coins, jewellery and other pieces. Obviously Ayelet Gadot was rendering these gold pieces into their elements: separating gold from gems and other materials and selling the gold and precious stones on the black market. The official going rate for gold was US$35 an ounce – what the von Appens and Helmut Gruen were paying to those who were selling was anyone's guess, but if Helmut Gruen and company were buying, they were paying Ayelet at least 20–40 per cent more. Eugene needed Magrete's knowledge on several fronts: where did all the money go, when they sold their combined property holdings to von Appen Pty Ltd? And what did she know about the sale of Wannsee to the Nordhav Foundation? Did they exchange their cashed-up wealth for Jewish gold?

The problem that Eugene faced was Magrete's resignation from the board of directors on 11 October 1943. Clearly after that date Magrete would always claim she was out of the loop. What interested him was when Anna told him that just prior to leaving for Tailfingen, Helmut met Anna at Beelitz and gave her a heavy locked satchel. He needed to know what was in it.

Eugene had interrogated von Papen when he was attending his brother's trial in Nuremberg. Von Papen confirmed that Magrete would be unable to give him information about the company's transactions after 11 October, but Eugene wanted to know why Werner Best was made a director of the company and quickly dumped. He knew that Deutsche's bank was dealing in Jewish gold in the course of the so-called Reinhard Operation and that Werner Best had instructed the bank to vet a proposal to purchase properties from von Appen Pty Ltd during that time.

When he first came to Tailfingen Fritz Hauptman had wanted Magrete jailed for being a Nazi. When Eugene eventually interviewed Hauptman, a man he thoroughly disliked, Hauptman said that it was rumoured that Magrete had harboured two criminals on Gross' farm when she was managing it for Julianna Gross. However, Fritz could not tell him the source of these rumours. Unfortunately, Frau Gross had died in the last Allied air raid on Ebingen and so could not be interviewed. Whenever Eugene mentioned Gertrude and Helmut being in Tailfingen to Anna, she was uncooperative, denying that they were there, instead talking about how good Gertrude had been to her, saving her from Herbert's approaches and protecting her from him, Magrete and their Nazi friends. Eugene had decided to lie to Magrete about what Anna had told him, and gauge Magrete's reaction to his simple deception.

14

Magrete arrived at the villa a little earlier than required, and so she stopped before the perimeter fence that would lead her to where the guard stood. She could feel Anna's presence, and when she closed her eyes she could sense Anna looking at her with great distrust. It was awful to be so close and not close at all. Magrete had started to attend Catholic Mass because she did not know what sins Anna thought she had committed against her, but felt by attending she might find a path for a more universal forgiveness. Magrete knew she was starting to act like Ilse – hoping for a spell to lift a curse.

Magrete started to focus on the interview ahead. If she failed this test, she would fail her children and her husband. She needed to be focused and strong, to lie when she needed to in order to protect those she loved, and to tell the truth when the truth could not bring harm to them. Eugene, she felt, was a fair and just man, but also a man who was driven to uncover the truth. Magrete braced herself as she greeted the guard. He ushered her into Eugene's study.

The private stood at the door as she sat in front of the desk. Magrete could see a lot of papers, years of investigations, and she was sure it was about her family, about her and her Nazi friends. She prayed that her family would remain free and intact after this interview.

After fifteen minutes the door was flung open and the private saluted. Eugene returned the salute and said, 'That'll be all, thank you.' The private left and Magrete stood up to greet Eugene. She knew that First Lieutenant Pierre Thomas would not be coming; Eugene Gould did not even acknowledge his absence. He walked around the desk, sat in the chair, and said to Magrete in a perfunctory but polite manner, 'Please be seated.' He carefully placed the papers in three separate piles, and took the first set in his hands.

'In America,' Eugene began, 'we're fairly informal. I'd prefer if you'd call me Eugene and, if you feel uncomfortable with that, just "Captain". I'll address you as Frau Nagy, or Magrete, if that's okay with you.'

'Thank you, Captain, Magrete will be fine,' Magrete said.

'I didn't bring you here to talk about your Nazi friends. First Lieutenant Pierre Thomas has given me a transcript of your first interview and of course I interviewed Marga Himmler when I was in Nuremberg, so we have a good understanding of your Nazi associations. What I do want to talk to you about is the business transactions that you've been involved in. When your first husband died in November 1938, who was running the business affairs of the von Appen company?'

'It wasn't a company then, just a private firm,' Magrete said, slightly apprehensive at correcting Eugene in their first interaction. 'Peter von Appen was doing a lot of the day-to-day decision-making, which he found tiresome, so he promoted the firm's solicitor, Helmut Gruen, to take over the running of the firm.'

'What was your role in the firm at that time?'

Magrete remembered Helmut's note to her under the rock in Beelitz about their discussions in Wannsee, and lied: 'I had no role.'

'But you were the heir apparent,' Eugene observed. 'You birthed Herbert's child, you had a diploma focused on business and accounting from the Vienna Commercial Academy for Girls, and you had been employed in the business and accounting section of the Kaiser Wilhelm Institute for Chemistry. Why wouldn't they use your expertise?'

'Captain,' Magrete said emphasising his rank, 'in those days, as now in the French zone, women were not expected to be employed after they got married and in particular after they had a child. Peter von Appen was a Prussian aristocrat, so Elfi and Peter expected me to manage the household when Elfi was unable to.'

Eugene doubted her answer, although it did appear plausible. He would play his next card. 'But Anna told me there were lots of times when Peter, Helmut and you were at meetings, presumably about the running of the department stores, because Elfi would come to the top apartment and compete with Anna for Ilse's time.'

Magrete felt disappointed with Anna, but masked it; the unity of her family was now at stake. 'Anna has got it wrong,' she said confidently. 'Yes, Elfi did go to the upstairs apartment, but for an entirely different reason. I found giving orders to elderly servants such as Gertrude problematic, and Elfi knew that, and she knew that I had to overcome that fear if one day I was to run the household, so she would instruct me about what needed to be done and leave me to do it and that meant dealing with Gertrude alone, on my own terms. To give me the needed confidence, Elfi would purposely be absent whilst I was directing Gertrude on household matters and so she would go upstairs and spend time with her only grandchild, Ilse.'

'So you were never in any discussions with Peter and Helmut as to why a privately listed firm became a publicly listed company?'

'No, never!'

'Why did Helmut and Peter publicly list the company and sell off all their combined properties to von Appen Pty Ltd?' Eugene asked, thinking he knew the answer.

'As I said to you before, I do not know. I was not involved in the business at that time.'

Now Eugene shouted, 'Come on! You and Herbert had an apartment in Vienna and when he died, he willed it to you. Surely Peter and Helmut couldn't sell your apartment to von Appen Pty Ltd without discussing it with you, or without your consent!'

Magrete knew she could not hesitate; she had to ride with her instincts, because he was getting very close to the truth. 'Captain,' she replied, with a sigh, 'the property was never in my name. It was always in Herbert's or Peter's name. Like Elfi, I trusted any decision

Peter made. Believe me, I had an extremely fortunate lifestyle at that time. I could go into any of the von Appen department stores and take whatever I wanted, when it was a private firm. Peter did not need to ask me for advice on how to make money – he was a very wealthy man, long before I met Herbert.'

Eugene could not argue with her logic, but from everything Anna had told him about Magrete's character, she had not seemed to be just a devoted housewife and homemaker. 'If you were so unknowledgeable about business matters,' he said sarcastically, 'why did you take up the position of chair of the board of directors of a major publicly listed company?' Answer that contradiction, he thought.

'After the death of the von Appens, I was sole heir to their wealth and, of course, to Herbert's. I held 39 per cent of the company shares and Helmut had 13 per cent, so in total we owned 52 per cent of the company. Helmut felt, and I agreed, that I was more than capable of chairing a committee, and because of my qualifications, I was more than capable of understanding a balance sheet. Most importantly, with Herbert, Elfi and Peter no longer alive, the three biggest obstacles to my appointment as chairperson of the board of directors had sadly passed away. It was as simple as that.'

Eugene could see she was upset at the thought of their deaths. He tried another line of enquiry. 'Tell me about your time during the sitting war. The von Appens had amassed a large amount of cash from publicly listing the company, loading von Appen Pty Ltd with a large amount of debt. Where did the cash go? Have you any idea?'

'No, I have no idea.'

'Have you ever heard of a Jewish woman named Ayelet Gadot?' There was no response from her, he observed, and so he was disappointed.

Magrete replied, 'Her name is not known to me.'

'Her maiden name is Ayelet Sulzer,' Eugene said.

'Anna's name is Sulzer,' Magrete responded.

'She was Anna's aunt,' Eugene said, watching Magrete closely. 'She was a Jewess who bought and sold gold or precious jewellery on the black market.' Eugene's eyes lowered as he exchanged a pile of papers from the desk and in that moment a tear trickled down Magrete's cheek as she realised that Anna's aunt was dead. She quickly wiped the tear away with the back of her hand. Eugene did not notice her show of emotion.

'She lived in Scheunenviertel, Berlin,' Eugene added, reading from the new pile of papers. Show him not a flicker, Magrete said to herself. 'She bought gold from prison guards, from Jews who wanted to flee the German Reich, and from Jews who wanted to eat. Do you know of her – if not her personally?'

'I do not know her. I have never met her,' Magrete answered truthfully.

'She was murdered by her husband,' Eugene said, leaning towards Magrete. Show him not a flicker. 'It made the newspapers,' he added. 'Did you not read about her?' His voice was growing louder.

'No,' Magrete answered truthfully. 'Captain, I am not an avid reader of newspapers, nor do I like listening to the news on the radio, as anyone who knows me will testify.'

Eugene knew from Anna's accounts that her last statement was true, but he persisted, asking in a softer tone, 'Have you ever heard of Dieter Fuchs?'

Magrete answered truthfully, 'Never.'

'He was a lowly German Reich diplomat,' Eugene said, 'who was used as a courier to smuggle gold into Switzerland and was shot by the Nazis for doing so. Have you heard of him?'

Magrete lied this time. 'No, I have never heard of him.'

Now he asked in a normal tone, 'You lived in Beelitz, didn't you?'

'I did, with Anna and Ilse,' Magrete answered, relieved he had changed tack.

'Before or after Helmut lived there?'

'Both. Initially Helmut lived there alone, and when he moved back to Berlin, Anna, Gertrude, Ilse and I took up residence. Gertrude later left and lived with Helmut in Berlin, leaving Ilse, Anna and myself there, and when we moved to Tailfingen, Gertrude and Helmut came to live in Beelitz again.'

'When Helmut initially lived there, the SS were looking for a person they thought was involved with Ayelet Gadot. Could that have been Helmut?' Eugene leaned over the table, looking at her intently.

Show him not a flicker. 'Helmut was a solicitor in his first incarnation. He loved the law and was very legalistic in all of his business dealings, so I would be very sceptical of it being him,' Magrete answered, lying in a measured tone.

Eugene suddenly asked, 'What is the colour of Helmut's hair?'

'A mousey brown.'

'Not blonde?'

Magrete smiled. 'I am a brownish-blonde. Helmut was definitely not a blonde.'

This line of questioning appeared to be a dead-end.

'What happened to the money that Helmut and Peter amassed by selling off their combined properties to the von Appen company when it was a private firm?'

'I do not know. I can only guess that when the Wannsee villa was bombed, all of it might have been lost.'

'But the von Appen jewellery was not lost, according to Anna. Why not?'

'Elfi kept a safe in the lounge room behind a fake wall,' Magrete answered truthfully. 'It only housed her and my jewellery and some of our most important documents, no money as such. After the bomb destroyed the villa, Helmut recovered the safe and so the jewellery and some documents were also recovered.'

Eugene was studying her face very carefully. 'Tell me about Wannsee. Why was it sold to the Nordhav Foundation, and why was

Werner Best made a director of the company, but resign after just one meeting?'

'All of that is in the company records-'

Eugene shouted, 'Which you know, no longer exist!'

Magrete was shocked by his revelation; she immediately suspected he had been in the room next-door when the French administrator had interviewed her. She regained her composure and answered, 'Werner Best was initially appointed, as we felt – Helmut and I – that the Foundation might be of use to our public company, because of their interest in acquiring property. However, when they bought a parcel of properties from our company it would have been a conflict of interest if the sale went ahead approved by a director who sat on both boards, so Werner Best had to resign. As von Papen said, the shortest appointment to the board of directors in German Reich history!'

Eugene asked, 'Did they buy the properties with Jewish gold?'

'As I understand it, the properties were bought from loans given to the Foundation by Deutsches Bank?'

Eugene decided to change tack again. 'What do you know about the law firm Meier and Schmidt?' Eugene was sure this question would throw her.

'When I was chair of the board of directors, I was not sure why they bought the company's flat in Basel. I assumed that they were using it as some sort of safe house for their Nazi clients when they were in Switzerland. From my perspective, it helped to lower our exposure to banks, and so I did not investigate the matter any further. The board approved of the sale based on the Finance Committee's recommendations.' Eugene had heard exactly the same argument when he interviewed von Papen in Nuremberg. He had also read a Nazi report of a clandestine raid on the offices of the Swiss firm Meier and Schmidt, in which they could not find any accounts associated with Helmut Gruen. However, he intuitively felt that somewhere a connection did exist to Helmut Gruen.

‘Why did the Nordhav Foundation purchase a bombed-out villa?’

‘They were going to hold a major conference there, from what Helmut told the board of directors. They did not want the presence of neighbours and they needed a first-rate bomb shelter, and where the von Appen villa was situated was the perfect site for one. They also liked our servant quarters and a large garage shed, both of which were spared during the air raid.’

‘Anna told me that before you left for Tailfingen, you left her in Beelitz to meet with Helmut. Why?’ Eugene sensed that every time he mentioned Anna to Magrete it disturbed her.

‘Helmut wanted someone to be there to hand over the keys of the Beelitz house to him,’ Magrete said, ‘because he did not want to travel to Berlin and back again. George and I saw no difficulty with his request, because we were staying in Berlin in George’s flat, with Gertrude in Helmut’s flat.’

‘Anna told me that Helmut gave her a heavy locked satchel to give to you. Did the satchel contain gold?’

Magrete answered truthfully, ‘No. The satchel was heavy because it contained the residual cash of my sale of the 39 per cent share of von Appen Pty Ltd to Helmut on the 11th of October of that year, when I resigned as the chairperson.’

‘So you’re telling me you got a huge amount of cash?’

‘Not such a huge amount,’ Magrete answered. ‘The company was continually selling off its properties to lower its debt, and the actual value of the company was continually being eroded by these fire sales. Helmut figured out early in the piece that in a war property was worthless. He sold off properties on a leaseback arrangement, which meant that the company who bought the properties took the risk if the premises were bombed, and not von Appen Pty Ltd. The other properties we transformed into hospitals, because we reasoned that Allied bombers would shudder at the thought of killing wounded soldiers. We relied on the large red crosses on their roofs to protect them from being destroyed. But the Munich hospital was eventually damaged anyway.' Magrete paused to try to subdue her emotions about the bombed out department stores.

'As I understand it, von Appen Pty Ltd went bankrupt,' Magrete continued, 'and the Nazis were seeking to arrest Helmut to charge him with embezzlement and fraud related to a company called Argentina Property Trust. The cash that Anna brought in the satchel was what was left after the three-year lease in Tailfingen was paid up-front. That cash kept my family going for the two years when George was unemployed in Tailfingen. What is now left is worthless. Nobody wants the Nazi Reichsmark, and even today's German currency buys you very little in this barter economy.'

'Tell me about Elderly Care.'

'I do not know that much about Elderly Care, because it was Helmut who did all the negotiations with them. What I do know is when I chaired the board of directors of von Appen Pty Ltd, Elderly Care purchased three of our DRK hospitals - in Magdeberg, Munich and Leipzig. I also know that some time later they purchased the Tailfingen house from von Appen, because my lease was transferred to Elderly Care, who by the way are trying to evict us.' This was the first time Eugene had heard of Magrete being under an eviction notice. He decided it might become useful to him at a later date.

He looked at her and suddenly saw how thin she had become. He recalled that when he had first met her she was lithe but had weight that suited her figure.

Eugene was beginning to feel more than a little exhausted. 'When did you last see Helmut Gruen?'

'The last time I saw Helmut was early October 1943, when I sold him my shares in von Appen Pty Ltd. The last time I heard of him was when Anna met him in Beelitz.' She hoped her lie would stick.

Eugene decided to pull out one last trick. 'Anna told me that Helmut and Gertrude had visited you in Tailfingen. Exactly when?'

Magrete immediately thought, rely on your instincts, because Anna would never place Gertrude at risk. 'Anna would never make such a claim,' she said, 'because Gertrude and Helmut have never been in Tailfingen.'

'Fritz Hauptman told me he saw them hiding in the Gross farmhouse,' Eugene lied. 'Why do you think that's funny?'

'Because Fritz Hauptman would not know what Helmut and Gertrude looked like! Anyway, he hates me, because he thought I got him sacked when he failed to properly investigate Michael Gross' attempted rape of Anna.' She knew the last phrase would shock him, and she hoped that would bring her some reprieve. 'Ask Julianna Gross about Fritz,' she added.

'Unfortunately, she died in the last Allied air raid of Ebingen,' Eugene said. Magrete gulped and a tear trickled down her cheek – the first piece of emotion, he noted, that she had displayed in front of him all day.

'One last thing. Anna claims she is two years younger than her papers indicate, and, more importantly, that she is a Jewess. That her real name is Anna Sulzer and her aunt was Ayelet Gadot neé Sulzer. Have you any official documents that can confirm Anna's account?'

Magrete could hear from the tone of his voice that Eugene doubted Anna, and although Anna had truly tried to damage her as much as possible, Eugene needed to be assured that Anna was not deceiving him. He needed to know the truth. 'My father, who was the Deputy Commissioner of the Vienna Police, Hans Holweg, stole the identity papers she now carries in order to save her from the Nazi regime,' Magrete said. 'She is two years younger than her false identity. Her mother Rachel was a non-resident housekeeper in my father's household, and she saved my mother's life when my mother had a miscarriage. Anna's father is Joseph Sulzer. Her grandmother is Ester. All have since died. The last time I saw Ester she gave me Anna's birth certificate and identity papers, which prove who she is, and prove that she is Jewish. They were stored in Elfi's safe at

Wannsee and were retrieved with all of our jewellery. I can give you her identity papers, which you can return to her.'

Eugene was shocked and grateful for her honesty, which had greatly simplified his personal life. He knew she could easily have lied to him, especially since Anna clearly wanted to damage her. Eugene looked at Magrete and knew he was defeated. Every test he had put her through had steered him to the conclusion that there was insufficient evidence to incriminate her of any wrongdoing. On the other hand, Helmut Gruen was the culprit, and needed to be found and arrested.

After the interview was complete Eugene drove Magrete home, and waited in the car as she retrieved Anna's birth certificate and identity papers. He was Jewish and now he had documentation to prove Anna's real Jewish identity. Despite this, they still could not marry.

On the following Saturday at the weekly dinner, Pierre agreed to amend Anna's papers to her proper name of Anna Sulzer. There were approximately 1700 so-called 'U-boats' – Jews who had managed to survive the Nazi period submerged beneath the surface of everyday life – and Anna was one of them. Anna felt exposed and yet happy that she had resurfaced with her correct identity. She knew Magrete was responsible, and was grateful to Magrete for being honest with Eugene, but could not forgive her for being involved in the death of her last surviving relative. The township hated Anna, but for the first time Anna felt unashamed of being Jewish; she could not care less. Eugene, on the other hand, felt an increased respect for Magrete. Her parting words to him typified her attitude: 'Everybody sees me as a problem to be solved, but I see myself as following my own destiny, wherever it takes me.'

Eugene was now working for the Office of Special Operations (OSO) and his report concluded that Magrete Nagy (neé Holweg) was a person of no further interest to the United States. He recommended that Interpol issue an immediate red notice for the detention and arrest of Helmut Gruen. Still, Eugene decided to intercept every letter sent to Magrete. Sooner or later, Eugene hoped, Helmut Gruen would try to contact Magrete, and when he did Eugene would arrest him and find out where the von Appen wealth had resurfaced.

15

By 19 December 1946, the marriage of Americans to Germans was permitted, but only under exceptional circumstances and after humiliating scrutiny. Few Military Government authorities maintained historical records for marriages longer than one year after the completion of the application process. Hurdles were even higher if the marriage was between a German and an American of another race. As the chain of command would approve or disapprove which marriages would be allowed, privates were usually denied the privilege of marriage, due to the lack of financial resources required to support a new family. Officers were in the best financial position to support such an endeavour, but very few did, in fear that such marriages might curtail their promotional prospects. Captain Eugene Gould had no such qualms. Anna Sulzer was his soul mate. He never tried to inhibit her passion, but occasionally tried to smooth out her excesses.

Eugene needed to have a private conversation with Anna, and knew that when they sat together out on the back verandah overlooking the garden of the villa, his army personnel and cook would leave him alone, unless an urgent matter arose. Anna and Eugene had coffee and biscuits, and she was now smoking a Marlboro cigarette with an elegant ivory tip, the latter being part of the cigarette. She had started smoking one month previously, and mostly did so after meals and during tea or coffee breaks. He hated the habit personally, but tolerated it in her because smoking tended to calm her.

'The Bizone started yesterday,' Eugene observed.

‘What’s a Bizone?’ Anna asked as she elegantly drew some smoke into her lungs. When she exhaled, a whisper of smoke outlined the direction of her breath.

‘The Brits and us have combined our occupying zones – which means there’s a new tension between the Soviets and us. We’ll start rationalising our administration and reducing the armed forces that we need in the two occupied zones.’

Anna butted her cigarette out in the ashtray. ‘Does that mean you might be sent home?’

Eugene looked up and saw she was worried. ‘No. My duty in Occupied Germany will end in January 1949, in about another two years.’ He could see she was relieved. ‘However, there is one drawback. We can’t get married until July of ’48.’

Anna went around the table that separated them, sat on his lap and kissed him as sweetly as she could. He could faintly taste the tobacco on her breath as she said, ‘I hope that’s a marriage proposal.’

‘It is,’ he answered, and kissed her back. Then he cheekily slapped her on her rear and said, ‘The neighbours might be looking, and kissing your residential housekeeper is never a good look in public, especially with my command and my cook nearby.’

Anna stood up and patted the area between his legs, saying, ‘Oh well, your loss.’ He was glad he was sitting down.

‘On another matter,’ Eugene said, ‘when I interviewed Magrete she told me about an incident where you were nearly raped. What happened?’

‘Magrete! What a gossip! This senile ex-mayor of Tailfingen, Gross I think was his name, suddenly jumped off his bike and pushed me into a vacant block in Goethestraße. He started to pull down my pants, and as he tried to undo his pants, Magrete kicked his backside, and he fell on the ground, and we ran back to the house. He was an absolute filthy swine!’ Anna fumbled for another cigarette and placed it in her mouth. Eugene took it out of her mouth and placed it back into her gold cigarette case.

'So she saved you from a possible rape?'

'Yes, but then in typical Magrete style, she undoes her Good Samaritan stuff by going to that creep's funeral. They claimed he died accidentally, although rumour has it he committed suicide. She publicly showed her disrespect for me, because she knew I was Jewish, of course,' Anna said, with disdain.

'I love you, but your take on events amazes me. When I mentioned Julianna had died during the last air raid on Ebingen, Magrete shed a tear or two. That would lead me to believe she empathised with Julianna, rather than with her husband.'

'Eugene, I love you, but' – Anna said, mimicking his tone – 'the problem is you think like a lawyer and not like a woman who nearly got raped.'

Private Lindsay Sommers suddenly appeared, saluted Eugene, looked at Anna and said, 'Sir, can I talk to you?' Anna understood what that meant, and retreated into the kitchen to talk to the cook.

'We've intercepted this letter that was sent to Frau Nagy,' the private said.

Eugene took the letter, said 'Thank you' and saluted. The private saluted, turned on his heel and left. The letter was from Herr Johann Leo Harisch from 2/5 Wiedner Hauptstraße, Vienna. It was an eviction notice, giving Frau Nagy just four weeks to leave the premises. The company letterhead was that of Argentina Property Trust, with Elderly Care clearly being a subsidiary of APT.

Eugene thought about the consequences of the eviction notice from his perspective. He had only heard of APT once from a witness, and that was Magrete. He had enough evidence to suggest that its subsidiary, Elderly Care, was an Argentinian company that Helmut Gruen had probably set-up for Martin Bormann. The world was looking for Bormann. There was lots of speculation that the Nazi underground might be hiding him and preparing a route for him to go to Latin America.

There were a huge number of DPs – displaced persons – in Occupied Germany, from Poles to Czechs to Greeks to Yugoslavs to Hungarians to Jews, and every European nationality. The migration from Eastern Europe to Occupied Germany continued en masse after the war. The camps that the Allies set-up for the purpose of housing DPs varied in size and character. Camps were established on sites that had previously served as barracks, hotels, hospitals, schools, apartment buildings, warehouses and private homes. In 1946, the camps came under the International Refugee Organization (IRO). A single camp might accommodate anywhere from fifty to over 7,000 DPs at any given time. There were 800 camps in the Bizone; forty-five in the French zone; twenty-one in Austria; and eight in Italy. The French were setting up a new DP camp in a large old warehouse at 62–64 Hechinger Straße in Tailfingen. The camp was to house 100 DP families, who had originally worked in the Tailfingen district when the local German men went to war. As soldiers were discharged from internment camps and returned home, they took their jobs back from the DPs.

The massive movement of men in both directions – DPs relocated in camps and discharged soldiers returning home – was a perfect camouflage for the next layer of Nazi perpetrators to escape Occupied Germany for Nazi strongholds in Latin America. Eugene reasoned that Argentinian Nazi sympathisers would want to have a foothold in Tailfingen in order to provide an orderly escape route, and Elderly Care's eviction notice to Magrete Nagy would provide them with such a foothold because, of the three western zones, the French were the least zealous, and the least efficient in vetting DPs. He needed someone on the inside who the Nazis would trust, or at least a person who would know of the new arrivals, which the OSO and not the French might be able to vet. Clearly George Nagy was a DP, but the Soviets were seeking his return to Hungary. How could he convince Magrete to become his operative on the inside of the DP hostel? First he needed to contact his superior for approval. Then he needed to secure Magrete's services. Thirdly, he needed Anna, George and First Lieutenant Pierre Thomas to be kept in the dark.

Five hours later he was given approval. The first DPs were to be housed in the refurbished warehouse in a week's time. He needed to work on Magrete, but first he wanted to make enquiries to confirm George's scientific past, and his role in the Institute. He also needed an operative to penetrate the Soviet line – a line that Winston Churchill had referred to as the Iron Curtain. For the first time since Eugene came to Tailfingen the OSO allowed him access to Krystyna Skarbek (also known as Christine Granville), a professionally trained spy. He sent OSO coded instructions outlining what he wanted her to investigate and sent her to Moscow. He would need to wait for her report. Meanwhile, he forwarded the eviction notice on to 1 Neuweilerstraße.

16

On 1 February Magrete got her second eviction notice, but this time it was from Vienna lawyers Hemple and Sporn of Elderly Care. It was carbon copied to First Lieutenant Pierre Thomas. Magrete was given two weeks to vacate the premises. She feared that they would become homeless, because there were no rooms available in Tailfingen, and the winter weather would make being homeless a dangerous circumstance, especially for her children. She was prepared to throw herself on the mercy of the local Catholic church if need be, but they were already inundated.

Magrete rode her bike to Ebingen and posted the empty letter that Helmut had given her. On the way home she realised she needed to put in place another strategy, because Helmut and Gertrude might not be alive. She knew Anna despised her but George had always got on well with her. When she arrived home, she begged George to see Anna in the hope that Eugene Gould might use his considerable influence with First Lieutenant Pierre Thomas to delay the eviction.

Anna agreed to see George, Ilse and Elisabeth, but not Magrete, at the villa at 10 am on 8 February, Magrete's birthday. Anna had consulted with Eugene, who was pleased that she might be rebuilding a bridge to a family that had harboured her during the Nazi regime. He suggested that they stay for lunch. Anna thought about it and agreed. She would love Magrete to be told how well she was faring compared with the circumstances Magrete was presently experiencing.

George, Ilse and Elisabeth arrived just as Eugene was about to leave. The men shook hands, and Eugene left. Anna waved him farewell from the front steps, then Eugene saw her turn and lead George and Elisabeth into the villa, with Ilse by her side.

Magrete had just fed Eva when her doorbell rang. She opened it to see Captain Eugene Gould. 'May I come in?'

'Of course,' Magrete said. 'Please make yourself comfortable in the lounge room, while I bed down Eva.'

Eugene chose to sit on the sofa, because he knew that would force her to sit in the armchair, nearer to him. Magrete entered the lounge room and realised that this was the first time he had entered her home since she had known him. This worried her.

'May I get you something to drink?'

'No, thank you. I said goodbye to George and your children at the villa, and so I've come here because I wanted to talk to you privately. I've some vital information that will affect your stay in Tailfingen, the source of which I can't reveal to you. The Soviets via the Hungarian government will officially demand that the French repatriate George back to Budapest-'

Magrete interrupted him. 'But they cannot do that, because I am an Austrian citizen!'

'Unfortunately, you're not! Under the unification, Austria became a province of Germany, and so according to the law, you take on the nationality of your husband. You and your family are therefore Hungarians.' He could see the revelation shocked her. 'The reason they're desperate to have George,' Eugene continued, 'is that they've already located his ex-team members, Dr Frank Bacskay, Dr Attila Pulay and Dr Mark Czár, in Hungary, and have relocated them to Moscow.'

'Why do they need George when they have the team?'

'I don't know if George told you what he did at the Institute. He lied to me, claiming he was a mere technician, when in fact he led a research team. You only need one technician, without a PhD, to manage the uranium stockpile, but you need a team of scientists with PhDs to investigate how to purify radioactive uranium or plutonium.'

Magrete saw Eugene had uncovered the truth. 'He is a scientist,' she said, 'and in my education I did very little science. I have no idea what he did.'

'George started to learn how to purify radioactive uranium from non-radioactive uranium,' Eugene said, not sure whether to believe her. 'They need George to oversee the process, because the other three research scientists he worked with aren't sure of the exact steps involved, nor the design of the equipment that's needed, unlike George. The Russians are determined to build their own atomic bomb, and they want him to head his old team.'

'If he is so clever, surely you Americans would need him?'

Smart woman, Eugene thought, and then countered, 'We don't need him because we've already perfected the technique – remember, we have atomic weapons!'

'But if you send him to Hungary you will be helping the Russians to produce an atomic bomb,' Magrete reasoned.

'It will not be our decision, because he's located in the French zone, and they're convinced he's just a technician. If they do send him to Hungary, or if they find out what I know and send him to France, his life will be terminated by forces that don't want the Russians, or for that matter the French, to have nuclear weapons.'

Magrete understood he was referring to the United States and Great Britain.

'How can we stay in Tailfingen and remain safe from these forces?'

'If I can convince Pierre to move George into the DP camp in Tailfingen, he and your family will be safe, because they would come under the United Nations Relief and Rehabilitation Administration (UNRRA), and as a DP family you might one day be eligible for refugee status, and immigrate to a country that is willing to accept refugees, and who have no desire to build nuclear weapons. George would then pose no threat to the countries who do possess nuclear weapons and want the club to remain at two.'

Magrete understood there would be a price to pay for Eugene's help. 'So what do you want from us?'

'I only want help from you, not from George. I want you to work for me, but to do so undercover.'

'What do you mean?'

'I want you to work for my unit and inform me about any Nazi officials who are in the DP camp, or people you know or suspect are Nazis, or people who others in the camp talk of as Nazis.'

Magrete felt a little disgusted. 'You mean, work for you as an informer?'

'Magrete, the people I'm talking about are not just Nazis who hate Jews. There are lots of Americans who hate Jews, Catholics or people from other races. The people I'm talking about killed innocent children, women and men, and did so just because they were Jews, Romani and homosexuals etc. We're talking about murderers who believe that they shouldn't face trial for their criminality.'

Magrete, accepting his proposal asked, 'Can I tell George?'

'The fewer people know, the safer it'll be for your family. As a woman, people won't suspect you so readily, whereas if George is seen to be snooping he'll be immediately suspected, especially because he isn't German. Also, you had Nazi affiliations in the past, so you'll be accepted as being one of them. George would never be considered one of them. Not even Anna will know.'

Magrete felt that her life was taking a significant turn. 'How long will I need to do this work for you?'

'Until January 1949, approximately two years from now. You'll get paid in cash and only in US dollars. We'll have a briefing once a month in a halfway house, when you'll get paid. Well? I need an answer.' Eugene did not want to be in Magrete's home when George returned.

As Magrete saw it, she had little choice. If her family went back to Hungary, George would be targeted by Britain and America. Magrete also knew her family could imminently be homeless, with winter coming on. She looked at him sadly. 'When can we move into the DP camp?'

'Give me a week,' Eugene answered. They both rose and he shook her hand. Magrete was now one of his operatives and, although he was ethically right, because of the secretive nature of her assignment she still felt soiled.

When George came home he was full of news about Anna and how well she was doing. He told Magrete that Anna was now a smoker and that she had provided lunch for Ilse, Elisabeth and himself. He held out a small bag and said that Anna had asked the cook to make some baby food for Eva. Magrete was eager to know if Anna had told George why she was angry with her. George told Magrete the subject had not come up. Finally, he said that Anna could not help them.

One week later George received a letter from First Lieutenant Pierre Thomas stating that he had two choices: to return to Hungary or to move into the DP camp at 62–64 Hechingerstraße. George was relieved that, rather than being evicted, they were leaving 1 Neuweilerstraße of their own accord. Magrete realised that even if Helmut and Gertrude were alive, they were not in a position to rescue her family.

17

Johann Leo Harisch headed the APT; their headquarters was in Buenos Aires. Helmut Gruen had structured the company under the loose supervision of Martin Bormann. The company acted as a conduit to safeguard German Reich wealth gained from pilfering the gold reserves of conquered countries. APT had initially bought the von Appen Pty Ltd DRK hospitals in Magdeberg, Munich and Leipzig. What angered Bormann was that Helmut Gruen, without Bormann's consent, and using Elderly Care's resources, had purchased on their behalf von Appen Pty Ltd's Prague hospital, apartments in Vienna and East Berlin, houses in Tailfingen and Beelitz, and the department store in Budapest. When Bormann realised that fraud and embezzlement had been committed he immediately issued a warrant for Helmut's arrest. Bormann's men had nearly captured Helmut in the Berlin Bahnhof, but he and his female accomplice had disappeared. APT could neither access nor sell the properties in East Berlin, Magdeberg, Leipzig, Prague, Budapest and Beelitz, because they were now within the Soviet zone of influence.

In 1947 APT had three assets that they could access: a bombed hospital in Munich, an apartment in Vienna and a house in Tailfingen. Harisch decided that APT would re-establish Elderly Care first in Vienna, where he would coordinate possible recovery of their property in countries under communist control, and facilitate a loose underground network to enable SS officers to escape Allied prosecution. Under his leadership the office in Vienna would procure false identity papers, provide accommodation in temporary safe houses with families sympathetic to the Nazi cause, provide employment in Nazi-friendly businesses, and secure placement in DP camps. SS officers once given refugee status by the UNRRA would be eligible to immigrate to such continents as North America, South America, Africa and Australia. They also were in close collaboration with the Bishop – a vital link for the exit strategy of Nazis travelling from Europe to Latin America.

The headquarters of APT needed further funds to invest in housing properties for these escapees, especially in Argentina, so the property in Munich and the properties in the communist-influenced zones would eventually be sold, they figured, when Europe's economy recovered. They never entertained the thought that communist regimes might one day nationalise their holdings.

The Tailfingen house was APT's next crucial asset. It was in close proximity to the Tailfingen DP camp, and was in the French zone, where scrutiny was lax. Tailfingen, they knew, was also where Helmut Gruen had last been sighted. APT directors were determined that Helmut Gruen would suffer their wrath. It was decided that Cédric Bacri would oversee the Tailfingen operation. Bacri was fluent in French, German, and English. He was a French Algerian Nazi not known to European authorities.

Cédric Bacri took up residency on 22 February and immediately sought an interview with First Lieutenant Pierre Thomas. Pierre said they could meet in the Mayoral Office at 3 pm, as he was having dinner with Eugene at the villa at 6 pm and he did not want this meeting to interfere with his longstanding dinner arrangement.

After introductions and shaking of hands, both were seated, Pierre behind his administrator's desk and Cédric in front of it.

'I'm a representative of Elderly Care,' Cédric said. 'It's a subsidiary of Argentina Property Trust, or APT, as we call it. We have properties in Munich, Vienna, Beelitz, East Berlin, Prague, Magdeberg, Leipzig and, of course, Tailfingen.'

Pierre did not like French Algerians: they were uncouth and generally arrogant. The locations of the APT properties amused him. 'You've one property that is in a zone where all four occupiers are in control, namely Vienna. You have one in the French zone, Tailfingen; one in the Bizone, Munich; and a whopping five in the Russian zones, under the control of communists, who don't believe in private ownership of property. Aren't you a little worried about your investment strategy?'

'We bought during a war, so you can't predict the outcome on a business model alone,' Cédric answered in French, looking embarrassed but undaunted. 'We're in particular interested in Helmut Gruen, who was the managing director of von Appen Pty Ltd, with the unfortunate von Papen being the chairman of the board of directors. Our company contends that Helmut Gruen embezzled and defrauded us of a considerable amount of money. He was last seen in the Tailfingen region, so we'd be most appreciative if you try to locate him.'

'We've at best twenty men acting as local police in a village of around ten thousand people. We don't have the manpower to go searching for an alleged criminal,' Pierre said.

'I understand your situation, First Lieutenant, but Elderly Care would make your endeavours worthwhile,' Cédric said, with a smile.

Pierre knew what that smile meant, and was happy to be bribed. 'Tell me what you know of Helmut Gruen.'

'Very little actually! I have a grainy photograph of him in the late 1920s and various documents we've acquired from the fraudulent transactions he made.' Cédric handed over an old newspaper clip displaying a grainy photograph of a twenty-something Helmut Gruen and several documents. The one document that was of interest to Pierre was a lease that Frau Magrete Nagy had signed from the lessor von Appen Pty Ltd, which had then been transferred to Elderly Care, once they acquired the property.

Cédric saw Pierre looking at the Tailfingen lease and added, 'We understand that Frau Nagy wanted to lease the Tailfingen property because her husband, George Nagy, was a team leader of some research group-'

Pierre interrupted, 'The Kaiser Wilhelm Institute for Chemistry.'

'That's right, the Kaiser Wilhelm Institute for Chemistry,' Cédric re-iterated.

Pierre considered the downside of a bribe. 'If I do locate Helmut Gruen, what happens next?'

'We've already sought extradition orders for his arrest, and for him to stand trial in Argentina for fraud and embezzlement. We'd invoke them!'

'I've a number of French charities that I'll donate this income to, so any money you wish to donate needs to go into my Paris bank account. I'll furnish you with those details soon.'

'Thank you,' Cédric replied, fully cognisant of what Pierre had conveyed.

Pierre escorted Cédric out of his chambers. He needed to refresh his understanding of the reports that Eugene had written about his interviews with Magrete Nagy. It was clear that APT had no interest in her, because they had not made the connection to her past business history with von Appen Pty Ltd. Pierre decided that he needed someone on the inside to keep him informed of her movements, in case Helmut Gruen tried to contact her. Meanwhile, Eugene Gould did not need to know of his meeting with Cédric Bacri, and Cédric did not need to know about Magrete Nagy, or Eugene Gould, for that matter, Pierre reasoned.

Pierre had a wonderful dinner that evening with Eugene. Neither Elderly Care nor Magrete Nagy were mentioned in any conversation.

18

George had not been truthful with Magrete about what had transpired when he met Anna on 8 February. George had asked Anna if she could persuade Eugene to talk to Pierre about delaying their eviction notice. Anna had said she could not intervene on their behalf, because she had been told that Pierre and Eugene's relationship was strictly codified in an agreement between the two occupying powers. While Ilse and Elisabeth played out on the back verandah, Anna enquired about the family's finances. George revealed that financially they were struggling. They discussed various options. Her salary was US$2,000 per year as a resident housekeeper. Anna suggested she gift George's family US$5 per week from her weekly wage of roughly $38. She asked that George and Ilse visit the bottom of the alleyway every Friday afternoon after he picked up Ilse from school so that she could hand over that sum. George was ecstatic, and hugged and kissed her. Anna made it dependent on one condition: that he will not reveal this arrangement to Magrete, which George readily agreed to do.

Eugene notified Magrete he would not need to see her for a month in order to allow her family to settle into their new community. In the intervening time he wanted to know more about Elderly Care and of its parent company, APT.

Within a week Magrete's family had moved out of the house and into the DP camp. As a family of five they were given a larger room than smaller families. The room contained a sink, with a cold-water tap and a small pot for human waste. There were five small mattresses, all the same size, in a row against a windowless wall. There was one five-drawer dresser with a mirror also situated on a windowless wall, next to the door. Magrete's suitcases and bags contained clothing that would not fit in the dresser. On the other side of the door to the dresser was a single window.

The woman next door, Helena Kempa, took an instant liking to Magrete and showed her around the camp. The camp had two large standalone toilet and shower blocks: one for women, girls and boy toddlers, and another for boys and men. There was a standalone laundry, a large kitchen and a communal dining room. The dining room, if not in use, could be used for meetings or, if the weather was foul, as a children's playroom. It could not be used for religious purposes, for it was deemed that Tailfingen had a variety of churches to accommodate people's religious beliefs. Women were expected to work in the laundry and kitchen as well as keep their rooms tidy and men were expected to tend the garden and do small repair jobs in and around the premises, as well as seek employment in Tailfingen. Herbs and other foods, such as potatoes and carrots, were grown in the garden for use in the community kitchen.

When the tour was complete, Helena Kempa found a quiet corner of the garden, indicated that they should sit on the grass and whispered to Magrete, 'We have no privacy in these rooms, so there's a golden rule about the toilets. They can be locked from the inside and if you find the women or men's toilets locked after 9 pm, you know that a couple is inside making love. The camp rule is you give one knock on your first visit, to let them know you need to use the toilet. After fifteen minutes you can go back and try to open the door. Most times you'll find it open, but if it isn't you might need to visit the garden. Manure is a wonderful fertiliser for most plants! In the morning the boys always inspect the garden first and spade the manure into the soil.'

Magrete looked horrified. 'Helena, I cannot imagine myself making love in a toilet block!'

Helena laughed. 'Those were my exact words when I was told. In a year from now, if I'm still in Tailfingen, I'll ask you – have you made love in the toilet block? Whatever you say, I promise I'll know by your face if you have.'

Magrete shook her head and laughed, as did Helena, and in that instant they became friends.

19

Eugene Gould had heard of Simon Wisenthal, who was employed by the OSS and the Counter-Intelligence Corps in 1946. Wisenthal assembled evidence, which proved of great value in the preparation for charges of war crimes against personnel held in the US zone. By 1947 he had left the OSS and established the Jewish 'Historical Documentation Centre on the Fate of Jews and Their Persecutors' in Linz, Austria. Eugene's idea to protect Magrete as a source was simple – any credible information she collected in Tailfingen would be shipped to Simon Wisenthal. He would mask its origin and combine it with his own research before he acted on it. Magrete might learn the whereabouts of some wanted SS escapees, but Wisenthal would collect the evidence to secure their prosecution. On Wedenesday 7 March Eugene could wait no longer. He needed to brief Magrete and give her instructions.

On Thursday 8 March 1947 at 8 am Frau Susanne Raba knocked on Magrete's door in the DP camp. Magrete opened it to see a stout woman unknown to her, who handed her a card. Magrete read: 'Your medicine is available at Kaiser Apotheke 5 Lange Straße'. When she looked up, the woman was no longer there.

George enquired, 'Who was it?'

'Just a woman telling me my medicine is ready,' Magrete said, searching for her in the distance.

'What medicine?' George asked, who was now standing behind her.

'I usually get hay fever in spring, and the medicine unblocks my nose and relieves the slight fever I get with it.'

George gave her a peck on her cheek. 'I learn more about you every single day.'

Clearly someone was trying to get in contact with Magrete in a clandestine manner. She suspected it might be Helmut Gruen, because she had never had a reply to the empty letter she had posted in Ebingen. She went off alone, leaving George to mind Eva and Elisabeth as Ilse was at school.

Magrete stood outside 5 Lange Straße, surprised to see that it was exactly what the card stated – Kaiser Apotheke. She opened the door and a bell rang. There were no customers in the shop. A man in his fifties wearing a white coat stood behind the counter. He looked over his glasses to see who was there, and then said, 'Frau Nagy, please step in the back.' The hairs on the back of Magrete's neck started to rise, as she took a deep breath to steady herself. As he parted the curtains Magrete could see Eugene Gould, and felt disappointed, but relieved. Eugene led her through a back door into a small closed verandah where there was a table and four chairs. On the table was a pot of tea, milk and sugar. He pointed to the tea and they sat down.

'Sorry about bringing you here in the manner I did, but there was no other way,' Eugene said, as he poured them both a cup of tea. Magrete indicated she needed no milk or sugar and started to sip her tea. Eugene continued, 'The first thing I need to know is who is behind Elderly Care and APT?'

'I really do not know. Helmut Gruen did all the negotiations with them, but when I was chairperson of the board of directors, we did approve sale to them of three of the DRK hospitals: Magdeberg, Munich and Leipzig. The lease on the Tailfingen house was initially with von Appen Pty Ltd and not Elderly Care, but at some time von Appen Pty Ltd must have sold it to Elderly Care, because they became my lessor. I have got the lease somewhere in my document file. I could show you the exact date they took over my lease.'

'No, that won't be necessary. The last time we met, you said to me …' Eugene paused as he flicked through a transcript in his notebook. 'Here it is. You said – "as I understand it, the company went bankrupt and the Nazis were seeking to arrest Helmut to charge him with embezzlement and fraud related to a company called Argentina Property Trust." Who told you that?'

Magrete had to think hard, and then it came to her. 'In late July 1944 Nicolaus von Below interviewed me at the Tailfingen police station and he told me that there was a warrant out for Helmut's arrest because he had embezzled a large sum of money from APT.'

'You do realise he was an adjutant to Adolf Hitler?'

'Yes, he told me so.'

Eugene changed the direction of the conversation. 'This is your safe house. If ever you feel threatened, you come here. The proprietor is Wilfred Raba, and his wife, who you met earlier today, is Susanne. If I need you to come here, Susanne will give you a message, or leave one with George, asking you to pickup your medicine. If she says it's urgent, leave as soon as you can. I've put protection in place for you, George and your children. I can't tell you more than that, for security reasons. So don't be alarmed if I need to see you here urgently. If you need me urgently, order Bayer's Baby Soothing Syrup. If you need me the following day, order Bayer's Ease, for a woman's monthly cramps. Otherwise, we meet the first Monday of every month at 11 am. The sign on the door will read: "Closed! Back in ten minutes." Just walk in and come to this room. We'll disable the bell at the front door to quieten your entry.'

'What if people see me walk in?'

'Act confidently, as if you've been given permission by the owner to walk in even though the shop is closed. Generally, you'll not discuss matters with Wilfred and Susanne. They might let you know that the meeting is not on today, but they would tell you that in this room and nowhere else. Have you any questions?'

'No, it seems straightforward.'

'What I want you to do in the camp is not to enquire about anybody,' Eugene said. 'Befriend people and let them talk to you about anything and everything. It's important that you sit on the steering and management committees and that you get involved with the organisation of most events. I have an up-to-date list of the DPs, employees and UN personnel in the camp. If someone recognises you, or you recognise somebody, we should meet urgently. If you feel threatened, or feel your family is threatened, we should also meet urgently. Remember, we're looking for people who have no compunction about killing helpless children, women and men. If they believe you'll compromise their freedom, you'll be an immediate target. If you suspect that someone is an SS henchman, and they are unaware of you, that is cause for us to meet the following day. Do you recognise this man?' Eugene showed Magrete a photograph taken in 1945.

Magrete looked at the photograph, inspected the man's uniform and realised how little she knew of the Nazi hierarchy. 'He looks familiar, but not really,' she answered.

Eugene assumed she knew Bormann, but was too ashamed to admit it. 'His name is Martin Bormann. He controlled who could see Hitler and so he gained immense power over the Nazi hierarchy because of that control. He's on our most-wanted list and is extremely dangerous. Keep the photograph hidden in a safe place.'

He showed her another photograph. Magrete knew she had never laid eyes on this man. She said emphatically, 'No!'

'He was a Nazi SS-Obersturmbannführer and one of the major organisers of the final solution,' Eugene said. 'His name is Adolf Eichmann. He was the bureaucratic implementer of a plan that Heydrich and company had formulated in the Wannsee conference of 1942. We caught him in 1946 and let him go. He was using the alias Otto Eckmann. I want you to keep this photograph too. If you see either of these men, go directly to the villa and give the private at the gate the codename P-A-N, for "Pay attention now!" Are there any questions?'

Magrete shook her head.

'You'll always leave first from any of our meetings. I know this is not what you wanted at this stage of your life, but believe me, a lot of Nazis will escape judgement for what they've done if we don't do this.' Eugene passed Magrete a sealed envelope, which contained a small amount of US dollars.

When Magrete had left, Eugene felt uneasy. He reasoned that individuals or persons occupying the Tailfingen house needed to be investigated because Magrete was a von Appen, and most of the villagers knew of that link and moreover, she was involved with a company that had defrauded APT. Both these issues might become problematic. He decided to send Krystyna Skarbek on a mission to East Berlin to find out if there was any link between Martin Bormann, the warrant for the arrest of Helmut Gruen and APT.

20

Magrete campaigned hard to get on the all-important Central Committee, basing her campaign on the fact that women needed representation. Most of the DPs were women and she was the wife of a prominent scientist, who had held a position at the Kaiser Wilhelm Institute for Chemistry. More importantly, she had a Diploma in Business and Accounting from the Vienna Commercial Academy for Girls. Helena Kempa was her biggest supporter and campaigned for her, winning over most of the Czech, Polish and Yugoslavian vote.

On 2 April the Central Committee met for the first time. There were six men and only one woman on the committee. The positions that were available were president, vice-president, secretary and treasurer. The rest of the committee wanted Magrete to take up the position of treasurer because of her qualifications, but she refused. Instead, Magrete invented the position of events manager, and the men assumed it would probably suit her better, because she was a woman and so voted for the creation of this new position. The elected positions were: president, Chaim Rosenshaft; vice-president, Zalman Sneig; treasurer, Jovan Divis; secretary, Georg Corak; and events manager, Magrete Nagy. Magrete announced that Helena Kempa would be her assistant in the portfolio. The committee members who did not hold positions heatedly debated her decision. President Zalman Sneig placated them by creating two more positions: assistant secretary, Fenec Banki, and assistant treasurer, Hans Balzhauser.

Magrete wanted to integrate herself fully into the social fabric of the DP camp. She had known that by becoming treasurer she would have been isolated from those who were working or staying in the camp. As events manager she would be at the epicentre of activity and therefore of chatter. She decided that the main events would be held in the dining hall every Saturday and Sunday evening.

Helena was older than Magrete, but nevertheless was flattered that Magrete had appointed her to the position of assistant events manager. She insisted that Magrete write her a formal letter appointing her to the role.

Helena and Magrete met on the following day to discuss their roles and what events should be considered. 'The obvious thing is for us to organise a dance every Saturday night in the dining hall,' Helena suggested.

'I think a dance night might be a bit premature,' Magrete said. 'We would need a band or a music player. At any rate, most of the DPs here are women with small children, who have lost their husbands. That would make it awkward for the married women who are with their husbands. I think we should return to your idea a little later.'

Magrete sensed Helena's disappointment and made another suggestion. 'What you could do is organise the formation of a band. Find DPs who can play music, and see if they have their musical instruments with them, and perhaps they could teach the children of DPs how to play as well. Once we have our own band, a dance night would be more feasible. And what about a choir?'

'That's a great idea because once we've a band and singers we can hold concerts as well as having dance nights. That's so clever, Magrete!'

'I think I will organise an after-dinner speaker for every Saturday evening,' Magrete said.

'Do you think that's wise? Most of the DPs aren't educated and so won't have much interest in hearing someone talk about a subject they know little about, especially after they've eaten.'

'But most DPs want to immigrate to another country. They do not want to go back their homeland, to a communist country or where their countrymen are starving, and they do not want to stay here, because of what they have experienced. What they want is a new life, a new future in a different land. They want their children to be educated, well fed, clothed, sheltered and happy. We could start by hearing in German what the UNRRA is doing to resettle them in a new country. After the lecture we could take a survey to find out which countries they wish to immigrate to, and try to locate someone who can tell them something about that place, like its history, and the language that is spoken there etc. Later we can ask them about topics they are interested in. What do you think?'

Helena was dumbfounded. 'You're right, Magrete,' she said. 'A DP in the camp convinced me that Argentina was the place to go, and I don't even know what language they speak. I knew his mother when I was working in Bisingen and saw him in the camp the other day. He calls himself Jan Binek now, though I always knew him as Franz Hofmann.'

Magrete realised she had her first piece of information to report to Eugene Gould.

21

Magrete's first meeting with Eugene Gould was on 7 April. For nearly a week she had felt conflicted about letting Eugene know what she had been told. She wondered if Helena could have been mistaken. But the more she thought about it the more she knew Helena was not – if you know the mother, you know the family. She wrestled with the idea that Franz Hofmann had a mother, father and probably sisters, brothers and an extended family, and how their reputations would suffer, if he was accused of a war crime. She knew that many Germans just wanted to forget the Nazi era and move on with their lives. The war had created so many losses for so many, on all sides, and now she might inflict a further loss.

She suddenly remembered Julianna Gross. The violence inflicted on Julianna had been horrific and yet everybody had ignored her husband's crimes. The crimes that the SS guards had committed were far more horrific, and she shuddered at the thought that she was contemplating turning a blind eye. She decided to tell Eugene what she had heard, and to ask him for a favour that he might not grant her.

At 11 am Magrete was in front of Kaiser Apotheke and saw the sign: 'Closed! Back in five minutes.' She opened the door silently and went immediately to the back room, where Eugene was waiting for her. He looked very pleased with himself, as if he had received some unexpected good news.

'Magrete, I understand your Saturday night lectures are really taking off. The word on the street is that Tailfingers are jealous that the DPs are getting information that's not readily available to them. That lecture by Padel from Officer de Movements Neuenbürg was the talk of the town.'

'He gave a wonderful talk,' Magrete said.

Eugene could see she looked distracted. 'You look a little tired. Have you anything to report?'

'I do, but I want to ask you a favour. I took on this work for you on selfish grounds. I wanted to keep my family intact in a western country. I feel uncomfortable spying on people's private lives and saddened by the fact that I could be doing innocent people tremendous harm. On the other hand, I know that to be a bystander when a horrific wrong has been committed makes you culpable as well. If I give you any information about any person, could you please tell me what crimes they are accused of having committed? I need to know, because during the war I had buried my head in the sand.' As she spoke, the stick figures of Bisingen returned to her memory.

'I promise I'll do my best, but the person I'm delivering the information to might not want you to know these people's crimes prior to their arrests.'

Magrete decided to relay what she knew. 'Helena Kempa is my assistant events manager. She told me that a DP called Jan Binek was in fact Franz Hofmann. She worked in Bisingen and knew his mother. So clearly he is using false papers to escape from Occupied Germany. At the lecture you were talking about, I was with Padel when Franz approached Padel, pressuring him about his refugee status. Padel took down his name and left.'

'I know you're struggling with this,' Eugene said, 'but think of the families who have lost loved ones whose only fault was that they were born Jewish, Romani or homosexual.' He was thinking of his mother's family and Anna's, whereas Magrete thought of all those, including those who were never thought of as Holocaust victims – the Romani and homosexuals.

When Magrete left, Eugene opened up the report he had commissioned from Krystyna Skarbek. She had sent him a copy of the warrant for the arrest of Helmut Gruen. It was signed by Martin Bormann. Her report concluded that there was no extradition order from Argentina for Helmut Gruen's arrest. He could now let Wisenthal know that APT and its subsidiary Elderly Care were Argentinian companies set-up by Bormann. The second piece of information he sent was that Fritz Hofmann of Bisingen was in the Tailfingen DP camp and using false papers in the name of Jan Binek. He asked Wisenthal to inform him of the war crimes Franz Hofmann might have committed in Bisingen.

22

Eugene's next meeting with Magrete was on 5 May. He told her that the Bisingen camp had resulted in at least 1187 deaths. The conditions in the camp were so appalling that a superior SS officer had reported it to Berlin, resulting in an inspection by the head of the SS-Wirtschaftsverwaltungshauptamtes (SS – Economic Administration

Main Office), Oswald Pohl. Even he, who had an appalling record and would eventually be executed for war crimes, recommended the dismissal of camp leader Franz Hofmann.

After the war, the French occupying force ordered the exhumation of the dead, who had been thrown into a mass grave, to be placed in single coffins and buried in the newly opened cemetery. Inmates of war criminal camps in Reutlingen and Balingen had to dig out the bodies. Former members of the National Socialist German Workers' Party, especially those who were teachers, clergymen and former mayors from all councils under French occupied terrain in Württemberg–Hohenzollern, were brought to Bisingen to learn about the existence of the concentration camp in Bisingen and its many victims.

Fritz Hofmann was definitely a person of interest to Wisenthal. Magrete once again thought of the stick figures and felt more secure that her work was a reminder to herself that everyone was responsible for their own actions no matter what the circumstance. She gave him four more names that day.

Just before Magrete left, Eugene asked, 'What was the address of your apartment in Vienna?'

'2/5 Wiedner Hauptstraße, Vienna. Why?'

Eugene ignored her enquiry. 'Do you know if von Appen Pty Ltd sold it to Elderly Care?'

'I do not have a clue,' Magrete replied, and Eugene believed her because he now trusted her.

Eugene made a note to himself after Magrete had left – he needed Krystyna Skarbek to find out which properties APT had supposedly purchased from von Appen Pty Ltd. He feared Krystyna might have to break into the Tailfingen house or the apartment in Vienna, which ever was easier for her.

23

At 4 pm on 4 June Cédric Bacri left the house to travel by bike to Ebingen. He was careful about which streets he took in order to avoid being followed. He might be picking up a very important person with the code name 'Bishop'. His instructions were that he had to be at Ebingen station on the first Wednesday of every month and wait outside for the 6 pm train. A man would approach him and say, 'I'm the Bishop.' In the company of the man he would wheel his bike to an appointed house, where another bike would be leaning on the inside of the front gate for the Bishop to pickup. They would then cycle to Tailfingen. The Bishop would hand him a letter giving him further instructions.

That evening, after the train had left, no one had approached him and after waiting thirty minutes Cédric decided to cycle back home.

Within ninety minutes Cédric wheeled the bike into the backyard and approached the back entrance only to see that the kitchen window was broken and open. He placed his bike on its stand, and went into the greenhouse to a flowerpot where he retrieved an Astra Model 600 pistol. He gingerly opened the back door and carefully inspected every ground floor room. With the pistol in his left hand, he proceeded up the stairs, his eyes fixed on the corridor that was within his range of vision. He inspected all of the upstairs rooms, and all were vacant.

He came down the staircase shoving the pistol into his belt and went to check the secret vault. Its contents were untouched. He closed the vault then closed the section of the wall that hid it. He sat down at his desk and opened all its drawers, inspecting each one carefully – nothing was missing. Cédric re-entered the kitchen, opened the pantry and was shocked to see that a large cache of food had been stolen. He was satisfied that the cause of the break-in was that the culprit or culprits were hungry. But when he opened the back door and saw that none of the produce in the greenhouse had been taken, he started to rethink his initial assessment. He hid his pistol back in the flowerpot and went into the house, locking all the doors that led to the outside. Tomorrow he would see First Lieutenant Pierre Thomas.

At 10 am the next day Cédric cycled to the Mayoral Office and requested to see Pierre Thomas. The secretary entered the office, closing the door behind her. Within two minutes she reappeared with Pierre who said, 'Cédric, my friend, come in and tell why you've come.' Pierre closed the door behind them, and they immediately took up their usual positions, Cédric sitting in front of the desk and Pierre behind it.

'I want to report a break-in which occurred yesterday between 4 and 8 pm,' Cédric said.

Pierre immediately opened a drawer and took out a pen and pad and started scribbling down notes. 'How did they get in?'

'They came through the back of the property via the greenhouse, smashed a kitchen window, and opened it to get into the house.'

'What did they take?'

'Only food from the pantry,' Cédric said.

'No money, no jewellery, no valuables, no clothes and no decorative items?' Pierre asked. 'No valuable documents?'

'No! All my documents were there, and none of the other items you have mentioned were taken. I rechecked everything this morning before I came here.'

'We're in a region where orphans are starving. Maybe one of these delinquents stole your food.'

'I thought about that, but the problem was that no produce was stolen from the greenhouse,' Cédric said, looking confused.

'You came in through the back, right, not the front?'

'Yes, I came in via the back entrance through the greenhouse to the back door and that's when I noticed the kitchen window had been smashed.'

Pierre enquired, 'Was the back gate left opened?'

'No, when I left it was shut and when I returned I had to open it.'

'Did you see any unfamiliar bikes or other modes of transport in the alleyway at the back of your house?'

'I can't remember. I should have looked, but I wasn't expecting a break-in.' Cédric was annoyed with himself for not being more observant.

'Are your fingerprints on the back door entrance, on the kitchen door and pantry handle?'

Cédric, looking mortified, answered, 'I think so.'

'Nevertheless, I'll send down a team to record and identify fingerprints on all the downstairs door handles, and we'll see what we can uncover. Is there anything more?'

Cédric felt he needed more security, especially if he was to look after the Bishop, and he knew exactly the man he wanted, but he needed to let Pierre make the decision. 'I wonder if it's possible for you to provide one of your soldiers to guard the front and back entrance of my house when I'm away for an hour or more. It needs to be someone physically large, who could handle one or two intruders on his own account, and someone who can speak my native tongue. It's only likely to be once or twice a month. I'm willing to pay you handsomely.'

Pierre's eyes lit up. 'There's a man in my group, Jean Fanier, who is on secondment from the 4th Group of Moroccan Tabors. He speaks Arabic, French and Algerian. He'd be perfect for what you have in mind. Of course, you must make payment to me in the usual manner.'

Cédric smiled. 'Of course, in the usual manner. And in the meantime, please let me know of any developments with respect to yesterday's break-in.'

They parted and immediately Pierre called for his secretary. 'Tell Helena Kempa I want to speak to her on Saturday morning.'

24

As Helena Kempa was ushered into the Mayoral Office, Pierre rose to greet her. Helena felt nervous because of Pierre's authority and because he always spoke French, a language Helena was not fluent in.

Pierre began the conversation in French. 'I asked you to look after Magrete when she entered the DP camp and I'm pleased that the two of you have become friends - '

'Friends!' Helena said in German. 'Oh, we're far more than that! I've been made her assistant events manager, and we've come up with some wonderful - '

Pierre interrupted in French, 'That's not what I - '

'As I was saying,' Helena said, who tended to gabble when she was nervous, 'Magrete has put me in charge of organising the choir and the band. Well, the choir was easy to organise because the vice-president of the Central Committee, Zalman Sneig, used to conduct a choir in one of those labour camps during the war, and so he has taken over, and they meet every Monday afternoon in the dining room after dinner, and he told me there were six women and six men, but he has been having trouble finding a baritone, as they're really rare, and so what he has decided is to ask if there are baritones in Tailfingen who'd like to join our DP choir so that he has a proper balance - '

Pierre interrupted again in French. 'That's very informative, but what I was going to ask you - '

'Of course! I should've told you about our new band! How silly of me! Our band is not the kind of band you'd find in a big city. Most of the DPs come from small villages in their homeland and worked on farms; that's why they're here, because the German Reich was fighting and didn't trust anyone to do their fighting for them, so they brought us here to labour for them. It's a piano accordion band!'

Pierre had enough. He rose from his chair, banged his two fists on the table and shouted in German, 'Stop! Stop!'

Helena stopped talking immediately.

Pierre then asked, in broken German, 'Has anyone outside the camp tried to contact Magrete?'

Helena realised that he had not been listening to her. 'As I said to you, First Lieutenant Pierre Thomas,' she answered more slowly in German, 'I have been busy organising the piano accordion band. Magrete organises the Saturday night dinner speakers, so lately we really haven't seen much of each other - '

'Thank you, Frau Kempa,' Pierre interrupted her in German. 'That's all I wanted to know.' He wrote something on a small piece of paper, and handed it to her. 'Show this to my secretary, and she'll give you a small token of our appreciation.'

Helena left his office and two minutes later his secretary found him lying on the couch next to the window. 'Please get me a glass and a full bottle of George's red wine,' he instructed his secretary in French. 'I need to erase that woman's voice from my mind forever!' He never interviewed Helena again.

25

Eugene was looking forward to the dinner with Pierre. After breaking into the Tailfingen house Krystyna Skarbek had used Deutsche Einheitskurzschrift (German shorthand) to copy a sizeable number of documents, including a letter written by Johann Leo Harisch to Cédric Bacri, informing him that the Bishop would stay at the Tailfingen house for days, if not weeks. Eugene had decided to withhold this information from Wiesenthal until he had a clearer picture of the operation, and a better idea of who the Bishop might be.

Krystyna Skarbek's report had given him so much more ammunition. Eugene now knew that Elderly Care owned the DRK hospitals in Munich, Prague, Magdeberg and Leipzig as well as houses in Beelitz and Tailfingen, and apartments in Vienna and East Berlin. He also knew who lived in the Vienna apartment and in the Tailfingen house. He immediately conveyed this information about their assets to Simon Wiesenthal.

When Pierre arrived the two men greeted each other cordially and sat down at the dining room table. Anna would sometimes join them for pre-dinner drinks, but she never shared a meal with them. Pierre trusted Eugene and tonight he decided he would use him, as a sounding board regarding the recent mystery of the break-in. Eugene would speak to him frankly and decisively on most topics.

Pierre enquired, 'Anna is not here tonight?'

'No, she's attending George's English class that he gives after the Saturday night lecture. Lately he's been giving her a bottle of Egri Bikavér once a month, because Anna has been topping the class,' Eugene said, not knowing that George was trying to repay in a different way Anna's generous financial support of his family.

Pierre had brought a bottle for them to share tonight. 'Rumour has it,' Pierre said, 'that somewhere in that bombed Kaiser Wilhelm Institute there exists a cellar that's well-known to George, but hidden from the rest of us, hosting a large cache of his Hungarian wine.' Eugene smiled at the thought of an underground wine cellar, missed by the German scientists, the Americans and the French, and known only to George.

'I don't understand why they're not giving French lessons,' Pierre continued. 'Most of these Eastern Europeans and Tailfingers can't understand French, which makes my job so much harder.'

'Perhaps Pierre, because none of the DPs have a chance to immigrate to France or French colonies, because France won't accept refugees.'

'That's not our fault,' Pierre countered. 'France was never invited to attend any major conference on the refugee problem.' Pierre wanted their conversation to centre on Magrete. 'From what I gather Magrete is doing a marvellous job of being the events manager. Everybody in Tailfingen is now using the DP camp as a resource. The Saturday night lectures she organises are a real hit and the locals love the choir and the piano accordion band.'

'The more I see of Magrete, the more I appreciate what she does,' Eugene observed. 'She seems to just make things happen around her. She walks into a place and energises it.'

As Pierre started on his entrée, he said, 'The break-in at her last residence is quite strange. The resident came home through the back gate, found the back window smashed and the pantry raided, but the robbers left the greenhouse in the back undisturbed even though it contained a lot of edible produce. It just doesn't make sense.'

'Perhaps,' Eugene proffered, 'the robbers broke in through the back and opportunistically raided the pantry, thinking they'd raid the greenhouse on their way out, but then they were disturbed by the resident coming in from the back, and so they left via the front door.'

'That makes perfect sense,' Pierre said. 'I wonder if the robbers were some of Magrete's past Nazi friends who thought she still lived there, and when they realised she didn't they robbed the place instead.'

'Could be,' Eugene said, 'but highly unlikely.'

'It'll only be a matter of time before Magrete's Nazi friends realise she's in a DP camp,' Pierre concluded.

'And when they do, she'll be considered useless for their flight to safe havens, and she'll be out of the loop. When you're in a DP camp you don't have access to money, influence, counterfeit documents. No, I believe Magrete is the least of your concerns.'

Pierre was comforted by this perspective.

'Speaking of Magrete,' Eugene continued, 'she has asked me to meet her at 4.30 pm Monday afternoon in the administration block to discuss whether I could give a Saturday lecture on the way American democracy works.'

'Ah, American democracy,' Pierre said and then smiled, 'inspired by the French Revolution!'

'Yes, and that's why the French designed the Statue of Liberty but we Americans mostly paid for it!' They clinked their wine glasses and laughed.

'Anyway,' Eugene continued, 'she asked me to deliver it in English, because some administrator gave his Saturday night lecture in French, and no one in the audience understood him.'

Pierre smiled, knowing that he was the butt of Eugene's humour, and replied, 'Only the cultured ones did, and they are the people who matter most.'

The evening ended on a jovial note. But what concerned Eugene was that Krystyna Skarbek had reported that she had picked the back door lock when she saw Cédric leave the premises at 4 pm and had completed her mission by 7. Between 7 and 8 pm someone had smashed the back window and entered the house. He suspected that someone was Helmut Gruen and his female accomplice. He reasoned that they were searching for Magrete, and when they realised she no longer lived there they opportunistically took food and left. Eugene knew that Pierre had got it wrong; everybody was fixated on the Nazis Magrete knew, not realising, as he did, that she had known only a few important Nazis via her first husband.

He continued to intercept Magrete's mail, just in case one letter would steer him to the whereabouts of Helmut Gruen.

26

On Saturday 6 September Magrete had scheduled George to deliver a lecture titled: 'A Simple Explanation of an Atomic Bomb and Its After-Effects'. When word got out, the camp had many enquiries about it and Magrete knew it would be the best attended event of the year.

What had stimulated so much interest was that the Americans on 15 April 1948 had reactivated nuclear weapons testing at Enewetak Atoll, in the northwest region of the Marshall Islands, in order to test an improved bomb design.

To ease the attendance numbers, Magrete decided to charge Tailfingers a small entry fee rather than a donation as well as to ask DPs for a donation. This would deter some people from attending, and provide funds to support future events. By 7 pm the dining room had been cleared and seats arranged, with a small table in the front acting as a lectern. Helena was sitting at the door collecting money as the hall quickly filled. By 7.30 pm it was packed. There were at least fifty people who could not get in. Magrete apologised to each of them personally.

First Lieutenant Pierre Thomas introduced George to the audience in French and mentioned his work at the Kaiser Wilhelm Institute for Chemistry. Everybody in Tailfingen was proud of the Institute and in particular of Otto Hahn. He was the first Nobel Laureate who had lived in their village. The applause was loud and respectful.

'Ladies and gentleman,' George began in German, much to the relief of the audience, 'I know most of you have not studied nuclear physics' – the audience sheepishly laughed – 'so I'm not going to stun you with my scientific knowledge by discussing the TNT/hexogen implosion lens design' – here the audience audibly sighed with relief – 'but rather give you some insight into the purification of radioactive material, how fission works, how an enormous amount of energy is released, and how people die of its after-effects from what we call radiation sickness.' George paused. The audience was absolutely silent.

'Uranium is extracted as an impure substance and so in order to get enough pure radioactive uranium to make a nuclear bomb, we must isolate it from its non radioactive components. A substance is said to be radioactive if you can put it on a photographic plate and it forms an image of its own accord. We need to purify the ore so that we get close to 100% of the radioactive component. We do this by making it into a gas. For example, if you want to purify dirty water you transform liquid water into steam and then condense it. In the case of uranium ore, we react it with a fluoride compound to make uranium hexafluoride, which is a gas. Once it is in the gas phase, we spin it and the heavy radioactive uranium compound spins to the bottom and so we can separate the radioactive part from the rest. Eventually we accumulate near to 100% of the pure radioactive uranium.'

George paused again, and then called out, 'Ilse, please come in now.'

The audience parted as Ilse led in ten children carrying containers. In the containers were mousetraps, each holding a ping pong ball where the cheese is normally positioned. The children carefully made a small rectangular playing field of mousetraps.

'Thanks, Ilse. What I've tried to simulate here is a fission experiment. If the ping pong ball is released from the mousetrap, energy is released, and it will make the ball fly high in the air. Now, watch carefully.' George stood on the small table, and dropped a ping pong ball onto a mousetrap in the middle of the field. Initially a few ping pong balls flew into the air, but then a huge number of the ping pong balls were released, creating a clattering sound which eventually subsided. 'Now imagine a sample of pure radioactive uranium in which billions of these reactions take place, releasing an enormous amount of energy. That's what happens within radioactive uranium when it reaches critical mass. The energy manifests itself as a massive explosion. In Hiroshima alone it's estimated that 140,000 people died from one atomic bomb explosion, and in Nagasaki three days later 80,000 people died.' George paused and saw the fascination on people's faces.

George commanded, 'Ilse and friends please clean up the mess.' He waited until the all the mousetraps and ping pong balls were cleared.

'But not all of these people died from the explosion,' George continued, 'or from the results of the explosion, like buildings collapsing. Radioactive material itself causes radiation sickness. The effects can last for years, and can include loss of hair, nausea, headaches, vomiting; the skin can be irritated or burned. In the long-term, people can experience infertility, memory loss and cancer. To end this talk, let me repeat what a great man once said: "No one can saves us but ourselves". This great man knew that our destiny lies in our hands and with this added responsibility we must use our knowledge for good and not to cause harm. Thank you for listening.'

Everybody stood up and applauded loudly; a few people whistled. Only Magrete knew whom George had quoted. He must have read one of my yoga books, she thought.

When the clapping had subsided, Pierre asked the audience in French if any of them had any questions. Most were intimidated by the content of the talk and so held their counsel. After a few awkward moments Captain Eugene Gould stood up and asked in French, 'What effect do you think having an A-bomb will have on the world and the way wars will be fought in the future, especially if the Soviets produce a nuclear weapon?' Magrete had not seen him come into the dining room, but she was pleased to see Anna sitting next to him.

'Interesting question,' George said, replying in German. 'Clearly it's in everybody's interest not to engage in nuclear warfare; all will suffer in such a war. However, that does not mean that they'll not engage in indirect warfare. Consider the game of chess. The Queen, Knights, Bishops, Castles and Pawns are there to protect the White and Black Kings. Let us equate the White King to the US and if the Soviets build a nuclear weapon, assign the Black King to them, and all the rest of the playing pieces can be considered as other countries that are in alliance with them. Hence, to lose a white pawn to the Soviets, such as Hungary, is not as important as to lose a white Queen, such as England, to the Soviets. Conventional wars will be fought amongst the playing pieces with the backing of their respective King. Heaven help us if there are more than just two Kings on the chess board.'

Pierre could see that most of the audience was uneducated, and so asked in French, 'Does the creation of an atomic bomb mean that people will come to distrust science in general, because they'll be dismayed by scientific discoveries falling into the hands of ruthless men?'

George thought about the question and said in German, 'I'm no oracle. But a scientific discovery that can lead to harm can also be harnessed for good. It's our ethical and moral behaviour that determines how we make use of a discovery. There are two threats that might lead to the disillusionment of science amongst the public in the future. The most obvious is the outside threat. I call it the Pope Urban threat, because he believed the Sun revolved around the Earth for he reasoned that the Earth was central to God. He should not have been allowed to have a scientific opinion, because he was ignorant of the scientific facts available in his time. Hence, we should realize not all scientific opinions carry equal weight.' George paused and could see some in the audience did not understand his explanation. Nevertheless, he ventured on.

'The second threat for Science is the inside threat. In the future, some scientists will announce scientific discoveries they claim will one day cure cancer, knowing fully well that their mediocre science will never make this stride. These inside scientific pretenders might help to destroy the credibility of science to the public at large.'

Pierre rose and said in French, 'I wish to thank Dr George Nagy for his illuminating lecture today. Please accept this small token from the Central Committee.' He handed George a wrapped gift. 'Ladies and gentleman, thank you for attending.'

As the audience streamed out of the dining room many stopped and congratulated Magrete and Helena for their contribution to the intellectual fabric of Tailfingen society. Anna made sure that Eugene and she avoided crossing paths with Magrete.

27

Corporal Jean Fanier was 6 foot 4 inches tall, and solidly built, weighing sixteen and a half stone. He usually wore the Moroccan military uniform, with a red fez and matching balloon pants. He was bored guarding Cédric's house and occasionally stole glimpses of Goethestraße.

He noticed a woman cycling from the Einsenbahnstraße to Neuweilerstraße and then into Hechingerstraße. She was very attractive, brownish-blonde hair and lean, with a large pointed bosom small waist and a tight rounded rear. He liked this type of Germanic woman; when he went to the local brothel, this was the type of woman he sought. The local prostitutes were afraid of him because he enjoyed his sex rough. Jean loved to dominate his female partner, and he liked the fear he could feel rippling through their bodies when he had hard sex with them.

Jean heard a noise from the back gate, and immediately positioned himself on the kitchen floor aiming his MAS-36 rifle directly at the door. There were three knocks on the door and a voice said, 'Jean, it's me, Cédric.'

Jean replied in Algerian, 'Open the door, enter, and close the door behind you.' It was his way of making sure that Cédric did not have a gun to his head. The door slowly opened, and Cédric walked in and closed the door behind him. Jean motioned Cédric away from the door and whispered, 'Have you brought someone with you?'

Cédric nodded and whispered, 'Yes, one guest.'

Jean, still not moving, whispered, 'Tell him to come in.'

Cédric did so and in walked the Bishop. Once Jean had looked out the back door and checked that everything was clear in the lane, he lowered his rifle and uncocked it. Cédric and the Bishop went into the lounge room, while Jean stood guard in the kitchen. The Bishop was none other than Bishop Alois Hudal, who Simon Wiesenthal had labelled the 'Black Bishop' because of his pro-Nazi views.

'Sorry about Jean, Right Reverend,' Cédric apologised. 'He's a bit trigger-happy, but he's a fantastic guard.'

'Is it safe to talk while he's in the house?'

'It is. He joined the 4th Group of Moroccan Tabors after the war on our instructions, and through a number of intermediaries we were able to get him seconded to Tailfingen. He's one of us, and he gives us regular, valuable information about First Lieutenant Pierre Thomas, the local administrator. Fanier is a valuable asset.'

'We need to talk about your next visitor,' the Bishop said. 'He's very much a practising Catholic. His name is Vinco Pavlowitch. He was wrongly accused by the west of mass-murdering several hundred thousand Serbs, and tens of thousands of Jews as well as Romani, all of whom were communists that he fought against in the Kingdom of Yugoslavia. We want him to stay here for two days, then we'll move him to your Vienna apartment, and after that to Naples and Argentina. These are the arrangements I've made. Read them, memorise them, and then destroy them. He'll be disguised as a priest and go under the name Don Pablo Gonner. You'll pick him up next month. Here are his papers, which I was able to secure from the Austrian Office in Rome, where we've the necessary cards for migration to Argentina. Guard these documents with your life. In the future, we'll be sending all exit documents via the local Catholic Church. Priests moving across borders and zones are invisible to border guards.'

By 11 September Right Reverend Alois Hudal had left Tailfingen, without the knowledge of Eugene Gould.

28

On 3 December Magrete was cycling from Langestraße into Goethestraße and then into Hechingerstraße when she noticed three bedrooms were lit up in her old home of 1 Neuweilerstraße. It was the regularity of the event that struck her. On 10 September, 8 October, 5 November and 3 December the bedroom lights suggested there were more people living in her old home than the one person who occupied it. It always began on the first Wednesday of every month. Sometimes the bedroom lights were on for two nights running, and at other times for three nights, but the sequence was too regular for it to be a coincidental visitor or two. Ever since Magrete had been meeting Eugene on the first Monday of every month, she had been more sensitive to non-random events. The lights aroused her curiosity, so she decided to visit her old next-door neighbour Sofie Wörm the following day.

When Sofie opened the door to Magrete, she was clearly delighted to see her. 'Come in, Magrete! You're the talk of the village. The Saturday lectures, the language classes, the band and the choir – it makes us Tailfingers jealous that we're not in the DP camp.'

'Sofie, you're so kind,' Magrete said. Sofie ushered Magrete into the lounge room and seated her in the armchair.

'A cup of camomile tea, the way you normally have it?'

'Love one,' Magrete replied.

When Sofie went to the kitchen, Magrete moved to the side window, and pushed the curtain back a little. Sofie's side window looked directly into the front lounge room window of her old house. Magrete could see a man looking down Goethestraße and that man was not the occupier of the house. Magrete had seen the man's face before, but she could not remember where. She could hear Sofie returning, and sat back in the armchair.

'Here,' Sofie said, handing Magrete her tea and placing her cup on the coffee table between them.

'I haven't seen you for a while,' Magrete reflected, 'and the other day when I cycled past your place I promised I would drop in.'

'We've all been so busy. I guess when the men returned from the war they had to make-up for lost time,' Sofie winked at Magrete, 'because I've been delivering one baby after another. We're definitely in the midst of a baby boom.'

'Hopefully my three will be enough for us,' Magrete said. 'By the way, how is your new neighbour?' Magrete knew that Sofie loved to gossip.

'Nothing like your family! He's the quietest neighbour I've had since Helmut. Occasionally when he's out of the house, he has some foreign soldier guarding it, and lately he's been having a few visitors. They're as quiet as church mice, though. You'd think I was living next to a morgue.'

'I cycle past your place often,' Magrete said, 'and I have noticed the visitors seem to come on a Wednesday and leave on a Thursday or Friday.'

Sofie thought about it. 'Funny you should say that … they do come on the first Wednesday of every month. Isn't that peculiar? They always visit the Catholic Church; they must be very religious.'

Magrete had just finished her tea when the man she had seen at the window flashed back into her mind, and she said softly to herself, 'Adolf Eichmann.'

'Who?'

'Never mind,' Magrete said coming back into the moment. 'I hope you do not think I am rude, but I have just remembered that I have an appointment in the next ten minutes. I wanted to see you to give you a ticket to the next concert at the DP camp.'

'Magrete, you shouldn't have! But thank you. Off you go to your meeting.'

Magrete handed her a ticket and gave her a kiss on either side of her cheeks, which Sofie responded in kind. Magrete slowly walked out the door and then cycled furiously to the villa.

29

At the villa Magrete said to the private at the gate, 'This is an emergency! Tell Captain Gould that Magrete Nagy has enquired about P-A-N.'

The private said, 'What's pan?'

'Never mind,' Magrete said, disappointed by his reaction. She took a piece of paper and pencil out of her pocket and wrote: 'PAN, the back gate at 1 Neuweilerstraße'. 'This is urgent! Give this message to Captain Eugene Gould immediately.' Magrete handed the paper to the private and rode to the alleyway at the back of her old house.

When she opened the back gate she immediately felt a sharp pain across her face, and collapsed face down on the ground near the birch tree. She heard a man say 'Deal with her!' Two men walked away, and she sensed another man standing over her. The man shoved a rag into her mouth and secured it with a band around her head to prevent her from screaming. Magrete felt him lifting the back of her skirt, then kneeling behind her as he brought her underwear down to her knees. There was a pause, and she felt him attempting to turn her over. Magrete went with the movement and whack! She hit the man on the side of the chin with a fist-sized rock she had seized from the ground next to the birch tree. The man collapsed on top of her, unconscious. Magrete slid from underneath him, stood and stripped the rag from her mouth, her underpants now down near her ankles, and that is when she noticed one flowerpot had an awkward tilt. Suddenly the back gate opened – it was Eugene. She raised her finger to her mouth to indicate he should remain silent. Eugene was stunned to see that her underwear had been nearly removed. Without a trace of embarrassment Magrete turned her back to him, lifted her underwear to its usual position and pulled down her dress.

Eugene watched transfixed as Magrete placed the unconscious soldier's arms around the birch tree and locked them together using the soldier's handcuffs, then placed the key in her pocket. She placed the rag the soldier had shoved into her mouth over his head, ripped off his belt and tied the belt around his neck to secure it. Eugene noticed that the soldier's exposed foreskin had been torn when she ripped the belt from him. Magrete now pushed his pants down further, grabbed a birch sapling and lashed him six times on his exposed backside. Welts appeared with each lash, and with each one the soldier was regaining consciousness. Magrete now extracted his wallet, took a handful of notes, then placed the wallet back in his pocket. She removed his rifle and leaned it against the back door. Magrete motioned Eugene to step into the alleyway, and she whispered to him, 'Get Pierre to come and rescue this sex fiend. I'll see you tomorrow at 11 am at the Apotheke.' She hopped on her bicycle and rode back to the DP camp, sore and worried.

Eugene finally understood what Magrete was doing: Pierre, being Catholic, could understand most men's urges, but paying a sadist to give you some masochistic pleasure was not one of them. This man was in serious trouble, Eugene thought, which would only be exacerbated by the fact that they would have to spend a considerable amount of time and effort to remove his handcuffs.

The next day they met at the Apotheke. Eugene apologised, 'Sorry about my dumb private! Are you alright?'

'My face is sore where that man struck me.' Eugene could see the bruise on her cheek. 'I told George I fell off the bike, and he laughed. Other than having a headache last night, I am all right. He never touched me, but the thought of him trying to, kept me up for a few hours. What happened when I left?'

'I went and got Pierre and told him that I'd heard a man groaning while I was changing a punctured tyre near 1 Neuweilerstraße and looked in through the back gate ... When Pierre saw him, he was furious and it took them an hour to get the handcuffs off. The soldier said a woman had attacked him, but Pierre didn't believe him. He then claimed it was a man and woman working in tandem, because they wanted to rob him. Pierre took his wallet and asked him how much money he had and since most of it was still there, it looked more likely that he'd hired a male prostitute for a sordid affair. Then Pierre raided the house and found many incriminating documents – evidence that Corporal Jean Fanier and Cédric were in cahoots, and operating a halfway house for Nazi fugitives. Cédric and Fanier were arrested, sent to Ebingen and charged with aiding and abetting criminal activity. They've been sent to Baden-Baden for further questioning.'

Magrete asked, 'Was Cédric alone when he was arrested?'

'Yes, but why do you ask?'

'The reason I desperately wanted to see you was because Cédric's guest was Adolf Eichmann.'

Eugene whistled and said, 'Eichmann! Are you sure?'

'I am certain. I recognised him from the photograph you gave me. Unfortunately, he definitely saw me, even if it was for a fleeting moment.'

Eugene looked concerned. Magrete had been responsible for a dozen arrests of SS officers and prison officials, and Eichmann being on the loose could be a big problem for her. He decided to increase security around her and her family.

30

On the morning of 5 December Magrete stole into the backyard of 1 Neuweilerstraße and went straight to the tilted flowerpot. She lifted it and took the Astra Model 600 pistol and a small satchel from a hole covered by the pot. Magrete placed the pistol in the satchel, returned to the DP camp, and headed for the women's toilet block. She went into the furthest cubicle from the entry, opened the satchel and read its contents. Then she lifted a paver and placed the satchel and pistol in a hollow underneath. She carefully replaced the paver, left the toilet block, and cycled to St Elizabeth Catholic Church in Lammerbergstraße.

Magrete walked into the confessional box, knelt in front of the screen, made the sign of the cross and said, 'In the name of the Father, and of the Son, and of the Holy Spirit, my last confession was three months ago.' The priest, Father Barth, read a passage from Holy Scripture. Magrete then said softly, 'I've sinned a great sin, Father.'

'What sin did you commit, my child?'

'When I was questioned by First Lieutenant Pierre Thomas about the activities that were going on in my old home at 1 Neuweilerstraße, I told him I had no idea. But I saw Adolf Eichmann enter this church, after leaving my old home, and he left carrying a satchel. Yesterday, I happened to find a satchel that contained forged documents in a rubbish bin in the alleyway behind my old residence for a hunted man, Franz Stangl. They were probably hidden there, before the French soldiers arrested the resident for being part of the ratline. The Americans captured Stangl this year, but he escaped. The documents were issued by Bishop Hudal, which provided this man and his wife accommodation in Rome, and a visa for him and his family to go to Syria, as well as a wad of money. These documents put you and this church in so much peril that I have sent them to an associate of mine in Vienna for safekeeping. I hope my family and I will be in God's hands. I am sorry for these and all my sins.'

Father Barth was no fool. He understood that the Roman Catholic Church could not be seen to be implicated in helping Nazis escape from criminal prosecution, and he knew Magrete had deposited evidence with a third party. He also knew that Tailfingen could no longer be used as part of the ratline; its operation at 1 Neuweilerstraße had effectively ended with the arrest of Cédric Bacri. Now that Frau Nagy had this evidence, St Elizabeth Church could no longer be used as a place to pickup safe cards – something that would make Bishop Hudal furious. But Father Barth liked Magrete and her family, and felt an obligation to protect her from Hudal's anger. He would tell

Hudal that First Lieutenant Pierre Thomas had given him the choice of bowing out of the ratline or having the church implicated in organising the escape of criminals. He knew this would be consistent with the charges laid against Cédric Bacri and Jean Fanier.

Father Barth said to Magrete, 'Your family will be safe in the hands of God. Say ten Hail Marys for the sin you've committed.'

Magrete made her act of contrition, realising that Father Barth had indirectly assured her that her family would be protected from retribution. She left the church elated. Father Barth felt relief that Tailfingen would no longer be a node in the ratline.

31

The International Refugee Organization (IRO), like its predecessor UNRRA, was limited under its Articles of Agreement to assist in the 'repatriation or return to their home countries of displaced persons.' It transported millions of former concentration camp dwellers, forced labourers and other victims of the German Reich to countries of their origin, including France, Belgium and Greece. The Western Allies returned over two million Soviet citizens to areas under Soviet control. They were moved in batches, generally in return for equivalent numbers of citizens of Western Allies, an equivalence that was insisted upon by the Soviet authorities. Many of the Soviets departed willingly, but others did not, and their forced return conflicted with the non-refoulement principle. Many citizens of East European States that had been taken over by communist regimes resisted repatriation, and most of the DPs in Tailfingen were in that category, so there was little movement in or out of the DP camp in Tailfingen from 1946 to 1948.

By 20 February 1948 1 Neuweilerstraße remained empty. Baden-Baden had decreed that the house had been used for criminal activity, confiscated the premise, and handed it to First Lieutenant Pierre

Thomas. He loved the house's central location, and his secretary/mistress and four other female administrators were relocated there. His secretary occupied Magrete and George's bedroom on her own. Pierre would often visit the house after hours and as he was not fraternising with a German woman, most of the female bureaucrats accepted his affair as part of the French way of life.

Magrete asked Pierre if she could reclaim her piano, and he readily agreed. She installed it in the DP camp dining room, and started to practise with the piano accordion band. Whenever Magrete had chores to do, her children were looked after either by George or by Helena's two children, Zofia and Claudia. There was a community understanding that co-operation and pooling of human and other resources would make life much easier for all DPs.

One of Magrete's simple but effective initiatives was the installation in the dining room of an old bookcase that the men had retrieved from the local garbage dump, repaired and repainted. She placed two books on the shelves, both in German: The Chivalrous Art of Archery and the Bhagavad Gita. Every day new books were added to the shelves, written in every Eastern European language imaginable, from Yiddish to Czech to Hungarian to Polish to Serbian to Croatian, as well as books in English. There was even a German–French dictionary, which everyone assumed Pierre Thomas had donated. Within a month, another bookshelf was needed to house the books that were being offered.

Magrete saw that Ilse was becoming depressed because she was seeing Anna less often, not due to ill will, but due to circumstance. Magrete had been teaching Ilse yoga in Anna's absence. She decided to approach Helena.

'Helena, I have been noticing that many of the women here are not getting enough exercise.' The DPs did not now do the hard physical work they had been required to during the war years.

Helena said, 'Many of us don't work as hard as we used to.'

'Did you know that Anna, who is the residential housekeeper

of the villa, was a yoga teacher? If I arrange with Captain Gould for you to see her, could you ask her to give a one-hour yoga class every Tuesday night after dinner in the dining room? You could mention to her that Ilse has already signed up. Of course, we cannot pay her, but we would give her free entry to her English classes and other events in the DP camp.'

'That's a brilliant idea!' Helena said. 'We could ask the men to look after the kids that can't attend, so the rest can go. I'm sure she'll do it.'

'I also wanted to tell you that I'm pregnant,' Magrete said, looking sheepish.

Helena went into fits of laughter and once she got control of herself said, 'Frau Purity, welcome to the bathroom couple scene! Those toilet blocks have created many a child!' They both laughed.

The following day Eugene was more than happy to allow Helena to speak to Anna, because he could see Anna was gaining a little weight, and he wanted the wedding in October to be without this worry. When Helena said Ilse had signed up, Anna immediately consented.

Every Tuesday evening, the women of the DP camp assembled to do yoga under Anna's instruction. Some men tried to peer through the windows in the hope of getting glimpses of women in their underwear only to be thwarted by women patrolling the area. Anna quickly became aware that Magrete had taught Ilse well, and asked Ilse to demonstrate some of the more difficult yoga exercises for the class. Ilse no longer felt depressed, because she was now seeing Anna twice a week – once for her English lesson and the other as Anna's assistant in her yoga class.

32

On 26 February 1948 the Max Planck Society was formed in Göttingen. Professor Otto Hahn was the first president of the Society. The Society initially encompassed only the institutes in the British and American Occupied Bizone. From the beginning, the Society was entirely dependent on public funding in order to finance its activities. George Nagy, in the French zone, was not aware that the Society and its institutes existed. In the same month Trizonia was formed, combining the occupied zones of America, Britain and France.

At 11 am on 1 March Magrete met with Eugene at the Apotheke. Magrete had decided she would not report that St Elizabeth Church had been used to issue exit cards to Adolf Eichmann, Franz Stangl and others. She reasoned that the local church would no longer be involved and, moreover, she liked the support Father Barth was giving to her and her family.

'Now that Pierre has arrested Cédric Bacri and Jean Fanier,' Eugene said, 'it seems that the operation in Tailfingen has come to an end, and that Tailfingen is far too hot for Nazis to come here. What do you think?'

'I agree, especially now that they have lost the house in Tailfingen. But it will not hurt to keep my ears to the ground. You never know what may slide in,' Magrete said, sadly realising that her monthly payment from Eugene was at an end.

Eugene knew that Magrete was pregnant. He did not want her to find herself in another dangerous situation. 'I think these Monday meetings should also come to an end. There are fourteen SS officers who, because of your work, have been convicted or who are facing a conviction. But the P-A-N code will still be operative and if you need to see me urgently on any matter, use it! Everybody in my command is aware what it means, so what happened to you on the first occasion won't happen to you again. Wisenthal has also got the authorities to shut down Elderly Care's Vienna operation, since the arrests here suggested that the Vienna apartment had been used for criminal activity. They could only expel Johann Leo Harisch rather than arresting him. Eva Peron intervened on his behalf and made certain that no charges would be laid against him.'

'I have one last piece of information for you, that I cannot make head or tail of,' Magrete said. She handed Eugene a letter. 'I found this in the piano when I retrieved from 1 Neuweilerstraße after Pierre had occupied the house.' It was a letter of introduction from a Herr Ricardo Klement to the director of APT in Buenos Aires, and contained one curious sentence: "I may have to go to Syria before I can temporarily enter Italy on my way to Argentina, so it may be a few months before I can finally meet you."'

Eugene asked, 'Do you know if Klement is a real person or an alias?'

'I do not know who Klement is, or who is hiding behind that name. The fact I found it in the upright piano could mean that Cédric Bacri was going to give it to a future guest, or that he had forgotten to give it to a past guest. I'd guess the former is more likely.'

Eugene felt uneasy about this letter. 'I'll send it to Simon Wiesenthal. He can research it far better than we can. He'll need to investigate this Syria–Italy–Argentina link.'

Magrete arrived back at the DP camp just after lunch. When she opened the door she was furious – there was her husband, drunk, snoring and reeking of alcohol. Eva and Elisabeth were sleeping. Magrete kicked George's backside as hard as she could, but he merely turned over and snored some more. Magrete saw an envelope on the floor, and she recognised Mimi's handwriting. The letter said that Mimi was pregnant and her child was due in October, as was Magrete's. Mimi also asked whether she should answer an enquiry from a Herr Horváth Márton, who had written asking the whereabouts of a Dr George Felsőbüki Nagy.

When George woke the following morning, Ilse, Eva, Elisabeth and Magrete were nowhere to be seen. He searched the camp but could not find them. He returned home and paced up and down the room, sometimes looking out the window waiting for his family to return.

Finally, Magrete walked in alone. She walked up to him, shoved her finger in his chest and shouted, 'You will never – and I mean never – leave my children to fend for themselves because you are blind drunk! Do you hear me?' George was convinced the neighbours were listening to their row.

'Look, I'm sorry Magrete-'

'Sorry does not cut it with me, George. Sorry does not do it! You have no excuse.'

'I drank the last bottle of Egri Bikavér, so trust me, it can't happen again.'

'Trust you? You have got to be kidding me! What were you expecting Elisabeth to do if anything had happened to Eva?'

'I promise it won't happen again.'

'George, this is your second strike. Remember the first strike, when I had Elisabeth and you were too drunk to know? Now this! Do not do this to the children and me ever again! We are in a DP camp, for God's sake. There are some very seedy characters living here.'

'I was stupid, just plain stupid. It won't happen again.'

'And on another point,' Magrete said, still furious, 'since when are you opening letters that are addressed to me?'

'I guess when you're drinking and bored you do stupid things. I promise I won't get drunk in future, so I won't do the other stupid things. Let me make it up to you in some way. Please.'

'Who the hell are Felsőbüki Nagy and Horváth Márton?' Magrete was looking at George as if she did not know him.

He avoided her eyes. 'I don't know either one of them. Maybe I'm being confused with someone else. Please write to Mimi and tell her that it's a simple case of mistaken identity. With so many DPs, and with my name similar to someone else's, such a confusion is understandable.'

'How did they know Mimi's address?'

George could sense that Magrete was not convinced. 'Yes, that's puzzling. I can only imagine that when my team returned to Hungary someone might have mentioned that you and I were married, and that you are the daughter of the Deputy Commissioner of the Vienna Police, and so a person mistakenly sent the letter to your parent's address enquiring about Felsőbüki Nagy – a person I've never heard of.'

Magrete was still not convinced, but decided to let it go for the sake of her children.

On a Saturday a few weeks later, George, Ilse and Elisabeth delighted Magrete and Eva by staging a special musical performance in their room, and George was officially forgiven.

However, George had remembered the gypsy prophecy, and felt he had chosen another fork along the road.

33

President Harry Truman signed the Marshall Plan on 3 April 1948, granting $5 billion in aid to sixteen European nations. It became effective from 3 June 1948. The Plan addressed key obstacles to post-war recovery. It looked towards the future, and in doing so focused on repairing the destruction caused by the war. The barter and black economy in the Bizone and the French zone was slowly diminishing as the real economy gained strength. The French now supported the reconstruction of Occupied Germany. The Soviet Union prevented countries in Eastern Europe from taking part in the Marshall Plan. Instead, the Soviet Union offered its own post-war program of economic aid.

On 24 June 1948 Soviet troops blocked all road and rail connections to West Berlin in a reaction against the introduction of a new currency in Trizonia. Within a few days, shipping on the Spree and Havel rivers was halted; electric power, which had been supplied to West Berlin by plants in the Soviet zone, was cut-off, and supplies of fresh food from the surrounding countryside were suddenly unavailable. The Four Power status of Berlin, agreed upon by the Allied victors, had not included any provisions regarding traffic by land to and from Berlin through the Soviet zone. It had, however, established three air corridors from the western zones to the city. The three Western powers acted swiftly: an airlift of unprecedented dimensions was organised to supply the 2.5 million inhabitants of the western sectors of Berlin with what they needed to survive. The United States military governor in Occupied Germany, General Lucius Clay, successfully coordinated the airlift, which deployed 230 United States and 150 British aeroplanes. Up to 10,000 tons of supplies were flown in daily, including coal and other heating fuels for the winter.

The first confrontation in the Cold War had begun and Magrete, now five months pregnant, prayed in St Elizabeth Church that her and Mimi's children would not experience another world war, and that her family might be permitted to flee Europe to a safer destination. Escaping Europe to a distant land now became a priority for Magrete. She never wanted to grieve again for lives lost because of armed conflict.

34

On 16 July 1948 Captain Gould filed a petition for marriage to an Austrian citizen, Anna Sulzer, as in six months' time he would be discharged from the US armed services and returned to the United States. While US military men were no longer barred from marrying

German or Austrian women, the paper trail was deliberately complicated in order to ensure that such occurrences were rare. What the authorities that invoked these hurdles had not foreseen was Eugene's legalistic mind and his determination to marry the person he loved, Anna.

First, Eugene filed an affidavit for the military government in Occupied Germany, which was his application for marriage. In this he had to provide personal information with respect to his address, previous marriages (none), and blood relations. The next few steps became progressively more invasive. Eugene's immediate commander was required to recommend approval or disapproval of the marriage. The commander approved, knowing that Eugene, an American Jew, and Anna, an Austrian Jew, would experience far less discrimination in an enlightened city such as New York – where Eugene lived – than elsewhere.

The petition had to begin no earlier than six months before he was scheduled to leave Occupied Germany. Eugene was scheduled to leave on 16 January 1949. The marriage itself would be conducted in the last sixty days of his tour, and was scheduled for October 1948. He gave the authorities very little time, but he had worked hard on the key personnel that needed to be on side from early January 1948.

After marrying an Austrian, Eugene knew he would no longer be eligible to be stationed in Occupied Germany. The unit chaplain, a Protestant, interviewed Eugene and Anna in Stuttgart and approved of the two getting married, especially because they were of the same faith. His OSS commander also supported the marriage, and wrote in Eugene's application form, 'The marriage will not bring discredit upon the military service nor be contrary to the public good.'

The medical screening of the bride-to-be was purposely designed to humiliate, but Anna was past humiliation. She was medically screened, primarily to ensure that she was free from communicable diseases, especially venereal diseases. She was found to be disease-free.

The civil marriage was set for 10 October 1948 in Tailfingen, under the supervision of First Lieutenant Pierre Thomas. Eugene had already prepared papers applying for a US travel permit for Anna, and for a military government marriage certificate from Bamberg after the marriage. The final application was twenty pages long. Eugene also secured travel documents allowing them to honeymoon in Switzerland. He was finally free to marry Anna.

The first Soviet atomic test was internally code-named First Lightning (Первая молния, or Pervaya Molniya) and was detonated on 29 August 1949. The Americans code-named it Joe 1. The design was very similar to the first US Fat Man plutonium bomb, using a TNT/hexogen implosion lens design. George Nagy's Hungarian colleagues' expertise was critical in purifying the fissionable material.

President Truman responded by calling for the United States to build-up its conventional and nuclear weapons, as well as to halt the spread of Soviet influence around the globe. While many historians argued that the Cold War had begun prior to the Soviets' first nuclear test, without nuclear weaponry the Soviets had not been able to match America's military might. A nuclear standoff in any third party conflict was the new political reality. This made Magrete even more determined to flee Europe for a distant country, in order to ensure the safety of her family from armed conflict.

35

On 10 October Eugene's sergeant, corporal and three privates attended his civil wedding. First Lieutenant Pierre Thomas conducted the ceremony, and Ilse and George Nagy were also there. While Anna and Eugene had both invited Ilse and George, only Eugene had invited Magrete. She officially declined the invitation due to her pregnancy, now in its ninth month, but in her heart she declined because she wanted Anna to have a perfect wedding day, which sadly she knew her presence would spoil.

'Why are you crying, Mum?' four-year-old Elisabeth asked. Magrete was silently weeping in their Tailfingen room.

Magrete wiped away her tears and said to her girl, 'Because I'm happy.'

'But when I'm happy I giggle and laugh,' Elisabeth said. 'I never cry.'

'Sometimes you are so happy that giggling and laughing aren't enough,' Magrete said.

Elisabeth, observing her mother carefully, asked, 'So why are you happy?'

'Because a most beautiful girl has grown into a beautiful woman, and she is getting married today, and she is so happy that I cannot help thinking about how happy she must be. These are tears of joy.' Magrete wiped away a few more tears.

'Is that beautiful woman Anna?'

'Yes, it is Anna,' Magrete said, before exclaiming, 'Oh my god! Get Helena next door – quickly, quickly!'

Helena knew why she was being summoned and placed Magrete's two children in the care of her husband and children. She then rushed to get Frau Sofie Wörm. It was 11 am, just as Anna and Eugene were exchanging their wedding vows.

Sofie rushed into the room. She checked Magrete and found she had only dilated to 3 centimetres. After three hours there had been no progression, despite Magrete's contractions being a sizeable time apart. Sofie again examined Magrete and discovered that the baby was in an awkward position, unable to easily enter the birth canal. She wrapped a large sarong-like cloth around Magrete to manoeuvre the baby into a better position, and internally used her fingers to rotate the baby's head into a more favourable position. Within forty-five minutes Magrete was checked again – this time the cervix started to dilated. Magrete pushed for three and a half hours to finally deliver a baby boy. The child was born after a total of six hours of labour.

After the birth, Sofie noticed that Magrete seemed to be going into shock – her pulse was rapid, she looked pale and felt extremely dizzy. When she carefully examined Magrete again, she discovered that her cervix had been badly bruised and weakened. Sofie knew that this could mean that Magrete might become infertile. It took another five hours of constant attention to get Magrete's vitals back to normal.

At 8 am the following day, George, Ilse, Elisabeth and Eva finally met the new addition to their family, a boy named Francis George Nagy, and he was very unlike the other three – a screamer from the beginning of his life. Magrete had finally honoured a pledge she had made to her mother: that her firstborn son would be named Francis, after her mother's favourite Saint.

By now, Anna and Eugene were on their way to Switzerland. For the first time since their separation, Anna felt guilty that she had not invited Magrete to her wedding. To ease her guilt, she constantly reminded herself of Magrete's involvement in the death of her aunt.

On 16 October, Mimi gave birth to a girl. They named her Matilda Magrete Kuebler, Matilda being her mother-in-law's mother's Christian name.

The planning committee for the Christmas Eve party at the DP camp consisted of Magrete (chair), Helena (assistant chair), Hans Balzhauser (conductor of the accordion band) and Zalman Sneig (conductor of the choir). It was decided that the celebration would be graced with a high table of Tailfingen dignitaries and members of the Central Committee, including First Lieutenant Pierre Thomas, Captain Eugene Gould, Chaim Rosenshaft and Zalman Sneig, and their wives. Hans Balzhauser would conduct both the choir and the accordion band on the night.

All wanted Magrete and George to sit on the high table, but Magrete flatly refused, telling the committee that the birth of her child had left her unwell, so she could not guarantee how long she might be present. Also, Ilse at nearly ten years of age would babysit

Magrete's other three children for a short period of time, so Magrete would need to return to her room as early as possible. Helena offered Magrete either of her two daughters to mind Magrete's children, but Magrete refused, knowing that Zofia and Claudia wanted to enjoy the event.

The committee knew that the food would be minimal, but because of the importance of the event, and due to previous events having netted them a reasonable surplus, they secured ingredients that would enable the kitchen to bake Christmas cakes and biscuits, which would be a real treat for the invited guests. They would also source and decorate a Christmas tree. All those in the DP camp who were attending the event were asked, if possible, to wear their traditional national dress. The evening entertainment would begin with the French National Anthem, 'La Marseillaise'. Magrete suggested that after a selection of Christmas carols were sung, they should end the night with some fun dance music. They all agreed.

As Magrete walked back to her room she suddenly felt a cramp, and knew she had bled. She hurriedly made her way to the bathroom/toilet block, and after cleansing herself and her underclothes she headed back to her room, where she found her family fast asleep.

36

Christmas Eve 1948 fell on a Friday. Dinner was quickly consumed, then the hall was cleared and the tables and chairs completely rearranged to produce a high table, flanked on one side by a large decorated Christmas tree and on the other side by space for the choir and seating for the accordion band. In front of the high table was a square dance floor. There was a table next to the Christmas tree that was set with plates of cakes and biscuits, treats that many of the children who were old enough to be present were seeing for the very first time. Those who had children too small to attend took it in turns to look after a pool of them, located in various rooms throughout the DP camp. Magrete had decided not to join the pool, for she was not feeling well, and so she left Ilse in charge with the promise that Ilse could attend after Magrete and George had returned to their room. George would escort Ilse back to the dining room.

Magrete, Helena, their children and their husbands were seated near the high table on one side and the rest of the Central Committee and their spouses who were not on the high table were seated on the opposite side. By 8 pm the dining room was packed, with many of those attending wearing their traditional national costumes. It was a sea of Eastern European nationalism, colourful and yet so odd. All rose when the guests of the high table entered the room.

Magrete's eyes never left Anna. She marvelled at how marriage sat so easily with her. She looked more content, more at ease than Magrete had ever envisaged Anna could be. She had lost a little weight, but in all the right places. Through her dark complexion shone a radiance Magrete had not seen before. Anna smiled and talked to each guest on the high table with confidence. Anna and Eugene together gave a sense of a new future that was waiting on the horizon.

Anna also took side-glances, now and then, at Magrete. A couple of times their eyes nearly met and Anna knew that if they had she would be impaled. Anna thought Magrete did not look well; she looked drawn and tired, almost listless. Her appearance disturbed and saddened Anna.

Pierre stood up and said in French, 'French National Anthem: "La Marseillaise"'. The conductor rapped his baton on the lectern in front of him and at the wave of his baton the choir sang and the band played 'La Marseillaise'. Pierre's voice was drowned out by the choir much to the relief and delight of the audience.

Zalman Sneig stood up and in German gave a short history of each Christmas song before it was sung. What surprised many was that he was proudly wearing a Jewish Kippah (skullcap) and knew more about the history and meaning of German Christmas songs than most in the audience.

When interval arrived, people were asked to go to the side table and collect biscuits and cakes. As the high table was being served, Anna glanced towards where Magrete and George had been sitting, only to find two empty chairs. She quickly raised her eyes to the exit door and saw Magrete and George leaving the dining room.

Magrete had not been feeling well, but had not wanted to miss this opportunity to see Anna. She felt another cramp, but this time no blood flowed. When George and Magrete reached their room, Ilse rushed to George demanding he take her to the party, and with a wave of Ilse's hand both were gone.

The dance music was a huge success. People got up and shed years of unhappiness, dancing in different ways, but with great enjoyment and vigour. A piano accordionist was playing and he twirled in amongst the dancers. Anna had Ilse on her lap at the high table as Eugene danced with Pierre's wife. George was talking to a fellow Hungarian he had never met before. There were so many different people, with so many different religions, talking in so many different tongues. They had never celebrated Christmas on Christmas Eve before, but tonight everyone was just happy to wash away hardship and the war from their lives. Laughter and jovial conversations were heard throughout the hall.

At the end of the night Pierre sought out George, who was talking to Anna. 'George, the Central Committee and I were planning to give Magrete this small token of appreciation for what she has done for the DP camp. I had a prominent UN administrator here tonight, and he told me he has never seen a DP camp that is so happy and more like an adult centre of learning. In most camps, DPs feel depressed and hopeless, but here we're going to find it difficult to relocate them! Please give Magrete our many thanks.'

George took the present and said to Pierre, 'Without Magrete I would have not survived this war. I'm the luckiest man in the world to have her and my family.'

Ilse looked at Anna and then to her father. 'We're not complete as a family, Dad, but we will be – trust me, we will be!' All of them laughed at her determination, though they had no idea what she was alluding to.

37

Since March 1948, George had refused to accept Anna's US$5 weekly contribution to his family. He did so because he could no longer repay her in other ways, such as by giving her a bottle of his red wine. Anna tried giving the money to Ilse to give to George during her yoga classes, but George would always return it. Once she was married, Anna accepted his position. She had also stopped attending his English classes, so there were fewer opportunities for her to interact directly with him. For the first time, Ilse accepted not seeing or being with Anna.

On 12 January George visited Anna at the villa alone. They sat in the dining room and she offered him biscuits and coffee, which he would have normally accepted, but this time he refused.

'Anna, you're leaving Hamburg to go to America as I understand it on the 16th of January.'

'No,' Anna said, 'we're leaving Tailfingen to go to Hamburg on the 16th.'

'You've been wonderful to this family,' George said. 'Ilse loves you like an older sister and I know you're aware that the day you will leave Tailfingen is her birthday. I wonder if she could see you before you leave.'

'Of course,' Anna said. 'I was going to arrange it with you.'

In the past George had always been able to get past any shield Anna placed between them. He hoped that Anna's marriage to Eugene had not tempered her defences. 'I've a much bigger favour to ask of you.' Anna looked apprehensive. 'I want you to allow Magrete to bring Ilse here and so be present when you meet.'

'George, you're asking far too much of me!'

'Magrete is not well,' George said. 'She has not bounced back after Francis' birth as she did with her other children.'

Anna's eyes moistened; Francis was the first child of Magrete's who had been delivered by another midwife. 'I know what you're trying to do, but there is no common ground between us anymore.'

'Anna, what could Magrete have possibly done to offend you so badly? Didn't she look after you when you were in danger? Didn't she put her children, her family, in peril by doing so? What could she have possibly done to you, for you to treat her so badly?'

Anna opened her mouth to speak but stopped when she saw Eugene standing behind George.

'George!' Eugene said, and George turned to face him. 'Ilse and Magrete are invited here for 3 pm on Sunday. Anna and I'll make sure they have a fond farewell.'

'Thanks, Eugene,' George said gratefully, and left the villa. When he got home he convinced Magrete that the invitation had come from both Anna and Eugene.

That night Anna and Eugene argued as never before. Anna hit Eugene several times on his chest with her fist – how dare he make arrangements for her with a woman she did not care for? The other soldiers in the villa left them alone. The argument was partially resolved at 1 am when Anna screamed, 'This is the first and only time I'll invite this woman! And I'll not look at her the whole time she's here!' Eugene was glad Anna had conceded, but he knew the price for this concession was going to be high.

38

The last Saturday dinner that First Lieutenant Pierre Thomas and Captain Eugene Gould had in Tailfingen was on 15 January. Anna joined them for initial drinks, able to follow only parts of their French conversation.

'We've come a long way, Pierre,' Eugene reflected.

'We have, mon ami,' Pierre agreed. 'We have witnessed a divided Germany developing into a Bizone Germany, and in June of 1948 becoming a Trizone, and on the road to recovery. The Ruhr valley will be the engine that drives the French–European recovery, thanks to your Marshall Plan.'

Anna poured them both a glass of George's Egri Bikavér red wine. 'Thanks, Anna!' Pierre said in his broken English. 'And why aren't you drinking a glass with us this night, our last night together in Tailfingen?'

'I find wine goes to my head far too quickly. It makes me tipsy,' Anna said in English, 'and extremely vulnerable to men.'

Pierre and Eugene laughed. 'I wish my wife was vulnerable to me under the influence of wine,' Pierre said, again in English.

'Gentlemen, this is where I need to leave you,' Anna said. Pierre tried hard not to look at her departing figure, but old habits were difficult to overcome. He liked the curvaceous body that was departing from the room.

Eugene snapped him out of his reverie, continuing in French, 'As an American, it would have been easy for you to be dismissive of me, and give me little assistance. I really appreciate the cooperative style that you adopted, Pierre.'

'You being fluent in French helped,' Pierre conceded. 'The only difficulty was when I had to shut down Elderly Care in Tailfingen.' Pierre smiled to himself. 'They were making some sizeable contributions to charities of mine in Paris. It was a pity that the sex fiend you found led to their demise in this town. I've never really believed your story about stopping while you were changing a tyre and seeing him handcuffed to that birch tree.'

'Well, it was a bit thin,' Eugene said. 'As we're leaving tomorrow I can tell you that my soldiers frequented the local brothel and the prostitutes just hated that brute, because he treated them violently, so someone had to keep an eye on him.'

'Ah, the local brothel,' Pierre mused. 'I could've shut it down long ago, but I figured that at least these women were getting paid for their services, which would hardly be the case for rape victims. You know the female population in our zone stood at 58 per cent.'

'No wonder you left the brothel untouched. Whatever happened to Jean and Cédric?'

'Both have been convicted and are serving time in a Fresnes prison. The irony is that the prison was used by the German Reich to imprison captured members of the French Resistance. Mariann Cohen, a Jewish Resistance fighter, was murdered there in July 1944. They'll have a long time to reflect on that fact. Also, because of their capture, and the recovery of the uranium ore, Baden-Baden has informed me that I'll be promoted to captain by the end of this month.' Pierre was glad he was now on par with Eugene's rank.

'Congratulations!' Eugene shook Pierre's hand across the table.

The meal was always delicious, the wine matched it perfectly, and the conversation always enjoyable. Not honest in some places, thought Pierre, but enjoyable.

'As a parting gift,' Eugene said, slightly intoxicated, 'I've got a dozen bottles of George's wine that he gave to my non-drinking wife that I'd like to gift to you. I can hardly transport a case of Hungarian reds into America. The army will wonder what my real mission was in Tailfingen.' Both men smiled.

'To the French–American alliance,' Pierre toasted. He knew he would miss Eugene, but every Saturday for the next twelve weeks he would toast him by drinking George's red wine in the bed of his mistress.

39

On 16 January, at breakfast, Eugene said to Anna, 'I don't want you to let Magrete and Ilse leave before I come back from Ebingen. I should be back by 4 pm. I might have some important news for all of you.' He would not elaborate.

This made Anna even angrier, because he would not be there for the beginning of the meeting. 'You know, Eugene, I won't look at her and I'll only talk to her through Ilse,' she said.

Eugene smiled at her and said, 'Don't forget what I've asked', and left.

Anna went to the cook and ordered afternoon tea for 3 pm. She asked for chocolate biscuits and a glass of milk to be served to Ilse. She ordered a chamomile tea for Magrete and herself and detailed to the cook how both cups should be prepared.

The rest of the morning was spent choosing the right clothes. Anna decided to wear long black gloves, just in case their hands accidentally brushed. She purposely wore silk stockings. She had heard that German women were having sex with American soldiers for silk stockings and cigarettes. Anna placed her Marlboro cigarettes into her expensive gold cigarette case. Her eye make-up was subtle, but highlighted her hazel eyes, and she reddened her lips a little more than usual with lipstick. She chose a red pillbox hat with a veil as an extra precaution, to shield herself from Magrete's eyes. She selected from her extensive wardrobe an expensive red dress with matching red high-heeled shoes that she had purchased while on her honeymoon in Switzerland.

During the afternoon, Anna carefully rearranged the back verandah table and chairs. She wanted to be able to look down the backyard to the alleyway that led to Eisenbahnstraße. She arranged each chair so that Magrete would at best view her profile and of course, Ilse could see Anna directly when Anna turned her head away from the laneway and looked directly at her. Magrete would be placed on Anna's right, and so could only see her back when she was talking to Ilse. She placed the ashtray so it would act as a further barrier between Magrete and herself.

Anna asked the private at the gate to bring Magrete and Ilse into the foyer together, but then to take Magrete alone to the verandah and, once she was seated, return to the foyer and bring Ilse to the kitchen. Here Anna would greet her and give her an expensive engraved gold bracelet for her birthday. Ilse and Anna, led by the cook, would then enter the verandah with the cook physically shielding Anna from Magrete's direct gaze. Anna showed the private which chair Magrete had to occupy.

Anna thoughts drifted to her Aunt Ayelet, and how Magrete was implicated in her murder. She planned to reveal this fact to Eugene once they were on the ship going from Hamburg to New York. Anna now felt ready to receive Magrete and Ilse.

Magrete had a frightful morning and early afternoon. She did her yoga exercises with Ilse to calm herself down. Ilse was the only child at home as George hated staying in their crowded room, and had taken Elisabeth, Eva and Francis on a long walk to the children's playground in Tailfingen. He was disturbed by Magrete's reaction to this meeting. He was also concerned about her health. He hoped that Anna and Magrete would, if not make amends, at least begin a journey of rediscovery.

Magrete decided to wear her cream swing trousers with a cream halter-neck top, flat-heeled white shoes and a heavy cream woollen jumper – the only clothes she had left from her Wannsee life. Her clothes were a little big for her, and so she had to acknowledge that she had lost weight. She possessed no make-up and her face was a little ruddy due to the coolness in the air.

Magrete looked at the clock and saw it was time to leave. She smiled at Ilse, who had chosen a black and white polka dot dress, with a matching waist bow and hair band. 'Come on, Mum,' Ilse said, 'let's go and meet my Anna!' Magrete knew that although Anna was lost to her, she would never be lost to Ilse. Her daughter's excitement and confidence gave Magrete some comfort, and she smiled at Ilse's unconditional love for Anna – something that Ilse had never offered her.

It was 3 pm and the private did exactly what Anna had ordered him to do. Magrete found herself sitting alone on the verandah with her daughter somewhere inside the villa. She reminisced about how life had changed since the last time she had sat in a villa. Wannsee seemed like a dream to her now, a lifetime ago, and a woman she no longer recognised – a woman who had led a luxurious life, but a life that drifted without purpose, focused only on privilege, prestige and prosperity.

The cook entered the verandah, followed by Anna and Ilse. Magrete immediately rose, but Anna's black-gloved hand demanded that Magrete be seated where she was placed. Magrete followed Anna's silent command and smiled. When Anna sat down, all Magrete could see was Anna's veiled profile, as Anna looked ahead to the alleyway.

'Anna,' Magrete said softly, 'how are you?'

Anna took out a cigarette from her gold case, tapped it on the gold lid several times, lit it, and blew smoke that billowed out into the garden vista in front of her. She stroked Ilse's hair with her left hand as Ilse drank her milk and ate her chocolate biscuits. 'Could you please serve us tea?' Anna said to the cook, in a friendly and familiar tone. The cook did so and Anna said, 'Thank you. That'll be all.' With her back to Magrete, she started to talk to Ilse.

Magrete understood their conversation was at an end. She gazed towards the alleyway as Anna and Ilse talked about Anna's trip to the United States and her excitement about embracing a new world and a wonderful life. She realised that Anna was treating Ilse as the adult and that she herself had the status of a child – to be seen but not to be heard. A tear trickled down Magrete's cheek, unnoticed by Anna or Ilse, as they chattered about the golden bracelet that Anna had given Ilse for her birthday. They talked about so many things that Magrete's mind whirled. She wondered again what had caused Anna to be so distant to her, and again felt ashamed for having cast Anna, a relative, in a servant's role.

Magrete looked quickly at Anna, and their eyes briefly met. At that moment Magrete realised that Anna was afraid of her - but why?

When Anna's eyes briefly encountered Magrete's, she had felt a sudden pain in her heart. This woman whom she had once loved, had admired and adored, who had always treated her like a younger sister, needed to be shed from her life forever. Her fear reflected the thought that although they were estranged, Magrete nevertheless was still within her province, but on leaving Tailfingen, life without Magrete would become a reality. Remember your aunt, she repeated to herself, but with less conviction.

Magrete heard Anna talking to Ilse about her love for Eugene, and what a difference he had made to her life. Magrete remembered Franz Stopper and thought, so young to have died for the German Reich. Magrete then heard Anna talking about living her life as a Jewess in New York, a city that would not judge her or her husband because of their heritage. Magrete thought about Rachel, murdered by the Nazis, and Ester, who was saved from hardship and torture, by a timely heart attack. Magrete heard Anna saying that life would be so much better in America, where clothing and food was plentiful. Magrete thought of Julianna, who had supplied her family with food and suffered at the hands of her husband. Another unnoticed tear meandered down Magrete's cheek; these many losses of the previous years weighed heavily upon her heart.

Ilse suddenly mumbled to herself, and Magrete smiled as Anna asked, 'What did you say?'

'Nothing, Anna, nothing really!' Ilse said, and then asked, 'How many children are you going to have?'

Magrete heard a flurry of words from an echo chamber, within her mind that were completely deconstructed to her. Suddenly without warning, Magrete, who could no longer bear being divorced from reality, rose and addressed Anna directly, with empathy and sadness in the tone of her voice. 'I hope you will not be offended if Ilse and I leave now. Do you mind if we go home via the alleyway into Eisenbahnstraße?'

'Of course not,' Anna heard herself say almost in a whisper. This was not the ending that Anna had planned nor expected.

Anna and Ilse hugged one another. Anna lifted Ilse into the air and kissed her through her veil and said to her in a whisper loud enough for Magrete to hear, 'Don't you dare forget me!'

Ilse kissed her back. 'Every day when I put on my bracelet, I'll think of you. You're beautiful, Anna! I want to be just like you. I love you, Anna!' Anna glanced at Magrete and saw she was smiling, without a hint of jealousy. It was a look Anna had often witnessed in the past.

Anna watched Magrete and Ilse walk down the path to the alleyway with her eyes welling with tears. Magrete did not look well, and Anna felt ashamed at the way she had treated her. She knew she would never see Magrete again, and the tussle between the realisation of Magrete's loss in her life and the cause of her Aunt's death, was conflicting her emotionally.

Suddenly, Eugene appeared and shouted at Anna, 'Where the hell are they?'

'They've gone,' Anna said remorsefully.

'But I told you to keep them here until I got back!'

The tone of Eugene's voice angered Anna. 'Magrete wanted to leave! And anyway, that bitch was involved in the death of my aunt Ayelet!' Anna blurted out her accusation without thinking.

'What are you talking about?'

'I read the note on your desk that said that Magrete was implicated in the murder of my aunt, Ayelet Sulzer, in Berlin in 1940!' Anna shouted. 'She caused the death of the only relative I had left!'

'I told you never to go into my study! Listen to me.' Eugene's tone grew calmer. 'My research showed that the Nazis proved that it was your Aunt's husband who killed her, because he had a gambling addiction, not Magrete. She had nothing to do with it!'

Instantly a large barrier of hate fell away from Anna's heart, but she clung onto another reason for her hate. 'She used me as her ticket to escape punishment, because she was a Nazi collaborator, and she knew her Nazi friends could never win the war!'

'She didn't need to save you to escape blame or punishment. She hasn't committed any crime! Also, her father was technically a Jew.'

'But they're Catholic,' Anna said.

'She has only known Catholicism,' Eugene said more softly, 'because that's the religion her parents practised. We intercepted a letter from her sister Mimi, which included a letter that her father wrote to Magrete, which he'd hidden in Magrete's old bedroom, telling Magrete of their heritage. Are you ready for this? You and Magrete are related. Her grandmother is your great-grandmother's sister. Her grandmother's birth certificate in the Vienna records was a forgery and that's what caused the delay in confirming it. This government document confirms the link between your two families. Her father is Ester's first cousin. Magrete is your mother's second cousin and you and Ilse are third cousins!'

'Ilse is my third cousin? I still have family alive? Oh, what have I done? What have I done?' Tears streamed down Anna's cheeks. She snatched the document from his hand and ran towards the alleyway, screaming, 'Magrete! Magrete!' She stopped to take off her shoes, then ran as fast as she could, screaming Magrete's name and waving in one hand two shoes and in the other a document. 'Magrete! Magrete!'

When Magrete and Ilse left Anna on the verandah, they were walking holding hands, with Magrete feeling totally depleted of all emotion. 'You know,' Magrete said softly, 'I heard you mumbling that Abracadabra spell under your breath. You know your spell does not work on me.'

'Mother,' Ilse stressed elongating her address, 'that Abracadabra stuff is for kids!'

Magrete softly boasted, 'Yesterday I heard you trying your spell, when you did not want to make-up the beds, but you know it did not work. I still made you make-up the beds.'

'Mothers are weird,' Ilse observed.

As Magrete and Ilse walked towards the camp, Ilse heard a faint sound that was growing in volume. She stopped, which made Magrete stop, and they turned to see the source of the noise. They saw Anna streaming towards them, screaming Magrete's name. Anna had no hat, no veil; she had her shoes in one hand, a piece of paper held high in the other, and her silk stockings were shredded up to her ankles. Magrete was transfixed. In no time Anna had rushed into her arms, slid to Magrete's feet and started to kiss them, crying, 'How could I have been so cruel to you? Please forgive me! Please forgive me!'

Magrete bent down and lifted Anna into her arms to comfort her. She said, crying softly, 'I am truly sorry for what I have done to you, Anna.'

Anna pulled away from her. 'You've done nothing to me! You've only cared for, protected and loved me! I doubted your love and that was my failing. Please forgive me!' Anna sobbed against Magrete's chest.

Magrete kissed her on the top of her head and said, 'I have missed you so badly. I am so glad we are together again.'

Ilse said, 'We're finally a family again!' They both reached to draw Ilse into their embrace.

As they were walking back to the DP camp, Anna explained why she had distrusted Magrete's love. At each point Magrete said, 'That is understandable. I would have felt the same in your shoes.'

When they reached the DP camp and entered Magrete's room, George and the children were still not home. Anna saw for the first time that they lived in one room with five mattresses on the floor, one sink, one dresser, bags of clothing and two suit cases, and she cried again, only to be comforted by Magrete. This woman, Anna thought, who gave so much to so many, now has so very little, but has never complained.

Ilse stepped out of the room to search for her father. Anna then showed Magrete the government document. 'Did you always know we were related?'

'Yes, I knew,' Magrete confessed, hanging her head in shame. 'I did not know if you knew, but under the Third Reich it was best to keep it quiet. After the war ended, I always thought we would all be one family, but I decided not to tell you about it until I could verify it. Then once we were estranged, I did not dare raise it with you, because I thought you would think it was just a callous trick.'

'Without you, I would not have survived the Third Reich, nor the time since the war,' Anna cried.

Eugene suddenly appeared with Ilse, who had returned without her father. 'We have to go!' he said to Anna. 'We have to get to Ebingen in order to get to Hamburg.'

'How much money do you have?' Anna said.

Eugene opened his wallet and Anna took all of his money and handed it to Magrete, saying, 'Don't you dare give it back to us!'

Anna then knelt in front of Ilse. 'Many years ago, when both of my parents were dead, I lived with my grandmother Ester, and when she died, a wonderful woman sat me down in front of St Mary's Church in Alexanderplatz and gave me this locket.' Anna took the locket off her neck, and placed it around Ilse's neck. 'Now this is on loan to you – it's only a loan.' Anna opened the locket. 'This wonderful woman,' Anna continued, 'your mother, placed a photograph of my grandmother, my mother and myself in this locket.' Anna opened the locket and Ilse saw two women and a young child who looked very much like her.

'I look just like you, Anna,' Ilse said in wonderment.

Anna could see that Ilse had the same hazel eyes, and a darker complexion than Magrete. 'You do, cuz,' Anna said, 'but this locket is only on loan. Guard it with your life, because wherever you and your mother are, I'll find you via your aunt Mimi and you'll give me back my locket. Is that a promise?'

'It's a promise,' Ilse said. 'I'll guard this with my life and return it to you.'

Anna rose and hugged Magrete, noting how thin she had become. 'I love you more than ever!' she said, teary-eyed. 'You mean everything to me. You saved my life, without making a single demand.'

Magrete, with tears in her own eyes, replied, 'I am so happy we are a family again.' They kissed each other on both cheeks to say goodbye. Eugene took Anna's arm and guided her out of the room.

After they left and the tears had subsided Magrete said to Ilse, 'Your spell seems to have worked.'

'Why did Anna call me cuz?'

'You will be happy to learn that you and Anna are related. You are third cousins,' Magrete said, knowing what this would mean to Ilse.

'I knew it!' Ilse said under her breath.

Magrete heard a knock on the door, and opened it. Helena informed her, 'While you were gone a bearded man knocked on my door and asked me to give you this. I think he's Swiss.' She gave Magrete an envelope that had her name printed on it.

'Thanks, Helena,' Magrete said. As Magrete closed the door, she opened the envelope to find a postcard inside. On the back of the card was written a single word – 'Australia'. She placed the card in her pocket and smiled to herself.

'Is it something important, Mum?'

'Not for now,' Magrete answered, happy at the thought that Helmut and Gertrude were alive.

When George returned and heard what had happened he told Magrete that Anna had given him US$5 per week for nearly a year to support them. Magrete cried, only for Elisabeth to ask if these were tears of joy.

That night, when her family was sleeping, Magrete felt a great weight had been lifted from her. She was not shackled to either happiness or sadness; she did not desire prestige and she was without material lust. Life had taught her how to be free!

The End

REFERENCES

WEBSITES

Numerous websites have been consulted in writing this novel, and in most cases only an odd fact was extracted, modified and/or used. On the other hand, there were some websites, which were heavily consulted, and these are referenced below.

The author wishes to acknowledge first and foremost, Wikipedia, as well as the following sources:

Google Books
Google Maps
https://www.chabad.org
https://www.cookpad.com
https://www.healthgrades.com
https://www.healthy.nethttps://www.histclo.com
https://www.historylearningsite.co.uk
https://www.holocaustonline.org
https://www.haydncorper.com
https://www.ideologic.org
https://www.jewishgen.org
https://www.jewishvirtuallibrary.org
https://www.news.nationalgeographic.com
https://www.spartacus-educational.com
https://www.ushmm.org
https://www.theguardian.com
https://www.history.com
https://www.historyplace.com
https://www.ncbi.nlm.nih.gov
https://www.pregnancybirthbaby.org.au
https://www.scrapbookpages.com
https://www.yogastudies.org
https://www.2worldwar2.com

REFERENCES

BOOKS

Airline Crashes and Fatalities since 1908.

A 1935 Timetable for a Girl's School In Nazi Germany, Bisingen by Christine Glauning.

Education for Death by Gregor Ziemer (1942).

Education in Nazi Germany, Everyday Life in Fascist Venice, 1929–40 by Kate Ferris.

Frau Marga Himmler's Diaries (1937–1945).

Forgotten Agents in a Forgotten Zone: German Women under French Occupation In Post-Nazi Germany, 1945–1949 by Katherine Rossy.

Freie Universität, Berlin, Otto Hahn by Klaus Hoffmann.

ART QUILL & CO PTY LTD

LAKE MACQUARIE, AUSTRALIA

Art Quill & Co Pty Ltd is located in Lake Macquarie,
New South Wales, Australia.
The company is primarily an art company
(see Art Quill Studio - http://artquill.blogspot.com -
a division of Art Quill & Co Pty Ltd).

The company also publishes limited edition artist printmaker's books as well as books not solely directed to art
(e.g. solution methodologies to novels).
We have listed the more popular published books below.

Kalle Gayn
4 Steps To Freedom
(Novel)

Dr Ellak I. von Nagy-Felsobuki
The Sudoku Solver
(Puzzle Solver)

Marie-Therese Wisniowski
Not in My Name
(Artist Printmakers' Book)

Marie-Therese Wisniowski
Beyond the Fear of Freedom
(Artist Printmakers' Book)